# THE SANDBOX TREE

Also by Thomas Fleming

HISTORY

THE MAN FROM MONTICELLO
*An Intimate Life of Thomas Jefferson*

WEST POINT
*The Men and Times of the United States Military Academy*

AFFECTIONATELY YOURS, GEORGE WASHINGTON
*A Self-Portrait in Letters of Friendship*

ONE SMALL CANDLE
*The Pilgrims' First Year in America*

BEAT THE LAST DRUM

NOW WE ARE ENEMIES

FICTION

ROMANS COUNTRYMEN LOVERS

A CRY OF WHITENESS

KING OF THE HILL

THE GOD OF LOVE

ALL GOOD MEN

# THE SANDBOX TREE

*by* Thomas Fleming

19 70

William Morrow and Company, Inc., *New York*

Second Printing, November 1970



Grateful acknowledgment is made to the following for permission to quote from the indicated works: to The Viking Press, Inc., and to The Society of Authors as the literary representative of the Estate of James Joyce, for eight lines from "O Sweetheart, hear you" from COLLECTED POEMS by James Joyce, copyright 1918 by B. W. Huebsch, Inc., renewed 1946 by Nora Joyce; to Mr. M. B. Yeats, The Macmillan Company, The Macmillan Company of Canada, and to A. P. Watt & Son, for five lines of "Among School Children" from COLLECTED POEMS by William Butler Yeats, copyright 1928 by The Macmillan Company, renewed 1956 by Georgie Yeats, and for two lines of "Into the Twilight" from COLLECTED POEMS by William Butler Yeats, copyright 1906 by The Macmillan Company, renewed 1934 by William Butler Yeats; and to Rytvoc, Inc., for two lines from "Wedding Bells Are Breaking Up That Old Gang of Mine," © Renewed Rytvoc, Inc. 1957.



Printed in the United States of America by
Quinn & Boden Company, Inc., Rahway, N.J.

Library of Congress Catalog Card Number 70-118341

Both nuns and mothers worship images
But those the candles light are not as those
That animate a mother's reveries,
But keep a marble or a bronze repose.
And yet they too break hearts—

*Among School Children*
William Butler Yeats

# Prologue

The story I am about to tell you happened twenty years ago. But it exists for me in a kind of timeless present, which is partly the product of personal pain and partly the tempo of this disjointed century. I think I am not alone in feeling that everything that has happened since the close of World War II remains somehow imprisoned in a great frozen block of time, a semi-eternal now. This book is an attempt to carve an image of truth from that neuter mass.

That word *truth* is a heady one. It should make every reader wary of me. There are many truths, as that reasonably honest politician Pontius Pilate pointed out. The one that fascinates me is historical truth. Without it we do not know where we are, where we are going, why or what we have become.

If I had to select one word to characterize those early postwar years, it would be fear. Not a craven, crawling terror but a subtle pervasive malaise. It stood like a substance between our wills and our ideals. From a depression that seemed to have no end, we had progressed to a war that suddenly, before we could begin to enjoy the fruits of victory, seemed to have had no purpose. We were as insecure, as threatened by poverty, disease, death as ever. The golden years of affluence that have transformed the attitudes of contemporary Americans were an unglimpsed, unrealized future.

If fear was the dominant American mentality, it is easy to see why those who still lived in the nation's ghettos were even more afraid. We Catholics, of course, did not know we were living in a ghetto, then. We did not know that we were embracing a very special brand of a European creed, brought to America's shores by the immigrant poor, built by pennies from the pockets of men and women who had sweated out their lives building railroads and scrubbing kitchens. By our time, the American Roman Catholic Church had grown with this stupendous nation into a world.

Yes, a world almost totally exclusive, with its own laws, philosophy, thoughts, and feelings, a world that seemed utterly irrevocable, immutable, transcendent. But it was, nevertheless, still a ghetto, built, like all ghettos, out of walls made of fear—fear that faced both ways. The fear of *them* by those on the outside and the fear of the *others* by those on the inside.

Today these walls are collapsing. America has been blowing them down, not with a Joshua-style trumpet, but with its steady insistence that fear must not become a way of life for any of its people. But as the walls crumbled, and the ghetto itself began to tremble beneath this immense metaphysical earthquake, personal tragedy became inevitable. Some would not, others could not escape from the collapse. Others, trying, became walking wounded. This is what I, historian writing as novelist (or novelist writing as historian), insist we must remember, *know*.

It was in the personal, the private, that the ghetto's failure first became visible. I have tried to focus on that cracked and wrinkled patch of time when the failure penetrated the minds and hearts that I knew best. The year, the month, the week, the day, the hour, yes, even the anguished moment when we faced the terrible truth about our world for the first time.

It is not only for those of us who have endured this failure that I write. It is for other Americans (some of them still trapped in their own ghettos) for whom this Catholic world remains mysterious and even menacing. Above all, it is for our children, to whom this will be truly history, in that blank world before their American lives began. Finally, for our children's children, for whom the word *American* will, I believe, have even deeper, more profound meaning.

# Chapter One

It began in sunlight, a brutal sun, baking the dusty asphalt street of weary one- and two-story houses. Down the scuffed steps of home came Margaret Connolly flanked by Mother and Father, a tableau out of Theodore Dreiser by Grant Wood, to the uneven slabs of slate sidewalk where Faith Kilpatrick stood waiting before a gleaming black Cadillac. "Are you sure you have enough of—everything?" Mother trilled.

"Yes, Mother," Margaret said. "For the third time, yes."

Mrs. Connolly was a large, plain-faced, broad-shouldered woman who wore her hair in two little waves on either side of her head. As usual, she completely ignored her seedy, sad-eyed husband, who stood only a foot away from Margaret, saying nothing, also as usual. Decades of petty defeats were lined into Bill Connolly's long, lean face. But a benevolent spin of the genes had enabled Margaret to acquire the best features from mother and father and combine them into a willowy dark Irish beauty.

"Oh, how I'd love to zoom off in this." Mrs. Connolly sighed, running her hand along the Cadillac's glistening fender. "It makes me wish I never saw our old heap again."

Faith Kilpatrick smiled. As the daughter of James Kilpatrick, Chief Justice of the state's Supreme Court, she was used to poor-mouth envy. "I prefer Fords myself," Faith said, giving the Cadillac's rear tire a contemptuous kick. "I keep telling my father these things are just conspicuous consumption."

Mrs. Connolly's smile was vacuous with non-comprehension. "Do you know," she said, putting one large arm around Margaret's shoulder, "she's never been away from home this long before? Twenty years old and I still think of her as my—my baby girl."

"Oh, Mother, please," Margaret murmured.

"It's only two weeks," Faith said. "We'll lock her in her bedroom every night and give the key to my mother."

"Oh, no, I want you both to have a *good* time."

"We'll try, Mother," Margaret said and gave her a perfunctory peck on the cheek. Then more deliberately she turned and murmured, "Good-bye, Daddy," and kissed him on the mouth. A moment later she was sinking into the gray cushions of the Cadillac's dim interior. Faith slammed the door. Mother waved frantically and cried, "Be sure and say hello to your mother, Faith." Father raised a slim hand halfway up his chest in a faint intimation of a blessing. The big car slicked through the melting asphalt toward the downtown expressway. A wave of thick moist heat engulfed them as they picked up speed. In its August dog days the city was an admirable substitute for purgatory.

"I really hope you didn't come up just for me," Margaret said.

"I told you I had to get my diaphragm fitted."

"Oh, Faith, stop."

"Don't worry, I had Father Malone bless it first."

Margaret shook her head. It was obvious that Faith had not reformed. But Margaret's reproval was more automatic than profound. In fact this instant resumption of their college relationship gave her a curious feeling of pleasure.

"What have you done besides read?" Faith demanded.

"Oh, go to the movies a few times."

"With whom?"

"Mother. Or Daddy. Or both."

"What happened to Tommy Loughran, the asexual intellectual?"

"He got a job as a camp counsellor."

"I'm going to introduce you to a decent male if it's the last thing I do on this planet."

"Don't you think it's better to let nature take its course?"

"Not your nature."

"Oh, you're being silly again."

The shore train's dim, airless coaches were practically deserted. They wound their way out of the terminal with the usual jolts and shrieks and were clicking past the leafy streets of the inner suburbs when down the aisle toward them zigzagged a big husky young man in freshly creased tan slacks and a brown-and-red-striped sport shirt. He was handsome in a rough, very masculine way. Too masculine. He looked directly at them with a knowing smile which Faith cheerfully returned. Flustered, Margaret stared out the window as he swayed above them.

"I'll be damned," he said. "When did they let you out of the asylum?"

"The same day they let you out of the alcoholic ward," Faith said.

"At last we've got something in common. Why don't you introduce me to your friend? That would give us one more thing to share."

Faith said nothing. She just sat there, giving him a steady, mocking smile.

"Come on, I'm harmless as long as the train stays on the tracks."

"I wouldn't put sabotage past you. But as they say in the old country, what harm? Margaret Connolly, meet Jake O'Connor."

"See how easy it is?" Jake said. "Now let's adjourn to the bar car. On a day like this it's the only place to travel."

"Shall we risk it?" Faith asked, crinkling her snub nose.

"I'm—I'm not thirsty," Margaret said. "If you want to go—"

Sunlight flashed in Faith's red hair as she threw back her head and laughed heartily. "I'd do it," she said, "but I don't want to see Mr. O'Connor's brilliant prospects ruined by a murder charge, especially when I'd be the corpse."

"Now, Faith, don't feel that way," Jake said, patting her on the head. "Just because every time I see you I have an insane desire to cut your throat—and extract the larynx."

His mocking blue eyes shifted to Margaret. "You've got to be thirsty, Miss Connolly. A day like this reminds me of the siege of Tobruk. It was a hundred and eighty in the shade and the water ration was one teaspoonful a day—"

"I'm sorry. I don't drink," Margaret murmured.

"You mean to say you're going to let me meet two girls, one of whom I know, and experience the trauma of not being able to make time with either one of them?"

"I may start believing in divine retribution," Faith said.

"This kind of thing could warp my whole personality."

"Baloney doesn't warp," Faith said.

"Neither does prussic acid," Jake said. "That's why we're such a perfect match." He pinched Faith's cheek. "God bless you both."

He vanished through the rear door with a magical hiss.

"Why didn't you want to go?" Faith asked. "Jake's a lot of fun in his peculiarly insane way."

"Who is he?"

"The playboy of the western wards. His father is Ben O'Connor, chairman of the county commissioners."

"Oh," Margaret said. The name and title meant nothing to her. "Was he really at the siege of Tobruk?"

"Of course not." Faith heaved a stagey sigh and let her eyes grow round. "I had a mad passion for him the year he came back from the Pacific. I even managed to get a date with him once, but it was a disaster. I'm not his type."

"I don't think I am either," Margaret said.

"Well, it really doesn't matter down here at the beach. Everybody fools around with everybody. You'll like it, Meg. If you'll just relax and let yourself go."

These words had an ominous ring for Margaret. Letting yourself go was not the way a Catholic college senior went about the business of living. It sounded as if the words could easily translate into yielding to temptation, ignoring occasions of sin. But if you disapprove, why are you here, Margaret? Why have you accepted this invitation? That was hard to explain. Politeness was part of it, an honest feeling of friendship for Faith and—admit it—a curiosity about this world of sun and sand where the city's rich played all summer. You want to taste this world, supposedly so complex and dazzling and challenging, ultimately you want to cure your ignorance, to *know* it.

"At least," Faith was saying, "that's the way it used to be. But this is the last time around for most of us and there's been an awful lot of pairing off."

Again Margaret could only know in the most distant, shadowy way what Faith meant. The word *summer* had no throb of deep emotion for her. Summer was dullness, reading, movies, day trips to the beach, weekend visits to suburban cousins. She listened, unimpressed, as Faith lamented the decline of summer as she had known it in its glorious prime.

"It hasn't been the same since the war. Nothing's been the same. And yet it's like *déjà vu,* visiting a strange place you could swear you've seen before in a dream or another life. We've gone right on playing the game the way we always played it. But not for ourselves. The parents are the real reason why we keep smiles on our happy, childish faces. What else have they worked and worried twenty years to accomplish?

"But, oh, the way it used to be, Meg. It was so perfect you were sure it was going to last forever. It was like one of those circles they talk about in philosophy. You know, the idea. But real. You laughed and swam and played crazy games and swam some more and went dancing at night and on the way home you kissed once or twice and that was all there was to it. A different boy every night. Now everyone is so damn serious."

"We are getting older," Margaret said, "and life is serious."

Faith groaned in mock despair and wrenched a copy of *The Naked and the Dead* from her suitcase. "See what he's got me reading?"

"Who?" Margaret asked, trying to conceal her dismay. The book was a best seller. She knew that much. She also knew that it was "dirty," full of sex and obscene language.

"Mr. Serious."

"You mean—you're going with someone?"

"In a way. A very offhand, inadvertent, unintentional, understated way. His name is Larry Donahue. You'll meet him."

"What do you think of—it?" Margaret asked, nodding toward *The Naked and the Dead,* and hating the prim note of withdrawal in her voice.

"Boring," Faith said. "And unbelievably derivative. Warmed-over Dos Passos with a few dashes of Hemingway."

"I've been reading this," Margaret said, and took a copy of *Seven Storey Mountain* out of her suitcase.

Faith glowered at it. "Larry says anyone who becomes a convert to Catholicism must have a screw loose."

"I don't think I'm going to like Larry."

"I'm not sure whether I like him either."

While the soot swirled through the train windows on the hot summer wind, Margaret and Faith retreated into utterly different worlds, Faith wading through jungles of four-letter verbs and adjectives, Margaret shadowing Thomas Merton through the sedate halls and smug classrooms of Columbia. Again and again she was awed by the scornful skill with which he refuted the worldly optimists and cynical atheists swarming around him. Father Denton Malone had called the author "a young G. K. Chesterton." But Margaret found Merton's description of his conversion more moving than anything she had ever read in Chesterton. The more she read, the more outrageous Faith's remark about converts became.

Margaret sighed, baffled once more by what passed for thinking in Faith's rebellious head. It was especially regrettable, because Faith had such a quick, almost brilliant mind. She got some of the highest marks Margaret had ever seen, with barely a glance at her textbooks. Faith also had a unique ability to say precisely the right thing at the right time—the gift that Margaret most envied. Wouldn't it be wonderful, always to have ready answers on your lips, answers that silenced the people Father Malone called the spokesmen of godless secularism and communism. . . .

"Thank God," Faith exclaimed.

"What?" Margaret asked, staring out the window at the same flat, sunbaked landscape she had seen the last time she looked.

"The air. Can't you taste the salt?"

"All I can taste is soot," Margaret said with a feeble swipe at the layer of grit on her sky-blue suit.

The conductor began bellowing unintelligible names and the train jerked and rattled to a series of neck-snapping stops. Finally came a shout which Faith seemed to understand and they seized their bags and debarked before an old wooden shack with "Paradise Beach" in faded gold on its weathered front. The sun beat down with late afternoon ferocity. Faith peered through the glare, muttering denunciations of her brother Jim who had promised to meet them.

"Ladies, ladies." Jake O'Connor beamed down at them from the steps of the train. "Your friendly porter has trudged all the way from the bar car to make sure you don't damage your delicate organs hefting those big bags."

He was slightly drunk, and Margaret found this somewhat unpleasant, at four o'clock in the afternoon. So did Faith. "You don't look capable of lifting anything heavier than a glass," she said.

Jake sighed and picked up their bags. "Why does alcohol bring out the Carry Nation in women? I could have cancer sores all over my face, but would either of you tell me to see a doctor? No. But a little alcohol on the breath and the prohibition instinct becomes uncontrollable."

"If you get any sores on your face," Faith said, "they won't be from cancer."

"Why didn't you tell me that last night, before we started undressing?" Jake said.

Margaret did not get the joke. She felt even more uncomfortable when Jake, having carried their bags to the shade of the station, began denouncing fashion's New Look. "It's going to lower the birth rate," he said. "Take your friend here. I've got to see her in a bathing suit before I find out whether she's got decent legs. You can only do that three months a year."

"It won't stop her from finding out you've got an indecent mind —twelve months a year."

A battered green station wagon scrunched to a stop beside them. The driver, a red-haired young man with a bony, rather handsome face, smiled cheerfully at them.

"You'll do anything to save some taxi fare," he said to Jake.

"Yeah. Even talk to your sister," Jake said.

Faith introduced Margaret to her brother Jim and got into the front seat with him. Jake threw the bags in the rear of the wagon and climbed into the back seat with Margaret.

"What's this you're reading?" Jake said, slipping the book out of Margaret's hand. "*Seven Storey Mountain*? Only Mount St. Monica's could make a good-looking girl like you read that drivel."

"I don't think it's drivel," Margaret said.

"The character joined a monastery, didn't he?" Jake said. "No booze, no girls. You can't even talk, for Christ's sake, for the rest of your life."

"Maybe you ought to consider joining," Faith said, "for those three reasons. One of them is going to get you in the end."

"Which will it be, and which end?"

"I've been rereading Chesterton's *The Everlasting Man,*" Jim Kilpatrick said. "It really makes you wonder about the theory of evolution."

"He should have called it *The Everlasting Woman,*" Faith said.

"I could write that one," Jake said. "It's the story of my life."

"I've got a better title: *Gone with the Whiskey.*"

"What is your problem, Faith? Irish puritanism, or good old-fashioned American lesbianism?"

"I don't think that's very funny, Jake," Jim Kilpatrick said.

"My apologies, Savonarola. But there's got to be some explanation for your little sister's virulent antagonism."

"It might be a simple lack of sanctifying grace in her soul."

"Now why didn't I think of that?" Jake said.

Margaret concentrated on looking out the window. The scenery of a typical shore town slid by, whitewashed boardinghouses with long, slanted porches full of rockers, a white, square-steepled Protestant church, a new red and yellow supermarket, an old-fashioned drugstore. In two blocks they were out on the open highway with scrubby grass and sand running down to a wide whitecapped bay on the right. On the left big fat houses squatted on top of sand dunes. The car slowed to a stop before a gravel road running up to one of these houses, and Jake climbed out.

"It's been a pleasure," he said. "Especially meeting you, Miss Connolly. You have restored my faith in Catholic womanhood. I'm going up to the house right now and call up my brother and tell him to reserve a room for me out at the seminary this September."

"Your brother joined up just to get away from you," Faith said.

"Wrong. He told me the real reason was his exposure to your personality, when he and old Smiling Jim here were buddies at Prep. Even then—at twelve—you were enough to drive him into perpetual chastity. If only he had met Miss Connolly here—"

"Home, James," Faith said, and slammed the door in his face.

*Stupid. Stupid. Stupid.* The words erupted across Margaret's mind like the cry of a prisoner as the door boomed shut. She did not want them. She did not understand them. They were simply there shouting: *Stupid, you are so stupid,* Margaret. Why didn't you let him buy you a Coke? Why didn't you make amusing conversation instead of freezing into your usual little ball of inferiority? It was such a perfect opportunity and you could have been so witty.

In that exchange about *The Everlasting Woman* you could have said: *Maybe women outlast men because they can relax and let the men do the running.*

And he might have said: *Maybe your kind of girl can.*

And you might have said: *Run? Don't worry, I will. In the opposite direction.*

Stop. Stop. Stop. He's gone and he won't come back and you are not witty, Margaret. Witty people say things when they should be said. People like you just don't fit into the bright witty world.

Why not? Why, why not? That was the question. Maybe it was

the querulous voice behind the door, maybe it is also the biggest reason why you are visiting the Kilpatricks. Maybe you want to prove, once and for all, the harsh, not necessarily sad truth you have just propounded.

Faith and Jim were discussing Jake O'Connor. "A lot of people are calling him a lush," Jim said.

"Oh, nuts," Faith said. "I know exactly what's bugging him. That idiot brother of his, your old friend Father Paul. He uses the same sour puss and detachable halo on Jake that you use on me. Did you take lessons from the same nun? I can't believe a man—"

Jim's head spun to the right to give Faith a fierce momentary glare. "Shut up," he said.

The station wagon swung abruptly off the highway and went bumping up a rutty road toward a squat weathered house with gabled windows and two huge chimneys.

"Can you feel the temperature changing?" Faith asked exultantly.

They hurried up the back steps into a wide, dim kitchen; the shades on the windows were drawn against the afternoon sun. Faith led Margaret through big rooms full of helter-skelter furniture—wicker chairs, rush rockers, worn couches and sagging easy chairs. The floors were littered with odds and ends of clothing, tennis racquets, beach balls, stray bathing suits, towels, even a surf-mat.

Upstairs was smaller and more orderly. Faith showed Margaret into a medium-sized blue-walled bedroom with conventional maple furniture. She threw up the window and a pungent sea breeze danced past the polka dot curtains. "Into the bathing suit, instantly," Faith said. "Unpack later."

"Faith! I've got to take a bath first."

"That's what the ocean's for," Faith said. "We never take baths down here."

Margaret was somewhat shocked. "Really," she pleaded. "I'm filthy."

Faith conceded and showed her to the bathroom. Twenty minutes later Margaret came downstairs, bathed and combed, wearing a new one-piece black and white print bathing suit. Finding no trace of Faith on the first floor, she picked up a magazine and dropped into an armchair to wait for her.

A tall gray-haired man rushed into the room from the kitchen. His vividly handsome face called for a top hat or a homburg, a dinner jacket or a Chesterfield. Instead he was wearing a baseball cap, a filthy once-white sweatshirt and equally unwashed khaki pants.

He glared at Margaret as if he had caught her pilfering the family silver.

"You," he roared. "What's your name—Margaret? Why the hell aren't you out on the beach?"

"I—was waiting for—for Faith."

"Waiting for Faith? What're you doing a damn fool thing like that for? She's probably out behind a dune necking with that Hollywood lifeguard."

"Oh, no," Margaret protested. "She said—"

He looked at Margaret as if she were his only daughter and had failed his fondest expectations utterly. "Who cares what she *said?* Haven't you found out yet what people *say* doesn't mean a damn thing?"

"But I'm sure—" Margaret began.

*"Sure!* Listen to me. I spend ten thousand dollars a year to keep this comic-book castle together. The sole purpose is to give people some sun! Are you going to sit around in that bathing-beauty outfit being sure and wasting my money?

"How long you staying?" he went on, before Margaret could even begin an answer. "You realize, of course, that you make my whole family look like a lot of misfits?"

"I think I'm staying two weeks."

"Impossible," he roared. "*Im*-possible! Nobody can get a tan in two weeks. Call your mother up tonight and tell her you're staying till Labor Day."

"But that's two more weeks," Margaret gasped.

"She'll go home tomorrow if you don't shut up," Faith shouted from the stairs. A moment later she appeared in a light-blue two-piece Lastex bathing suit.

"If somebody didn't speak up," he roared, "this girl'd go home looking like she just escaped from a monastery."

"It's people like you who'll drive her into one," Faith stormed. "And that's where we should have put you long ago." She rushed at him and began to shove him out of the room. "Beat it," she said. "Go down and play poker with the Commissioner."

"I can't afford it," he protested. "He took me for fifty-five cents yesterday."

He stopped at the door and pointed dramatically at Margaret.

"Young woman," he bellowed, "you heard what I said about calling your mother. Now get on that phone tonight or I'll have to do it myself."

Faith slammed the door in his face and turned to Margaret.

"That's my father," she said. "When he goes on that way it's a sure sign he likes you. Believe it or not. Let's hit the beach."

Still slightly dazed, Margaret followed Faith out on the front porch and stopped, dazzled now, not by sound, but sight. Sun and sand filled the air with an intense brightness, a blending of heat and light. Beyond the sand the sun played less whitely, but still intensely, on the flat dark-blue sea. Above was a different blue, light-drenched, crystalline, curving down the afternoon glow to meet the dark line of the sea's horizon. A soft wind played at Margaret's hair and the skirt of her bathing suit, adding a delicate touch of life to the scene, which was as empty of motion as a painting.

"It's all so—different," Margaret said, and stepped into the white sand. It was warm—almost hot—beneath her feet. She curled her toes into it and laughed with sudden inexplicable pleasure.

"Come on," Faith said, "you have to greet Mother."

They trudged across the beach to a woman sitting alone beneath a large pink and white umbrella. "Mother," Faith said, in a somewhat flat, unnatural voice, "Margaret's here."

"Oh my dear. *Finally*."

Mrs. Kilpatrick held out a slim, bony browned hand. The face was a shock, after the Judge's worldly good looks. It could have been copied from a saint in a medieval tapestry. The eyes were wide, deep and brilliant, the mouth, even when fixed in a formal smile, as now, was drawn and spiritual. There was no excess flesh. The skin seemed almost translucent against the skull.

"*Margaret.* It's so good to see you again. How is your *wonderful* mother? I don't know what I'd do without her, what any of us would do. Why, when I had to go in the hospital for that silly arthritis operation she simply *ran* that Marian bridge. And what she did for the White Fathers while I was recuperating in Florida! I told the Archbishop I was *ashamed* to see my name at the head of the committee, when Mrs. Connolly did all the work."

"Oh," Margaret said, "she—she loves it. I hope you're feeling better."

"Far better than I deserve." She held up the slim brown hand. "See. I can move my fingers now. They had to break each one joint by joint. It's a new treatment for arthritis. Horribly painful. But I offered up the suffering to the Little Flower for a special intention. And she heard me. I suppose Faith's told you the wonderful news about her sister Theresa?"

"No, I—"

"She's entered the novitiate. Her father thought she was too young, but her confessor didn't agree and I don't either. Do you? I was *so* thrilled. You know I've prayed and prayed for a vocation in our family, and she was my last hope. Now I can concentrate on *you,* Margaret."

As Mrs. Kilpatrick laughed in a small tinkling way, a strange combination of feelings assailed Margaret. Theresa Kilpatrick, that mousy little teen-ager in the convent? She had been barely visible around the Kilpatrick house the one or two times Margaret had visited. It was hardly surprising that Faith did not tell her the news, yet for some reason Margaret felt vaguely annoyed—or was it envious?

"Sometimes I think you're a witch doctor, Mother," Faith said in a cold, cutting voice.

Mrs. Kilpatrick's laughter trilled again, precise and exquisitely ladylike. "You skeptics, you'll all learn eventually that you can't fight the Little Flower."

"I haven't stopped trying," Faith said.

"Oh-h-h," Mrs. Kilpatrick said, dismissing her daughter with a wave of her hand. "Margaret, when are we going to convert her? We'll have to pray a little harder. But you've spent enough time listening to this ancient invalid. Go have fun now. We'll have lots more chats before you go, Margaret."

"I hope so," Margaret said.

As they continued down the beach toward the ocean, Faith said, "You have too many chats with her and you'll wind up keeping Theresa company."

"Would that be such a catastrophe?"

Faith made a strangling sound. She spread a worn green blanket out on the sand and flung herself down on it. "This hostess bit is going to kill me. But I've sworn not to argue with you. Especially on that subject."

"There isn't much you haven't said, anyway," Margaret reminded her, with a smile.

"True," Faith said, flipping over on her back. "Let's lie here in absolute silence till we get good and baked, and then make a dash for the water."

"Sounds nice," Margaret said, stretching out beside her. The sun beat fiercely on her legs and arms and face. But it was curiously pleasant.

"Do you think you might take the Judge's suggestion and stay an extra two weeks?" Faith said. "It didn't sound like an invitation but it was."

"Oh, I don't know, Faith, my mother—"

A male face appeared above them. The blond hair was short, almost crew cut; the blue eyes were wide and direct. The strong straight lips were parted in a half smile.

"I'm sorry, Miss Kilpatrick," he said. "Soliciting on the beach is forbidden."

Faith bounced to a sitting position with an outraged gasp.

"Is that any way for a loafguard to talk?"

Margaret did not move. Under lids half closed from the intense sun, she watched the young man stroll around the blanket and stand at the foot. He was about six feet tall; his build was slim and sinewy, strong without a bulky thickness. He had a tawny tan, against which the hair on his chest and legs and arms was golden. He wore faded blue trunks, and a whistle hung from a leather thong around his neck.

Faith looked up at him impudently, a grin on her round freckled face. She seemed to take intense pleasure in saying nothing. He dug his toes into the sand and smiled back at her.

"Nice day," he said.

"It was," Faith said.

There was another moment of silence. He continued to smile unabashedly down at them. Faith sighed and shook her head in mournful surrender.

"Margaret," she said, "I'd like you to meet someone. Margaret Connolly, Dick Thornton. Margaret's my roommate."

"Hello," Margaret said, sitting up.

His face became solemn and he said: "You've had a chance, then, to make a thorough study. . . ."

He nodded toward Faith. Margaret caught the smile in his eyes but did not understand what he was trying to say. She half smiled uncertainly.

"From your experience," Dick went on, "I'm sure you'll agree that it's a clear-cut case of megalomania, with overtones of delirium tremens."

"Do you really think so?" Margaret said, still only half rising to his mood.

"Listen to me, Miss Connolly," Faith said. "This is what is known as a lifeguard. But it isn't your life that you have to guard against him."

Dick pounced on her and casually shoved her face into the blanket.

"Hey, Larry," he called. "Take her away. She's starting to babble again."

Margaret looked over her shoulder and saw a thinner, shorter young man walking toward them. He was not good-looking but there was something definitely magnetic about his face. The nose was quite sharp and prominent, the mouth tight and sensitive. His dark-red hair was unkempt and uncut. There was something disdainful and challenging in his expression. Before anyone spoke, he looked to Margaret as if he was daring her to contradict him.

"Larry Donahue, Margaret Connolly," Dick said, still holding Faith's face in the blanket.

Larry nodded and said brusquely, "I've heard the name—frequently."

Margaret gave him a look which she hoped was cool and unimpressed. But he had already turned to Dick. "What seems to be the trouble?" he said.

"Your American Dream Girl here," Dick said. "Demonstrating once more the evil effects of after hours' drinking."

Faith struggled free and sat up. "Oh, God," she said when she saw Larry.

"Listen, Faith," Dick said. "I just want to give you a little advice. Like all intellectual types, Larry is very sensitive. If you continue this callous treatment, you will undoubtedly lose his heart."

"His heart is nonexistent," Faith said. "It died of virulent abstraction years ago."

"Do you really room with her, Margaret?" Larry said.

"I'm afraid so," Margaret said with another careful smile.

"Let us in on the secret," Dick said. "How do you shut her up?"

Margaret's laugh was forced. "Where do you go to college?" she asked.

"College?" Dick Thornton laughed wryly. "Wow, am I mortified."

"He's graduating from State's law school next June," Faith said cheerfully. "And he thinks he looks mature and thirty-fivish, so you've cut him to the quick and I'm glad."

Dick ignored Faith and smiled at Margaret. "I'm a doddering twenty-four. It's a compliment."

"You mean you don't want to look like our solemn balding intellectual here?" Faith said.

"Who's balding?" Larry said.

"You are," Faith said, and rubbed a handful of sand into his hair.

Larry seized Faith's arm and pinned her face down on the blanket. "Let's see, we were talking about college, weren't we, Margaret?"

"Yes," Margaret said, not quite sure whether she should continue the discussion with Faith in such a compromised position. "I suppose you're in law school too?"

"Not quite," Larry said in a dry, offhand voice. "My G.I. Bill expired and I've been forced to join the great army of the ungainfully employed. I'm working nights for our town's crusading newspaper."

"Oh, I'm sorry," Margaret said.

"There's nothing to be sorry about," Larry snapped. "I'll finish eventually."

"Oh," Margaret floundered, still trying to be friendly. "You live in the city?"

Dick glowered at her. "You mean it's obvious that he does and I don't?"

"Oh, no," Margaret said, completely intimidated now. "Does your family—have a house near here?"

"I freeload," Larry said.

"That's the understatement of the century," Faith said, still with her face in the blanket. "He's spent so much time at the O'Connors' house the dog bites Jake when he comes in at night."

Dick threw a towel over her head. "For God's sake, take her away," he said to Larry.

"Where?" Larry said. "No matter how far away I take her, she always finds her way back."

Dick pointed to the ocean. "How about that way?"

"That's a thought." Larry dragged Faith to her feet and started for the water. Faith pulled her hand free, scooped up her bathing hat, and ran down the beach ahead of him, tucking in her hair. Larry slouched after her, deliberately refusing to hurry.

"Come on, Muscles."

Faith stood at the water's edge, daring him to catch her. Suddenly Larry broke into a run, and before Faith could move, he had her by the hips and had flung her into an incoming swell. He dived in after her and they swam out together.

*It was all so different.*

Margaret stared out at the two swimmers for a long moment, and it was only after she had tried unsuccessfully to adjust her mind to such casual roughhousing that she realized she must cope with the problem of talking to Dick Thornton. She glanced shyly at him, deciding it would be best for him to speak first.

"How long are you down for?" he asked.

"Two weeks—I think," Margaret said. "Though Judge Kilpatrick just told me that it was going to be four. . . ."

"It might be four then," Dick said with a quick laugh. "What do you think of the Judge?"

"I've never met anyone like him in my life."

"Congratulations. You're an honest woman. Most people just jump back and say, 'Well, he's nice really, I guess—' "

"What do you think of him?"

"A lot. He loaned me the money for my first year of college, before the war. When my G.I. Bill ran out he got me a scholarship for these last two years of law school. . . ."

"I've never met him before."

Margaret drained a handful of sand through her fingers and drew a meditative circle around it. "Where did you go to college?"

"State. Would . . . you like to go out tonight? Maybe double-date with Larry and Faith?"

"Tonight? Oh . . . I . . ."

"Okay. Break it to me as painlessly as possible. You're engaged?"

"No."

"Going steady?"

"No!"

"Faith's got you a date already?"

"No."

"Well . . . then?"

Margaret shoved her hand slowly into the hot sand. It made a small white bulge, like a grave.

"All right," she said. "If Faith wants to go. After all, she's the hostess. . . ."

"I'll twist her arm," Dick said. "About eight, okay?" He looked down toward the water. "I've got to get back to work."

"All right," Margaret said.

He strolled away while Margaret sat numbly, her mind gripped by two thoughts. *He's probably not a Catholic. He's twenty-four.*

"Well, I'll be goddammed! Margaret!"

Judge Kilpatrick advanced across the sand toward her in a pair of knee-length khaki trunks. He looked even more formidable than he had in the house, as he ran his fingers through his wavy gray hair and roared down at her: "Haven't you gone in the water yet?"

"No," Margaret said. "Your daughter deserted me."

"I *told* you she'd do that." The Judge took her by the arm and hauled her to her feet. "Come on. Get your hat and keep me company."

He put his arm through hers and marched toward the water. A stocky man on a blanket a few dozen yards to the right waved to them, and the Judge bellowed, "I sure can pick 'em, can't I, Ben?"

Dick was standing at the water's edge with three small boys.

"Thornton," the Judge said, "you got any hopes of getting a date with this bathing beauty tonight?"

"I've got more than hopes, Judge," Dick said.

Margaret absorbed herself in tucking her hair beneath her cap.

"I don't care what you've got," the Judge said. "Give 'em up right now. I'm about to display my athletic prowess."

Moderate swells were forming a few yards out and breaking on the shore. Maintaining the same dignified pace, the Judge strolled toward one of these and suddenly flung himself into it, with the bellow of an overwrought rhinoceros. He surfaced on the other side, his gray hair a mop over his beetling eyebrows, and ordered Margaret to get wet. She dived into the next swell.

"Did you get a date with that Hollywood lifeguard?" the Judge demanded as she surfaced beside him.

"Yes," Margaret said. "I mean he asked me. I said yes. . . ."

"What the hell else would you say? Do you realize he's had half my family mooning around like a lot of love-sick giraffes since the middle of June?"

"Faith, you mean?"

"No. Faith's too damn busy making a fool of herself with that sourball Donahue. I mean Barbara and Helen."

"Oh, I haven't met them."

"You will any minute," the Judge said. "They're on your blanket now, waiting for a progress report. They're my wife's nieces. Only fourteen and fifteen, and it kills them to admit it."

The Judge spent most of his time bobbing along on his back like a buoy. While he bobbed, he talked. He amazed Margaret by knowing all about her family. How her father had been forced to give up his hopes of becoming a lawyer when his father died, and he, the oldest, had to support his mother. "He's the best damn law clerk in the city," the Judge said. He knew her mother's family too. "The Gahagans. What a screwy bunch they were. Do you ever see your Uncle Bart?"

"Not for years. He lives out West now."

"We were good friends in the old days. Many is the night I sat up with him until dawn tearing the Catholic Church apart."

"Oh," Margaret said.

Uncle Bart was a forbidden topic in the Connolly household. He had divorced his wife and remarried. The family had declared him a moral pariah.

"What do you think of Mount St. Monica's?" the Judge asked.

"I like it. I mean—I have no complaints. I wouldn't have gone to college at all if I hadn't won a scholarship there."

The Judge proceeded to cross-examine her, demanding her opinion of this teacher, that course. Margaret could see her answers did not satisfy him. His only comment after five or ten minutes of probing was, after a walrus-like snort: "The worst mistake I ever made was sending Faith to that damn school." Whereupon he flipped into a sidestroke and announced that their swim was over.

On the beach the Judge ignored Margaret and made for the stocky man, who was now dozing on his blanket, a newspaper over his face. He woke up rapidly when the Judge gave him an enthusiastic kick. Margaret walked slowly up the sand toward her own blanket. Barbara and Helen Brophy watched her approach with expectantly excited eyes. They were both overweight, round-faced and snub-nosed, so homely that even Margaret, who did her best to avoid uncharitably harsh judgments of people, winced inwardly at the sight of them. They greeted her with a gush of simultaneous excitement.

"Did he ask you for a date?"

"Who?" Margaret said with deliberate evasion.

"Dick!"

"In a way."

Margaret took off her bathing cap and shook the water from her hair.

"Tonight?" Helen whispered, glancing nervously down the beach to make sure the subject was not within eavesdropping distance.

"Yes, I think so," Margaret said, determined to be offhand. "If Faith can go with someone."

"Oh, she'll go," Barbara said, "with Larry Donahue. She's *crazy* about him. But why go out with her?"

"Yes," Helen said eagerly. "Why don't you ditch her? There might be a full moon tonight. You could drive down to Manasquerry. . . . Isn't that the most romantic name?" She sighed and gazed mournfully at Margaret. "If only I had your figure."

Margaret pretended to be absorbed in drying and combing her hair. To her immense relief, Faith and Larry appeared, strolling along the water's edge holding hands. She seized on them as a subject.

"Does Larry like Faith, do you think?"

"Absolutely not," Barbara said. She glared belligerently at her sister. "Helen thinks he does, but I can tell."

"I think he's rediscovering Faith. They've known each other a long time," Helen said.

"Bunk," Barbara said. "You think love is like the *Woman's Home Companion* says it is. There's nothing to his interest but sex. And you know how *sporadic* that is."

Dick came down the beach from the opposite direction and met Faith and Larry at the water's edge. They exchanged a few words, and the three of them strolled toward the blanket. Barbara and Helen grabbed frantically for their bathing caps and towels and fled. "We can't *endure* being too close to him," Helen whispered before she scampered after her sister.

"Well," Faith said as she and her two escorts approached. "You *are* the ideal guest. You even arrange the hostess's social schedule."

"It was arranged for me," Margaret said lightly.

"What did he do, use hypnosis?"

"She was blinded by the sun," Dick said.

"Let's hope she's not similarly affected by moonlight." Faith picked up a corner of the blanket and began to pull it out from under Margaret. "We had best retire to our boudoirs, Miss Connolly, to properly prepare ourselves for an evening with these two horrors."

As they came up the porch steps Margaret heard a familiar voice calling her name. Esther Sugrue, president of their soon-to-be senior class at Mount St. Monica, sat complacently in a glider at the far end of the porch. A dumpy figure, stringy black hair, a face dominated by a beaked nose, none of these disadvantages ever seemed to trouble Esther. Poetry, literature, the world of the mind, enabled her to ignore her formidable deficiencies. Being the daughter of one of the city's wealthier businessmen also helped.

"Have you ever seen anything worse in a bathing suit?" Faith said, smiling savagely.

"Oh, Faith, you never stop," Esther giggled.

It was not Esther's usual reply to Faith's barbs. Jim Kilpatrick appeared, carrying two tall frosted glasses of Coke. "It's not so funny when you have to live with it," he said. "Poor Margaret must know that."

"Margaret happens to have a sense of humor," Faith snapped.

"So do I," Jim said. "That's why I don't laugh at your jokes."

"You lost yours in a philosophy class," Faith said.

"I saw Margaret talking to that handsome lifeguard," Esther said kittenishly.

"She not only talked to him, she has a date with him," Faith said.

"Oh, Margaret, you do work fast," Esther simpered.

This was a new Esther, obviously manufactured for Jim Kilpatrick's benefit.

"He's a very thoughtful guy," Jim Kilpatrick said. "I'd be willing to bet he becomes a Catholic someday."

"Oh, for God's sake," Faith exploded, "what's that got to do with it?"

Jim gave his sister another contemptuous look. "I think Margaret could be a very good influence on him."

Upstairs in Margaret's bedroom Faith was still fuming. "My brother never stops trying to convert the world."

"We're supposed to, aren't we?" Margaret said.

"What?"

"Convert people. Aren't we all supposed to be apostles?"

"Meg—anyone who tries to be an apostle on her first date with a man like Dick Thornton will never have a second one."

"What's so terrible about that?"

"Oh, nothing's terrible about anything," Faith snapped. "If you think that way before you've even dated him, what's the point? You had exactly one date all last year—with that sickening creep Tommy Loughran. I'd just like to see you meet one intelligent, attractive man—"

Alone in her room, Margaret dressed slowly, watching the shadows creep across the white beach, the light dissolve on the placid sea. It was easy enough to finish the sentence Faith had begun, ". . . meet one intelligent, attractive man—before you go into the convent."

Yes, whispered that voice behind the door, there was the familiar question, Margaret, sometimes spoken, more often unspoken. This vocation that so many people (but not Faith) were so certain you had—didn't it explain why you were always reduced to tongue-tied panic when you met a man? Why you preferred to watch while others had fun? Wasn't it a sign that you were meant for other, more important things, beyond and above the idle amusements of this world? Was it satisfaction that you felt flooding your mind at this thought, Margaret? Or only its pale younger sister, consolation? Or was it all explained by your father's shyness—his reserve, you preferred to call it? How many hours you have spent trying to answer those questions, Margaret.

Dinner with the Kilpatricks annihilated this impulse to solemn reflection. It was like eating at a table loaded with exploding fireworks. Seated next to Jim Kilpatrick, Margaret inadvertently lit a fuse by asking him what he planned to do when he graduated.

"I'm going to get a master's in philosophy and then go into social work."

"And he shall be known as St. James the Least," Faith said.

"I hate to think what you'll be known as, if you keep hanging around with that slob Donahue."

"He thinks, which is more than you can say."

"If anyone had told me, ten years ago, that I was bringing up a social worker, I would have punched him in the mouth," Judge Kilpatrick said.

"Because they're a threat to political machines? They are, you know."

"Because it's a job for pinheads," the Judge snarled, "pinheads who think they know enough to tell other people how to live their lives."

"When you give people a sense of dignity, they won't be so inclined to take a handout from the ward boss."

"Nobody can give anybody a sense of dignity," the Judge growled. "If he can't find it on his own, he'll stay in those goddamn slums forever."

"The Christian takes a different view of human nature—"

"I am so damn sick of hearing you use that word *Christian* as if you owned it," the Judge roared. "How the hell does that give you a leg up on understanding reality?"

*"Credo ut intelligam,"* Jim said.

"What the hell does that mean?"

"I believe in order that I may understand," Faith said. "St. Anselm. He screwed his head on backwards, and everybody from Thomas Aquinas to Jacques Maritain has been imitating his marvelous example."

"Maybe your brother was born to be a social worker," the Judge said. "They've got their heads screwed on backwards too."

"Well, *I* think social work is wonderful," Mrs. Kilpatrick said. "Its inspiration, as Jimmy often says, is fundamentally Christian. Even Catholic. After all, the first social worker was St. Vincent de Paul, right?"

"Who gives a damn what some Frog did in the eighteenth century?" the Judge said. "I'm talking about the United States in the year 1948."

"Somebody's got to do something about this country," Jim Kilpatrick said.

"What the hell's wrong with this country?" the Judge asked.

"What's right about it? Its whole philosophy, from the Declaration of Independence to the United Nations Charter, is nothing but corrupt Protestantism, Pelagianism really. Unless we can infuse some Catholic substance into it, there's really no hope."

"Catholic substance," the Judge snorted. "What the hell does that mean? We all should start eating spaghetti and meatballs, and then march around giving the Fascist salute? That's what they were doing up at Our Lady of Messina parish, till we dragged Monsignor Monteleone and a couple of his fellow spaghetti benders down to City Hall and told them to start saluting the flag or else."

"There's a lot to be said for Mussolini's corporate state," Jim said loftily. "Several Catholic thinkers praised it highly, until he made the mistake of getting involved with Hitler."

"Sure they praised it highly," Faith said, "because your so-called Catholic thinkers are a bunch of Fascists just like him."

"Oh, Margaret, I must show you Theresa's first letter from the novitiate," Mrs. Kilpatrick said. "It's so full of happiness. They're scrubbing floors on their hands and knees. Imagine! But every scrub of the brush is a prayer, she said."

"Yes," Margaret said, still struggling to make sense out of the cross-fire crackling among the other three Kilpatricks. She sided with Jim, of course, and Faith's skeptical sniping hardly surprised her. But she was appalled and bewildered by the Judge's assault on his son. In her infrequent visits to the Kilpatrick home in the city she had never met the Judge. It was startling, yet somehow subtly reassuring, to discover that these powerful, important people were obviously unhappy and divided. Did it mean that Father Malone was right—no one could succeed in this world without compromising or at least confusing his spiritual values?

The argument subsided with a final volley of insults, and Margaret was able to concentrate more enthusiastically on Mrs. Kilpatrick's ecstatic description of her daughter Theresa's novitiate. Her slim, surprisingly cold hand clutched Margaret's wrist as she said, "I often wish that I had made that choice. Not that I haven't had a happy life. But even when you have everything you can possibly want in this world, there is always the feeling that you aren't doing enough, you aren't truly giving back to God all He has given you. Sometimes I even think that everything I have and use so selfishly, like the car, the servants, is somehow a subtraction from what I could be doing—"

"Goddamn it," the Judge said, "is there one saltcellar on this table that works?"

After supper the family scattered. The Judge took a walk on the beach, Mrs. Kilpatrick retired to her bedroom, Jim departed in pursuit of Esther Sugrue. Faith led Margaret out on the porch, and they sat in old wicker rockers, watching the last light fade on the dark-blue sea. Suddenly the hood of a bright-red car appeared on the side road, the shiny bumper almost touching the steep slope of the dune. A horn sounded a single summons. Faith proceeded to vault over the porch railing onto the sand below. Margaret, a little appalled, walked around to the front steps. Dick Thornton was standing beside the car door wearing gray slacks and a blue linen sport jacket. He took a long look at Margaret as she walked toward him and for a panicky moment she wondered if her year-old white piqué dress looked absurdly unfashionable. The skirt flared much more than the New Look. It was impossible to tell from the small smile on Dick's lips as she slipped into the front seat and he closed the door behind her.

Dick got behind the wheel and they bumped down the sandy drive to the highway. Larry, in the back with Faith, announced in train dispatchers' tones, "Adjust your safety belts everyone."

They drove very slowly through the town of Paradise and proceeded at a sedate forty-five along a broad four-lane ocean parkway. Faith gave the back of the seat a violent kick. "Stop trying to make an impression on her, you fraud in your Ford. Scare her to death now and get it over with."

"I beg your pardon," Dick said, and slowed to forty.

"Do not accept this as any resemblance to how this man really drives, Margaret. This is the first time I have ever ridden with him at a sane speed."

"He feels sorry for you," Larry said. "He knows a retarded adolescent when he sees one."

"That's why I find your conversation so fascinating."

Dick kept the speedometer below fifty until they swung off the highway and rolled past a series of illuminated signs welcoming them to a place called Barberry Park. Margaret had heard of it, of course. It was the state's Coney Island, crammed with fun houses, whoopee rides, hot-dog stands, dance pavilions, all festooned with garish red, yellow, purple and green neon. The sea breeze itself seemed drenched with roasting popcorn as they mounted the boardwalk and contemplated the miles of lurid sound and color.

"Here it is," Larry Donahue said with an oratorical gesture, "the apotheosis of the American Dream, the pursuit of happiness reduced to twentieth-century terms. Fun."

"Some of us happen to like fun," Faith said.

"Yeah, we can't all be intellectuals," Dick Thornton said. "Let's go burn some patriotic dollars."

To Margaret's amazement she enjoyed the next two hours. Dick and Larry avoided the more childish rides and supplied most of the amusement in the games they chose. They argued and fooled through a ridiculous round of miniature golf in which Larry cheated outrageously, poured several dollars into skee ball and won nothing, put a single dime on greyhound 13 in a wheel of fortune game and walked off with a panda almost as big as Faith. Dick named him Kilpatrick because, he said, pandas were rare too.

"What's so rare about the Kilpatricks?" Faith asked.

"Like mackerels in the moonlight, they both shine and stink," Larry Donahue said.

"Oh, that's so funny," Faith said. "Another joke like that and Dick may have to give me artificial respiration."

"Don't try to understand them, Margaret," Dick said with a smile. "Just be glad you're normal."

"I'm thirsty," Faith said, "and besides we should baptize the Kilpatricks' new arrival."

She gave the panda a maternal pat.

"And, of course, there's only one place," Larry said grimly.

"Not Mario's again," Dick said.

"She likes the lighting," Larry said. "Nobody notices when I carry her out."

"Just remember, Margaret," Dick said, "any resemblance between this joint and some place I'd take you is strictly accidental."

"Let's hurry or we'll miss the midnight orgy," Faith said.

Mario's was on a side road about twenty minutes from Barberry Park. Booths and tables crowded a long, low room shrouded in cigarette smoke and shadow. Nothing particularly orgiastic seemed to be happening. The patrons, all young, huddled along the walls talking noisily. In the nether darkness of the rear a jukebox emoted mournfully.

> You are too beautiful, my dear, to be true.
> I am a fool for beauty.
> Fooled by the knowledge that because I have
>     found you
> I could have bound you, too.

"I understand this place is negotiating a contract with the home for the blind," Dick said as they sat down in a booth near the front.

"Also the foundling home," Larry said. "What are we drinking?"

Margaret ordered ginger ale and the two men ordered beer. Faith chose Scotch on the rocks. "Why can't you be pure like your roommate?" Larry said. "It's cheaper."

"I'm sure that's the only thing about purity you find attractive."

"I'm reassured about convent girls," Dick said. "If Margaret is more typical, that is."

"She's typical all right," Faith said.

"I am not typical," Margaret said. "No one is typical."

"Everyone is typical," Larry Donahue said, "but no one wants to admit it. We all think of ourselves as fabulously unique."

"And only a few of us are," Faith said. "What do I typify?"

"The successful Irish politician's daughter."

"And what do you typify?"

"The Irish Catholic who has learned to think."

"And Dick?" Faith said. "Let's not leave anybody out."

"The Wasp in search of his acre of diamonds."

"Not bad. Not bad at all," Dick said cheerfully. "Won't you be surprised when I find it?"

Larry smiled sardonically. "But I think Margaret is our most interesting type by far. It takes at least a sentence to explain the rest of us, but you can sum up Margaret in just one word: Catholic."

"What's wrong with that?" Margaret said uncertainly. There was a nasty undertone in Larry's voice, a kind of muted anger, that disturbed her.

"There's nothing wrong with it," Larry said. "It's kind of marvelous to meet someone who has completely accepted the system."

"And you don't?"

"He doesn't accept anything," Faith said. "Not even money."

"Seriously," Larry said, "don't you ever get tired of being told what to do, what to think, what to feel?"

"I'm sorry," Margaret said, "I don't even know what you're talking about."

"Lawrence, my boy," Dick said, "maybe it's about time for you to face up to a hard fact: not everybody is as bugged by religion as you are."

"I am not bugged by religion," Larry said. "I am bugged by fraud masquerading as religion."

"That's your version," Dick said. "Margaret gets a lot of satisfaction out of it. I say three cheers for Margaret."

"Listen to him," Larry said. "He sounds like a ruling elder. When's the last time you visited your little whitewashed cathedral down there on Main Street?"

"Okay. But I don't hold anything against those who do go—there or to any other church."

"Ain't tolerance beautiful," Larry said. "But the more I think of it, the more I suspect it's really mental leukemia."

Margaret struggled, largely in vain, to follow this conversation. It was obvious that she had been rather thoroughly discussed before she arrived. It was also obvious that Larry Donahue was one of those disenchanted Catholics, similar, if not identical, to her Uncle Bart. Faith leaned the same way so naturally there was no help forthcoming from her. Amazing that her only defender was Dick, a Protestant.

"I'm going to solve it all," Faith said, "by inventing a new religion. Impuritanism."

"How does it go?" Dick said.

"We very sternly support all the Commandments except the Sixth—for you the Seventh. Impuritans will be very serious about making money, upholding law and order with public hangings and an occasional stake burning, but virginity will be absolutely forbidden from the age of sixteen and adultery will be an act of profound religious significance."

"You could sweep the country," Dick said.

"Yea verily, the anti-intellectual has spoken," Larry said.

"Do you hear that sour note?" Faith sighed. "I call upon you all to witness the fact. Here I am, the personification of allure, preaching orgy as a way of life, and what do I get from him—paranoia."

"As we all know from our recent military experience," Larry said, "the best defense is a strong offense. What do you think of Impuritanism, Margaret?"

"Margaret doesn't need it," Faith said. "She's not an intellectual."

"She doesn't think?"

"Of course she thinks," Faith said, "but not twenty-four hours a day like you, which means she is capable of having a genuine emotion occasionally."

"Why don't you go out with her instead of me?"

Faith laughed. "I'm not that kind of girl either." She rattled the ice in her glass. "Give me another drink and I may prove it."

They ordered another round and Dick said, "Quick, Margaret, change the subject. I'm bored."

"Why does the Judge call you a Hollywood lifeguard?"

"The Judge is like his daughter," Larry Donahue said. "He believes in slipping everyone the needle. It keeps them on the defensive."

"The Judge fascinates me," Dick said.

"He depresses me," Larry said.

"Why?"

"He's a phony like the rest of his cronies."

"True or false, Faith?" Dick said.

"I don't know," Faith said, her voice suddenly muted.

"The Judge has made it," Dick said. "He can afford to clown around. But I suspect he's pretty damn serious about a lot of things."

"The essential phoniness remains. He rings hollow," Larry said.

"Everybody rings hollow somewhere," Dick said.

"Not Margaret," Larry said. "She's solid and true all the way through. Do you know you fascinate your roommate, Margaret? You've become a symbol for her."

"Lawrence, cut it out," Dick said.

"I don't see how—that could happen," Margaret said.

"You're completely devout and completely happy. She isn't devout and she isn't happy. In her addled brain this adds up to a syllogism. Which says a lot for the logic they're teaching you at Mount St. Monica."

"Speaking of logic," Faith said, jingling her glass, "what do you deduce from this?"

"It's time to depart, lest my wallet become as empty as your head."

In the car Dick started the motor and said, "Well, Margaret, now you've seen what life is like in our enchanting little summer colony, what train are you taking home tomorrow?"

"Don't mention that disgusting word," Faith said from the rear of the car. "The night is young and all that jazz. On to Manasquerry."

"Have a heart," Dick said. "I have to get up at seven o'clock tomorrow morning."

"Oh, let's humor her," Larry said.

"Okay," Dick sighed.

Manasquerry. Margaret suddenly remembered Barbara Brophy's paean to its romantic possibilities. *Alone on the boardwalk. . . . The full moon.*

At first Margaret was not sure whether it was an illusion created by the darkness, but Dick seemed to be driving much faster. Billboards, houses, road signs leaped up in the headlights and vanished instantly. A hot wind tore in through the window and played havoc with her hair. She finally stole a look at the speedometer. It read eighty-five.

Margaret turned to see why Faith was saying nothing about this suicidal speed. And when she turned she saw an unbelievable sight in the back seat. Larry had Faith in his arms. They were deep in a passionate kiss.

For ten minutes Margaret sat in numb silence. Then Dick began asking her where she lived and other harmless vital statistics. She answered him in monosyllables. But the conversation helped her to regain her equilibrium.

"What does your father do?" she asked.

"Real estate. Summer stuff mostly."

"He's sweet," Faith said from the back. "The little notes he always leaves in the house—telling us to have a nice summer."

"Yes," Dick said, "everybody loves Rob Thornton."

*But not you,* Margaret thought, catching the flat, falling note in Dick's voice. It was bewildering—and at the same time it filled her with unexpected pity. How difficult it must be, not to love someone so close to you. It must involve so many hours of masquerading, of trying not to cause pain.

They rolled through Paradise Beach at a sedate speed. Then the road was a long pale line in the darkness. Dick sent the car leaping down it in a terrific burst of speed. Margaret caught a glimpse of the dark bulk of the Kilpatrick house on the dunes. Then there was nothing but windswept blackness with house lights in the distance or an occasional car which they passed as if it were standing still.

Margaret's uneasiness mounted with the speed. What would Dick do on this dark boardwalk? What would she do? She dreaded having to do anything. He was mysterious, confusing. Her mind skipped frantically over the day. *Twenty-four and not a Catholic. When was the last time you visited your whitewashed cathedral? On the boardwalk in the moonlight. Supposed to be an apostle.* Ridiculous. You don't know what is going to happen. You are certain of only one thing; you are not going to neck with him or let him paw you, no matter what Faith and Larry do.

A moment later Dick turned off the highway and they crunched up a pebbled side street to the boardwalk. As they got out of the car Margaret murmured an aspiration. *Immaculate heart of Mary, pray for us.* They walked up the steps to the boardwalk.

Above, the sky was lavish with stars. Below, the beach was a dull grayish white and beyond it the calm sea stretched blackly. Manasquerry had no amusements. The beach and boardwalk were totally deserted.

"But—where's the moon?"

The words hung there like something in a comic strip before Margaret realized she had spoken them.

"Dick has it in his pocket," Faith said. "He forgot to hang it up."

Margaret tried to join in the laughter. But she was more inclined to weep. There you go again, Margaret, from bad to worse this time. From tongue-tied silence to outright, total stupidity. She tried to explain about Barbara and Helen Brophy, but everyone was laughing too hard to listen.

"If you don't feel it's safe, Dick," Faith said, "we'll be glad to go home."

"This is a very long boardwalk," Dick said. "Why don't you two start walking?"

"What are you going to do?"

"I'm going to sit right down there." Dick pointed toward the sand. "Just yell when you come back. And don't worry about us. We have Kilpatrick for a chaperone." He plopped the panda onto the railing in front of them. Margaret had not noticed he was carrying him.

"Okay," Faith said. She seized Larry's hand and dragged him a few reluctant steps.

"If you come back alone, Larry, we won't ask any questions," Dick said.

"I may," Larry said.

"I'm wearing my scapulars," Faith said. "I'm not afraid."

Margaret stood tensely for a moment, wondering whether she should refuse to go down. But when Dick took her hand and led her to the nearby steps, she followed him obediently. Her heart was pounding and a tiny pulse in her temple beat in a reflected rhythm, a syncopation of uncertainty and dread. *You can always run,* she told herself.

"Take off your shoes," Dick said as they reached the sand. "It's easier walking."

"No! I mean—I'm all right," Margaret said. In the next instant she floundered clumsily against him, and he laughed and said he had warned her.

Dick stopped about a hundred feet from the water. "Terrific night, isn't it?"

Margaret answered late, awkwardly, "Yes, wonderful . . ."

"I love the sea at night," Dick said. "It's best without a moon. There's something dark and huge about it that gets inside you."

He sat down on the sand, and Margaret sat cautiously down beside him at what she estimated was a safe distance. Dick took Kilpatrick off his hip and set him down beside them.

"This gentleman is here to guarantee my propriety."

Margaret laughed nervously. "Do you really think a Kilpatrick can guarantee anything like that?"

"Okay, I'll guarantee it," Dick said easily. "Does that make you feel any better?"

"I've read or heard somewhere," Margaret said hastily, "that the sea is—an image of the soul."

Dick laughed. "Does that mean I have a lot of darkness inside mine?"

"I didn't say that," Margaret said. She picked up some sand and rubbed it between her palms; it felt cool and soft, as if some of the starlight had gotten into it. Dick picked up a small piece of driftwood and played with it for a moment.

"Stupid argument in the bar," he said. "I felt sorry for you."

"I'm afraid I don't understand Larry Donahue."

Dick shook his head. "Larry's a strange guy. He got some of the highest marks in the history of the law school. But—he needs something right now that Faith could give him."

"What?"

"Understanding—sympathy."

"Maybe he's not giving her any."

Dick shrugged and flung his piece of driftwood down the beach.

"Who's supposed to do what first? No one likes to make a fool of himself. There are ways—of saying things, of saying enough. . . ."

"Why should she—how can she? When their beliefs are—entirely opposite."

"You think two people shouldn't disagree, is that what you're saying?"

"Of course not. There's bound to be some disagreement—on incidentals. But there has to be an agreement on the essentials—the principles people live by."

"Come on. You mean Faith—Larry—two people—can't get along if one believes Thomas Aquinas is a lot of baloney and the other thinks he's a great philosopher?"

"You put it in the worst possible way. I mean two people—for instance, one doesn't believe in God, and the other's very religious. What could they agree on?"

"They could agree that they loved each other."

For an instant Margaret felt a whirling, fluttering sensation—as if a bird or a large winged insect were frantically trying to escape from her body. She fought it desperately and was calm again. "But there has to be a basis for love."

"Just being a person is a basis for love, isn't it?"

"But it's the kind of person that matters. Isn't that determined by—what do you think?"

Dick pointed to the dark sea. "Do you think that's beautiful?"

"Yes."

"Why do you think it's beautiful? Because God made it? I mean is that how you arrive at the conclusion that it's beautiful? Step by step—God made it, therefore it's beautiful?"

"No," Margaret said. "It just is."

"That's right. I think it's beautiful too, for the same reason. There's a lot more to being a person than thinking. If you see life as it really is—see what's good in it and try to live that part of it—that's the important thing."

Margaret stared stubbornly down at the pale sand. "I still think—what you believe is important."

"Sure it's important. But there are other things just as important."

"You down there," Faith shouted from the boardwalk. "I'm going to call the police if you don't stop—"

Margaret's feelings were a strange mixture of relief and disappointment. One more failure, Margaret? One more time when you have met the world—didn't this man personify it in a way with his vague optimistic philosophy—and failed to summon the swift, devastating replies?

"Need some help?"

"What?"

He was standing above her, his arm outstretched. Without thinking she accepted the offer. As his fingers closed over hers and he pulled her erect, Margaret realized for the first time that Dick had not even tried to hold her hand.

# Chapter Two

Judge James Kilpatrick lit his cigarette and descended the stairs quoting Shakespeare.

> "O thou weed!
> Who art so lovely fair and smell'st so sweet
> That the sense aches at thee, would thou hadst ne'er been born!"

In the dining room, his daughter Faith greeted him with that new mixture of amusement and disapproval in her eyes. The Judge threw up his hands and took a backward step, astonishment on his face. "I took you for that cunning whore of Venice."

Beside her at the table, Margaret Connolly poised her cereal spoon in mid-passage, aghast at what might come next. But Faith coolly replied, "Whose solid virtue the shot of accident nor dart of chance could neither graze nor pierce?"

"Not bad. Not bad," said the Judge. "As for your friend, is she still 'a maiden ever bold, of spirit so still and quiet that her motion blushed at herself'?"

" 'Do not put me to't for I am nothing if not critical.' "

"Ah!" said the Judge, lifting his morning coffee and taking a long, deep whiff. "You're all the same—pictures out of doors, wild-cats in your kitchens, saints in your injuries, devils being offended, players in your housewifery and housewives in your beds."

"Get thee glass eyes," Faith said, "and like a scurvy politician seem to see things thou does not."

"You're out of the play," the Judge said.

"It still fits."

The Judge chuckled. "I will be hanged, if some eternal villain, some busy and insinuating rogue, some cogging cozening slave, to get some office, have not devised this slander."

Finishing his coffee with a loud, satisfied smack, the Judge returned the cup to the saucer with an equally emphatic clank. "Well," he said, "now step I forth to whip hypocrisy."

He paused at the door to take one last look at Margaret Connolly. The thick dark hair, the wide dark-blue eyes, the high prominent cheekbones and rich-lipped brooding mouth–it was almost unbelievable that Bill Connolly, poor spavined reed that he was, could have fathered this girl on that cow of a wife. It was enough to make a man believe in witches and warlocks. The girl was simply too fine, the beauty too elemental, to believe blood was responsible. Look at your own daughter. The very caricature of the peasant; the pug-nosed, puckish, freckled face that broke your heart every time you looked at it. And how many times would it break her heart before long? That was her worry, not yours. They were out of the nest, flapping and fluttering here on the beach like the gooney birds, and you could only watch them flounder and fall and urge them to fly again. If you still believed in God, it was only because He had proven to you, again and again, His sardonic sense of humor.

Yes, said the Judge to the empty morning beach as he seized a cane from the rack at the door and stepped over damp beach towels and abandoned life jackets, who would believe this broth of a boy with the soot of the coal yard barely scrubbed off his neck could have married Madeline Brophy, heiress to meat-packing millions? Those were the days, James, when you thought a pair of broad shoulders and a Barrymore profile were the answer to the woes of the world. Didn't they seem to be? Who could have foreseen that the bumbling Brophys with their Hispano Suizas and Packards, their summers in Europe aboard the latest Cunarder, their New York fashions and their resident Monsignor, were the worst collection of boobs since God goofed up Adam? It wasn't the big Depression of '29 that finished them; no, those sawdust heroes came apart at the seams in the little dip of 1919–20. There you were, James, with your dreams of genteel corporate law exploding in your face like the rotten sausages those meatheads (the perfect name for them) sold to the Army. There you were, with a wife who thought she was still the ideal combination of the Little Flower and Lady Bountiful, and all the sponging relatives who had gnawed out the guts of the company over the years trying to get in bed with you.

Which was just as well, the Judge thought as he slammed the door of his custom-built five-passenger Cadillac and turned on the radio. With a wife like the Little Flower, a man might as well have company in bed. There wasn't anything else to do.

He paused, his hand on the starter button, and looked up at the slice of his face in the rectangular mirror. What the devil, James? Whence comes all this rumination? You know your motto. *I am a kind of burr; I shall stick.* Some men must love my lady and some Joan. You have no regrets about the way life has treated you. You just feel entitled to make some explanations. Whatever made you think your smartass son and brat of a daughter would want to listen?

It was Margaret Connolly's fault. Her totally innocent gaze aroused memories of those halcyon days when you envisioned a lifetime of wedded bliss with the Little Flower. And of course Margaret's father, Bill Connolly, was a kind of symbol, like rebellious slaves and criminals the Romans used to crucify at crossroads. Bill Connolly with his resigned service in the halls of Stapleton Talbot, wiping the balls of the Protestant scions. No thank you. Better to cheat, steal, if necessary murder, to avoid that fate.

The Judge pressed the starter and the motor thundered into throaty life. Watch it, kid. You haven't carried on these kinds of arguments with yourself for decades. This goddamn younger generation is getting on your nerves. Especially that ratty little sourball, Larry Donahue. Every time you see him talking to your daughter, you want to kick him in the groin. The way he talks to you, with that mixture of contempt and good humor. Old Willie the Shake nailed his type a long time ago. *Yond Cassius hath a lean and hungry look. Such men are dangerous.*

*Jesus Christ.* Out on the highway he shifted quickly from second to third and slammed the motor up to sixty in ten seconds. It's a good thing you're getting away from this goddammed overgrown kindergarten, back to the real world where what matters is not a lot of half-baked opinions cooked up by synthetic Jesuits and oddball adolescents.

About ten miles beyond the town of Paradise Beach, a cluster of incredibly tiny bungalows squatted along the dunes. The Judge slowed to a stop as he reached the center of this settlement, and a stocky, bland-faced man in a cheap summer suit scrambled into the car beside him. "Hello, Jim," said Bernie Brophy in his usual half whine. The Judge barely nodded to his brother-in-law. There were times when he wondered why he had allowed his wife to talk him into acting as Uncle Bernie's chauffeur. He couldn't stand the sight of this faded marshmallow of a man, much less the sound of his wheedling voice. When he wasn't wheedling, he was drinking, and more than one morning he smelled like a spittoon in a waterfront bar. But this morning, with his inexplicably heightened self-consciousness, the Judge knew exactly why he did it. It was the satisfaction, still payable after twenty-five years, of seeing this human caricature humbly scrunching his fat ass into the Kilpatrick Cadillac.

"Goddamn it, Bernie," said the Judge, "I hope those shanties float. One good northeast storm and you'll be in the bay. Are you sure all the kids can swim?"

Bernie had eight kids. A nice sensible number for a man with a $4500 job in the county finance department. The Kilpatricks mercifully reduced the congestion in the cabin by boarding two or three of the older ones for several weeks at a time.

"Oh, we rode out last year's blow," Bernie said. "Remember that northeaster the end of August? Almost a hurricane. Just got a little flooding."

"Little flooding, hell. You were in the goddamn bay but you were too drunk to know it. Then the wind shifted and it blew you back where you started. I got the whole story from that lobsterman who fishes off the next dune."

"Oh, sure," said Bernie without enthusiasm. "How are Sis and the kids?"

"Sis is wonderful," the Judge said. "When I saw her at dinner last night her arthritis was causing her terrible pain. But she sprinkled Holy Water on it, as usual, and was smiling through. I didn't ask about her emphysema or her colitis, but I would say from the sound of her voice that she had definitely gotten rid of her cold. And of course the best news of all is she hasn't had a migraine headache in a month."

"Gee, that's great," Bernie said, either completely missing the sarcasm or diplomatically ignoring it.

"You know, when I look at those bungalows I think to myself how crazy life is. The Brophys started out living in shanties like those, and naturally they thought it was absolute hell. Now they're vacationing in the goddamn things, and they think it's wonderful."

"It's better than the city at this time of year," Bernie said.

"I can remember your old man telling me how his father used to slaughter the pigs he stole from the stockyards underneath the kitchen table. The blood drained into the dirt floor."

"Yeah," Bernie said faintly, "I remember those stories too."

"Shanties to shanties in three generations."

"We can't all be lucky," Bernie said. "We have to take the good with the bad."

Suddenly the Judge hated himself. You are truly despicable, Your Honor. Why in hell are you browbeating this poor sod who only had the bad luck to be born a Brophy? Sure he shit all over you when you came to call on his sister, practically threatened to run you down in his Stutz Bearcat, and talked endlessly about the swells he was meeting in Georgetown. What does that mean now, after twenty-five years? He's done his penance, and the poor bastard is still in purgatory.

"Oh, for Christ's sake, I'm only kidding, Bernie."

"Sure, Jim. I know."

Was that sarcasm? Was there, after all, a brain behind those frightened rabbit-eyes ticking off the profits and losses, the pros and cons of those around him? Maybe you've spent so many years thinking about the Brophys as a feeding problem, you've forgotten they're human after all. It's the truth, you have no more insight into them than the keeper has into the animals at the zoo. You know the tame ones and the ones that bite, and not much else. Goddamn it, life was fundamentally insane.

Bernie slumped in his seat and the Judge pushed the speedometer up to eighty. That's better, take out your frustrations on the car, you bastard. For twenty miles they swirled along, with the wind pounding the windshield, the tires humming slickly on the white concrete. Then a familiar sound jerked the Judge's foot off the accelerator: a siren. In a moment a police cruiser was alongside them. Local cops, two lean, mean-eyed Wasp hicks, obviously gloating at the capture of an enemy Cadillac. The Judge cursed slowly under his breath, simultaneously noting a small smirk on Bernie's spoiled mouth. That made him take back all the sentimental pity he had just lavished on him. Suck eggs, you greasy little crumb, he thought as he flashed his brightest smile into the cop's hawk-nosed face. "I plead guilty. But don't take out the book, my friend. I think we can settle this some other way. I'm Jim Kilpatrick, Chief Justice of the State Supreme Court. This is one of my associates, Justice Botein," he added, nodding toward Bernie. "We're on our way up to see the governor."

"Gimmy ya license, Judge," said the cop in the flat, nasal twang of his dialect.

The Judge reached inside his coat and handed him his billfold. "Dick Kemper still judge of the Superior Court down here?"

The black beady eyes narrowed but did not quite cross. "Yep," he said.

"He's up for reappointment next year."

"None of my business."

"It will be if you write out that ticket. I'll see to it that he hangs your ass higher than that telephone pole."

The brow furrowed under the visor. The tip of the tongue appeared for a split second, to lick the sun-dried lips. He handed back the billfold to the Judge. "Just be careful," he said. "We can't 'low eighty-mile stuff in this township. Just cause you're a big man don't give you no leave to risk other people's lives."

"I'm sorry, really sorry," the Judge said. "I don't usually. My mind wandered. Here, you and your partner have a drink on me tonight."

Ten dollars slipped out of the billfold and into the law's grasping hand. "Why, thanks, Judge."

"Tell Judge Kemper next time you see him I said hello."

"Why, sure. Listen, they're tearin' up the road ahead. Why don't you follow us? We'll get you right through it."

Ten minutes later they rode past a mile of waiting cars and trucks behind the patrol car, with its siren howling and red dome light flashing. At the end of the line, the Judge gave his escort a cheerful wave and slammed the motor right back up to eighty. "Goddamn clam diggers," he said.

After another twenty miles, Bernie began talking politics. He professed himself worried over the future of the organization. The Republican governor had moved the attorney general, a tough no-nonsense lawyer, into the county as special prosecutor and he was using the state police to break up the organization's gambling operations. It was an unprecedented move. Usually the Republicans let the organization have its own way inside the county.

The Judge scoffed at Bernie's fears. "They've tried it before. They won't get anywhere."

"But I hear all the action's moving out of the county. That's gonna hurt, right?"

"We're going to initiate a taxpayers' suit, to force the governor to appoint a local prosecutor. He can't find one, Democrat or Republican, that isn't on our side."

"Naturally you'll hear the suit."

"Of course."

"What would he do without you up there? You've pulled his chestnuts out of the fire more times."

The Judge grunted noncommittally. "He owes me a few."

"That 1942 ballot box decision. How the hell did you get away with that one?"

"What the hell do you mean?" said the Judge. "I cited thirteen precedents for that decision. It was a model of jurisprudential logic."

"Sure," said Bernie, "but when you got right down to it, you said they could open the ballot boxes and look into them, but they couldn't take any ballots out."

"Precisely," said the Judge. "As I read the law, that's all I was empowered to let them do."

"How come they don't take somethin' like that to the U.S. Supreme Court?"

"The U.S. Supreme Court rarely interferes in state elections."

They rode in silence for a while. Then Bernie said, "You mean to say there isn't a lawyer in the whole county that you guys haven't got in your pocket?"

"There may be one or two—some drunk like Dick Donahue. But no one that the state senate would accept."

"Fantastic." Bernie sighed.

It was, when you thought of it, a little fantastic to the outsider. But to the insider, the man who was sitting beside the seat of power watching the process from the beginning, it was not very surprising. Thirty years was a long time, so long it was easy for men to forget there was ever another way of running a city. Slowly, steadily, using all the dirty and clean tricks in the book, the organization had penetrated into every corner and crevice of the city's life—the churches, the banks, the corporations; none of them made a move without at least thinking about the organization's reaction to it, and more often than not checking in advance. From the city they had reached out into the state, shaking the long, cold grip of the Republicans on judgeships, commissions and agencies. State power had brought federal power. The congressmen representing them in Washington acquired clout beyond their numbers because there was this big meaty state waiting to be delivered to the right candidate.

No, it was not surprising, unless you remembered the handsome valedictorian with his Jesuit scholarship and absurd dreams of playing Christian gentleman, the fighter for the oppressed, unless you pondered his role in the creation of this organization. Only those on the very inside of the inside, Bernie, know that without Judge James Kilpatrick's brain power, big Dave Shea, the bullvoiced, bullheaded leader—the man the newspapers called "The Boss"—would have been in jail twenty years ago. No politician with a third-rate education can control a modern industrial state teeming with savvy lawyers and tough businessmen. Dave Shea had started out with the arrogant assumption that you could get your way by hitting people on the head. That was how he and his plug-uglies gained control of the First Ward. If it worked in that dockside jungle, it would work everywhere else, right?

Wrong, said James Kilpatrick. They had wrangled it out in a hundred roaring, cursing arguments until Shea saw the proof and the payoff—victory after victory, governors, senators, congressmen, prosecutors, judges, marching to the organization's music up and down the reach of this big wealthy state. Not fear, but judicious favor, the right job to the right man in the right place at the right time, was the formula. It called for the kind of exquisite judgment that Dave Shea totally lacked, once he got beyond his grubby native boundaries. It was Jim Kilpatrick, in various guises—corporation counsel, presiding judge of the Superior Court, Chief Justice of the state Supreme Court—who performed the delicate surgery that refined Irish political muscle into statewide power.

But Bernie, with his pea-brained moralism (still trying, however feebly, to look down on this slum-born upstart who had dared to violate his sister's purity), did not ask the important question, the one sanctimonious James Kilpatrick, Jr., and his sister Faith, *sub silentio* through that wiseass Donahue, were asking: What have you done with this power? At first it seemed best to treat the canard with the contempt it deserved. "We're eating pretty well," His Honor had snapped. But when his son made the astonishing declaration that he was not going to law school Judge Kilpatrick realized the question was fundamental—and at the same time still irrelevant.

Irrelevant, goddamn it, because that was the goal of the whole lousy organization—eating, drinking, sleeping, dressing, driving well. Forty years ago, faced with a lifetime of doing none of these things, it was enough. What the hell, they had taken care of their own kind. Thousands of Micks who would have spent their lives with greasy collars and sooty necks were wearing $150 suits and sending their kids to the best schools in the country. They had taken the best of the Wops and the Polacks with them too. So what if the rest of them and the boogies were still in the slums? Let them find their way out, like we did—the hard way. These goddamn kids with bleeding hearts and their bleats about social justice and the papal encyclicals. Wait a minute. Not all of them. You've got two lemons and Benny O'Connor, a ward leader with a third grade education, gets a son like Jake. There was your kind of kid, living it up while he can, under every skirt in town, drinking the saloons dry and sizing up everything and everybody, just waiting to make his move. Why couldn't you get it through your offsprings' ivory Irish skulls that life was made to be lived?

You know why. The goddamn Catholic Church with its squirrel-house ideas stood between you and them, between them and reality. You say to your son, Become a lawyer and you'll be worth a million before you're thirty, and he looks at you as if you'd just told him to suck your cock. Making a million before you're thirty—or eighty for that matter—was despicable according to the so-called Catholic intellectuals. To do it you had to become tainted by the world, which meant that you would probably give way to the sins of the flesh, and wind up in the hands of the devil. It was so goddammed idiotic, you almost threw up every time you heard your son spouting his arrogant, moralistic vituperation on everything from Dave Shea to the American Constitution.

"You still go to church every Sunday, Bernie?"

Bernie almost jumped out of his shiny-assed pants. "Do I still go to church?" he echoed incredulously. "Of course."

"Why?"

"Why? It's one of the Commandments."

"The Protestants don't go every Sunday."

"So what?"

"I mean, do you still buy the whole roll of baloney—hell, heaven, infallibility, acts of contrition?"

"Of course, why shouldn't I?"

The Judge shrugged. "I don't know. You've lived long enough to see how it screws up people's lives, haven't you?"

"People's lives get screwed up when they fail to follow a moral code," Bernie said.

"Jesus Christ," the Judge said, "I wish I could be as confident about my philosophical ideas. I mean, what do you tell a guy when his wife kicks him out of bed and says no more kids, the One Holy Catholic Apostolic way—abstinence?"

Bernie's voice suddenly went up a notch. "We have to learn to control our carnal desires."

"How are you doing in that department, Bernie? You haven't had another kid for five years now."

"I really don't think I want to discuss—"

"I think you're getting a little queer myself. That happens, you know."

"Ah-haha." Bernie's laugh was more like a cough. "I never know when you're kidding, Jim."

"Neither do I," the Judge said. "I always envied you, Bernie. You know I went right from prep school into Stapleton Talbot as an office boy, and from there into law school. You could do that in those days. But I used to wish I'd had a chance to go to Georgetown and feel up all those Trinity girls and learn all that wonderful Jesuit philosophy. I mean it really used to bother me, Bernie. But now I'm beginning to think it's the luckiest thing that ever happened to me. Judging by what those goddammed Jesuits have done to my son, I'd be one of two things right now—a classic drunk like poor Dick Donahue, or the chief counsel for the Archdiocese. I don't know which version I'd hate more."

Bernie sighed. "I never have been able to figure you out, Jim."

"There have been times when I've even puzzled myself," the Judge said.

They were on a six-lane highway now, and ahead of them the city was visible across miles of river marsh on its long, low hill—a gray, shapeless mass surrounded and surmounted by a pall of lighter gray. Through the car windows on the booming wind came the stink of burning garbage.

"Ah," said the Judge, "me nose is in the city. That's what my mother used to say, Lord rest her soul, when we were coming home."

Soon they were in the worst of it. On both sides of them, mountains of burning garbage sent murky clouds of smoke billowing across the highway. The Judge and Bernie hastily closed the windows of the car and the Judge slowed to a safer fifty miles an hour. For more than four miles, the smoke shrouded the highway, making trucks loom up in the other lane like paleolithic apparitions. "It's terrible down in the West End when the wind blows the wrong way," Bernie said. "You swear sometimes you're gonna choke. My doctor said it was no good for my emphysema, I ought to move, and I asked him where."

"Goddamn doctors are more trouble than they're worth," the Judge said. "That Jew I went to told me I had arteriosclerosis, whatever the hell that is. Said I should quit smoking and gave me a diet that had me living on skimmed milk and radishes, for Christ's sake."

"I can hardly breathe some nights," Bernie said, "when the wind is the wrong way and in the summer when it's muggy. My doctor says it's bad for the heart."

"They don't know what the hell they're talking about and they never did," the Judge said. "I remember one told me I was going blind. The son of a bitch said I'd be blind in six months and I should start to learn Braille. Can you imagine that? I was just out of law school. I told him to shove his Braille and his bill, got some eye drops from a druggist I knew, and I've never had any trouble since. I still don't wear glasses."

Bernie wasn't listening. He was too deep in his emphysema. "Move, I said, where can I move? That's your problem, he said. I wish you didn't tell me, I said. I got enough troubles with eight kids."

"Have a cigarette," the Judge said.

"The doctor said I should cut down."

"Jesus Christ," the Judge said. "If you don't live before you die, Bernie, how are they going to know when you're dead?

"Yeah," the Judge said as he took the bright-red whorl of the lighter from Bernie and lit up. "I told that kike specialist I've been smoking two packs a day for thirty years and it hasn't hurt me. Why the hell should it start bothering me now?"

He dropped Bernie at the courthouse and watched him mount the steps toward the huge grilled doors. In five minutes he would be sitting in the tax office, scrawling illegibly in the ledgers for another eight hours a day. Thirty goddamn years of it. How did he stand it? It had to be his inherited brainlessness. Bernie was a born automaton.

Ah. You heartless bastard. He was trapped like all the rest of them. Like you too, for all your gorgeous bullshit.

He swung the Cadillac into a savage U-turn at the red light and glared at the slit of himself in the mirror above his head. "One more crack like that and I'll issue a writ of mandamus for you."

Down the long gradual eastern slope of the city's hill he rolled to the private parking lot behind an obscenely ugly building, a Victorian jumble of spires and imitation buttresses topped by a once copper, now sickly green dome: City Hall. Inside that ugliness sat the man who translated words into power. Through the side door and up the back stairs trotted the Judge. The old legs that took more than one Prep team to glory still have some spring in them. The second flight? Instinctively the Judge stepped through a door into the rotunda and strolled casually across what he liked to call the forum.

Pols big and little stood in clusters murmuring confidentially. Not one failed to raise an eye or a hand in salute to Judge James Kilpatrick. "Hello there, Judge." "Jim, howzit?" "Morning, Judge." In the center of the massive replica of the city's seal on the marble floor, a big splay-foot on each of the eagle's claws, stood mighty Bill O'Brien, the handsomest, dumbest Irish cop on the force. Six-foot-four with muscles of iron and a head to match, the weight-lifting champion of the state. Instead of patrolling the streets and enforcing the laws, which he looked like he could do single-handed, he stood here day after day like a dummy on display. The Big Man, Dave Shea, wanted it that way. Approaching from behind, the Judge threw an arm around O'Brien's massive neck and grabbed his gun.

"Jesus Christ, O'Brien, asleep on your feet again."

A chuckle rumbled in the huge chest. "Sure, let me off aisy, Judge. I was countin' votes come election day."

The Judge planted his right foot against Bill's stupendous left brogan and held out his hand for some Indian wrestling. "Come on, I'll take you two out of three."

"Ah now, yer Honor, I couldn't take your money."

"One for a buck. And give me some odds."

"I think a hundred to one might be fair."

"You're on," the Judge said, and they went to work.

By now people were coming out of offices on all sides of the rotunda to watch the show. Hand to hand, leg to leg, the two antagonists stood for a brief moment in muscular tension. Then the Judge tried to knock O'Brien off balance by jabbing him in the stomach with his cane. O'Brien deflected the foul with one iron arm and spun the Judge around until they were facing in the opposite direction.

"Sure, y' don't even fight fair, yer Honor," said Bill, taking his dollar.

"Why the hell should I," said the Judge, "when the odds are a hundred to one?"

"What the hell's going on here?"

A small, needle-nosed man with a bald head came strutting into the middle of the rotunda. Johnny Kenellen, the deputy mayor, the most hated man in City Hall.

"What the hell does it look like?" the Judge said. "I've just been showing up your goddamn crummy police force."

"Yeah, yeah," Kenellen said, while his fish eyes circled the rotunda. People hastily retreated from the doorways to their desks. "We're tryin' to get a day's work done around here."

"What the hell would you know about that?" the Judge said. "You haven't done a day's work since they took you off the spittoons."

The murderous hatred in Kenellen's eyes was like early morning champagne to the Judge. "As a matter of fact," he continued, "you never did more than three of them a day."

"The mayor's waitin' to see you," snapped Kenellen, and strutted back to the private elevator which only he and Mayor Shea were permited to use.

"Someday," the Judge said to Bill O'Brien, "I'd like you to pick up that little bastard and play him like an accordion."

O'Brien shook the building with a bellow of laughter. "Sure and it might turn out to be murder. Can you get me off, yer Honor?"

"Guaranteed," said the Judge.

Tipping his hat at an exorbitant angle, he trotted up the marble stairs to the second floor, breezed past the startled secretaries in the outer office, and shoved wide the huge oak doors to the mayor's office. There was Kenellen in front of Dave Shea's big desk, squawking like Donald Duck. "Indian wrestlin' with a cop inna middle of the lobby. What would reporters say if—"

"They'd say the old organization is showing some signs of life, you two-bit Judas."

For a moment Dave Shea was annoyed. But he controlled it. The massive bald head, with the square jaw and flattened prize fighter's nose, swung around like the snout of a weapon—a weapon he had used so often, its devastating effect was now a conscious, controlled performance. The blank gray eyes of the poker player par excellence drilled into Judge Kilpatrick. "Hello, Jim. Feeling good?"

"Never felt better."

"Johnny's got a point, you know. The goddamn reporters never pass up a chance to take a crack at us."

"Who the hell are you trying to kid?" Judge Kilpatrick said. "There isn't a reporter left in the city that isn't on the pad in one way or another. What's on your mind?"

"This Barton thing."

Johnny Kenellen dropped into one of the huge, carved-oak chairs that lined the walls of the immense office. His feet did not even touch the floor. He looked like a first grader in a dentist's waiting room. The Judge glowered at him. "Don't you think this is something we should discuss alone?"

"I don't say nuthin' here that Johnny can't hear."

The Judge had heard Dave Shea assassinate English grammar for thirty years. Why did it still make him wince?

"If you spent more time in that chair, maybe there wouldn't be so many goddamn things he had to hear."

"Now listen, Jim," Dave Shea growled, "I've taken a lot of shit from you over the years but I ain't gonna let you insult Johnny here. He's done a hell of a job for me. And for you too. For all of us."

"He's a penny pinochle player in a ten-dollar game. I've never seen anything more screwed up than this Barton thing."

"We're runnin' an organization. An organization's gotta have discipline," Kenellen shrilled.

"Why the hell didn't you let the little boogie talk till his brains fell out?"

"Because people were listenin' to him, that's why," Dave Shea rumbled. He was losing his temper, and Judge Kilpatrick knew from long experience that there was no point whatsoever in making Dave Shea lose his temper. But for some reason the Judge did not care.

"Then why the hell didn't you get him on something that would stand up? This goddamn rap is ridiculous. Bribing an election officer. That's what I mean. When you let this two-bit tinhorn run the show—"

"Shut up!" Dave Shea roared. "It was my idea. It was the quickest and the best. Since the war, that coon vote is nuthin' to sneeze at. They've doubled, maybe tripled, Johnny tells me. And they're restless. We wanted to get Barton the hell out of the way and we want him to *stay* out of the way. That's why you're down here. When that hearing comes up next week I want you to give that nigger the maximum. Five big ones."

"Five years for a twenty-five-dollar bribe? You're out of your goddamn head. Appeals courts reduce sentences like that. They never sustain them."

"I want this one sustained."

"You're not gonna get it sustained. You're going to get it reduced."

Judge Kilpatrick was shouting now. Right back in the coal yards. You can see the soot on your old man's neck, the beery, stinking sweat on his dirty undershirt as he swore to God he'd beat the bejabers out of Puggo Moran for insulting the honor of County Cork. It never ends, it never ends, whined a voice, like something from outer space, as Dave Shea roared back, "You son of a bitch, we're gonna see who's runnin' this show, once and for all. Without me you'd all be still down on Second Street scrounging coal from the roundhouse."

"Without me you'd be in Atlanta doing ten to twenty."

"The hell I would, you wiseass cocksucker. I could have bought up shysters like you by the dozen any time and now I can get 'em by the hundreds. I made you and your whole lousy family, and the minute you forget it, I'll make you remember it."

"You try it and I might remember a few things that a certain senator down in Washington would love to hear."

"See what I said, Mayor? You can't trust the son of a bitch," Johnny Kenellen squawked.

"I don't take that kind of shit from anybody," Shea roared. He was on his feet, the massive fists closing. For a terrible moment Judge James Kilpatrick felt raw fear. He lunged to his feet, not quite sure whether it was to fight or run.

Then he saw the two of them, eyeball to eyeball there in the gloomy barn of an office, faces flushed, pulses pounding, and hated the day he was born Irish. "Goddamn it, Dave," he said, "when are you going to grow up?"

"Are you gonna give me that sentence?" Shea ranted.

"Eighteen months."

"Five years."

"Eighteen months."

"That's the minimum under the goddamn statute."

"He's a first offender, for Christ's sake. It's basic judicial practice to reduce a maximum sentence for a first offender. The whole court will vote for it. They have to. They'll get laughed out of the goddamn state."

"The hell with the rest of the state. I don't want to see that coon for five years."

The Judge picked up his hat from the table, stood a bookend up against the large unread volumes of the city's statutes, and walked to the door. "See you around, Dave."

"Five years," Shea roared.

"Eighteen months," the Judge said, and slammed the big oak door behind him.

As he strolled through the outer office, nodding to the wide-eyed secretaries, he could hear Shea kicking the door and cursing like a man in a padded cell. Strolling down the marble stairs, the Judge hummed a tune and noticed that his undershirt was soaked with sweat. His collar was wilting. He felt like he had just spent a half hour in a Turkish bath with his clothes on. "Goddamn son of a bitch," he muttered while he gave a cheerful wave to Officer O'Brien, and swept through the revolving doors to the moist, glaring sunshine of the city's summer streets.

As he opened the car door, he noticed a strange throbbing sensation in his chest. Not a heartbeat, but something that felt vaguely like an extra heart beating in its own rhythm. Each beat sent a twinge of pain running up his shoulder and down his left arm. What the hell did that mean? No more Indian wrestling with that big ox O'Brien. You've probably pulled six muscles in there, he told himself.

He rolled uptown for a lunch date at the Garden Square Hotel with Monsignor Eddie O'Donnell, the muscular Vicar General of the Archdiocese. After years of patient wheedling, Eddie had talked his brother onto the Court of Errors and Appeals. The letter of endorsement from Chief Justice James Kilpatrick had had considerable weight in the governor's decision. The nicest thing about Eddie was his absolute lack of interest in religion. He never mentioned it. Politics was his passion, and as he drove the Judge mentally selected some choice tidbits of gossip from the last legislative session that he knew would please Eddie's palate.

After lunch, the Judge tooled over to the main public library and spent three hours in the cool interior of the law room doing research for an opinion he was writing on a disputed will. It was a fascinating case. The illegitimate daughter of one of the state's most prominent politicians—an ex-senator—was suing his heirs for a share of her father's estate. The judge's widow had disinherited her by name in her will. The state's two lower appeals courts had upheld the supposed sanctity of the owner's right to dispose of her property. But Judge Kilpatrick had found a precedent for a contrary opinion in the seventeenth-century colonial records of the state. A man who had fathered a child on an Indian squaw had had his will revoked by a tough old Puritan judge because he had made no provision for the infant.

Although the suitor in the present case was no infant, the Judge was planning to astonish the big brains at Stapleton Talbot who were defending the ex-senator's heirs by citing the forgotten old case as a precedent. Then, as they reeled from that right-cross, he would hit them with a powerhouse left full of precedents from English common law, on the rights of so-called "natural" children. *True, the American Revolution had created a breach between English and American common law in many cases, but the great tradition of protecting the rights of the helpless and innocent, particularly in this state, where commentaries of Chancellor Kent of New York are still revered. . . .* Gleefully, the Judge envisioned the frenzy in the eyes of Stapleton Talbot's legal eagles as they racked their Harvard and Yale heads for an answer. They thought they knew all the law in the state, thanks to their goddamn ancestry. The Judge loved to spring such learned surprises on his erstwhile employers. Besides, the poor bastard of a plaintiff's name was Dougherty.

Leaving the library about four, the Judge drove briskly across town to the Parkway and parked his Cadillac in the driveway of a big bay-windowed house with a broad old-fashioned porch. It was on a side street only a few doors away from the Parkway's six lanes, around which the city's wealthy and socially prominent clustered. He went into the empty house, dark with the shades drawn, and for some reason he could not quite fathom, wandered from room to room not thinking of anything really but somehow mourning all the years of his life and the lives of his children these rooms had seen. He avoided Theresa's room. He never did understand that wispy, faery little girl who clung so obsessively to her idiot mother. Now she had her reward. He stood first in Jim's room, then in Faith's, examining the sentimental photographic history with which his wife covered their walls. There was Jim at three, a grouchy cherub, and Faith at five with an impish smile on that button of a face. There she was in white, with her First Communion veil, and Jim in his dark-blue confirmation suit and the red tie which the lousy color processing of those days had turned purple. Graduations, birthdays, diplomas, their scrolls for first honors and bests in Latin, French, Religion were all there. But not the five-dollar bills he had handed out to them for every report card, none of the hard-nosed advice he had given them about the importance of getting high marks, to prove to yourself how good you were. No, Judge Kilpatrick, the fathering voice was strangely missing from these childhood walls, indeed from this whole house. And of course you know why, your Honor. So why brood about it?

Hurriedly, in his own bedroom, where the walls were devoid of pictures, the Judge pulled off his sweat-soaked underwear and shirt, still damp from his encounter with Dave Shea, and took a shower. He was buttoning a fresh shirt, humming a sardonic "Mother Macree" to himself in the mirror, when the telephone rang. It was brother-in-law Bernie. "Jim," gasped the panicked voice on the other end of the line, "what the hell's going on? I'm out of a job."

"Who says so?"

"Toolin, the sheriff. He just came downstairs and told me to get the hell out of the courthouse. I mean he was nice about it. But he said it was orders. What the hell's going on?"

"Where are you?"

"Home."

"I'll call you back in five minutes."

The Judge dialed a private number which he did not have to look up. Dave Shea answered the phone. "You are a no-good worthless prick," Judge Kilpatrick said.

"Is that boogie gonna get five years?"

"Honest to Christ, you ought to wear a condom instead of a hat."

"Answer the goddamn question."

"That poor, ball-less bastard up there in the courthouse has got a heart condition, don't you know that?"

"I didn't know that," said the stony voice on the other end of the line. "You still haven't answered the question."

"Okay, Dave. Just call it off."

"Okay. Tell him I'm sorry—about his heart condition."

The Judge slammed down the phone, hoping it cracked one of Shea's corroded eardrums. He telephoned Bernie and told him to report for work tomorrow as if nothing had happened. In the gnawing, empty silence, he finished buttoning his shirt, tying his tie, finally realizing that he was averting his eyes from the face of the man in the mirror. *Jesus Christ.* He stormed out of the house, up the street to the Parkway. Hailing a cab, he rode out to the northern rim of the city where the Parkway was less fashionable and the fat mansions gave way to red-brick apartments. He strolled into the one numbered 1301 and used a key to let himself into the bare, drab lobby with its whitewashed walls and dirt-stained tile floors. A tiny elevator, scarcely large enough for two persons, carried him to the fifth floor. Again using a key from his ring, he let himself into the apartment marked 6F. "Margaret," he called. "Marg?" With a growl of disappointment, he threw his hat on a chair. What was it this time? A summer dramatic club? Or a counseling session with some thick-lipped boogie who couldn't speak the English language, much less read or write it? There was always something—what the hell was the word—noble that kept her in that lousy school later than anyone else.

The Judge gave himself another lecture. Goddamn it, you are not going to let that clown in City Hall ruin your disposition. After thirty years you are immune to the son of a bitch.

Humming a cheerful tune, he mixed himself a Scotch and soda, and turned on the big bulky air-conditioners that stood in the living room and in the bedroom. From a bookcase that lined one wall of the living room, he took a much-thumbed copy of Boswell's *Johnson* and began flipping the pages, reading his favorite passages. It was amazing how many of them he had underlined in the course of twenty years. They leaped out, two and three to a page.

The Irish are a fair people;—they never speak well of one another.

If I had no duties, and no reference to futurity, I would spend my life in driving briskly in a post chaise with a pretty woman.

He who praises everybody praises nobody.

I have, all my life, been lying till noon; yet I tell all young men, and tell them with great sincerity, that nobody that does not rise early will ever do any good.

I inherited a vile melancholy from my father, which has made me mad all my life, at least not sober.

Sir, are you so grossly ignorant of human nature, as not to know that a man may be very sincere in good principles, without having good practice?

Politics are now nothing more than a means of rising in the world.

Soon he was deep in that marvelous argument between Johnson and Goldsmith about toleration, where Johnson drove Goldsmith and all the other liberals crazy by arguing that the state had every right to suppress opinions it considered dangerous. The Judge sipped his Scotch and let the words and the liquor suffuse him with a sentimental glow. Face it, you were born in the wrong century. This was your era, when men treasured a hard, glittering phrase and wasted no tears on women or good causes, a time when the grimy underbelly of life was both visible and ignored. And religion, like other public rituals, was performed without the tiniest expectation of personal belief.

The sound of a key in the lock. The Judge put down his Scotch and soda, and his bushy gray eyebrows rose expectantly. The door opened and a tall, rather willowy woman appeared in the dim foyer. Her arms were full of books which she tried to deposit, without much success, on the small table opposite the door. Several crashed onto the floor, and she made a wordless sound of annoyance. She picked them up and stood there for a moment, fussing with her hair in the murky mirror above the table. A woman first, last and always, the Judge sighed to himself. "Come on," he said, "I don't give a damn how you look. I just want a good passionate kiss."

She stood in the doorway of the living room, while the fading sun turned the tan wallpaper, with its French Provincial scenes, to gold. "You're hopeless," she said. "You'll never learn any manners—much less acquire any sensitivity."

"The hell you say," the Judge said. "I'm one of the most sensitive jurists in the state. I cry all the way to the electric chair every time I sentence one."

"Monster," she said, and came slowly across the room. It was always a moment of pure pleasure, to see her walking towards him. She had a marvelous natural grace. There were swatches of gray in her thick dark hair, but her eyes were still as liquid and alive as the day he first saw her in surrogate's court, trying to find out why she hadn't received any money from her father's estate. Mickey O'Hanlon, the crookedest Irish lawyer in town, had been playing the horses with it, that was why.

She bent over him, and for a moment there was the tiniest pause. Was it hesitation, or simply a wish to see him, hold him with her eyes as he so often wanted to do—and did—with her? Then her mouth came down on his, warm and soft against his cold, wet lips. For a moment his fingers were in her hair, touching the back of the long slender neck. Then she was strolling past him, to the bar. "Good God," she said, "I'm drunk already, just from your breath. Are you drinking it straight these days?"

"It's my privilege," the Judge growled, dropping *Samuel Johnson* on the floor. "I've had one hell of a lousy day."

She slipped into a chair opposite him and crossed her legs. He let his eyes travel down the long curving line of stockinged flesh while she sighed breathily and said, "Poor dear. So have I."

"Tell me what disasters have erupted in the world of the retarded," he said, raising his glass in a toast. "I'm sure it will make my troubles seem trivial."

She laughed in her low throaty way. "We had a knife fight in the cafeteria."

"Goddamn it," the Judge said. "Why don't you let me get you a transfer out of that rotten school?"

"—And I was the monitor," she went on as if he had said nothing. "It made me wish I knew some judo. Fortunately, one of my star pupils decided he didn't want to see me get killed, and stopped it."

"Margaret, what the hell do you get out of teaching them? You admit fifty percent of them can't read, and they're in high school."

"But fifty percent of them can."

"Some one of these days I'm just going to pick up the phone and have you transferred without your permission."

"And I'll get myself transferred right back."

The Judge glowered and drank his Scotch. He loved the defiant tilt of her chin in an argument. He also knew why she insisted on teaching English in the worst high school in the city, a crumbling nineteenth-century pile that was 95 percent Negro. Guilt was the answer, and you were the cause, James. Yet when it had begun, fifteen years ago, she had seemed to be the cause, an uncaused cause, a kind of goddess with that serenity which he had finally realized was innocence. Night after night they had sat across candlelit dinner tables, ostensibly together to discuss the complications of that absurdly simple will which he could have solved with a single phone call. Endlessly they talked about Shakespeare and Johnson, Fitzgerald and Philip Barry, making literature into a lie that conveniently obscured the enormous echoing love he felt groping out of his soul for her.

Soul, no other word. There was a sickness raging in Judge James Kilpatrick that she cured with those long entwining arms, that convalescent laugh, with the cool calm of those perfect eyes. There were times when it still astonished him how quietly, almost humbly, she became his mistress. He had been so warped by the crude terminology of conquest, it took him months to realize that this love that had transformed so much of him had also happened in her.

She was telling him, with not a little annoyance in her voice, that he was disgustingly prejudiced. Negroes were human beings, Americans. They needed all the help they could get if they were ever going to escape from their slums.

"I agree with every word of it," the Judge said, "but they've got to do it themselves. They're never going to learn anything from you."

"Why not?"

"Because when you read them Hamlet's soliloquy and tell them it's great poetry, they're just taking old mistress's word for it all over again. They've got to have somebody black stand up there and say I read this and it really grabbed me."

"Oh, sometimes you make me furious. Do you think there's really that much difference in the color of somebody's skin?"

"When the color means what it's meant in this country, yes. You'd do a lot more good teaching a course in Negro literature to white kids. Which gets us back to the old argument about you wasting your time in high school."

"I thought we settled that years ago."

"We did, but not to my satisfaction."

"If you could produce a Ph.D. degree for me by waving your judicial gavel or something, I might consider it."

The Judge smiled quizzically. "It could be arranged."

"No."

The Judge sighed. "Honesty, that's your real problem."

"Sometimes I wish it was yours. What does our Imperial Caesar want you to do now?"

He told her about the Barton case and watched her face whiten with anxiety. Fortunately, she did not know him. He was not an ex-pupil, thank God for small favors. Her reaction was bad enough. "Jim, you can't. You'll—you'll be disgraced."

He told her about brother-in-law Bernie. "There are six other Brophys on the pad. So he's only warming up."

"But it's so totally—wrong. I mean—against an individual." She got up and fixed herself another drink. He handed her his glass, and she poured him one. He noticed it was much lighter than the one he had fixed for himself. Eternally maternal, they can't help themselves.

"I don't know," he groused. "Nobody told that little jig to stick his woolly head into the concrete mixer. He did it on his own."

"But his intentions are—good."

"You mean respectable. He just wants a slice of the action. He might have gotten it too, if he asked for it in a nice way. We need some young Negro leaders."

She stared into her drink. "It doesn't get any better, does it?"

"What do you mean?"

"I thought—I guess it was silly of me—that as the years went on and you became more powerful—you wouldn't have to do these things. I thought—you could really do something with your power. I mean besides elect governors and hand out jobs. Build a new school downtown, for instance. Get people out of the slums into housing projects."

"Not a chance," he said, hearing his own voice dry and hard, a dismaying sound in his ears. "The city's broke. The Depression flattened us."

She sighed—more mournful, strangely touching. "At the very least I thought—that you would eventually be more independent—from him."

"It never occurred to me," he said in the same heavy, harsh voice. "As far as I can remember I never even suggested it."

"I didn't say you had. It was just my own addled, unrealistic female thinking."

That second heart suddenly throbbed in his chest. He felt a pain run down his arm again. He shifted in his chair. "Where would you like to go to dinner?"

"Oh, it's too hot to go out. Let's eat here. I have some chicken tetrazzini all ready. I'll just pop it in the oven."

"Any wine on ice?"

"Of course. What sort of a courtesan do you think I am?"

The smile was forced. The words, the look on her face, clanged against the Judge's mind like a deflected knife blade. Appalling, the intricacies of the female mind. All these years she had been nursing this small, futile dream—that someday he would be free to make her the second Mrs. Kilpatrick. Either God would conveniently dispose of the current Mrs. K., or Judge K. would rise up in independent judicial majesty and shuck her like yesterday's underwear. Incredible. All that bravado, that high-hearted defiance of conventional morality, was it all an act? No, don't be so crude. It was time, eating away at this and all the other parts of your life, James. What did Yeats say?

> Outworn heart, in a time outworn
> Come clear of the nets of wrong and right.

While the chicken tetrazzini baked, they had another drink and talked about a half-dozen things. They debated what plays they would see on their annual fall trip to New York. As usual the Judge wanted to see the musicals and she wanted the serious dramas. Also as usual, they settled for a fifty-fifty compromise. They argued over Ingrid Bergman's *Joan of Arc*. "That dumb Swede is smarter than I thought," the Judge said. "But it's still a lousy picture." Margaret shook her head. "I still say it was the best Joan I've ever seen." What about the impending trial of the leaders of the American Communist party in New York? "Bad law and good politics," the Judge said. "The Supreme Court is sure to reverse the conviction. But it smokes out the Wallace Democrats. It'll help get Truman elected." Margaret looked dubious. "Can Truman get elected?" The Judge drained his drink. "Dewey couldn't carry this state if he campaigned here for the next three years." Margaret listened, fascinated, while the Judge explained why the labor vote and the various ethnic and racial blocs were certain to ignore Henry Wallace and treat Thomas E. Dewey with the contempt he deserved. Sometimes the Judge wondered whether she enjoyed politics as much as she said she did. If not, he loved her for pretending.

"What did you think of Saul Bellow?" It was her latest attempt to convert him to modern literature. The Judge grunted. "The guy can't write. And to read him you'd think the whole world was Jewish."

"What's wrong with that? You think the whole world's Irish."

"But I'm right and he's wrong."

"You *are* hopeless."

The dinner was delicious. The wine, Pouilly Fuissé, was full-bodied but dry, a perfect contrast to the creamy chicken and the endive salad. It was somehow comforting to the Judge to contemplate the probability that there weren't ten people in the city having a comparable dinner. Maybe when all is said and done you are nothing but a snob.

The hours after dinner were spent in their favorite fashion, each with the book of his choice. Occasionally, they read aloud passages that struck them. The Judge preferred biographies, although Margaret never ceased to ply him with the novels she felt were required reading. When eleven o'clock chimed delicately on the Louis XVI gold clock he had bought her in Paris, they had one more drink while her bath water ran, and reminisced drowsily about their last trip to Florida. The Judge made fun of the Jewish furriers, imitating their Bronx accents, until she laughed in spite of her disapproval of his offhand anti-Semitism.

Alone, while she bathed, he began to tell himself he was being idiotic to read so much into that passing remark about Dave Shea. Maybe your guilt was the problem, which made it a conundrum, because you can't even phrase an indictment. He finished his drink, went down the hall to a second bathroom and showered quickly. By the time she came out of the bathroom in a blue negligee, he was sitting on the edge of the bed, in his purple and blue bathrobe. His royal robe, she called it.

"You look tired," she said as she sat down beside him.

"I'm not that tired." He drew her against him with an authoritative squeeze while his hand slipped softly through her hair and down her neck and along the cool scented flesh of her arm. His lips found hers, and time vanished. Wish and desire, possession and more possession, words flooded his mind banishing years, denying loss, disappointment, pain beyond this circle of fragrance, this cool island of love. Outside the windows the city sweated and groaned in the grip of August. The Wops down on Christoferro Street hunched over their card games; the Negroes crowded, eyes, teeth gleaming, around the dice in their littered alleys. Dave Shea dined on prunes in his Parkway mansion, and Barton beat his head against the bars in the county jail. Nothing made any sense out there compared to this total moment, these touches, kisses, this giving and taking. The only truth that was visible, past and present, then and now.

Out of his body coursed at last the joyous response, the wish made act, the deep throbbing release that banished anger and anxiety. They lay together, perfectly still, for more minutes. Then she went down the hall to her bathroom to remove her diaphragm, and he to flush his condom down the spinning, silent toilet. Fifteen years, and yet they were still careful. Margaret was only forty-three. Menopause in five years? Perhaps. In five years you will be sixty-two. Not a pleasant thought, your Honor. Sentence it to solitary confinement.

He slipped into his pajamas, lit a cigarette and strolled back into the bedroom. He put the cigarette out when he heard her footstep in the hall. She did not look at him as she came in the door. She might have been a stranger in a pink nightgown hurrying past the foot of the bed—a figure from a dream. Quickly she slipped beneath the covers. His hand reached out and tentatively touched her arm. She did not come to him, her arms open for one last kiss. It was not really an inflexible part of the ritual, but still the Judge asked, "Anything the matter?"

"No."

"You're sure?"

"My sister, maybe. I went to see her on the way home and got the usual lecture."

Beatrice Halloran, the original Irish spinster, with a face like the prow of the U.S.S. *Missouri* and a temperament to match. "Someday I'm going to shoot that battleax right between the eyes," the Judge said. "I'll handle my own defense and plead justifiable homicide."

"She means well," Margaret said, in a voice that was so toneless it was like ice water on his skin.

"The hell she does. She means the exact opposite of well. She means rotten. She wants you to be as miserable as she is, crawling down the street every morning to daily Mass, and folding altar linens for some moron monsignor every night."

"She never gives up. She's convinced that God has put her on earth to save my soul. From you."

"Tell her I accept the challenge."

He put out the light, socked his pillow and stretched out in bed beside her. Inevitably his thoughts drifted back over the day. Dave

Shea's bellowing face thrust at him through the darkness, brother-in-law Bernie's voice whined in his ear. Then a new sound. Margaret was weeping. At first he could not believe it. It was almost smothered by the air-conditioner's rumble. But he heard it again, and again, a small gasping sound deep in her throat. He put out his hand and his fingers found her wet cheeks. "Maggie," he said, "what the hell's the matter?"

"Nothing," she said. "I'm female. I've got a right to cry whenever —I feel like it."

He turned to her, slipped one arm beneath her and rolled her against him until she was cradled in his arms.

"All the way home," she said, "I kept remembering all the years we've had together. All the happiness. Then when I saw you waiting for me there in the chair for the first time, instead of—being proud, I was sad. It frightened me. I don't know how to explain it. I don't ever want to be sad about you—no matter what happens."

"You never will be," the Judge said.

"Just hold me. I'll stop in a minute."

"There's no hurry," he said. His lips brushed her wet cheeks, authenticating the tears. Salty on the tongue and in the mind.

Slowly she stopped crying, but made no attempt to escape from his arms. He did not know how long they lay there, but suddenly his mind was seeing a kaleidoscope of faces. Young, dark-haired, with shining, innocent eyes. It was Margaret, of course, that first night when he leaned across the restaurant table toward her, saying, *"Miss Halloran, you don't seem to realize you're extraordinarily beautiful."* How could he remember so clearly, so acutely over fifteen years, the limpid quality of her innocence? Why did it suddenly torment him now, remembering it as something toward which he lunged, greedily, desperate to cure his spirit, rancid with call girls and compromises? Was it simply because the formula no longer worked, the innocence had vanished, beyond memory even, into a marriage that was not a marriage, one more of Jim Kilpatrick's compromises with the world of Things as They Are? No. All true, but the answer was more absurd. There was another face in that kaleidoscope of hair and eyes and unspoiled mouths, a face that was haunting you because it was real and it made you remember irrevocably the other reality, that other innocence which had wept its secret hope away here in your arms. Suddenly to both the faces, both Margarets, Judge James Kilpatrick found himself whispering, "I'm sorry."

# Chapter Three

Dick Thornton drove slowly down the sunbaked main street. Middle-aged women in slacks idled past the chic shops that flourished each July and August, when the dollar bills fell like a blizzard on Paradise Beach. Summer people—aliens—the enemy. To be fleeced, suckered, swindled, and otherwise defrauded. That was the way Paradise had taught him to see these well-padded women with their big cars and husbands who spoke with the unmistakable authority of wealth. But that was the hick's philosophy, to chortle over cheating an extra ten or twenty-five dollars for repairing a roof or fixing a toilet—clutching at the pitiful illusion that the rich did not have the brains to know when they were being taken. As if the rich cared. The hick did not see that his petty larceny simply made him more picturesque. He never dreamed that he was only supplying the rich with more condescending anecdotes for their cocktail parties and dinners.

Off Main Street, Dick drove into a different world. Gone were the bustle and traffic, the neon, the storefronts. Huge old trees shaded the hot drowsy streets. The rambling houses sat back, solemn and sedate, skirted by wide, screened porches. Women in unfashionably long cotton dresses pulled weeds in flower beds, girls in shorts sat on porch steps. "Hi, Dick," they called as he rolled past. "Hi." Often a toddler wobbled across the lawn waving his arms brainlessly. Amazing how many of his high school classmates were married. It seemed only last year they were rattling around these same streets in their jalopies. Now married, going steady permanently, settling down to the routine of babies and small-town jobs without even a murmur of complaint. Amazing how easily people accepted things. But not Dick Thornton.

He emerged from the residential streets to catch the last explosion of the sinking sun on the bay. Past the fresh-fish shacks and the docks he rolled, to the big iron gate of the Paradise Yacht Club. He stuck the car in the parking lot and ambled into the bar. Tall, boyish Bill Whitfield gave him a welcoming wave.

"Where can I scrounge a ticket for the dance tonight?"

"The old man bought about twenty extra, as usual," Bill said. "You can have mine and I'll pick up another one."

"Thanks," Dick said, and reached for his wallet.

"Forget it."

"Why should I forget it?"

"Because we're not supposed to sell the damn things, for reason one, and for reason two, I want you to sit with me so I can get a close look at Victoria Sand."

"You'd better bring your field glasses."

"You mean that beautiful unplatonic relationship is over?"

"I gather you've been talking to Slocum."

"Who else? He was practically green telling how you cornered the best thing on the campus from September to June, seven nights a week."

Dick accepted a bottle of Löwenbräu and poured it slowly into the long-stemmed glass. "You should know better than to take Dwight literally."

"Even subtracting fifty percent, it still sounded pretty good."

Dick shrugged. "It was pretty good."

"But it's all over now?"

"Believe it or not, Bill, getting laid can get boring."

"Great below the neck, but not much topside, huh?"

"That's one way of putting it."

He took a long, deep swallow of cold beer, thinking to himself, I cannot tell you or anyone else, Bill, the multitude of lessons I've learned from Victoria Sand. They would constitute quite a list. To number just a few: in spite of all my intellectual pretensions, I still believe in old-fashioned fidelity; intellectual pretensions, especially with girls who sleep around, are too often just that—pretensions; never, never, never should you try to mix sex and social climbing.

"So who're you dragging?" Bill asked.

"A girl I met on the beach. Quiet, but damn good-looking."

Bill grinned. "That's always been kind of important to you, hasn't it, Richard?"

Why not? You looked in the mirror and you knew what you saw there was above average. Why settle for less? But you cannot be that frank with Bill Whitfield. "What's the great Slocum doing with himself?"

"Oh, racing that goddamn souped-up surfboard," Bill said.

Dick shook his head. "He's got fifty thousand dollars' worth of real boat out there just rotting away. I'm the only one that's used it all summer."

Bill laughed. "When you've got Dwight's dough, why worry about fifty grand? If he ever decides to sell that damn thing at a bargain price, let me know, will you?"

"I will—if I can't raise the money myself."

"Big Dwight said he might drive down for the dance. He's got some Italian movie broad he wants to display to us Yacht Club squares."

"I could do without that."

They compared law schools for a while in a carefully neutral tone. Bill didn't want to imply that Yale was better. That would have placed him in the difficult position of the rich boy talking down to a fellow American. Bill wasn't even rich, just upper middle class. It was amazing how easily you could put these city people on the defensive. The hicks never learned that lesson.

Leaving the bay's cool breeze, Dick drove back into the thick murmurous heat of Paradise's residential streets. Familiar figures strolled home from the day's work. There was Buzz Cramer, still lifeguarding down at Jorgensen's beach, teaching physical education in the winter. Two kids already. And rotund Cal Curtis of hardware-store fame, the very model of a pompous church elder with his big belly and booming baritone voice. And librarian Sally Flagg with her plain solemn face and straight black hair—the brightest girl in the class. And Fat Sammy Jacobs, the town's only Jew, his drooping moon-face staring plaintively in his endlessly hopeless search for a friendly hello.

Dick pulled into the Thornton driveway. The old house peered at him through the trees, the two gabled windows on the third floor —his sanctuary—like protruding insect eyes. It resembled a praying mantis hunched there, thin and narrow, reaching out invisible arms to devour the unwary. Thou shalt not devour me, Dick thought grimly. Let that be the first commandment of the new law.

His grandmother was sitting on the screened porch in her favorite rocker shelling peas. "Hi, Momma Glad," he called as he came up the steps. The childish words came naturally to him. He did not really think about how silly they sounded. Once he had refused to pronounce them. But that battle had ended a long time ago. He accepted this square-jawed, cold-eyed old woman as a substitute mother, the best his father could manage under the circumstances.

"When you want supper?"

"Pretty soon if you don't mind. I'm going to the Yacht Club dance."

"They ever do anything down there besides dance?"

"Drink."

"I don't think that's funny and you know it."

The anger was still real in the old voice but there was also a plaintive note. Once the threat of that anger had turned his brain to jelly. She could still do it to Rob Thornton, her dutiful son, but not to grandson Richard. Before her horrified eyes he had flung into the fire the teetotalist pledge she had made him take at fourteen, shattering the carefully worked out dream of sainthood she had constructed for him with the aid of the Reverend Henry Goss.

"I'm only kidding."

"Alcohol is not a kidding matter."

She struggled to her feet clutching the bowl of peas to her well-rounded bosom. She had been a handsome woman in her day and, he suspected, a bitch practically from the cradle. She was a living, walking, and especially speaking, embodiment of that Protestant America which was fading so rapidly from the national scene. Carry Nation was one of her heroines and America's failure to embrace prohibition was a national sacrilege. Drinking, gambling, smoking were sins, and sex was even worse than sin—it was unmentionable.

After years of lecturing, raging, punishing, she had wearily accepted his rejection of the God she had taught him to worship so fervently in his youth. They had stopped arguing toward the end of his college days and a kind of respect, a ghost of their old affection, had grown between them. Flawed though it was by that awful righteousness, there was a stubborn love in the old woman and he knew most of it went, almost against her will, to him.

"Sally Flagg's giving an organ recital at the church tonight. I was gonna ask you to come."

"No thanks, I'm all dated up."

"Who, some city girl as usual?"

"Is there a law against it?"

"No law. Just seems to me it wouldn't harm you to look around your own town a little."

If I did that, Momma Glad, I might get into that car and head for the city and never come back. It was impossible to tell her how totally he disdained Paradise and its ways. But it was pretty obvious, even to her. His careful cultivation of city friends, both the Irish Catholics on the beach and the Protestants at the Yacht Club. His preference for city girls. How could he tell her that it was part of a plan to escape the multitude of traps she and others had set for him on these somnolent streets? He was not going to grow into middle age and old age with the stamp of small-town inferiority in his eyes or on his tongue. He was going to escape, he was going to conquer the conquerors and come back ten or fifteen years from now to dock his own fifty-thousand-dollar sloop at the Yacht Club and hold court in his own mansion on the dunes. Yes, he vowed. He could match this old woman's intensity, match it and surpass it with his own wanting, his own loving.

She came out on the open porch and confronted him with a glare that would have paralyzed him ten years ago. "Come on, picklepuss," he said, "smile."

"I don't think it's funny. I never will think it's funny, you drinkin'."

She stalked into the house. Dick was about to follow her when he heard his father coming. Around Paradise you heard Rob Thornton coming two, three, and often four blocks away. He drove an ancient black 1923 Buick which huffed and puffed and wheezed and clanked along Paradise's quiet streets like a twentieth-century one-horse shay. He claimed the car was a clever business gimmick. Customers who went out to see a house in Rob Thornton's mechanical relic would not be likely to forget him. Whether it made them more inclined to rent from him was another more dubious question.

With a series of shrieks, shudders and explosions the Buick trembled to a stop. His father strolled up the lawn toward him, a roly-poly smiling figure out of Sinclair Lewis. The Panama hat was perched at a jaunty angle over the round cheerful face, the seersucker suit was hopelessly rumpled and the tie fell away from the neck just far enough to destroy any suspicion of gentility. A regular fella, Rob Thornton. No airs about him. No class either.

"Hello, son," he said. "How's the kid?"

"Just dandy."

Rob Thornton trotted up the five porch steps and clapped Dick heartily on the back. "Just gettin' home?"

"Yeah, I stopped off at the Yacht Club for a beer."

"Oh." Rob Thornton had never been inside the Yacht Club in his life. "Goin' to the dance down there tonight?"

"I think so."

"Big shindig, I gather. Ned Ames tells me he's got every room in the hotel rented and half of them are looped already."

"It's getting toward the end of the summer. The urge to celebrate gets stronger."

"Yeah." Rob Thornton glanced hastily up at his son and then glanced past him into the screened porch. "Don't drink too much. You know how it upsets the old girl."

"Don't worry. I promised you I'd keep her in a good mood for the rest of the summer and I will if it kills me."

Rob Thornton clapped him on the back again. "Thanks, kiddo. She gives me the old harry after you go. As if I could tell you what to do these days."

They laughed, but there was a twinge of sadness in those words. Dick knew what Rob Thornton wanted him to do. Come back to Paradise, law degree in hand, and open up an office on Main Street. Become the low man on the local legal totem pole and starve for five or ten years until some of the old hacks died off. Eventually, after maybe forty years, you might rise to that sublime point where the Farmers National Bank entrusted itself to your legal care for a whopping ten thousand dollars a year. Then you could buy a Chrysler Imperial and have your wife drive you to church on Sunday like Adam Barkley—by then your eyesight would be too feeble to handle a high-powered car yourself.

"If this weather holds, it'll be the best summer in ten years. I tell ya, this town is gettin' rich, kiddo. There's real money around. Buzz Ackerman's just about ready to build a motel out on Route Twenty. Thirty-six rooms. And Ames is talkin' about doublin' his capacity.

If I had me some capital I'd buy up every acre of empty land I could find."

"Yeah," Dick said.

"If I was you with all those contacts over there at the Yacht Club, I'd talk one of them filthy rich into settin' you up as a real estate development corporation. With me snuffin' out the bargains and you handlin' the legal and financial end—"

"Yeah," Dick said. He had heard it all before. "I've got to get through another year of law school, Pop. That's all I'm worried about right now."

"Well, that's probably sensible."

No hurt in the voice, just a little sadness. He knew he was being let down easy, but that was better than being let down hard. Rob Thornton had had just about enough of life letting him down hard. He, too, had dreamed of big city money and had taken it on the chops early in the Depression. Back he had crept with his flashy big-city wife minus the inheritance his father had saved from a thousand, penny-ante real-estate deals. Back to the only shelter in sight, this old devourer, this house. And Mother Gladys welcomed the prodigal there with the icy eyes and iron arms of righteousness, welcomed him but not his wife.

That subtle, silent, mysterious woman surrendered in six months, surrendered and fled three thousand miles, abandoning son and husband to start a new life in California. How many schoolboy years you had puzzled over that desertion before they finally let you visit her, that sixteenth summer. Then you understood, you understood so much, in so many incredible ways. But you could never explain any of these understandings to Rob Thornton. He had become someone totally different in those years between desertion and discovery. The man who had sought the challenge and money of the city had vanished utterly in that gray depression decade. He had meekly accepted a job as a clerk in his father's old office and waited fifteen patient years for the partner to die. Fifteen years of churchgoing and small talk on Main Street corners, of radio listening and house hustling and lease signing and handshaking, of clipping little jokes from *The Reader's Digest* and *Grit.* And all you can say to him now, standing on the front porch of the only home you can remember, on the porch where he too stood as a boy, and a young man your age, all you can say is, How in Christ did you stand it?

But you did not really start asking those questions—and so many other questions—until you came back from California. After thirteen years of silence, his mother had announced that she wanted to see him. Hours of whispered conferences between his father and grandmother, and finally a negotiated consent, conducted entirely by the two women, stipulating to the second how long he could stay. Ten days. That was, they thought, a fairly safe compromise between the month she demanded and the five days they were inclined to grant. Simpletons. Five days, or one day, would have been enough. One hour would have been enough to see that in his blood there was a dream of power and importance that leaped the boundaries of their little seashore town. But ten days gave her enough time to awaken the dream in all its dimensions.

Everything he had heard or seen in his boyish imagination had been a myth. She was not especially beautiful. But she was utterly honest. She told him that she regretted leaving him behind her. It had been a mistake. She had not been thinking clearly at the time.

"But nobody was thinking clearly in 1930," she said, with a wry smile.

It was like stepping into a modern, fully lighted room after years of fumbling through rooms lit by the feeble lamps of 1910—which were, in fact, the chief illumination in the old house of his boyhood. His mother was in the twentieth century. His father was still trapped, a hundred years, or at least fifty, behind her, driving the sandy streets of Paradise Beach in his prehistoric Buick, spouting his corny little jokes to the summer visitors as they wandered from room to room of the cold empty houses, deciding whether to cross his palm with a commission.

His mother had explained, in that hard, matter-of-fact voice, how impossible it had been for her to change herself enough to live in Paradise Beach. She told him about the day she had worn slacks on the main street and how the next Sunday the minister had preached a sermon on degeneracy, quoting from the fate of Sodom and Gomorrah, where the sexes had a penchant for switching costumes. She made him see, for the first time, just how dreadful his grandmother was as a human being. And, of course, she had introduced him to her second husband when he came home from that discreet business trip which gave them a chance to begin bridging the years.

Dick's hand gripped the porch railing just a little more tightly as he remembered that long Hebrew face—heard once more his mother's casual voice. "This is Sam. Sam Stone." *Stone, hell,* he had almost shouted at her. You mean Stein. That pudgy, hawk-nosed Hebrew face was as obvious as the yellow stars that Hitler had made them wear. His mother had married a *Jew.* It was hard for him to believe, sometimes, how narrow he had been, how trapped within the mental alley of Paradise Beach with its absurd hick arrogance masquerading stupid prejudices. Now he could remember with bittersweet sadness how much he had come to like Sam Stone in the five brief days of his stepsonship. A theatrical agent, Sam had money and enjoyed spending it. This was a phenomenon almost as incredible to sixteen-year-old Richard Thornton as his Jewishness. Sam took them to five of the best restaurants in Hollywood on five consecutive nights. He arranged for Dick and his mother to visit the production lots of every major studio. He took them swimming at a private beach club south of Los Angeles.

"Are you surprised that Sam's Jewish?" his mother asked in that same dry, offhand voice, as they sat on the beach watching the huge Pacific rollers. Sam was up ordering them lunch in the club restaurant.

"Yes."

"I was afraid you would be. Growing up in that miserable town. That's what I regret more than anything else, leaving you to the mercy of those dreadful people. Learn to judge people by their actions, Dick, by what they think, feel, say. Not by what they happen to be born.

"I do like him," he had said, hot tears in his idealistic eyes.

For the first time since she had kissed him hello, his mother showed emotion. She squeezed his hand. "I'm glad," she said. "He's a good man, Dick. He'll help you if he possibly can. All you have to do is ask him. Remember that."

There had been a certain tension in her voice, as well as warmth. He had wondered about it momentarily but had quickly forgotten when Sam returned spouting funny jokes and wild unbelievable stories about the big names of Hollywood. Three months later, back in Paradise, he had read Sam's grief-stricken words.

Your mother died this morning at 3 A.M. She asked to be cremated, so there won't be any formal funeral service. There is no need for you to come out. I thought you would want to know. It was cancer, Dick. She had it when you were out here. She was a great woman. I'm proud to have been able to call her my wife. Believe me, if you ever give me a chance to show you a father's feelings . . .

Now he could look back on all those days and nights of anguish with gratitude. It had been his awakening to the smallness, the meanness of Paradise. Without that parousia of pain he might have mouldered here as smugly content with himself and the world as the rest of them. But the guilt that twisted in him had at last opened his eyes to its real cause. A year later, in that famous seventeenth summer, he had quit the church, to his grandmother's still-vocal grief. It was his first step toward freedom, freedom of body and mind. He had groped blindly, clumsily, at first, lugging his guilty secrets with him. But it was soon clear that the only way he could escape these furies and achieve that way of relating to people that his mother had praised, was to escape from Paradise. So, coldly, consciously, he began separating himself from the town's ways of thinking, feeling, acting. That was the summer he stopped being a good boy and started collecting his share of the local girls. Oddly, they liked his style, even when he took them with cold contempt.

It was a highly individual rebellion without any of the usual American symbols, such as blue jeans or black jackets, hot rods or alcohol. This was not the standard equipment of the people who ran the banks and corporations and political organizations. He ignored the juvenile idiocies and set out to acquire the standard equipment —the right education, the right accent, the right manners, the right clothes and the right girls.

But the girls were a problem once he extended his range beyond the local crop. At the Yacht Club and on the private beaches they had displayed from the start a kind of ruthless discrimination that was as educational—and as shocking—as a pail of cold water in the face. He would never forget that seventeenth summer, when he had asked Dolores Talbot, the shore's reigning blonde, to go steady. She had laughed and laughed. Blithely, Dolores had let him riffle through her datebook, already crammed with the most expensive names in the state. "I could put you down for a year from next Saturday," Dolores had said with her sweetest, most devastating smile. "But that's the best I can do." He had told her not to bother and henceforth tried to avoid the mistake of over-reaching—perhaps the hardest thing a small-town type must learn. In some ways—perhaps too many ways—Dick thought grimly, you are still learning it.

But at least the unpleasant knowledge is being acquired. That was the important thing. Not to stand still, either mentally or spiritually, like the rest of his generation in Paradise seemed almost determined to do.

An hour later he drove down a neoned main street into the wind-swept darkness of the ocean highway. Paradise, father, mother, grandmother, vanished now in one consuming anticipation. Victoria Sand would be at the dance tonight with her current stud. He wanted to walk past her, dance past her, smile past her, through her, with Margaret Connolly on his arm and in his arms. He wanted to take Margaret Connolly, every lovely inch of her, and cram her down Victoria Sand's gaping mouth. Look your best, Margaret. You owe it to me; I've been spending money on you like it's going out of style.

Margaret more than fulfilled her obligations. She came smiling downstairs in a gauzy, all-white summer dress with a blue sash. She had tanned quickly and the white against the slim brown arms and graceful neck, the darkness of her eyes and hair, was electrifying. What have you got here, Thornton?

Ever since that first night on the beach at Manasquerry, Margaret Connolly had been slowly penetrating his psyche, like one of those radioactive dyes they use to X-ray the brain. Not Margaret really, but an image behind her, a shadowy intuition of someone or something that whispered happiness. Talking to her on the beach over the next few days, he had still found her distant and shy. On impulse one evening he had mentioned her to Larry Donahue.

With unconcealed delight Larry told him that Margaret was beyond him. "I meant what I said that first night, Richard. She is the living, breathing, walking personification of the middle-class Catholic. She really believes God is in cahoots with the Pope and all is right with the world as seen from Vatican City. Add to that the Irish dread of sex, plus instant panic at the word Protestant, and what have you got?"

"A damn attractive, likable girl," he had said stubbornly. "We've gotten along fine."

"Did she tell you she may go into the convent?"

"Jesus, no. When?"

"Next June, if she makes up her mind—and with mother, nuns and priests working on her—"

The thought of Margaret burying herself in some nunnery for the rest of the century had shaken him more than he admitted. He studied her now, smiling across the room at him, and found the idea even more dismaying.

In the distance Faith was ranting, "Twenty years down here and I've never been invited to the Yacht Club, and this creep gets an invitation in ten days. If that doesn't prove the universe is basically absurd—"

"My purpose is purely educational," Dick said. "I want to show Margaret how the other half lives."

"And I want to see it," Margaret said airily.

"You see how obnoxious she is already? She'll be worse than the Wasps before the clock strikes twelve. A Cinderella in reverse."

"Maybe you'd get an invitation if you took advantage of your membership and spent some time over there," the Judge snapped.

"I'll do that when they start admitting Jews and Negroes."

"For Christ sake, don't be ridiculous. The Hebes have got their own yacht club down at Bombay Beach. And what nigger is rich enough to own a boat?"

"It's the principle of the thing," Faith said.

"No guts is the principle in my opinion," the Judge said. "Your whole generation would rather sit around discussing the theology of picking your nose than go out and meet the real world. You're still clinging together like a bunch of greenhorns right off the boat."

In the car Margaret said, "I didn't realize this place was so exclusive."

"It is, a little."

"Faith says that the Kilpatricks were the first Catholics invited to join the club—and that was only when her father became Chief Justice."

"I don't think that stuff will last much longer. The town is half Catholic in the summer now, and the club needs new members. They've got to start letting them in."

"Oh," Margaret said. She still sounded unhappy.

"Don't worry, they won't burn you at the stake. They're more likely to name you Queen of the Ball."

The band was whacking out "Some One Of These Days" as they arrived. Ed Acheson, shorn of the bean-pole dignity with which he presided over the Paradise Beach grammar school during the winter, led them out on the sun deck in his most obsequious headwaiter's manner. In the far corner overlooking the starlit bay they found Bill Whitfield and his date. She was a Radcliffe girl, slim, dark, very cool and reserved. She asked Margaret where she went to school. When Margaret told her, she simply said, "Oh," and looked at Dick as if he had smuggled a Jew or a Negro into the sacrosanct confines of the Paradise Yacht Club.

Bill Whitfield was his usual easygoing self. "Mount St. Monica," he said. "I used to date a girl from there. Dolores Talbot. You know her?"

"Oh, yes," Margaret said. "She's in my class."

"Dolores has everything but taste," Miss Radcliffe said. "What are you majoring in at Mount St. Monica?"

She pronounced the name of the school as if it were a part of the anatomy not usually mentioned in polite company.

"English."

"Oh. What fun. I am too. We had the most divine course in Joyce last semester. Do you like him as much as I do?"

"I haven't read him," Margaret said. "We don't study modern literature."

"Really?"

"Let's dance," Dick said.

On the floor he could not help lecturing Margaret. "You shouldn't let her get away with that act."

"What act?" Margaret said.

"Studying Joyce and all that baloney. You should have said something like I prefer the nineteenth-century novel."

"I didn't realize—I was involved in a contest," Margaret said.

"You were," Dick said. "You always will be with that type of dame."

They danced in silence for about five minutes.

"What does your father do for a living?"

"He's managing clerk at Stapleton Talbot—a law firm."

"Not a law firm, *the* law firm," Dick said. "The one that every law school graduate in the state would sell an arm or a leg to join."

"Really? I didn't know it was so popular."

"Not popular, rich. How long has your father been there?"

"Oh, I don't know. Twenty, twenty-five years."

Fascinating. A managing clerk was hardly the most important man in a law firm. But he was far from the least important. He was the man who kept the firm on schedule, on keel, he knew all the partners intimately. He initiated the young lawyers into the mysteries of local court procedure, the minor routines that law schools no longer bothered to teach.

"I might take a swing at Stapleton Talbot myself."

"Oh—good," she said.

Amazing, how totally naïve she was. Why did that please you, Richard? Was it simply a reaction against Vicky Sand, who measured everything in creation by *who* was *doing it* and *what* they were *worth?* Or was it simply a rational desire to find a girl with solid values? Yes, that was it, you could add the sauce of social sophistication when necessary.

They stayed on the dance floor. You are being overprotective, Richard. Let her get a few more hard knocks from Miss Radcliffe . . .

Victoria Sand came swirling through the dancers in a cloud of blue chiffon. Astonishing, he had forgotten all about her. "Hello, Vicky," he said.

"Oh—Dick."

"I'd like you to meet Margaret Connolly."

He stopped dancing and swung Margaret around on his arm so that they were face to face. It could not have gone better. He watched Margaret flow over Vicky like a corrosive chemical. She shriveled down inside her chiffon, black eyes dulling, the small spoiled mouth pouting. She was no match for Margaret. It was cuteness versus beauty.

"How have you been, Vicky?" he said, savoring the hard arrogance in his voice.

"Fine. And you?"

"Never been better."

Flustered, she introduced her partner. The band blared and Dick missed his name. It did not matter. Vicky only wanted to escape from Margaret Connolly. Those luminous eyes, the unspoiled mouth, the long lithe body, were more than a cruel comparison, Dick suddenly realized; they were a reproach.

"See you around," Dick called as Vicky vanished into the crowd.

The evening was pratically complete. They rejoined Bill Whitfield and his date on the veranda and ordered drinks. Miss Radcliffe was telling Bill what was wrong with American education. "It's amazing how much our universities retain of their old religious orientation. I mean if you compare the restrictions at Harvard with a

Catholic college, it isn't that much different. In this era I think that's disgraceful—"

"Yeah," Bill said, totally bored.

She was obviously someone who had never overcome an inhibition in her life. The apostles of freedom, the screamers for female equality were almost always that way.

"I think freedom is a personal thing," Dick said. "If you don't have it, it's your own fault. There's no point in blaming schools or churches or society."

"Subjectively that may be true," Miss Radcliffe said, "but objectively—"

"And in the second place," Dick said, "I'm not so damn sure that freedom is such a great thing for college students. All they ever do with it, as far as I can see, is sleep around, and I never have been able to figure out what's so educational about that."

"It's much more complex," Miss Radcliffe said plaintively.

"From my experience I would say that Catholics, the religious colleges in general, have got a point when they recommend some self-restraint."

"Wait just a minute," Bill Whitfield said, "let me sprinkle some sawdust on the floor, Reverend."

"Okay, okay. I just happen to be a little vehement on the subject at the moment."

"Obviously," Bill said. "How about you, Margaret? You're the only witness we've got. Are you in favor of restraint and repression?"

"I'm in favor of restraint. Repression is sort of a loaded word, don't you think?"

*You can play the game, Miss Connolly. A delightful discovery.*

"Personally," Dick said, "I'm inclined to favor more religion in education. The objective study of it, I mean, so people can make intelligent decisions about what they believe. We've got too damn many cocktail-party atheists running around being cynical for all the wrong reasons. I took ten hours of comparative religion—"

Shouts, cries from inside the club. People stood up, craning, crowding the French windows. Suspecting the worst, Dick climbed on a chair. There was Dwight Slocum and a busty, wild-eyed girl with streaming coffee-colored hair doing a frenetic Lindy in the middle of the dance floor.

"It's Dwight," he said to Bill Whitfield.

"Drunk?"

"Very."

"Let's get out of here and go someplace quiet," Bill Whitfield said. "I'd rather not get listed by the rules committee again."

They escaped down the veranda steps and around the back of the club to the parking lot.

"I'm one of Dwight's best friends. So is Bill," Dick explained to Margaret. "But when Dwight gets drunk the best thing to do is stay away from him."

"Is he related to *the* Slocums?"

"The only son and heir."

"Oh. How–did you meet him?"

Should you tell her the truth, that a long time ago when you were a mere towel boy at the Yacht Club swimming pool you selected Dwight Slocum as your royal road to instant wealth? No, it was too soon for candor. "His family's been coming down here for years. I've known him since we were kids."

Neutral. That was the proper tone for now. And your feelings about Dwight are neutral, Richard. You are able to strike a very neat balance between revulsion and admiration.

They followed Whitfield's car for several miles. Bill was a nice fellow but there was no particular reason to waste any more time on him. Miss Radcliffe would spend the night seeking revenge for the creaming Richard Thornton had given her, and she wasn't worth the fight. He pulled up beside them at the first red light and told them he was heading home early.

"Why waste a perfectly good evening arguing with that dame?" he said as he pulled away. They drove down to Jorgensen's Pavilion, where there was always a name band holding forth for twenty-five cents a dance. It was a pleasant, well-run ballroom. They put tables out on the ocean promenade and you could hear, if not see, the water. He sat and listened to that vaguely mournful sound of the waves striking the beach and felt a kind of peace steal down his nerves into his flesh. From the moment you walked into that club tonight, Richard, you were slightly mad. Now you have had your revenge and the innocent instrument sits opposite you, wide-eyed, waiting–for what?

Come, Richard, analyze this girl. Make the effort. After all, are you or aren't you going to become the state's richest lawyer? That requires thorough knowledge of modern psychology. She was repressed. No doubt about it. She had a superego so huge it practically annihilated her ego. As for the id, she barely knew it existed, but her body must know. Those rising breasts and long slim thighs, that supple belly—no, Freud was really pretty useless when it came to personal relationships. Let us resort to poetry instead. There was something deep and still in this girl like the taste of good wine at a candlelit dinner. White wine, cool and elusive on the tongue. Victoria Sand had been house-brand whiskey, great for the first three or four jolts, less and less exciting the more you saw how easy it was to get a slug from the bottle. Remember what life is, Richard, a process, growth, learning. A long time ago you decided you were special. That was why you turned your back on Paradise. This girl was special, too, different in her silences, her reserve. And no arrogance. That was important, too. Life was too short to cope with arrogance. Too short for the Richard Thorntons of this world anyway, who had so many other things to do.

"We always seem to wind up listening to the ocean, don't we?"

Margaret smiled. "I like it," she said.

"What else do you like?"

"Everything," she said. "The beach, dancing, swimming."

He bought a dozen tickets and they moved onto the floor to a lazy fox-trot. A singer began to sigh about a paper doll while red, blue and yellow lights played on the walls and ceilings. "Are you staying those extra two weeks?"

"Just one, I'm afraid."

"Mother objected?"

"Naturally."

"You've got to learn to fight back."

"I'm not a very fast learner."

The band suddenly switched to imitation Glenn Miller and everybody started to Lindy. "I'm not too good at this," Margaret said.

"They're not giving out prizes. Relax."

She was better than she thought, and she liked it. There was no boredom in this girl. She was still discovering things. He heard her laugh as he switched from his left to his right hand and spun her behind his back. She swayed out there at arm's length, the willowy body full of grace and life, the face aglow with pleasure and excitement. She was definitely worth some time and trouble, Richard. Even a lot of time and trouble.

They danced for an hour and Margaret grew visibly weary. Jake O'Connor's beach party last night had lasted until dawn. "I'm taking you home," he said, "before you pull a Camille on me."

"I'm just not used to these hours."

"Give yourself a chance."

Main Street was deserted now. Only the drugstore windows still glowed as the last of the movie crowd gurgled their sodas.

"Is this—the whole town?"

He swung off Main Street into the residential section. The streetlights were barely visible through the thick, sighing branches of the trees. The old houses were mostly dark. But here and there a window still glowed in an upper story.

"This is the real town," Dick said.

"It's so peaceful," Margaret said. "Those wonderful trees."

"It is peaceful," Dick said. "Too peaceful."

At the Kilpatricks' they found Faith sitting on the porch steps thumbing her mandolin. Larry sat a few feet away.

"Welcome back to reality," Larry said.

"You're early," Faith said. "A dull party?"

"You might say that," Dick said.

"It's got to be dull," Larry said. "Do the Wasps ever do anything that isn't dull?"

"Count their money," Dick said. "I find that damn exciting."

"You're just jealous," Margaret said. "Both of you. We had a wonderful time."

"Good God, you're brainwashed," Larry said. "The next thing you'll be down there on Main Street Sunday mornings singing 'Come into My Garden, God.' "

"Not a chance," Dick said.

He left Margaret to undergo the rest of the interrogation alone and drove slowly home. Without turning on a light, he fumbled down the narrow side hall past the living room and dining room with their sliding white doors shut tight as they had always been since he came to this house, a whining five-year-old. After a couple of gropes, he found the cord to the kitchen light. The tin-topped white table with its three white captain's chairs greeted him with blank solemnity. He got out a bottle of milk and the last slice of weekend pie. His grandmother was an indifferent cook at everything but desserts. Her pies and cakes and apple turnovers were the best he had ever eaten anywhere. This pie was apple, sliced very fine with cinnamon threaded through it and a touch of brown sugar baked into the crust. Whenever he had a piece of her pie he was able to be more charitable about Gladys Thornton. There was a lot to admire in that fiery spirit. But like everything and everyone else you have confronted thus far in life, Richard, you must select what serves you and let the rest go. That always means something less than rapport, it always means a kind of loneliness.

It would be lovely to have someone with whom there was no need to select, someone with whom you could open your mind and feelings without the perpetual fear that they were going to use everything you said against you. You had tried it with Victoria Sand and it had all come flying back at you in a farewell fusillade, the revelations rearranged according to Sigmund Freud and his imitators to spell *neurotic*—the instant smear word of the era.

Yes, there is something to be said for Gladys Thornton and her total contempt for the modern world. It has put a streak of conservative caution in your bones that has saved you from swallowing whole the shibboleths and cant phrases by which too many people your age live. *Personal* is your key word, you intend to make your life personal, and that is why you were able to tell Victoria Sand bluntly, without apology, that you were not going to stand there grinning like an idiot while she slept around whenever her libido moved her. She had flung the shrill standard slogans at you about the rights of modern women and her need for the kind of fulfillment he was unable to supply. It didn't interest him. He had dumped her so hard she had fallen right out of Dwight Slocum's set. Yes, you could be a bit of a Puritan yourself, Richard, when someone pressed the right psychological button.

Now there was Margaret Connolly, as different from Vicky Sand as you could make the female species. He saw her again, laughing, her head thrown back, at the end of his outstretched arm—

Footsteps on the front porch, a fist banging on the outer door, while in the street a horn blared. In the doorway beneath the feeble porch light a girl with coffee-colored hair, a wide smile and very frightened eyes. Magnificent breasts bulged out of a low-necked black satin evening gown that fit her as if it was elastic. "Meester Thorn-ton?" She smiled while the horn blared in the background and lights came on in windows up and down the block.

It was Dwight and his entourage. "Thornton, you son of a bitch," he was roaring through the window of the white Cadillac at the curb. "Come on, you coxswain you, we want to go sailing."

"You'll go sailing right into night court if you don't lay off that horn."

"Yeah, yeah, yeah. Come on, coxswain, I got a date with a siren and I need you to keep me off the rocks."

Two years ago Dwight had taken the sloop out at night and run aground on a mud flat only a few hundred yards beyond the Yacht Club channel. He had had to sit there all night cursing and face the hoots and horselaughs of the morning. Ever since, he had made it a point to bring Dick Thornton along on his midnight sails. Dick was a perfect combination—local enough to know every shoal and inlet in the bay, good friend enough to keep his mouth shut about anything that happened on board.

And with Dwight, especially Dwight drunk, anything might happen. "It's one o'clock in the morning," Dick said, peering into the car.

"So the night's just warming up," Dwight chortled. "We even brought along company to make sure you warm up with it."

He flipped the car's overhead light and there beside a nuzzling pair of drunks smiled Victoria Sand. "Get in, will you, for Chrissake?" Dwight roared.

Dick held the door for the coffee-haired girl and got in the front seat beside her. "Meet Theresa Conti," Dwight said. "A big name in Italian movies. She got raped by five hundred Sabines in her last picture."

"I can see why," Dick said, staring down Theresa's decolletage.

"Theresa, meet Richard Thornton, the smartest son of a bitch I have ever met, and that includes my old man."

Theresa gave him a bright, vacant smile. Dwight gunned the motor and sent the car hurtling down the dark empty street. At the Yacht Club Dick got a good look at the nuzzling couple as they stumbled out of the car, and vetoed Dwight's idea of taking his sloop out on the bay.

"You lose somebody overboard on a night as dark as this and it's goodbye for good."

"Okay, we'll take the Chris-Craft," Dwight said. "More room in the cabin anyway."

The Slocum Special, as the Chris-Craft was called, was a glistening white thirty-five-footer with every conceivable comfort a rich man might want at sea. Dick went up on the flying bridge, started the motor, and they throbbed slowly past the rows of white hulls into the open bay. Soon they were plowing into a stiff west wind that sent spray splattering against the windshield. Dwight, Vicky and Theresa Conti joined him on the bridge. Dwight handed him a drink and raved about the joys of night-cruising. But his esthetic ebullience did not last. His mind was below decks.

"Hey," he roared down the hatchway, "you bastards through with the cabin?"

Muffled voices apparently answered in the affirmative. Dwight clapped Dick on the back. "Richard," he said, "you've been such a sport about losing a night's sleep, I'll let you and Vicky go first."

All he could see, by the glow of the binnacle light, was the mockery in Vicky's eyes. "No thanks," he said.

"What's this?" Dwight said, pretending total bewilderment. "I heard rumors. But I thought sea breezes—you know how I hate to see romances end."

"In that case you shouldn't have invited her."

"Richard," Dwight said, "you're making the little lady unhappy." He put his arm around Vicky. "Baby, don't look so sad. Believe me, I could barely stand watching you waste your time on this so-called intellectual for the last year."

"That's nice to know," Vicky said.

"I could suggest some even nicer things."

"You know where I live."

"But I'm impatient. Why don't we do some rehearsing right now?"

"I'd love it."

"Did you hear that, Richard? She wants to play switchees. Any objections?"

"Just sympathy."

"Wheew! He is in a nasty mood."

Dwight took Vicky's hand and they disappeared below. Theresa Conti stood silently beside Dick while he steered the Slocum Special in big lazy circles through a steady swell. Fifteen minutes later, Dwight reappeared.

"Thornton," he said, "you never told me it was that good. You've been holding out on me."

"I told you. But you were occupied at the time."

"Ah, mamma mia, poor Theresa," Dwight said, and gave her a bear hug. She tried to kiss him and Dwight laughed. "Not me, baby. I've had it for the night."

"Richard," he said after a moment, "her feelings are hurt. You got to console her."

"Thanks. But I'm not very good when I'm nervous. And I'd be damn nervous with you up here at the wheel."

Just enough independence but not too much. That was the formula for handling Dwight. You are getting good at it, Richard, you do it almost by instinct now. But Dwight drunk was not the same as Dwight sober. He reached over, flipped the ignition switch and killed the motor. "Now you've got nothing to worry about."

"With this wind we'll be up on the beach in twenty minutes."

"You know what I think, Richard? You don't like my taste. Either that or it's Queersville—I've been waiting for you to go that way like the rest of the intellectuals."

So it was down to that. He revived the motor and gave Dwight the wheel. "Use the Yacht Club lights to fix your position and keep moving in a circle."

Total darkness in the cockpit. The drunken couple were wrestling on the stern cushions. A few feet away, Vicky Sand stood smoking a cigarette, staring out at the dark water. Dick led Theresa Conti to the cabin door. If you want to stay in Dwight's club there are certain rules you must obey. How many hours you have spent guzzling with him until he was drunk enough to admire your capacity. How many times you have risked your life sitting beside him as he pushed the speedometer needle off the dial. How many nights you have strolled with him into elegant whorehouses in Chicago, San Francisco, Dallas. And each time you told yourself, The world is amoral, Richard. These kinds of acts are neutral. They do not touch your personal integrity. They subtract nothing from your determination to shape your life along essentially moral lines. They are a modest concession, nothing more, to the necessities of your peculiar position.

He opened the cabin door and descended the three small steps into the walnut-lined interior. Theresa Conti wiggled out of her dress and stretched out on the lower bunk. For a moment he stared unbelieving at the stupendous breasts. They looked unreal above the gamin waist and spindly legs. Theresa smiled. It was bright, automatic, empty. How many thousands of times will you use that smile from the same reclining position before you die, Theresa, and your eyes will still be full of that frightened bewilderment? We who think about life are responsible for that baffled pain. Yet there is really nothing we can do about it.

"You—like?" She ran her hands over her breasts and down her body.

He nodded and pulled off his shirt and pants and lay down beside her. The bay sloshed on the other side of the bulkhead, a lamp above them swayed as the Slocum Special pitched and rolled. Quick and fast. Quick and fast. And do not kiss her. You have never been able to kiss a whore and this is what you have here, Richard. He let his lips taste the thick perfume of Theresa's neck. He swung into the saddle and went to work, the breasts beneath his chest like half-inflated beach balls. He closed his eyes and shoved it in and out. An utterly meaningless performance, Richard, in a meaningless world. No God to swing thunderbolts at you or roast you in the flames of hell. Therefore, each act became meaningful only in terms of the actor's purpose, and in that sense there is almost a moral purpose in my fucking you so calmly, deliberately, Theresa. Because this is one more step toward the fantastically complex salvation of Richard Thornton's body and soul in a new dispensation, and we must save both, Theresa.

She bucked and wiggled under him, murmuring Italian. *"Carissimo, bellissimo."*

You are all woman, Theresa, and for you this performance has its own morality, some childish nirvana furnished from Macy's basement by a personalized Marshall Plan. All woman, and I am about to be a man in you.

As he trembled on the brink, a face swayed out of the darkness inside his eyes, dark hair, not coffee-colored, a willowy body and a bright laughing smile: Margaret Connolly there at the end of his outstretched arm. Crazily, as his semen gushed impersonally in Theresa's loins, he whispered to that other face there in the darkness, "It doesn't matter. It doesn't really matter."

# Chapter Four

*"Those wedding bells are breaking up*
*That old gang of mine."*

Faith kept humming the song all the way to the station. Margaret ignored her and talked casually about going back to school. On the train she took out Thomas Merton's *Seven Storey Mountain*—ruefully noting that her place in the book had not changed since she had closed it as the train pulled into Paradise Beach three weeks ago. Three weeks. It was impossible to believe in three weeks. It was either three days or three years. She sighed and began to read. But she could not concentrate on the earnest prose for more than ten seconds. Something else kept speaking incessantly in her ears and finally she realized it was the train's clicking wheels saying, *Dick Thornton—Dick Thornton—Dick Thornton.* Ridiculous. She slammed the book shut and stared out the window at the flat sandy landscape.

Margaret, Margaret, what has happened? You were so sensible before you entered this crazy world of sunlight and blue water. Your mind was as neat as one of your dresser drawers, where blouses and underwear were folded in precise rows. You knew exactly where to find everything. Now this alarming jumble of images, sounds, touches, that race through your whole body, without warning, like currents from a berserk switchboard. *Dick Thornton—Dick Thornton—Dick Thornton,* mocked the wheels. Nights on the porch listening to Dick and Larry Donahue telling funny stories about the war. Larry Donahue and the Kilpatricks singing "The Minstrel Boy" and a dozen other Irish songs while Dick sat to one side, a small uneasy smile on his face, and your sudden rush of sympathy, wanting to say, *I'm outside too.* Then looking hastily away, blushing, when Larry Donahue, his mocking eyes on Faith, sang one of James Joyce's poems.

But one unto him
Will softly move
And softly woo him
In ways of love

His hand is under
Her smooth round breast
So he who has sorrow
Shall have rest.

Sailing the bay, golden moonlight on miles of water. Dancing in another brightness, storybook laughter to a Stan Kenton beat. Drifting down, down in the cold watery darkness with the feel of his arm around your waist. The mind refusing to take it seriously, scoffing at possibility, while a voice whispered *yes.* And all the time there was no overwhelming sense of escape. There was still that voice, speaking to you behind the door there in the darkness of your mind, remembering answers you could have made, funny remarks that always came too late. But somehow the sense of disdain, the smell of failure was removed. You were still the same Margaret Connolly, but you were *accepted* by these relaxed, laughing, teasing people. Even Larry Donahue seemed to grow less acid, more wryly bantering as the days floated effortlessly into each other, and Dick spent more and more time with her. The voice behind the door became at worst a hollow, silly haunt and at best a delicious, if equally silly, daydream.

*I'm really a good girl,* said Margaret, smiling up at the man of the world while the orchestra chirped merrily. *What are you good at?* he said with a knowing smile. *Try me and see,* she whispered with a mocking toss of her dark head. Movie dialogue. Fred Astaire Thornton pursuing Ginger Rogers Connolly up miles of marble staircase, around forests of fluted columns. You could always laugh yourself out of earlier daydreams, Margaret, there was always Mother announcing something sensible like a shopping expedition or a cooking lesson or a relative to visit. Maybe all you need is a healthy jolt of Mother's common sense now, Margaret. A half-dozen dates do not make a romance. *Dick Thornton—Dick Thornton—Dick Thornton,* clattered the wheels past small towns and patches of shining sea, past white boats and grassy dunes, past suburban developments spreading down the small valleys and up the undulating hills like collections of dollhouses. *Dick Thornton—Dick Thornton—Dick—*

The train gave a weary groan and slowed to a crawl. Suddenly out the window there was only a great blank wall of warehouses, then acres of empty boxcars and switchyards, and dozens of scrambling men in overalls. Now they were rolling past streets of tenements with the third-floor windows open in the heat, which began to penetrate the car with soggy persistence. Block after block slid past, eye after blank eye, with the dingy interior of other lives wearily open to casual view. Faces occasionally, as blank and empty as the windows without the faces, fat-faced women in bathrobes at noon, unshaven men in undershirts, staring down in the street. The city and its citizens.

The wheels no longer said anything. Glancing up, Margaret saw the vast, gray clutter of the houses, the black tracery of the streets, clinging to the long, narrow hill which the city engulfed. The rail line ran along the base of it, on the river side, so that you felt, almost physically, the city's tremendous mass. This was where you lived, Margaret, just one person in hundreds of thousands. Perhaps that is what makes you so sensible, Margaret. You are a city girl. You know that you cannot swallow the whole world because the world is just too big. It is so much safer to be sensible, neat, quiet, when you grow up in this world. Unless you grow up like Faith, of course, on top of it, you cannot avoid feeling its weight there all around you, all the time.

Darkness now. They were in the tunnel, gliding into the station by the river. There is Mother waving frantically, trotting along beside the window, an ecstatic smile on her face. Her little girl has come home in one piece. Mother was very sensible. She was waiting for you out there in the dusty heated air, waiting to help you rescue your sensible life, Margaret. Get up, haul your bag off the rack and walk toward your only possible future.

"Oh, you look so *tan,*" Mother cried as she hugged her.

Her father stepped forward and gave her a quick efficient kiss on the cheek. "Come on, I'm double parked," he said, and they followed him down the grimy gray platform to a creaking escalator which carried them into the dim station.

"Well, tell me all about your handsome lifeguard," Mother said the moment they were settled in the car.

Margaret was totally unprepared. "How—do you know about him?"

"Oh, I called Mrs. Kilpatrick to see how you were and we had a lovely chat. She told me you were a wonderful girl—oh, you should have *heard* the nice things she said about you. But she did complain that she hardly got a chance to talk to you after the first day or two —she said this handsome lifeguard practically *monopolized* you."

"That's hardly true," Margaret said, although she had to admit to herself that she had more or less avoided Mrs. Kilpatrick because all she wanted to talk about was her daughter Theresa. "I don't see any reason for talking about Dick that way, as if he was some sort of freak."

"I don't mean that, darling. But he is *handsome?* You have been dating him?"

Mother giggled. She was acting cute again. Margaret remembered with a twist of remorse that she had acted the same way over her pitifully few dates in high school. Mother did not seem to realize that a woman her size should never try to be cute. It was like watching an elephant dance a minuet.

Margaret, that is not very charitable. Answer Mother politely. "We went out five or six times."

"Well—that's pretty good for three weeks. It took your father three months to take me out that much."

"Honestly, Mother—it was just part of—summer."

"I hope so." The familiar voice was suddenly almost stern. "Father Malone was quite upset to hear about it."

"Upset? Why?"

"Well, for one thing the fellow's a Protestant, isn't he? And then you do have the possibility of—"

*A higher calling.* Are you wincing at those words, Mother? No, you are just being delicate; Father Malone has warned you against forcing me into a vocation. But I am wincing, Mother. I don't know why and I don't know what it means. But I am wincing.

"That's perfectly ridiculous, to start discussing me—or Dick—in those terms."

Her mother laughed uncertainly. "I'm only telling you how Father reacted. I don't know as much about these things as he does."

Margaret looked out the car window at the swarms of children playing along the downtown sidewalks and said nothing. Fortunately, there were plenty of other things to talk about when they got home.

Mrs. Kilpatrick had been appointed chairwoman of a statewide conference of leading Catholic laywomen to discuss religion in family life. Father Denton Malone, chaplain at Mount St. Monica's, and several other well-known clerics had agreed to give talks and head discussion groups. As usual, Mrs. Kilpatrick was calling on Mrs. Connolly, her favorite lieutenant, to do the hard work of mailing out the invitations and coordinating the committees. Sometimes, Margaret thought wryly to herself, her mother seemed to be getting more out of her daughter's college education than anyone else. Margaret's friendship with Faith had enabled Mrs. Connolly to enter that elite world beyond the parish, in which Mrs. Kilpatrick moved, organizing card parties and teas for the wealthy wives of the politicians, contractors, and trucking magnates whose names appeared on the Cardinal's committee for the laity, the board of directors of the CIO and Catholic Charities. The thought that she had given her mother entrée to this world usually pleased Margaret. But now, walking into the living room, and seeing the piles of papers running like a chain reaction from Mother's desk across the couch cushions to the radiator covers, Margaret felt just a little dismayed. They would all be swept up in the chaos before it was over. Although Mother was a willing worker, she was not very well organized.

But it was futile to protest against an accomplished fact. Margaret soon found herself typing letters to out-of-town delegates about hotel reservations, rushing across town with corrected programs for the printer, taking what seemed like an endless series of telephone calls from Mrs. Kilpatrick who was trying to run the conference from Paradise Beach. Whenever they found a spare hour off this merry-go-round, they shopped. Day after day they trudged from store to store and mother pondered her daughter in beige, brown, gray, even purple. She always had trouble making up her mind just what looked "right" for Margaret. All her clothes had to satisfy several somewhat contradictory requirements. They had to fit well and look reasonably expensive, even if they were usually on sale. At the same time they shouldn't and couldn't look too "alluring," as Mother was fond of saying. Tight sweaters and snug skirts were out. This year the New

Look, with its long full skirts and frilly blouses, was on Mother's side. But there were still the party dresses to fight about. Anything that showed too much bosom or back was banned. Mother did not fight with Margaret about these decisions. It was the saleswomen who felt that Margaret cried out for this kind of clothes. "But she's such a beautiful girl," one of them wailed when Mrs. Connolly turned down the third consecutive plunging neckline. "Such a marvelous figure!"

"Don't be ridiculous," Mrs. Connolly snapped. "There's nothing beautiful about her." Margaret blushed, because her mother was staring angrily at her, as if the saleswoman's words were her fault. "She's reasonably nice looking, that's all. There's absolutely no reason for her to get conceited over her looks." Again, the words were accusing and Margaret could not help feeling annoyed. She had almost wanted to point out that she was *not* conceited, that she had gone to a great deal of personal trouble to make sure that she never fell into this trap against which Mother had warned her so often.

Margaret came home from this combative experience feeling as if she had swum the Atlantic Ocean. Her father was working late as usual. He had planned to take his vacation during these last two weeks of the summer, but when Mrs. Kilpatrick called Mother to the colors, he had shrugged and gone back to work. Sometimes Margaret worried about the endless drudgery he seemed to perform, day and night, at Stapleton Talbot. He never seemed to do anything but work, and according to Mother, no one among his employers even vaguely appreciated his "contribution," as she called it. But that was typical of the Protestants. They were always ready to work anyone with an Irish name to death, if they gave them a chance. The trouble with Bill Connolly was, he gave them the chance. He didn't have enough gumption to quit his job, or at least ask for a raise. Margaret tried to think as little as possible about these harsh words because they made her sad. There were other reasons why her father stayed in his job, she was certain. Someday, when she was older, she was going to ask him about it. Life was strange, she thought, as she slipped wearily into bed. Her mother didn't really seem to *like* her father, yet she had married him. Why did people get married anyway? Wasn't love supposed to be the reason? How could you love someone and not like them? Suddenly she saw Dick Thornton, smiling at her as they danced to a slow fox-trot. She liked him, but you didn't necessarily *love* everyone you liked. Yes, that is a very sensible thought, Margaret. Think it again and again and again.

The next thing Margaret heard was her mother's voice, calling to her and simultaneously knocking on the door of her bedroom. "Margaret, Margaret, there's a letter here for you." Then Mother was standing beside the bed, thrusting the white envelope practically down her daughter's throat. Margaret sat up, sleepily staring at the unfamiliar handwriting.

"Who is it?"

"It says on the back: Thornton, Paradise Beach," Mother said.

For another moment Margaret just sat there dazedly with the letter in her hand.

"Aren't you going to open it?"

"I think I'll wash my face first, so I can see." She went into the bathroom and closed the door. Amazing, the instinctive deceit you have just displayed, Margaret. But now that you have come this far, keep going. She turned on the water, ripped the letter open and read:

Dear Margaret:

Summer is fading out with more whimpers than bangs down here. Faith isn't speaking to Larry Donahue for some silly reason (it's one way of protecting her virtue, I suppose) and Larry is ready to cut my throat when I ask him about it. We obviously all miss your benevolent presence. Even Larry, the original cynic, admits you are the most even-tempered woman he has ever met.

This is my favorite time of the year down here. The water is warm and the beach is cold, so that separates the men from the boys (and the women from the girls). Most of the city slickers have gone home, except for a few like the Kilpatricks, who really care about the place. I wish you could come down for a couple of days just before you go back to school. But that's probably impossible, so instead I'll be practical and let you know that I'll be in the city a week from this Thursday. Can I take you to dinner?

Best,
DICK

What do you think, what do you say, Margaret? She walked out of the bathroom and almost collided with her mother who was standing in the doorway.

"Have you read it?" she said.

"Yes."

"What did he say?"

"Nothing very much."

"Oh, let me read it."

Margaret said nothing. But she did not hand her mother the letter. Then she knew that she did not want to hand it to her.

"What's the matter? You don't want me to read it?"

"It's not really that important, or interesting, Mother."

Mrs. Connolly laughed uncertainly. "Well, my little girl is growing up, isn't she?"

"Oh, here," Margaret said, and thrust the letter at her mother. "You're being silly."

Mrs. Connolly snatched the letter and read it, so it seemed to Margaret, in a single glance. "Well, that's out of the question," she said.

A startling anger erupted in Margaret's mind. It alarmed her so much, all she could say was, "Why?"

"That's the last night of the conference. We're having a dinner and the Archbishop is speaking. I certainly expect you to come."

"Oh," Margaret said. "I—didn't know."

"As a matter of fact, I'm going to need your help all through that conference and the rest of the week will be just one mad rush of shopping. You haven't got half your clothes."

Later that morning, after Margaret had cleaned up her room, she sat down at her old desk where she had spent so many studious high school hours and wrote:

Dear Dick,

I would love to see you next week but my mother is running a statewide conference on Religion in the Family, and on Thursday they're having a dinner which I am "expected" to attend. Do I make myself clear? Aside from helping out on this project, I seem to spend all my time shopping. Getting ready for college is a very complicated business if you're a female—and have a mother who can't make up her mind about any item of clothing without seeing it four times. In short, it looks like I had best wait until I am settled in my cubbyhole at Mount St. Monica before I begin socializing.

Best,
MARGARET

At the corner, on the way to an afternoon of shopping, she asked Mother to stop the car, and dropped the letter in the mailbox.

"Who's that to?" Mother asked.

"Dick."

"Oh."

Did you want to read that, too, Mother? You missed your chance. That is neither kind nor charitable, Margaret, but probably true.

"You didn't really want to see him, did you?" Mother said as she put the car into first gear with an emphatic shove of her large arm.

"Well, it wasn't a matter of life and death, but—"

"But what?" Mother said, beeping impatiently at a taxi driver trying to read the numbers on the houses.

"I—guess I didn't."

A lie, Margaret. You have told a lie. But it was so much easier than telling the truth, which would only invite another inquisition on whether she was serious about Dick and how Father Malone disapproved and why summer romances were basically ridiculous and it was hard to understand how Mother's sensible little girl Margaret could possibly believe in them. Actually, Mother, she only believes she has a right to see Dick Thornton when and where she chooses.

For the rest of the week, no matter how furiously enthusiastic Mother waxed over the upcoming conference, Margaret felt vaguely ill and depressed. There was no answer to her letter refusing Dick's invitation and she went over every phrase she had written, trying to read into them innuendoes he might have read, signifying insult or rejection or indifference. Worst was the voice that kept whispering, *Yes, Margaret, he has probably read your letter and seen right through it. Not a grown woman but a little girl and Momma said no you can't go out with that bad man.*

Oh, so silly. Forget it, Margaret, forget him. You knew it was impossible right from the start.

When the first day of the conference finally came, she almost welcomed it. At least it was a distraction. She did not attend all the seminars, of course. Some of them, her mother explained, were discussing "adult problems" such as the causes of divorce or birth control. But Mother insisted she come to the opening day's luncheon. "Father Malone is speaking," she said triumphantly, "at *my* suggestion. I told Mrs. Kilpatrick he was not only the best chaplain Mount St. Monica's ever had—but he's also a wonderful spiritual guide. *You* can vouch for that, right?"

It was undeniably true, but Margaret somehow found it simpler to say nothing in reply.

The weather bureau had been predicting a September heat wave and it arrived in all its ferocity. By noon the temperature outside the Garden Square Hotel was hovering near 100°. Inside, it was almost as hot. Margaret wandered through a maze of third-floor conference rooms until she found the doors to the Dakota Suite, on which someone had hung an all-purpose sign, CATHOLIC CONFERENCE. Inside she found a swarm of perspiring women, most of them lumpy and fiftyish.

Mother hailed her across the room and dragged her over to a circle of women standing around Mrs. Kilpatrick, who was seated in a chair, her cane beside her. Obviously her operations had not completely cured her arthritis. "Here's my faithful helper," Mother said, largely to Mrs. Kilpatrick. "I couldn't have possibly handled all these details without her. I'm certainly going to miss her when she goes back to school."

"And of course," said Mrs. Kilpatrick, with one of her more angelic smiles, "you'll miss her even more if—"

"Oh, we don't even talk about that. I mean—if that's what God wants, He'll let us know. Right, Meg?"

Margaret nodded automatically, and only then realized they were discussing her vocation.

"He will give you whatever grace you need, let me assure you of that," Mrs. Kilpatrick said. "Believe me, it was a wrench when my Theresa came to me and told me she had made up her mind. Much as I had *prayed* for at least one vocation in the family, still when the time came to part with her—"

"But isn't this Marge's only daughter?" asked a short intense woman with hair on her upper lip.

"Only child," Mrs. Kilpatrick said. "That's why I think it's truly marvelous the way she feels so open about it."

"There's nothing marvelous about it," Mother said merrily. "I just decided a long time ago to resign myself to God's will."

"You can say what you want," Mrs. Kilpatrick grandly insisted, "I still think it's marvelous. And I'm sure everyone agrees with me."

Heads nodded, assents were universally murmured. A waiter came strolling through the crowd ringing a bell. "Lunch," he bawled.

"Oh, dear," Mother said, "and Father Malone isn't here yet. He's usually so prompt."

She handed Margaret over to the pudgy lady. "I'm up on the dais, dear, but I'm sure you'll enjoy talking to these ladies. Mrs. Carmichael here is a graduate of Mount St. Monica."

She squeezed the pudgy lady's short fat arm and moved swiftly into the crowd. "This way, ladies," she called. "Luncheon is this way. You can have more drinks inside."

Everyone followed obediently into an adjoining dining room. Margaret sat down at a circular table with Mrs. Carmichael and her friend.

"Your mother is so wonderful. I don't know how she does it," Mrs. Carmichael said. "And I understand you're just like her."

"Not really," Margaret said.

"I mean in school. I understand you get wonderful marks."

"Oh—fair."

"I was lucky to graduate myself," Mrs. Carmichael said with a hollow laugh. "But I think school was harder then. We had such small classes. They were always asking you to recite."

"Oh, that must have been hard," Margaret said.

"And you have a vocation," said the thin-lipped woman who was sitting on the other side.

"Well," Margaret floundered, "I'm not completely sure—"

"Your mother was telling us how you wanted to enter right after high school, but she decided you were too young."

"Yes," Margaret said, even if the story was not completely true. It was her father who had insisted that since she had won a full scholarship to Mount St. Monica she should wait until she graduated from college before making such a momentous decision. Her mother had acquiesced reluctantly, after long conferences with Sister Mildred, Margaret's homeroom teacher, who had been even more reluctant to agree. But her father had been adamant. It was the only time in her life she had ever seen him win an argument with her mother.

"I have five children," pudgy Mrs. Carmichael was saying. "Three boys and two girls. I would love to see at least one of them have a vocation. But I'm not so sure how I'd feel if I only had one."

"Oh, there's Father Malone," Margaret said.

The chaplain of Mount St. Monica had acquired a deep tan during the summer months. His smile was a flash of white as he moved briskly up and down the speaker's table shaking hands with the distinguished guests. He sat down between Mrs. Connolly and Mrs. Kilpatrick and they plunged into an animated conversation. Watching them from a distance, Margaret suddenly experienced a strange sinking sensation. Father Malone was her confessor at Mount St. Monica, the spiritual adviser with whom she had conferred repeatedly over the past three years as she struggled and prayed over her vocation. Why was it disturbing to see him so convivial and relaxed at lunch with Mother? You are being silly, Margaret. It's really a good thing to have a spiritual adviser who knows not only you but your family well.

Mrs. Carmichael and the thin-lipped woman fell into an exhaustive discussion of their children's marks. The food, chicken and tired peas, was as dull as the conversation. Margaret tried to listen to the women on the other side of the table but they were also talking about children. She was glad when Mrs. Kilpatrick finally tapped a spoon against a glass and rose to introduce Father Malone.

After hailing him as the most gifted young priest in the diocese, she yielded the microphone to him. He gave a superb talk, solemn, serious but with flashes of humor. Each family, he maintained, was a replica of the Mystical Body of Christ. It was the father's duty as head to direct a family, but the mother was the heart of the family and it was her duty to see that the spiritual blood of sanctifying grace was constantly pumped to every member. He ended with a soaring assurance that each mother could achieve in her own family the position which the Blessed Mother held in the greater mystical body of the church.

The applause was thunderous. Everyone at the table marveled at Marge Connolly's suggestion to have Father Malone as the keynote speaker. "We out-of-towners hadn't really heard him, you know," Mrs. Carmichael explained. "But she guaranteed us. And, oh . . ."

"I can hardly wait to get home and put that in my diary," said the thin-lipped woman. "I keep a spiritual diary. My confessor suggested it."

Mother swept down on them, towing Father Malone. She introduced him to everyone except Margaret. "I think you know her." She giggled.

"I certainly do and I'll be seeing a lot more of her soon." Father Malone smiled.

He was obviously in a hurry and after exchanging a few more pleasantries with the ladies at the table, he pleaded a meeting at the chancery office and fled. Mother gravitated immediately to Mrs. Kilpatrick's side and the two of them discussed in glowing terms what a superb success Father Malone's speech had been. Mrs. Kilpatrick declared it had "spiritual resonance," a verdict on which everyone was in total agreement.

Margaret, feeling like a lost waif, stood on the edge of the circle.

She finally summoned the courage to touch her mother on the arm and ask, "Can I go now?"

"Aren't you staying for the dinner meeting?" her mother said, pretending to be surprised.

"I don't see why Daddy should eat alone," Margaret pleaded.

"He'll be perfectly all right," Mother said, still trying to sound cheerful in front of so many listeners.

"I think that's sweet," Mrs. Kilpatrick said. "I wish Faith felt that way about her father. Or her mother, for that matter."

"Well–" Mrs. Connolly faltered.

Margaret met her mother's eyes. Unspoken was the knowledge they both shared now and her mother for some strange reason resented Margaret sharing. To leave Daddy alone for an evening could become an invitation to disaster. He had remained true to his last pledge for a long time, almost three years. But the mere possibility of another bender, the memory of her mother's raging vituperation, was enough to make Margaret shudder. No doubt Mother considered it a subtle reprimand. They had never really discussed Bill Connolly's drinking and Margaret sometimes wondered if that was why she was never able to justify Mother's rage when it happened. Sadness was Margaret's reaction. Her father did not become one of those angry, hateful drunks. He subsided even deeper into his silence. It was, she often thought, more like a man desperately gulping down some vital fluid that somehow involved his very survival. He would drink a bottle, even two bottles in a single night, and lie there stuporous on the couch while Mother bellowed and blustered at him.

It was worth braving Mother's disapproval, Margaret thought grimly as she rode home on the bus. She found a steak in the refrigerator, boiled some potatoes, then fried them with onions, and when her father came home she greeted him with a happy kiss. "Surprise," she said, "I've cooked your favorite dinner."

In the kitchen Bill Connolly beamed down at the steak. "By golly," he said as he chewed his first slice, "you could make someone a good wife."

"Oh," Margaret scoffed, "who'd want to marry me?"

Father stared incredulously at daughter. "You must be kidding."

"No, I'm not. I'm always so–ill at ease with boys."

"Give yourself a chance," Bill Connolly said. "You haven't spent much time with them. That's one thing wrong with a convent education. A big thing in my opinion."

He chewed his steak for another moment. "You met a fellow down at the shore, didn't you?"

"Yes."

"How'd you get along with him?"

"Fine."

"Have you heard from him since you came back?"

"Yes, he wanted to take me out tomorrow night but I couldn't go on account of the conference."

"Oh, for God's sake," her father said.

"The Archbishop is speaking and Mother thought I should come."

"You have my deepest sympathy."

And that's all I have. You know and I know that there is not much either of us can do about changing Mother's mind once it is made up. For a moment Margaret thought wryly about Father Malone's speech. In the body of the Connolly family the classic positions were reversed. Mother was the head. Father—what? A heart in a way. He drew love from you, deep pitying love, radically different from the obedient devotion you gave Mother.

The heat wave burned through the night and the next day. By evening the city was a furnace and the Garden Square Hotel was an oven in the center of it. Margaret suffered with the rest of the conference through an interminable speech by the Archbishop, who was no orator. Nevertheless, the conference was pronounced a success by Mrs. Kilpatrick, and Mrs. Connolly spent the rest of the week in a glow of exultation, which supplied extra energy for a series of whirlwind shopping expeditions. Most of Saturday was spent packing Margaret's bags. After Mass on Sunday her father lugged them downstairs and crammed them into the trunk of their prewar Ford. A quick breakfast and they were ready to escort daughter to her senior year in college.

All the way out in the car Mother talked incessantly. "I hope you've got enough slips. Do you think so? Aren't you looking forward to this year? Senior year is supposed to be the best. Father Malone said it's the culmination of all the things you've been studying for the past eight years. It must be a wonderful feeling to see everything coming together that way. Aren't you looking forward to it?"

"Of course," Margaret said.

"I guess you won't see any more of that handsome lifeguard," Mother said. "He gave up after one letter."

"Maybe," Margaret said.

"It certainly looks that way. If you do hear from him, I hope you'll discuss it with Father Malone."

"Honestly, Mother. Why should I do that? He has better things to do than discuss a casual date."

"You know Father has a special interest in you. Take advantage of it."

Margaret looked straight ahead and said nothing. Her mother talked for ten minutes about Father Malone's wisdom and kindness. Margaret managed not to hear most of it. She let her mind glide out ahead of the car down the long white curve of the turnpike, past the loop it made around Mount St. Monica and over the foothills to the state university where Dick Thornton was perhaps arriving today for his last year of law school.

Thinking what? About his job prospects, new courses. Certainly not about Margaret Connolly.

The absurdity of her pseudo-romance seemed even clearer to Margaret when they rolled through the big iron gates and up the wooded drive to the broad lawns and ugly old buildings of Mount St. Monica's. Here is a world, separate, complete, that is going to swallow you for nine long months. Your thoughts, feelings, hopes, fears, will be totally encompassed by these buildings and that formidable iron fence. Not Dick Thornton, but the principles of theology, the phases of Elizabethan literature, will be what matter and it was silly to fight against the sheer weight of their reality.

"Oh, look," Mrs. Connolly said. "There's Father Malone's car. He must be in. Why don't we say hello?"

It was impossible to oppose the idea. Mrs. Connolly found Father Malone's friendship enormously flattering. They pulled up in front of the small white cottage which served as the chaplain's residence, and Mrs. Connolly led them all up the porch steps to ring the bell. A moment later, Father Malone was smiling up at them. Face to face he was still a very handsome man, with wavy black hair, a fine high forehead, direct blue eyes, and a supple smiling mouth. If there was any defect, it was his size. He was rather short, and to make up for it he had a rather odd habit of rising on his tiptoes while he talked. He did it now because both elder Connollys towered over him, and even Margaret was a little taller.

Margaret watched her father give a brief wordless nod and hold out his hand. Father Malone pumped it warmly. You've never thought of it before, but isn't it odd, this habit of calling priests

Father, as if they could ever take the place of a real father with his mysterious power to evoke love.

Meanwhile, Mother gushed. "We just wanted to say hello, Father. I'm sure you're busy getting settled, like everyone else."

"I am, as a matter of fact," he said, and held up his hands, which were smeared with dirt. "Nobody's dusted in here for three months," he said jovially. "I saw the Archbishop last week. He was raving about your Family Life Conference."

"Oh, *really*," burbled Mother.

"I hope Margaret got something out of it."

"Oh, I'm sure she did, Father."

"Maybe she was bored by the whole thing. After spending a summer with the rich. And meeting a handsome lifeguard in the bargain."

"Oh, no, Father," Margaret murmured automatically, before she realized the full implications of his words.

"I was a little worried when that first letter arrived," Mother said, "but there hasn't been a peep since then."

"I wasn't worried," Father Malone said, giving Margaret's forearm a passing pat. "I was only teasing her just now. I've got complete confidence in Margaret."

"That makes me so happy to hear, Father. She can be a little—stubborn, with me."

"I was that way with my mother too," Father Malone said.

*My God, they talk about me as if I was thirteen years old. Or three.* But it was hardly new. You had heard Father Malone discuss your temperament, your spiritual gifts, with Mother before. What is new is your reaction to it, Margaret.

"We must get together for a chat very soon, Margaret," Father Malone said.

She murmured an assent and they said goodbye. In front of Sacré Coeur, the big main building, her father unloaded her bags and Margaret gave her mother a farewell kiss. The resignation with which she had entered the grounds was gone. She followed her father, burdened with bags, up the stairs to her room, feeling very much like an unwilling prisoner being led to her cell. *Silly*. You are letting a summer emotion disrupt the most important part of your life.

In the third-floor hall they were shaken by a shout from Judge Kilpatrick. "Well, I'll be damned. You've got your poor old man working too. Where the hell is that lifeguard you had walking on his hands by Labor Day? All these so-called boyfriends are never around to do anything useful, are they, Bill?"

"From what I hear," her father said, glancing warily at Margaret, "the lifeguard's kind of faded away."

"Faded away? Like hell," the Judge bellowed. He dug a snapshot out of his pocket and handed it to Margaret. It was a picture of her and Dick, smiling down from the Kilpatrick front porch. "He insisted I deliver this to you, *personally*. Why, he didn't even look at another girl after this one left," the Judge assured her father. "And he used to be the biggest skirt-chaser on the shore."

"Well," her father said, smiling at Margaret, "that's good news, isn't it, Meg?"

*He wanted her to see Dick.* These words, their conversation at supper, suddenly coalesced in Margaret's mind. Her amazement confused her. She glanced hastily at the picture. The two smiling figures in bathing suits looked utterly strange, even foreign. It might have been a news photo of two celebrities on the beach at Cannes. Or those unprofessional snapshots they publish of young couples who die in automobile accidents. "I don't know," she said. "The Judge is probably just—teasing as usual."

"Teasing? Listen," Judge Kilpatrick said indignantly, "if I'm not telling the truth, may Mother Superior strike me dead right here in this hall."

"Careful," Faith called from the doorway of their room. "I saw her outside on a broomstick a second ago, and I'm not carrying your body down all those stairs."

"You just watch," the Judge said, ignoring his daughter, "that lifeguard will be up here before the week is out, if he has to come on a bicycle."

Her father deposited her bags, kissed her goodbye and departed. Margaret looked slowly around the room. It was on a lower floor, but otherwise it was identical with last year's room. Along the faded green walls were two iron beds, scuffed brown dressers and small square brown desks. A sagging green Morris chair crouched beneath the only window.

Faith sat cross-legged on her bed looking sardonic. "Well," she said, "ready for another nine months of hell?"

"As ready as I'll ever be, I suppose."

"What do you hear from Mr. Thornton?"

Margaret told her the sad story.

"Marvelous," Faith said. "We can be miserable together."

"Oh, in his letter Dick said something about you and Larry—"

"Yes," Faith said. She threw herself back on the bed and stared up at the ceiling. "It was the damnedest thing that's ever happened to me, Meg. I don't know how to describe it—or whether I even should bother to try. All of a sudden I started taking him *seriously*. And that meant taking everything seriously, the Catholic Church, my father. It was like—being drunk twenty-four hours a day. Except you didn't feel good. You felt awful."

"You mean—you fell in love with him?"

"The word *love* is totally inadequate. I told you I don't know how to describe it. Most of the time we argued, insulted and sneered at each other. Then we'd talk about being in love—what it meant. To Larry it meant thinking, feeling—practically *being* the other person."

Faith struggled to a sitting position again. There were tears in her eyes. Margaret felt a rush of sympathy. Last year you would have lectured Faith. How different your feelings are now, Margaret.

"He wanted me to give up—everything. The Church, God, everything. He wanted me to believe—exactly what he believes. Nothing."

"Faith, that's horrible!"

"Horrible—or courageous, or maybe both. Anyway that's what we argued about most of the time. That and my father. He told me things about my father—"

Faith shook her head, fighting to hold back the tears. "He called it reality therapy."

"Oh, Faith, how could he love you and do a thing like that?"

"I don't know, but he does love me. And I love him." Faith managed a rueful grin. "And it's all your fault."

"My fault?"

"I think what broke me down was seeing how happy you and Dick were. I should have known better. That brand of romance is totally beyond my reach."

"There's no romance."

"It was a damn good imitation then."

"Well, it's over."

"How do you know?"

"He didn't answer my letter."

"The next time he'll telephone. You're obviously the type that has to be assaulted caveman style."

Dinner the first night was always a festive affair. The cooks made special desserts and the lower classes serenaded the new seniors who in turn serenaded the freshmen. Everyone, even Faith, was in a holiday mood. There was nothing to study and they crowded into various rooms and talked about the summer. Four-fifths of the conversation was about men. It was a little startling to Margaret—something she had never really noticed before.

"I met this crazy Michigan boy at a beach party—"

"And this Georgetown boy cut in—"

"He was so suave I was sure he was from Yale—"

"How about you, Margaret?" asked thin, acerbic Rita Conboy. "Did you meet any interesting males since June?"

The question was obviously condescending. Margaret found it very pleasant to say, "I met one."

"Oh?"

Everyone in the room was suddenly listening. "He's not that exciting, though," Margaret added hastily.

"He excited me," Faith said.

"Come on, tell," beefy Helen Cudahy said, in her hoarse bass.

Margaret shook her head. "You'll hear it all from Faith anyway."

"They will *not*. I don't disburse confidences to these creeps."

The subject was dropped and stayed dropped until the following morning when they began classes. Father Malone's course in theology was first on the list. He spent the period outlining the ground they would cover—the attributes of the three persons of the Blessed Trinity, the angels and other orders of heavenly beings, the creation of man, the problem of evil. At the bell, Esther Sugrue and several other girls went up to the desk and began chatting with him. Margaret, whose second period was in another room, began collecting her books and was on her way out the door when Father Malone said, in a voice he obviously intended her to overhear, "I've been told that Margaret had the best-looking boy on the beach in tow."

For a moment she swayed in the doorway, transfixed by the inane smirks on every face. Say something witty, Margaret? No, she could only gasp: "I—have to go, Father. I'll be late."

She rushed into the hall, her face hot with embarrassment. Why was everyone so interested in her feeble little romance, which meant absolutely nothing and was, in fact, over? At lunch Esther Sugrue began teasing her about Dick, but was silenced by Faith. That afternoon Margaret met Father Malone as he drove past in his car. "Running in to the chancery," he said, smiling up at her. "When are we going to get together for a little talk?"

"Oh—as soon as I get settled, Father. You know how the first few days of school are."

"Of course."

He rolled away down the drive, and Margaret suddenly found herself wishing she had never become friendly with Faith Kilpatrick, never gone to Paradise Beach, never had a mother named Marge Connolly or a confessor named Denton Malone. She tramped up the three flights of stairs to her room, ready to demolish Faith if she so much as mentioned Dick Thornton.

"Phone call for you," Faith said from behind a book she was reading on her bed.

"For me? From who?"

"Someone named Thornton."

She handed Margaret a sheet of memo paper with a number on it. Margaret sat down at her desk, staring dazedly at the figures. "What did he want?" she finally said.

"Your lily-white body, naturally," Faith said. "But he didn't come right out and say it. They're very subtle, these Protestants."

"Oh stop, Faith. I thought—I thought it was over for good. I—was glad."

"I don't believe a word of it."

"I was."

"Call him up. He can't do you much damage long distance."

She dialed the operator and gave her the number. A strange voice answered.

"I'm returning a call from Dick Thornton."

"Hold on."

"Hello," Dick said a moment later. "How's the schoolgirl?"

"Oh," Margaret said, experiencing a mild panic. "I'm—I'm overwhelmed, as usual."

"Not too overwhelmed for a night on the town this weekend, I hope?"

"Well—there's a tea dance here at school. Maybe you'd like to come to that."

"When?"
"Sunday. In the afternoon."
"Sounds dull."
He was right. Sunday tea dances were dreadful. But having made her suggestion, Margaret felt bound to defend it. "It's not that bad. You can get to see the school."
"I want to see you."
No. That was coming too close, even long distance. "I really think you'll enjoy it," she said in a flat negative voice.
"Okay. What time?"
"Two-thirty."
"I'll see you then."
Faith raised an eyebrow over the top of her book when Margaret re-entered the room. "Well?" she said, when Margaret ignored her.
"I invited him to next week's tea dance," she said.
"For God's sake, why?"
"It seemed like—a good first date. Besides, I don't want to give him ideas."
*God, you're sounding like an idiot.*
"Ideas about what? The only idea he'll get from that silly shuffle can be summed up in five capital letters—C-R-E-E-P."
"Well—he made me mad the way he pooh-poohed the idea the moment I suggested it. As if he—looks down on going to a school like this."
"Why shouldn't he? I've spent the summer telling him how lousy it is."
"Look, I haven't asked you to take such a great interest in this—relationship, and I really don't appreciate it."
For a moment Faith's eyes came angrily alive. Then she bowed her head over her book again. "Touché. I just hate to see you relapsing into your convent-school personality again. I thought I saw a new you down there at the beach."
For some reason Margaret found these words both frightening and infuriating. "I really don't know what you're talking about, Faith. There's only one me, with one personality, and I am not conscious of any radical change."
"I thought I saw one," Faith said without looking up from her book. "I guess I was wrong."
Margaret snatched her coat and fled. For an hour she walked alone

around the rim of the campus lawn with Faith's words echoing in her mind and quivering in her body. Was it possible to become a new person? No. She had no faith in the idea. She had no faith in a new Margaret. There is only one Margaret and she is walking here, suddenly weeping for no special reason, just weeping.

# Chapter Five

Judge James Kilpatrick parked his car in the stall marked "Reserved for the Sheriff," outside the county courthouse, and lit a cigarette. He strolled casually into the courthouse and onto the central elevator. Squint McElroy, the operator, a stump of a man with an absolutely bald head, practically saluted. "Hello, Judge," he said. "You gonna reprieve that Barton character?" Squint was a close student of the city's politics.

"The governor gives reprieves, Squint. I grant stays of execution, or reversals. How the hell are you going to pass the goddamn bar exam if you don't know that?"

"Who wants ta pass the lousy bar exam," growled Squint. "I never met a lawyer or a judge yet I'd wanna shake hands wit afta dark."

"I never met an elevator man I'd turn my back on at high noon," the Judge said, exhaling a cloud of cigarette smoke that all but obscured the large "No Smoking" sign on the wall behind him.

"I say give that boogie the maximum," Squint said. "There ain't none of them any good."

"Our esteemed prosecutor is the guy I'd like to burn," the Judge said. "He suppressed enough evidence to acquit that poor nigger a dozen times."

"You mean you're gonna let him off?" complained Squint, as the elevator jerked to a stop on the third floor and he rolled back the big brass doors with a hairy dead-white arm.

"I may order a new trial and a change of venue. Do you know what that means?"

"Sure I know what it means," shouted Squint as the Judge strode down the corridor. "It means you're chicken. You and Big Dave are chicken. You're scared of the nigger vote, that's what it means."

Good old Squint. They had grown up together in the shadow of the coal yard. Their fathers had been drunks together. They had been running that gag about the bar exam for thirty years now but there were times when the Judge wondered how the Squinter really felt about his old hookey-days buddy. Christ, you are getting soft as a grilled marshmallow.

Into the chambers of Judge Edward Dinsmore strode Judge James Kilpatrick. They had belonged to him for ten years, when he had been the presiding judge in the courthouse, and he still acted as if his name were on the door. He caught Judge Dinsmore in the act of pouring himself a shot of bourbon from a silver flask. "Well, I'll be a son of a bitch," the Judge said, and charged across the crimson carpet to snatch the flask from Dinsmore's paralyzed hand. In flowery Spenserian script was engraved the Judge's intials, E.D. Beneath it, in plain American type, "to Eddie from the boys at O'Dowd's." The Judge put the flask back down on Dinsmore's gleaming mahogany desk and glanced around the familiar room. The portraits of earlier presiding judges, with their pompous Van's and De's beneath their beefy phizzes, the atrocious painting of the city during the age of sail in an even more atrocious gilt frame, were as familiar as the furniture of his own house. He suddenly found himself wishing he had never left this room for the tightrope world of the state capital, where the Supreme Court sat, surrounded by sullen, hostile Republicans. This was home. The city outside with its warm sooty embrace, the familiar faces in the elevators and corridors.

"I thought we were going to have lunch," the Judge said, absently.

"I thought I'd have it sent in, Jim," Dinsmore said in his hoarse croak.

"So we can get really schnozzled?"

"It's just that I can't walk too far on this foot, Jim. Gout is a funny thing."

"So is booze."

Eddie Dinsmore fell back in his padded swivel chair until his head touched the back and his eyes were on the carved-oak ceiling.

Eddie Dinsmore. Hustling Eddie, they called him down at St. Francis Prep in 1915. Cheerleader, basketball manager, always on the run, kissing every ass in sight. Hustling Eddie. And now Judge Dinsmore, with the flushed, blotched face, the sad, squashed button-nose, the popping little eyes, the same Eddie, and not the same. Jesus, totally different. Were they all?

"I'm doing the job, Jim," Dinsmore said.

"You're doing *shit*. I've got letters from half the Bar Association about what you've been doing. They say you're pie-eyed at nine in the morning. You don't know a tort from a turd."

A tear dribbled down Dinsmore's raddled cheek. "I'm trying, Jim. So help me God, I'm trying."

"Trying isn't enough, Eddie. This is an election year and they're talking about another Grand Jury investigation. We can't afford a guy sitting up there with a head like a barrage balloon."

Eddie Dinsmore maintained that weird slumped-back pose, his eyes still on the ceiling. "You want the piece of paper. It's in the drawer all signed."

"I don't want any goddamn piece of paper," Judge Kilpatrick roared.

"He sent you up here to get it, didn't he?"

"If he did, I'd tell him to get it himself and shove it up his fat Irish ass in the bargain. Eddie, I want you to promise me you're off this goddamn stuff." He picked up the flask and poured the contents into the silver inkwell on Dinsmore's desk. "Not another goddamn drop for two years and then you'll have the pension and you can get stoned and stay that way for the rest of your life."

Like a puppet on a string, Eddie Dinsmore swayed forward, his shoulders twitching, and slowly lowered his head onto his desk between his cradled arms. He was crying like an incredible four-year-old. In between the sobs the man's voice came in static gasps. "I—can't—Jim—you know—why—the kid—I keep seeing him—lying there on the beach—oh, Jesus Jesus Jesus—"

Goddamn every miserable German in this rotten stinking world, the Judge thought, and particularly goddamn the Kraut who put a bullet through the head of Edward Gregory Dinsmore, Jr., on Omaha beach. The Judge threw hat, coat and cane on a polished mahogany table, and walked up and down doing some ceiling staring of his own. Dinsmore's sobbing was the only sound in the big carpeted room. "I know it's tough, Eddie. But that was four years ago. People don't remember, Eddie, they don't forgive after four years."

Judge Dinsmore continued to weep.

"It happened to other guys, Eddie. Joe Delaney. Pete O'Neill. Sure they were stoned for a couple of months. But they pulled out of it. You can do it too. You've got two other good kids."

"They don't mean a thing to me. They never did. He was the only one. I often think it's God punishment for the way I've—"

"For *Christ's* sake," the Judge roared. "Did it ever occur to you that if he was alive he'd probably be prancing around town shitting all over you and your so-called reputation? That's what they're all doing, don't you know that? Shit on daddy, it's the big local pastime. I don't think you give a real goddamn for that kid, I don't think you ever did. You never spent five minutes with him when he was growing up. Christ, I know that. I've spent more time in third-rate nightclubs and crummy gin mills with you than anybody else in the goddamn city."

Eddie Dinsmore's head was up now, his wet bruised face puckered up like a baby about to bawl.

"You're really eating your guts out because you never had the balls to stand up to King David downtown. You took his goddamn shilling like all the rest of us and you play the grief-stricken drunk to keep your other two kids off your back, and in between you have alcoholic dreams about running a good grand jury investigation just once. But you'll never do it because you know goddamn well he'd come up here and kick the shit out of you personally."

"Goddamn you," Eddie Dinsmore said. "Goddamn your rotten soul to hell for all eternity."

"I'll take my chances on that," the Judge roared. "I'm trying to save your crummy soul now."

"How? By crucifying me?" Dinsmore screeched.

"By telling you the goddamn truth. Swallow it like the castor oil your old lady was always cramming down your skinny gullet. Maybe it will clean out some of the shit you've been feeding yourself."

"If you were my size and weight, I'd kill you," Dinsmore screamed. "I'd wipe up this goddamn office with you."

"The hell you would," the Judge said. "I'd take you with one arm and both legs tied."

Eddie Dinsmore stared up at him, with one side of his face sagging like a stroke victim's, the eyes red-rimmed, the raunchy cheeks wet with tears, and suddenly the Judge was back forty years, seeing the same face after a gang fight on the way home from St. Patrick's Parochial School. The same little Eddie, game but scared. But in this new gang fight, this epic brawl with that bully called Life, gameness and hustle were not enough. You also needed luck and a special kind of staying power that went beyond gameness.

"This is the last time, Eddie," Judge Kilpatrick said. "The next time, I'm asking for the paper."

Eddie Dinsmore's head went up and down, signifying acceptance.

"Let's go have lunch," the Judge said. "We'll go up to the State Club and split one of those thirty-six-ounce steaks. You look like you haven't had an honest meal in a month."

"Okay," Eddie said.

He went into his private washroom, snorgled some water into his face and came out looking reasonably calm. "I'm sorry, Jim," he said.

"Sorry for what?" the Judge growled. "If we can't call each other names, who the hell can? Besides, you've called me a son of a bitch so often in the past, I hardly even notice it any more."

Judge Dinsmore laughed and tried to stretch his small arm around the Judge's bulky shoulder. "Jesus Christ," he said, "what would I do without you?"

Lunch was a bore. The Judge found his mind wandering repeatedly while Eddie yacked about the latest political gossip. Shea was feuding with Matty Blair, the leader of the First Ward, over Blair's habit of grabbing too much of the monthly horse-parlor handle. The Republicans were trying to tempt Blair into a fusion ticket against the organization. The Judge had heard it all before, with different names, and it always ended the same way, with the organization rolling over those suicidal enough to stick out their necks, with majorities of 8 and 10 to 1. Even less appealing was Eddie's usual roster of the sick and dying. Eddie seemed to specialize in collecting the latest news on who had cancer, heart disease, gallbladder trouble and crippling arthritis. In desperation the Judge changed the subject to something really serious.

"Why the hell did you give that boogie Barton five years?"

Dinsmore looked astonished. "Orders from downtown."

"Now the commissar wants me to sustain it. Why the hell didn't you call me first? I could have twisted a few arms and sustained three. But five is ridiculous."

Judge Dinsmore looked scared: "You think they might try for a reversal? You wouldn't let that happen, would you, Jim?"

"Don't sweat. On that it would be a straight party vote. But a hell of a lot of people in other parts of the state are pretty sick of Old Iron Balls and his billy-club approach."

"So what do we do?"

Judge Kilpatrick studied the portrait of Judge Ludwig De Peyster, who looked like he had just swallowed a tomahawk. "When the prisoner continues to show defiance and contempt for the law . . . I gather this coon is still out throwing mud."

"On street corners, in parish halls, you name it."

"Get one of the court officers to follow him around for a few days and make a report to me."

"Sure."

He drove Eddie back to the courthouse and left him on the curb vowing eternal sobriety. Making a U-turn while the traffic cop on the corner glared helplessly, the Judge drove downtown to the Second National Bank. He eased the big car to a stop beside a long yellow stretch of curb, with big red and blue NO PARKING signs at either end of it. Inside the dim old bank with its grilled iron windows and marble floor, he saluted bulky Buster O'Toole in his familiar blue uniform. "Jesus Christ, don't you ever get tired of playing cops and robbers?" the Judge said. "You've got to be the richest bull in this city."

O'Toole had been president of the PBA for years, before his retirement. "Listen," he said, "that crummy pension don't keep a guy in cigarettes."

"Change brands," the Judge said, and fled from an imminent diatribe.

He reached through a grilled iron door in the back of the bank, pressed a buzzer, and pushed it open. Twirling his summer Panama he strolled casually past clerks and secretaries into the president's office. Joe Higgins looked up from his desk, his square, red, hypertense face first frowning, then smiling. Suddenly the Judge was back twenty-five years and there was another face behind that big mahogany desk and he was standing in the same doorway, hat very much in hand. Old Ben Brainard, Wasp power personified, with his haunted eyes and sour accusatory mouth. What a knack he had for making you feel like a nigger. He had even said it once right here in his office when you were negotiating with him and a few of his high-collared friends to put some more Irish names on their payrolls.

*I've always thought of the Irish as our Negroes. But you're different. Why don't you play ball with us? Open your own law office. I'll give you an option on enough bank stock to make you independent, plus half the bank's real estate work.* You had told him to shove it and ten years later in the worst of the Depression you had stood in the same doorway and heard the state auditors tell the desperate old man that he could no longer juggle his way out of the truth: his bank was busted. Into receivership had gone the Second National, with Irish Democrats holding every chair on the State Banking Commission. When the doors opened again, the Wasps were gone and men like Joe Higgins now sat in the president's chair and other chairs getting high blood pressure and sour mouths from the same worries that had bugged old Ben Brainard and his friends. You never really won in this crazy game; you were just ahead or behind.

"What the hell do you want?" said Joe Higgins.

"I want my goddamn money," the Judge said. "The Most Reverend is getting impatient."

"I've got it right here," Joe said, and whipped the check out of his desk drawer. He read it aloud. "Pay to the order of The Most Reverend Terrence McGuire one million dollars and no cents."

"No sense is right," said the Judge. "I'd rather give it to the Ku Klux Klan."

"Now, Jim," said Higgins sadly, "you don't mean that."

"Sure I do," the Judge said. "The Klan would at least put the dough into bed sheets, and that would mean a few more jobs down at the mills. Most of this will go to some second-rate Wop sculptors in Perugia."

"Jim," said Higgins, "sometimes I worry about the state of your soul."

The words were serious but Higgins was smiling. He and the Judge had been religious sparring partners for years.

"I worry about the state of your head," the Judge said. "You and all the other daily communicants."

"Listen, Jim," said Higgins as the Judge started for the door, check in hand, "some people from the State Board were in the other day with another warning about confidentiality. Times are changing. We just can't get away with sending a man's files down to City Hall every time Shea or Kenellen hears a rumor. I'm still willing to cooperate on a really serious problem, but from now on all requests have got to come through me."

"What the hell am I supposed to do about it?" the Judge said.
"Can't you talk to him?"
"Nobody can talk to that thick Mick."
He left Joe Higgins standing there behind his desk, fumbling in the drawer for his hypertension pills, and strolled away, pausing to show Buster O'Toole the one-million-dollar check. With a wink he took it over to Mary Brogan behind the bars in teller's cage Number One. Built like a Wagnerian soprano, she was famous for her renditions of "Mother Macree" at innumerable parish smokers.
"Give me this in fives and tens, and make it snappy," the Judge said.
"Jesus, Mary, and Joseph," Mary shrieked.
Several people at nearby windows thought the bank was being robbed. The Judge departed while Buster O'Toole calmed the incipient panic. The Judge rolled across town and then north on the Parkway, past the big fieldstone mansions built at the turn of the century by the Protestant rich. Some of their descendents still clung to these broad-beamed symbols of success, like doomed defenders of bypassed forts. But more than half of the names on the mailboxes were Irish. Higgins, Kennellen, Flynn, Sugrue, they drifted through the Judge's mind like a vague litany as he rolled past them. You had helped to put them there. As if anyone, the beneficiaries included, gave a damn, or would lift a hand or a checkbook to help Jim Kilpatrick if he needed it. What the hell, he was getting his too, wasn't he? Sure he was.
Almost cheered by the savagery of his cynicism, the Judge made a sharp right off the Parkway past the huge white marble and limestone cathedral. He shot across a parking lot as big as a football field and pulled up behind the chancery office, which was in the same unique architectural style as the cathedral. He parked before a sign which read "Reserved for the Military Ordinate" and glowered for a moment at the white elephant, as everyone in town called the Archbishop's ghostly, ghastly house of worship. So far it had cost five million dollars and the scaffolding still clung to its sides, innumerable niches for statues remained unfilled, and windows intended for radiant stained glass were blank, black panes. Depression, war, nothing daunted the Archbishop in his dogged determination to make St. Mary's "the most magnificent cathedral in America." He was fond of pointing out that the city had a higher concentration of Catholics than any other city in the country. It behooved them to show Amer-

ica and the world what American Catholic culture could produce. The Judge maintained that this and the idea that the cathedral should be white as a symbol of the Virgin Mary's purity were the only two ideas the Archbishop had had in the last twenty-five years.

The grilled iron windows and the heavy brass door of the Chancery Office reminded him of the Second National Bank. Logical, the Judge thought. The dowdy, dumpy receptionist led him upstairs past sitting rooms full of faded French furniture. Pictures of earlier Archbishops stared formidably from the walls. Through the big oaken door, not unlike the mayor's office, into a spacious corner office full of sunshine. There was His Excellency, over in the far corner of the room between two glowing windows, waving a watering can. Flowers grew in window boxes all around the room. The last time he visited, the Judge had gotten a fifteen-minute lecture on the problems of raising African violets.

"My dear Judge, how are you?" said the Archbishop, abandoning his can and advancing down the room in short quick steps that inevitably reminded the Judge of a penguin in a hurry.

Now came the moment of pure regurgitation. The stubby peasant hand came out, and the Judge went down on one knee and made a very quick pass at the episcopal ring. He was amazed by the intensity with which he detested this performance, every time he did it. The feeling never seemed to diminish. Remarkable. Meanwhile he was saying, "How the hell do you do it, Your Excellency, you're looking younger every time I see you."

"I don't know, I never think about it," said the Archbishop, with the tiniest touch of a brogue in his voice. It was phony. He'd been born on New York's Lower East Side, and his passion for things Irish was pure tourism.

"But I sometimes think," he said as they ambled down the room toward his desk, "that maybe it does have something to do with faith. Peace of soul, Jim. It's a lot more important than the peace of mind that writing rabbi is selling these days."

What's the difference, the Judge thought, but he said, "That's a very profound observation."

The Archbishop beamed up at Judge Kilpatrick. His Excellency's bald head, with only a few wisps of gray hair slicked left and right above the forehead, barely reached the Judge's shoulder. "I've been telling all my pastors to preach at least one sermon about it. That rabbi—what's his name, Liebman?—is selling nothing but cheap psychology with not an iota of religion in it. It's dangerous. It tempts people to think they can get along without God."

"Fascinating," the Judge said. "You ought to write a book on it."

"Oh, I'll let Fulton Sheen do that." The Archbishop chuckled and sank into the massive leather-padded medieval chair behind his desk. He fiddled with his ring, and then with an almost girlish giggle said, "I hear you've got a present for me."

"You might call it that, Your Excellency," said the Judge. "I think of it more as a gesture of affection. This comes not just from the city and the county, Your Excellency, but from people who admire you and your work in every part of the state."

The Archbishop's hand moved just a little too quickly and he practically snatched the check away from the Judge. "A million dollars again." He beamed down at it. "Really, Judge, as I was saying to Monsignor O'Connell only the other day, I don't know what the church would do without the help of its dedicated laity. Please tell the mayor how grateful I am."

"I certainly will, Your Excellency. He wishes he could give it to you personally. But you remember the last time—those reporters."

"Oh, yes, I do. They were vicious. The secular press is simply vicious. They never miss a chance to strike at the Church."

Three years ago Dave Shea had presented the Archbishop with another of his million-dollar thank offerings at a Holy Name dinner. That was the year that the Archbishop had denounced the new state constitution which the Republicans were trying to ram through in a referendum. The state needed a new constitution, but Dave Shea couldn't quite see why it needed one with a clause which stated that all public officials would be required under subpoena from a grand jury or the legislature to make available records of their personal wealth. If the constitution had gone through, Big Dave would have had to retire to Florida or even to a few years in durance vile. But the Archbishop's denunciation had demolished the reformers by better than two to one in the referendum. Several of the state's influential papers had muttered nasty things about the need for more separation between the state and the church.

"What is the status of those constitution-makers these days?"

"In disarray, Your Excellency. I don't think we'll hear from them for another ten years."

"Good. Good."

"My wife sends you her best regards, too, Your Excellency."

"Ah, that dear woman. I hope the sun and the salt air have done her some good. I have seldom seen anyone suffer with such patient, truly religious resignation. You're a lucky man, to live beside such a soul, Judge."

Oh so lucky, the Judge thought. So lucky I used to lie awake at night planning getaways to Mexico and California. But the Judge said, "I know. I hope you'll remember her in your Masses."

"I always do. Be sure and tell her that now."

A quick shake of the soft, stubby hand, a final God bless you, and the Judge was out in the hot parking lot staring at the white elephant again and thinking, *What can you eat for dinner when you've been shoveling shit all afternoon?*

# Chapter Six

Why did he keep thinking about her? Dick Thornton was impatient at his inability to control his own mind. She was just the most beautiful thing he had come across in his travels thus far, and he had an eye for beautiful things. To consider marrying her, at this point, was ridiculous.

He wound the car through the tight lanes on the Expressway's approach to the city and was soon downtown, rolling past the gray scabby fronts of the piers. The city's stubby skyline mounted into a blue October sky on his right.

The city made him think even more ironically. He was worrying too much about Margaret Connolly. She could be important, but at the moment she was nine-tenths question mark. Like the city; a challenge worth going after, but to be faced with a coldly realistic eye.

She was still incredibly naïve in many ways. And there was the religious problem. He did not object to either of these facts. She was eager to learn, that was the important thing. Besides, he was tired of girls who were so damned sure of what they wanted. About her religion he had not a little personal repugnance, but no prejudice. Catholics he had met at school and in the service were no different from any other group. The few devout ones repelled him, just as devout Protestants did. More so, in fact. Catholics were more subservient, more full of standardized thinking and stock arguments.

But Margaret seemed somehow outside this aberration. She was not determined to drive her faith down everyone else's throat, as Faith's brother, Jim Kilpatrick was, for instance.

He turned off River Avenue and drove slowly through the crowded downtown streets. He never entered this part of the city without realizing how shockingly different it was from his world. The garbage in the gutters, the scrawny, yelling kids trying to play ball on the black asphalt, the honking cars and rumbling trucks, the bedding on the fire escapes. It made him grateful for Paradise Beach, even obliquely grateful to the beaten man who had taken him down there in those grim Depression years. At least he had had the open fields, the beach, the ocean, the salt air and blue sky. He was an alien in this world, and even now, driving through it, a faint claustrophobia touched his chest.

The buzzer opened the outer door of the decrepit brownstone and Dick climbed a creaking staircase to the dim second floor. As he pushed open the door of Apartment 2A he heard Larry shouting, "Let's drink out here." His ex-roommate was standing in the middle of a newspaper- and book-littered living room in his undershirt. He ran his hand through his uncombed red hair and grinned cheerfully at Dick.

"Well, I'll be damned," he said, "if it isn't old Horatio Alger Thornton himself, the thoughtful lifeguard."

"You get more degenerate every time I see you," Dick said.

"This isn't degeneration, it's a celebration." Larry grabbed Dick by the arm and led him down the hall into the kitchen. "Look who I found trying to pick the locks down at City Hall. Mistook it for a saloon. They released him in my custody."

Jake O'Connor smiled up at Dick from a chair tipped against the icebox. "Greetings, classmate," he said. "How are things on the Law Review?"

"Great," Dick said. "I'm sorry you didn't make it."

"Who needs it?" Jake said.

"Some of us will have to work for a living," Dick said.

He tried to make the remark offhand but failed to entirely dilute its acidity. Like many other people in Paradise Beach, Dick Thornton had disliked Jake O'Connor from the day he met him. Not that Jake ever did or said anything deliberately offensive. On the contrary, he always treated the locals with breezy good-natured friendliness. Which was precisely why they disliked him. Instinctively they saw the implied superiority in Jake's smile, the swaggering condescension in his cheerful hello. Over the years this dislike had only grown as they watched Jake handle, with blasé unblinking confidence, sports, school, girls, the war. Nothing fazed Jake. He had seen it all the day after he was born in the big city.

During the last year and a half of their cram-school law course, Jake had made several friendly overtures to Dick, inviting him to parties and once even on a double date. Dick had accepted because Larry Donahue guaranteed him that some day Jake O'Connor was going to be a very important man. But Jake's cheerful cynicism about everything from female virtue to hard work only revived Dick's old dislike. He did not really try very hard to disguise it. His future went far beyond Jake O'Connor's greasy world of political pull to the heart of the heart of things. The boardroom of Slocum Industries and other boardrooms in other cities, still turning points at the center of fortune's whirling wheel, where the really big men and the really big money lived.

"Did you hear Jake's on his bicycle after Dolores Talbot?" Larry said.

"How silly can you get?" Dick said.

"Don't worry," Jake said, "I'm buying a motorcycle."

"It better be gold plated," Larry said.

"Are you getting anything?" Dick said.

"Richard—have you ever tried to do it on a bicycle? These things take time."

"What's happened to Hilda the wholesome whore?" Larry asked.

"Gone the way of Peggy the perfect prostitute. Reformed. I have an unfortunate effect on women. They all want to reform me. And they end up reforming themselves."

Jake had Larry laughing now. "You stupid bastard. When are you going to cut it out and take life seriously?"

"I am taking it seriously. Just as seriously as it deserves to be taken."

They eyed each other for a moment, and Larry said "Crap," and threw a dirty dish towel at Jake. Dick had seen that faintly mocking, almost antagonistic look pass between them before, and he still did not understand what it meant. It encompassed years between Larry and Jake that he, the outsider, the small-town boy, could not share. Feelings that wound deep into the past, and tinged the present too.

"But let's not talk about me," Jake said, tipping farther back in his chair. "Let us consider Lawrence Donahue, the austere apostle of social reform, chasing Faith Kilpatrick, the biggest little bitch in town."

"Yeah," Larry said sourly.

"She is a bitch, isn't she?"

"I think she's a hell of a girl," Dick said.

"That's a good word for the life she'd lead you," Jake said. "But our apostle here likes to suffer. He has a crucifixion complex."

"I haven't felt a twinge of pain yet," Larry said.

"Any twinges of pleasure?"

"A few."

"I always kind of wanted to make her," Jake said. "I suspect she's a reluctant virgin. Or was."

"Our man Thornton here has the original reluctant virgin," Larry said.

"The one who visited the Kilpatricks? She's a looker. What's her name again?"

"Margaret Connolly," Larry said.

"Is she converting you, Thornton?" Jake asked.

"She's one hundred and two percent Catholic," Larry said.

"I'm betting on her," Jake said. "Remember I used to tell you, Thornton, that either the Jehovah's Witnesses or the Jesuits were going to get you? You're made for the Holy Name Society, kid. The one, holy, Catholic and apostolic church is your spiritual home. Am I right, Larry?"

"Are you ever right about anything?" Larry said. "Richard here believes more or less what I believe about the Christian religion."

"Yeah, I know. That's in his head. But in his guts he's still ready to hit that sawdust trail."

"Nobody's going to convert me to anything," Dick growled.

"Brave words," Jake said. He offered his glass in a toast. "May you still be able to utter them as you go up the aisle of the cathedral."

"Who the hell is going up an aisle?"

"Thornton, when are you going to admit that you're true-blue? You never went out with a girl in your life that you didn't measure for a wedding dress."

"I believe in marriage," Dick said. "Is that a crime?"

Dick kept a smile on his face but inwardly he was writhing. Why do you get into these arguments with cynics like Jake O'Connor? They always ended the same way—with you sounding like a pompous, earnest hick.

"Sometimes I think I ought to go back to being a good Protestant," Dick said. "Hanging around with you two would make anyone think that way."

"A man should always be grateful to those who restore his illusions," Jake said.

Dick turned to Larry. "Are you coming to the dance? I presume you're invited."

Larry looked at him, amusement flickering on his lips. Jake grinned unabashedly. "I've had the tea-dance circuit, Richard. I had it by the end of freshman year."

The dismissed feeling came on strong again. The country boy was being sent off to play his games while the men stayed home for some serious drinking. Jesus, he would show them how far this country boy could go, before the game was over.

Careful. Careful. It would not happen tomorrow, or the next day, or the next year. It was a long, lonely road. While slobs like Jake O'Connor sat there with the world dumped in their laps. But it was ridiculous to get upset about it now.

"I'll see you around, big shot," he said to Jake.

"Don't drink too much of that Mount St. Monica's punch," Jake said. "They spike it with root beer."

It was one fifteen before he was out of the city's traffic. Margaret had advised him to arrive about two thirty. He drove fast, because he was late and because he was angry. It was exactly two thirty-nine when he nosed through the huge wrought-iron gates and rolled up Mount St. Monica's winding drive. In a moment he was out of the woods and the college was visible across a broad, sloping lawn. The buildings were a collection of architectural junk. But the moment he saw them, an odd thing happened. He stopped thinking about Larry and Jake—and became absorbed in the anticipation of seeing Margaret again.

He parked in front of the huge main building and went up granite steps into a large rotunda-like reception room. It had a marble floor and a domed ceiling with a mosaic of the Holy Spirit in the form of a dove.

A black-robed elderly nun with a round pleasant face framed by a pleated white coif sat behind a desk on the other side of the room. Behind her, a little to the left, double doors opened on a carpeted hall; a wide stairway began on the other side. The little nun nodded to Dick, and he went over and introduced himself and told her he was calling for Margaret Connolly.

"Oh, Margaret!" she chirped. "Of course. She's one of my favorites. I'm Sister Mary Rose."

"I'm very glad to meet you, Sister."

"Are you a relation of Margaret's?"

"No, I'm not . . ."

"Oh, a gentleman friend," Sister exclaimed. "Now isn't *that* nice! I'll call her." She picked up a phone that was fastened to the side of her desk and asked for Margaret Connolly. After a moment's pause, she told Margaret that Mr. Thornton was here.

"She'll be down just as soon as she possibly can, I'm sure," Sister said, smiling brightly. "So you just wait in the sitting room on the left."

The narrow sitting room was empty; it was lined with a variety of old-fashioned chairs and couches; the walls were done in white enamel, with panels of gold arabesqued wallpaper. There was an intriguing oil painting on the wall beside the door.

In the painting's foreground was a young, quite pretty girl wearing a long-sleeved blue dress. Her molded brown hair was vaguely in the style of the early twenties. Her eyes looked off into the distance and her lips were parted in a half-smile of dazed ecstasy. Her hands were folded on her breast in an attitude of humble submission. Behind her a brown-haired, white-robed Christ leaned forward to whisper in her ear. The figures floated in a background of pale yellow with a suggestion of clouds in the upper fringes.

"Hello," Margaret said behind him.

She was standing in the doorway wearing a belted dark-blue dress with a small white collar. Her face was lifted just slightly to greet him. He found he liked more than ever the way she wore her thick dark hair. It harmonized perfectly with the wide, strong-boned beauty of her face.

"Hello," he said, taking her hand. "Am I too early?"

"No. We'll take a walk around the campus . . . all right?"

She stepped back into the rotunda and called across to Sister Mary Rose:

"We'll be back, Sister. We're just going for a walk."

Margaret picked up a short dark-green coat from a chair by the door and led him out into the October sunshine.

"Why did we have to tell Sister where we were going?"

"Well, if I was going off campus, I'd have to sign out."

"Why?"

"It's a precaution."

"Against what?"

"Against anyone staying out longer than they should."

"At night?"

"Yes. We have to be back by ten thirty on Saturday nights, other nights, seven thirty."

"You're kidding," Dick said. "Do you mean we have to be back tonight at seven thirty?"

"Yes—but I didn't know—I mean I didn't think we were going out."

"I thought we'd drive back to the city for dinner."

"But the dance is supposed to last until six thirty."

"We have to eat, don't we?"

"I was going to eat here. At school."

"Oh." He shook his head, baffled by both her manner and her presumptions. "We could change our minds, couldn't we? About eating?"

"I don't see how we could get to the city and back."

"Isn't there some place near here?"

"I really didn't plan on it."

Dick laughed and gave her a skeptical look. "You mean to say you got me all the way out here and expected me to go docilely away after four hours?"

She dropped her eyes and said stiffly, "I'm awfully sorry. I have a lot of studying to do."

Dick withdrew to an awkward jocularity. "Okay. Let's get a look at this noble institution."

With methodical solemnity Margaret proceeded to point out the various buildings—the gymnasium, a two-story, rectangular red-brick building with a set of incongruous Ionic columns on the front steps; the science building, a square fieldstone structure with stunted Gothic battlements and corner turrets; the three-story gray clapboard auxiliary dormitory, a model of Victorian gingerbread; the small white cottage where the chaplain lived; the yellow-brick T-shaped convent.

Her manner puzzled him completely. She acted like a professional guide, limiting her conversation to the what and why of the buildings, and speaking in a curiously flat emotionless voice. It made him wonder if he had offended her. But he could not imagine how.

"What's Faith up to?" he said. They had turned off the path along the oval drive and were strolling across the wide green lawns behind Sacré Coeur. "She any happier at dear old Mount St. Monica's?"

Margaret made an unpleasant face. "Faith is a born complainer."

"Does she stand entirely alone?"

"No. There are always a few you can never satisfy."

"That's true," Dick said. "But I've found that the ones you can't satisfy are sometimes the ones who really have the brains and the courage."

"She's coming to the dance this afternoon."

"Oh . . . good."

They stopped before a small, oddly towered fieldstone structure. "This is the chapel," Margaret said. "It's quite old—it was part of the original property—this all belonged to the Grady family. It really isn't big enough for the whole school, now."

"Pretty sad looking, isn't it?" Dick said.

"What?"

"I said it looks pretty sad. The architecture . . . and so forth."

"I've—always liked it."

Another swing and a miss.

"Would you like to go in? For a minute?"

"Sure."

They steppped from sunlight to deep shadow. The church was wider and larger inside than he had expected. The stained-glass windows, each picturing one of the apostles, were incredibly bad. The altar flickered whitely in the glow of two banks of candles, one on either side, against the railing. Was there some reason why she was bringing him in here? Was she after all another Catholic out to get converts?

They stood in the back for a silent moment. "I like those stained-glass windows," he whispered.

It sounded almost as bad as the windows looked, but you had to say something. Margaret smiled faintly, genuflected and led him outside, blessing herself with holy water from the stone basin at the door as she went.

"Let's see," Dick said. "You bless yourself with holy water because you believe it contains sacramental grace—right?"

"Yes," Margaret said, obviously surprised. "Where did you learn that?"

"Comparative Religion 102," Dick said. "Very thorough course. I can lecture for hours on Jewish and Catholic dietary laws, Moslem fast days. You name it."

"I see," Margaret said.

They strolled back toward the main building, called Sacré Coeur, after the Sacred Heart, Margaret explained. Dick tried to study her as they walked. Something important was wrong. The radiance, the glow which had seemed to surround this girl at the beach was gone.

In the reception rotunda, Margaret hesitated. It was now crowded with young men and girls. "Where did you two go?" Faith said behind them. "As a spy for the local branch of The Inquisition, I demand an immediate confession."

Dick laughed, and turned to her with a grateful smile.

"I was afraid we'd meet you," Margaret said.

"If you can't get me a date, the least you could do is let me horn in on yours," Faith said.

"I could've gotten you a date," Dick said. "Why didn't you call me?"

"Why didn't *you* call me?" Faith said. "After all I should think you'd know by now that Margaret and I have a sort of Cyrano de Bergerac setup. I write all her dialogue, and so forth."

She took Dick's free arm and led him through the crowd. "I have him for the first three and a half hours," she said to Margaret, "and then you can walk him down to the gate."

"Why are you so silly?" Margaret murmured.

"How's the Judge?" Dick said.

"He's back selling decisions."

They marched down a long hall into a room on the right, filled with chairs and tables. French windows opened onto a stone patio, where several groups of girls stood and talked. A few other girls and several unattached young men sat here and there along the walls.

Faith dropped Dick's arm and whispered, "I see a potential victim." She strolled toward a young man sitting alone in the far corner.

Dick and Margaret sat down near the door; a dreamy fox-trot began in the megaphone above their heads. Margaret said nothing for a full minute. Then she leaned toward him and said solemnly, "You can dance with Faith if you'd like. I don't mind."

"Why should I do that?"

Margaret looked down at her hands. "I don't know. I just thought you'd enjoy yourself more."

It suddenly occurred to him that she might be jealous. "I can only take Faith in small doses," he said, with a quick laugh. "I can't keep up the running commentary. Besides, I came out here to dance with you."

He took her hand and led her out on the dance floor.

"There isn't anyone else—yet," Margaret said.

"So what?" Dick said. "The better to dance with you."

The room filled up rapidly, but no one joined them on the floor. The boys showed no inclination to become attached to girls, and vice versa. Faith was sitting next to a quite young but pleasant looking lad, not the one she had baited in the corner. She seemed to be enjoying herself, but the young man looked uncomfortable.

"I see it takes them a while to get to know each other," Dick said.

Margaret nodded. "That's why I never come to these dances. The boys make you feel like such a fool."

"You mean they even ignore you?"

"Yes. I'm not like Faith. I don't go over and talk to them."

"Why should you? If they ignore you, they must be unconscious."

"Oh, now—"

They danced silently for a few more minutes, and then Margaret suggested they stop. She led him over to where Faith was sitting. Faith introduced them to the young man, Ed James, from St. Jerome's College in the city.

"He came all the way out here just to see me," she said.

"And now he has to go all the way back to get away from you," Dick said.

"She told me she has her bag all packed," James said, with a somewhat nervous smile. "She wants to elope."

Dick asked Faith if she would like to dance, and she accepted.

"I feel like a grandfather around here," he said.

A few couples were dancing now, though the larger percentage of girls and young men still stood and sat in segregated groups.

"As long as it isn't a father," Faith said.

"How's your love life?" he asked.

"So-so," Faith said. "I just have trouble keeping track of them all."

He debated asking Faith what was bothering Margaret and decided against it. He also decided against mentioning Larry. It was, after all, none of his business.

"Get Margaret away from this place the next time," Faith said. "I almost choked when I heard you were coming to this."

Dick shrugged. "She asked me."

"Well, next time *tell* her."

A tall, dark, heavily built girl with a strong shrewd face was talking to Margaret when Dick and Faith returned. Margaret introduced her as Helen Cudahy. Ed James had vanished. Faith took Helen's arm and announced they were off to hunt down a few freshmen for tomorrow's dinner.

"That's the Cudahy Brewery family's only heir," Margaret said, nodding after Helen.

Dick pulled her to her feet and started to dance. "Listen, woman. Are you trying to get rid of me?"

"No."

"I don't like heiresses. They make me nervous."

"Oh."

"My old professor of philosophy, Dr. Sunglass, often told me that when a woman wants to get rid of a gentleman friend, she starts talking up all her girl friends. Have I done something wrong since I arrived? Forgotten to genuflect in front of a statue, or something?"

"Oh, no, Dick. Don't be silly."

"Well, what's the matter?"

"Nothing's the matter."

"It must be this dance. You don't belong in here with these kids. You look and act five years older than anybody here."

"So—do you," Margaret said, as if she were confessing something she had tried to conceal.

"Then let's leave."

"All right," Margaret said, to his surprise.

Outside, Dick led her toward the car. Margaret stopped and stared at him with a pained expression.

"Dick . . . I told you. I can't. . . ."

"I thought you said we were leaving?"

"But I'm not signed out. And it's too late, now. You're supposed to let them know—so they won't have dinner for you."

Dick slumped dejectedly against the fender. "What happens now?"

"I thought we could go for a walk. It's a school rule about signing out."

She looked so contrite he felt sorry for her. He stood up and forced a grin. "I'll live."

They strolled down the drive towards the woods. Pity had replaced his annoyance. The school was not Margaret's fault, any more than the absurd religion she had inherited. She was trapped in her past, her childhood, as others had tried to trap you. How could you convince her that escape was possible?

"There's a soda store about a half mile down the road outside," Margaret said.

"I haven't been to one in years," Dick said. "Let's go."

They discussed school as they walked. Margaret detailed the subjects she was taking in the coming year. Dick had to admit he was impressed by the terminology, at least.

"Ontology, Theology," he repeated after her. "I'll have to take a few special tutoring courses to keep up with you."

"Oh, they probably won't be quite as impressive as they sound," Margaret said. "They water it all down for us females, I'm afraid."

The soda store was clean and the brown booths were empty. A matronly woman in a gray uniform took their orders and went behind the counter to mix their sodas.

"That's an amusing character you have for a receptionist," Dick said. "Sister Mary Rose." He told Margaret about his brief conversation.

Margaret smiled warmly. "Yes. I love her. Faith is always teasing her. She's a little old and gets mixed up about things. . . ."

"Are the rest of the nuns like that?"

"They're a little more strict. But they're all right," she added hastily.

The waitress brought their sodas—chocolate for both, and Dick raised his for a toast.

"For a mild winter."

"Why?" Margaret said, smiling but puzzled.

"To keep the highways clear from here to the city."

"Oh." She began to eat her ice cream. It was impossible to tell whether or not she liked the idea.

"That reminds me, speaking of Sister Mary Rose. What does that picture in the front parlor mean?"

"The one with the young girl and Christ behind her?"

"Yes. Christ is whispering in her ear."

"He's calling her. It's the story of a vocation."

"To be a nun?"

"Yes."

"I thought it was something like that," Dick said. "Do you think that's what really happens?"

"Yes, of course."

"Including the expression on her face?" Dick said, with a quick smile.

"I suppose you think it's silly," Margaret said, in a low taut voice.

"The expression, or the idea of being a nun?"

"Both."

"As a matter of fact, I do," Dick said. "It seems a great waste. . . ."

"Don't you think it's possible that someone would *want* to serve God—Christ—to give their lives to Him?"

"Sure I think it's possible. Anything is possible."

Margaret was disconcerted. "What do you mean?"

"People can be induced to do almost anything for a religious purpose. Look at the Indian Holy Men who drive nails into their bodies. Or the snake cults down South."

"This is different. It's an answer to a call from God."

Dick smiled, trying to lessen the serious cutting tone. "It's exactly the same. You're just looking at it from a narrow point of view and calling it by another name."

"If you don't understand it, there's no need to make fun of it."

"I understand it," Dick said, irritated in spite of himself. "I didn't understand the stupid picture to begin with, that's all."

"I think it's beautiful myself," Margaret said. "It's always touched me deeply."

"You've been trained to respond to it."

"I have not. I just respond, and I'm not ashamed of it. As a matter of fact, I've been thinking of going in the convent myself—"

Admit he knew? Or pretend to be astonished? The second choice was easier. "You mean that?"

"Yes," Margaret said. "It's a perfectly sensible thing to do, if you have the vocation."

"Do you have it?"

"I don't know."

"How can you tell?"

"Well," Margaret said hesitantly, "it's hard to explain. You wait and pray for guidance—"

"From whom?"

"God. And the Blessed Mother."

"Oh cut it out."

Now he was really astonished—at himself. He knew those words were rude, crude, wrong. But he could not stop them. They had spoken themselves.

"Dick! Honestly! Just because you don't understand, there's no reason to sneer. It's insulting—"

Dick glared at a red, white and yellow picture of a banana split and realized she was right. "I apologize," he said. "I get worked up about things like this, that's all. My grandmother wanted me to be a minister. I had to fight her off."

"This is different. It's a free decision on my part. If I decide I have the vocation."

"My God, Margaret"—he caught himself—"I'm sorry. But try to see. It's not a free decision. You're not aware of what it involves. And that's what makes a decision free. You're being influenced. You *must* be."

"You just don't understand," Margaret said. "There's nothing unusual about it, to a Catholic."

"Religion is religion," Dick snapped. "It all adds up to the same thing. You give away your time and money, even your life, to something that probably doesn't exist. If it weren't so tragic it would be amusing."

Margaret's mouth trembled. For a moment Dick thought she was going to cry. But she controlled herself. "It's getting late," she said. "I think we'd better get back."

"It's only five."

"I have some studying to do."

By the time they reached the entrance to the main building, Dick was calm enough to take her arm and turn her to him.

"I had no intention of insulting you or your religion. I was talking about religion in general. I honestly believe what I said."

"I don't," Margaret said coldly.

"I'm not asking you to believe it."

"Then what were we arguing about?"

Dick stopped and thought it over. "You're right again," he said, looking up at her from a lower step. "But just let me say one thing. When I argue with someone, I'm trying to convince them, that's true. But I don't demand them to be convinced. I believe everyone has a right to think what they please. It's just hard to put it into practice when you disagree extremely with someone. . . ."

Margaret's eyes seemed to ask him not to complete the sentence.

". . . with someone you like," Dick said savagely, and strode off down the walk to his car.

An hour later Dick was pushing Larry Donahue's buzzer again. He opened the door with a drink in his hand. "You look unhappy, Richard. Come on in and absorb a little of the bachelor's consolation."

"Jake still here?"

"He left about an hour ago," Larry said, "when he finally realized he wasn't going to get me drunk."

Larry led him down the hall into the living room. "We have a little contest every time we get together—whose view of life will prevail. So far the score is nothing-nothing."

"The guy bugs me," Dick said. "I shouldn't let him—but he does."

"He bugs me too," Larry said, "a lot worse than he could ever bug you. But don't worry, I'll get to him just like I'm getting to Faith Kilpatrick."

He handed Dick a drink. Looking up at his ex-roommate, Dick felt again that sense of encountering an alien experience. Now the strangeness was redoubled by the liquorish glitter of Larry's deep-set gray eyes, the bitterness in his sardonic smile.

"From what I can see," Dick said, "you haven't made much progress with Faith."

Larry threw back his head and gave a sharp nasty laugh. "Negative, Richard. I'll get it all. I'll get it just the way I want to get it. No maudlin emotion, just pure surrender, the surrender of the self, Richard."

"I got the impression you weren't even speaking."

"The orgasm of self-surrender is physical, Richard, the little death. I want the soul. Metaphysical surrender. Larger death."

*Metaphysical* was one of Larry's favorite words. Dick rarely understood what he meant by it.

"I told you a long time ago, Richard, we operate on different levels, you and I. A Catholic like me is metaphysically infected from birth."

"Does that go for Margaret Connolly?"

"Margaret Connolly." Repeating her name formed a small smile on Larry's lips. "No. Margaret is a different kind of Catholic. The metaphysical content is unconscious. It makes for an appealing simplicity. I can see why she disturbs Faith so much."

"She disturbed me today."

"What happened?"

"I don't know. But she was like something off the polar ice cap. We spent most of the time arguing about religion."

"Did she tell you she was thinking of entering the convent?"

Dick nodded. "I said I thought it was stupid. That really froze things up."

"A mistake, old pal."

"I'm used to saying what I think."

"But you're not going to get anywhere that way. Which reminds me, where do you want to get?"

"I don't know, frankly," Dick said. "It's a little early in the game for that, isn't it?"

"True. But it's an important consideration." Larry put down his drink and held up three fingers. "There are the following possibilities."

He bent down one finger. "The kind of deal you had with Vicky Sand."

He bent down a second finger. "One big night à la Kierkegaard's *Diary of a Seducer*."

He bent down a third finger. "To have and to hold until death, et cetera."

Dick took a long swallow of his drink. "I've had about all I want of number one. I'm getting a little old for number two. So I guess it's number three."

"It's just as well," Larry said, "you'd never get number one and you could wind up in jail trying for number two. Not that number three is going to be easy."

Larry mixed himself another drink and returned to his chair. He was obviously enjoying himself.

"Give it to me straight," Dick said. "That's why I'm here."

"Margaret is the apotheosis of the middle-class Catholic girl. First you've got to understand the middle-class Catholic. They all *literally* believe what the Church teaches. In the lower class and the upper class there is an opportunity to discover through one's own experience exactly how fraudulent the whole operation is. But the spirituality of the middle-class Catholic is unsullied. They suffer neither the disillusionment of deprivation nor the corruptions of power. They remain devout, trusting, absolutely obedient to God's official spokesmen, the priests and nuns who tell you what to do and think."

"I follow," Dick said, "not enthusiastically, but I follow."

"Margaret has gone to Catholic schools all her life. She is, in other words, now in her sixteenth year of listening to these priests and nuns tell her what to think and feel. At home she gets the same diet. Her mother is the Catholic clubwoman par excellence. You can't put together a benefit committee for any Catholic cause in town without her winding up as the anchor lady. It should not surprise you, therefore, that Margaret reacts to her environment in a highly overdetermined way. Her image of you, for instance, is involved with all the stories she has heard about corrupt atheists and agnostics with no morals whose only purpose in life is doing a girl wrong. When you tell her bluntly that convent life is for the birds, you instantly conjure up that image of the atheistic lecher. Reaction: freeze."

"I'm still shivering," Dick said.

"Another compounding factor is the Irish-Catholic dread of sex as the supreme sin, the only thing really worth confessing. It reinforces the freeze." Larry leaned back in his chair and drank for a moment. "Sounds hopeless, doesn't it?"

"Very."

"But not completely. You've got two things going for you. One, the clerics have no control over Margaret's libido. She feels attracted to you, that's obvious. But don't ever try to bring the sexual side of it into her consciousness. Let it work at the unconscious level where it will do you the most good. Two, Margaret's an American which means she suffers at least slightly from spiritual schizophrenia. Americans are supposed to think for themselves. Catholics think what they're told. A man feels this schizophrenia much more acutely than a woman, of course. Girls like Margaret aren't much on the American side. But there's a spark of independence there that with a little luck you can fan into life."

"I like that idea," Dick said. "I like it a lot."

"But don't get carried away and think you can do it just by whistling 'Yankee Doodle' on every date. It's going to be a very slow and subtle operation. You've got to keep your head and maneuver. Above all you've got to avoid creating the freeze reaction by giving her a hard time about her religion or making any wild passes until the attraction is built up high enough—"

"Like the sandbox tree," Dick said.

"Sorry," Larry said. "I'm a city boy."

"They had a lot of them on that island where I won the war. When the fruit ripens past a certain point, it explodes."

Larry shrugged. "I prefer another metaphor. The womb. Margaret's curled up there in the womb of Mother Church. But she still has a chance to be born if you can persuade her to undergo the trauma of birth. Personally, I don't think you can do it."

They sat there staring at each other for a long silent moment. Again Dick felt, even tasted the strangeness of the world Larry Donahue had just described to him. But instead of revulsion he felt an intense excitement. This was more than the pursuit of a girl, it was a challenge, a chance to prove one last time, in the most absolute and final way, that he had overcome all the guilt, the dread, the narrow compulsions that had haunted his teen-age years.

Concealing his inner excitement from Larry, he said with a casual shrug: "I'm going to give it a whirl anyway."

"Good luck."

They were silent for another moment.

"But you don't follow your own advice," Dick said. "You're doing the exact opposite with Faith."

Larry nodded. "I know. Believe me when I tell you, Richard, that between you and Margaret and Faith and me there's a difference—as if we came from separate planets. And I'm *not* being condescending. Be glad you're not metaphysical. Be glad you're not mixed up with this."

He gestured toward the window and Dick knew instantly what he meant. "The city?"

"The city and the people who run the show. It makes everything—your values, your feelings, different."

"Come on, Larry. People are still people. When you start insisting that Faith should be some sort of echo or imitation of you, aren't you just being a Catholic turned inside out?"

"No," Larry snapped. "I am using religion because it happens to be the most convenient and—I'll admit it—personally preferable thing at hand to give me the controlling vote in the situation. How long do you think I'd last without it—with a drunk for a father and not a nickel in the bank, up against the Judge's daughter? I'd be another organization yes-man in ten minutes, Richard. Between me and Faith the key is power. Personal power . . ."

Dick shivered. The strangeness was total now and it involved something beyond psychology, something dark and ominous that transformed his friend's saturnine face. They are different, Richard, and you are suddenly grateful for Margaret's simplicity. Oh, problems, yes. And you are also grateful for Larry's stark analysis. But you must go it alone, Richard, and let Larry go his own strange road alone. What a crazy world.

# Chapter Seven

Faith Kilpatrick loathed morning Mass. Attendance was compulsory, and the punishment for the few who could not muster the energy to get out of bed was loss of late permissions. Since late permissions were a necessity if a girl had a date in the city and since dates, if they were to be had at all, were in the city, most of Mount St. Monica's came to Mass daily. But their reluctance was more than apparent. Hair uncombed, faces still fuzzy with sleep, they slumped in the pews, staring dully at Father Denton Malone on the altar. Helen Cudahy and several others simply put their heads down and slept.

In the middle aisle Margaret Connolly solemnly marked the absentees on a seating chart. As vice-president of the Sodality, she was responsible for half the church. Esther Sugrue, Sodality president, checked the other half. Margaret looked more than a little depressed. Her tea-dance date with Dick had been a disaster, from what little Faith could deduce from her veiled (à propos word) remarks. Faith watched her finish checking off the absentees and kneel down in a front pew to bow her head in prayer. When was the last time you prayed, Faith? Maybe you had better say a few good ones, not for Margaret, she really didn't need any, but for Faith Kilpatrick, the girl whose soul is suddenly in danger.

Absurd, to think those words could have genuine meaning. You have made jokes about them for so many years, giving them and all the other catechism clichés the Kilpatrick horselaugh. That marvelous gift for mockery, obviously inherited, had now become a terrible liability.

Faith loosened the scarf at her throat and unbuttoned the dirty brown raincoat she'd flung over her pajamas. It did no good. It was happening again, every vivid word of it, awakening in her body like jets of flame in an oven. Her face began to flush, the palms of her hands tingled with pinpoints of sweat. It was so absurd to let a piece of information, deliberately and viciously implanted in the mind like a saboteur's bomb, torment you this way. But it was no good. No amount of scorn or persuasion could prevent the whole scene from happening again.

There was the beach with the golden moon which Margaret Connolly had requested, staring blandly down on the shimmering sea. A scene out of *True Story,* except for the dialogue.

Larry Donahue: "I heard something about the Judge the other day that might interest you."

Faith: "Coming from you, I'm sure it isn't good."

Larry: "Why so defensive?"

Faith: "I happen to love him in a sort of confused, bemused way."

Larry: "It's the way you combine simplicity and cynicism that intrigues me."

Faith: "You're sweet too."

Larry: "Maybe I'd better forget it."

Faith: "You know I won't let you now."

Larry: "It isn't good. It isn't even nice. No, I'd better forget it."

Faith: "Coward."

Larry: "I'm not even sure it's true. But I'm inclined to believe it."

Faith: "Tell, for God's sake."

Larry: "The Judge has a mistress. He's had one for years."

Silence while Faith listens to the sea washing on the beach, and beyond it the grinding clutch of an accelerating car. Silence while Faith walks across the sea into emptiness, a land beyond the moon. Silence while the body escapes the mind (or was it vice versa?) for the first terrifying time and a voice mechanically asks: "Who is she?"

"A schoolteacher named Margaret Halloran. She lives alone in an apartment at 1301 Parkway. Out in the north end."

"I don't believe you, of course."

"Of course."

"But I admit it's possible. I know he and my mother—"

"The separate bedroom bit?"
"For years."
"He's not exactly devout either."
"No."
"Who told you?"
"An old pal I've gotten to know. Matty Blair, the leader of the First Ward."
"What would a thug like him know about it?"
"He knows a lot. He's been around a long time."
"It's been going on a long time?"
"About fifteen years, from what I can gather."
"Oh, that's ridiculous!"

You are screaming, Faith. There are hot, biting tears blurring your eyes. Your fists are clenched, nails driving into your palms. You want to walk into the water, quench this fire that is burning in your body. Jesus, how could he? All those years when he was alternately teasing and spoiling you, roughhouse on the couch, the silly jokes at dinner, the false teeth—have you ever laughed so hard?—a flick of the tongue, and presto, there he was, an Edgar Bergen dummy, and all the time this other unspeakable, vile thing was happening. Week after week, month after month this sin was accumulating in black immensity, spreading like a huge stain over those images to which you so desperately clung, clouding the clarity of that laughter, contaminating the affection of every rough kiss and offhand hug, defiling every touch, taste, smell of him. Oh, God, you thrashed in that inky sea, frantically clutching those ruined memories, swimming for a nonexistent shore, and all the time the voices kept talking.

"What do you expect me to say?"
"I don't know. Nothing."
"You expected something."
"Not really. I've learned not to expect anything from you."
"Thanks."
"The truth. It's our motto, remember?"
"Yes."

So home you went, with your charred chastity, a pillar of futile fire across the cool, shadow-pocked sand.

All right, it's over. You have lived it again and survived. Maybe it would be better not to fight it, to accept it casually as a kind of psychic rash that comes and goes, with no really dire effects.

First of all, you still don't entirely believe it. It was easy enough to picture the Judge falling from grace at some Bar Association convention. It was the *duration* that tormented you. The thought of it beginning when you were four years old, when you were totally helpless, too young to warn him or console him, somehow to save him from the enormity.

But it wasn't . . .

You have told yourself once, twice, a thousand times, *you understand.* You have watched with new insight, with an intensity that was almost affection, the utter emptiness of the Kilpatrick marriage. The mechanical words exchanged at the table, the expert nonlistening when Mother began one of her monologues on the politics of the Marian Guild, or what the Archbishop said when they lunched together. There was no antagonism, none of the sick bickering that was, Faith gathered, the status quo in the Connolly marriage. Quite simply, the Judge's attitude toward his wife was utter, total indifference. *Nothingness.*

Was that why you found it so unacceptable? From nothing, nothing comes, according to the philosophers, and that was why a throb of fear rode toward you on that word, like a surfer on a wave, a sudden draining sense of diminution, loss. What did it mean, to be born out of this nothingness? Were all the Judge's other imitations and intimations of love as empty as the act that created you? Poor Faith, you do not know, and you relapse into a kind of squishy self-pity which you also find repulsive. So you have swum around the circle back into mockery again. Except, dear God, the target now is so vulnerable.

*"Ite, Missa est,"* Father Malone was intoning from the altar. Go, the Mass is ended. If only the mess, too, was ended.

Breakfast after Mass was a helter-skelter rush. Disconsolately staring at the greasy scrambled eggs, Faith found herself grateful for Margaret's silence. Around them others complained about the food, school, men, and life in general.

Rita Conboy poked a disdainful fork at the obscenely yellow eggs. "I wouldn't give these to a cat."

Esther Sugrue narrated shrilly to mousy Eileen Becker, "And I went to see Sister Claire and said, 'Do you know we don't have a copy of Francis Thompson's essays in the library?' "

"Pindar," Eileen Becker said. "They have only one old copy of him, ready to fall to pieces in your hands."

Dolores Talbot, her lustrous blond hair in curlers under a bandanna, looked like anything but the school's reigning beauty. But she was at least good humored. "I gather you're still dating daredevil Dick Thornton," she said to Margaret. "Having fun?"

"Oh." Margaret grew flustered as usual. "Do you know him?"

"I've double-dated with him," Dolores said. "He's a good friend of Bill Whitfield and several other of my defunct fiancés." Dolores had been engaged at least once a term since freshman year.

"Oh," Margaret said.

"Anyway, when you start dating someone nice, Margaret, all the cats meow."

"Lick the milk off your whiskers and say something, Rita," Faith snickered. Paralyzed with hostility, Rita Conboy could only glare.

On the way to class they stopped at their mailboxes. Faith, expecting no communications, ignored hers and watched Margaret extract a letter that could only be from Dick. "Aha," she said. "Apologies to the unborn child and that sort of thing?"

Margaret tore it open, read it in one devouring glance and stuffed it into her jacket pocket. "Come on," Faith said, almost running to keep up with Margaret's leggy strides, "you can't leave me dangling. No matter what you say, we're in this together."

"I thought he'd never want to speak to me again. Instead, he's —sorry," Margaret said.

"About what?"

"About how rotten he was—or thought he was," Margaret said, "when it was really my fault."

"Is that all?"

"He wants me to go to a party next Saturday—at Paula Stapleton's house."

"Stapleton! Wow!" Faith said.

"Do you know her?"

"I know of her. She's the quintessential Wasp. Her family owns about half the city."

Margaret could not conceal her dismay. "What can I possibly say to someone like that?"

"Don't say anything. Let her do the talking."

Faith could see that Margaret's mind was miles away from the subject matter throughout the first two periods, a dull history of education and Sister Regina Mildred's course on Shakespeare. "Millie," as everyone called her, was much too absorbed in her Elizabethan historical background to notice whether anyone was paying attention. Faith found herself floating in a similar mental vacuum, in which she desperately attempted to apportion values to chaotic images. Margaret, Dick, Larry, the Judge, the unknown mistress swirled through her mind like figures in some psychic maelstrom. Was Margaret a perfect test case that in some sense of the word proved—or disproved—all the destructive things Larry said about Catholicism? Was it rational—or fair to Margaret—to think of her that way?

By now they were in their third period. It was ontology, taught by lumbering Sister Mary Concepta whom Faith had long asserted was really a reincarnation of St. Thomas Aquinas in drag. Sister Mary Concepta did not tolerate inattention when she explained the nature of things. She felt, remotely, that she was in the chair of Peter, handing down revealed truths, and for anyone to overlook them, even for a few moments, was heresy. In the heyday of medieval philosophy, heretics were burned, and Sister Concepta was distinctly of that spirit and time.

"Miss Connolly," Sister Concepta suddenly boomed in her basso profundo, "do you have such a remarkable understanding of the difference between essence and substance that you can spend your time drawing pictures in your notebook?"

"No. No, Sister," Margaret said, closing her notebook hastily.

"Let me see what you were drawing there," Sister insisted ponderously.

"It was really nothing, Sister," Margaret said desperately.

"Margaret Connolly," Sister boomed, as aghast as if she was watching an angel falling from grace.

Margaret opened the book and Sister picked it up to peer at it. She was very nearsighted. "A capital *D?* How can that be more interesting than the difference between essence and substance?"

A titter ran through the room. Margaret blushed agonizingly.

"What's so funny?" Sister Concepta said, raising her large oblong head to survey the room. There was, of course, no answer.

"Can you tell us, Miss Connolly, the difference between essence and existence? And explain substantial form, for good measure?"

Margaret stared miserably at the incomprehensible diagram on the blackboard, and whispered, "No, Sister, I'm afraid I can't."

"What is the matter with you, girl?" Sister Concepta lumbered back up the room to the teacher's platform. There, with a prehistoric rumble, she cleared her throat and picked up the textbook. "If you had taken the trouble to open your text you would have noticed that it is all very neatly explained in the first two paragraphs on page 109. I think you had better copy those paragraphs a hundred times tonight, Miss Connolly."

"Yes, Sister."

"And keep your writing legible."

"Yes, Sister."

Sister Concepta plodded on to the next point in her stifling exposition of what she called the Perennial philosophy and Faith called the catechism according to St. Thomas Aquinas. Margaret, her face almost drained of color, sat stiffly upright in her chair, her eyes riveted on the board, obviously too dazed with humiliation to understand anything that was said. Mercifully, within ten minutes the bell rang and they were dismissed for lunch. In the corridor, Faith fell into step beside her.

"If you want to daydream, the best thing to do is look straight at Concepta. Then she thinks that abstracted look in your eyes is philosophical."

"Save the advice," Margaret said. "I don't need it now."

"Well, for later. After the next date."

"Oh, stop. I don't think it's funny," Margaret said in a savage whisper as they went into the dining room.

At the table they were greeted with a round robin of inane smiles. Rita Conboy had just finished telling the story, and sat there, her feline eyes shining, her prim sadistic mouth twitching.

"How can a *D* be more interesting than substance and essence, Meg?" Esther Sugrue giggled.

"Please have mercy," Margaret murmured, lowering her eyes.

"Oh"—Esther giggled again—"we certainly have a right to know if anyone does."

"You might also have the good taste to shut up," Faith said.

"Listen to Emily Post," Rita Conboy sneered. "Of all people, talking about good taste."

"I must say that is incongruous, Faith." Esther smirked.

"What's going on?" Helen Cudahy said, arriving as usual five minutes late. Rita Conboy delightedly retold the entire story.

"Isn't it fascinating," Faith said. "I mean, have you ever heard anything quite so racy and dramatic?"

Helen got the hint instantly, God bless her. "It reminds me of the time I got caught with a condom on my finger in religion class down at Holy Rosary. . . ."

The rest of lunch was spent listening to the escapades which had gotten Helen expelled from three schools so far. Margaret's story paled into utter insignificance and she finished her lunch in obscure silence. Was she grateful? Did she realize how expertly her devoted roommate had managed her escape from stage center? Probably not, Faith thought, surprised by a sudden flash of bitterness. Instead it's all black marks for encouraging Cudahyism, synonymous in Margaret's canon with pornography. The saints of this world are difficult to live with. Maybe you should be getting that message across to Dick Thornton.

But there was an unsaint, an unfanatic, an un- (but not anti-) holy person inside this intense perfectionistic person that was Margaret. Faith had seen flashes of it, especially when she was angry. Last year, on the Student Council, when they were asked to vote their presumed-to-be-automatic approval of the expulsion of Mary Jane Comiskey, a sweet hapless girl who had drunk too much at the senior prom. Faith had appeared before the Council, as a committee of one, to make a blazing plea on her behalf, and Margaret, a voting member as a Sodality officer, had startled everyone by seconding Faith's invective with an eloquent outburst against the inhumanity of Mother President's decree. She had wept when the Council voted 10 to 1 against her.

Faith turned toward Margaret, hoping to read contrary evidence in her expression, as Helen's monologue began to run down. Margaret was gone, her food barely touched on her plate. Up in the room Faith found her at her desk writing. Looking over her shoulder, Faith saw she was doing her punish lesson. On page after page in her notebook, her small, careful handwriting repeated the monotonous words.

Essence is that in virtue of which a being is just what it is. The definition of a being according to its proximate genus and specific difference gives it its essence.

Existence is that state of a being in virtue of which it is present as an actuality and not merely as a possibility. It is opposed to mere possibility.

"Ridiculous," Faith said.

"What am I supposed to do about it?"

"Defy her," Faith said, with a melodramatic sweep of her arm. "Tell her you are not a child. That such treatment is moronic, tyrannic, archaic—how many have you got done?"

"Thirty-five."

"You should have consulted me before you started."

"I'm not in the mood for humor."

"Excuse me." Faith pulled up a blanket and snuggled down on her bed. "Wake me up when you're finished. We'll go for a walk."

"We have a catechism class."

"Oh, no," Faith said. "You've signed me up for that idiocy again?"

"It's so hard to get anyone, Faith. It's in St. Martin's."

The city's Negro parish. They had taught there last year. Margaret had shrewdly inveigled Faith into it by telling her that no one else in the school would take the job.

"We didn't do them any good, as far as I could see."

"The pastor didn't agree with you."

Esther Sugrue joined them for the trip into the city. Faith had embarrassed her into volunteering, last year. As president of the Sodality she could hardly decline. She had then proceeded to talk up the experience to Jim Kilpatrick, convincing him that he had an authentic saint on his hands. Faith, of course, found this even more nauseating than Esther's sentimental attitude toward "the little pickaninnies," as she called the black second graders.

St. Martin de Porres parish was, fortunately, not in the heart of the Negro ghetto, which the city's white majority called Nighttown. The name was not a tribute to James Joyce, but to a more obvious color comparison. The ghetto had grown immensely in the war years when thousands of Negroes had streamed from the South to work in the city's factories. St. Martin's was on the edge of the huge slum only a few blocks away from St. Aloysius, one of the city's larger white churches. It was called a "mission church" by the Archdiocese, but everyone knew it was a device to keep the Negroes out of the city's white parish churches and schools.

Father Matthew Carey, the small, gentle-voiced pastor of St. Martin's, greeted them with a shy smile at the door of the red-brick church. He was a priest Faith admired. He had volunteered for this job when he heard that a dozen other men approached by the Archbishop had turned it down. Father Carey led them down the middle aisle to this year's crop of First Communion candidates. Margaret and Esther divided the girls, who were much more numerous, and a few moments later Faith was staring down at four rows of small wide-eyed black faces. They stared back at her with the enviable directness of a seven-year-old. "My name is Miss Kilpatrick," she said. "I'm here to teach you about God."

*Yes, God, the person Larry Donahue does not believe in.*

"It's very important to know about God because if you don't know about Him, you can't love Him. If you didn't know your father and mother, you wouldn't love them, would you?"

*And when you do know a person, can you avoid loving them?*

"It's the same thing with God. When you know Him, and understand how He takes care of you, it's so much easier to love Him, and that helps you to be good, and if you are good, you can be sure you'll go to heaven and be happy forever."

*You don't believe one word of that, do you, Larry? And Faith? Now that Father (read God) (thank you, Dr. Freud) is something less than perfection incarnate?*

"But right now, we have another, very important reason for learning about God. Does anyone know what it is?"

Two hands shot up. Faith recognized a round, eager face with saucer eyes.

"So we can receive ah Fust Communun."

"Communion. Right. And that's very important. Because in communion, we come very close to God. We receive Him right into our bodies, like food. And that helps make us good, and happy."

*If you believe it, Faith, why don't you go to communion? Why do you sit there day after day starving God out of your body? Perhaps because He has already vanished from your mind? And you resent the schizophrenia of His intrusion elsewhere? You want wholeness (happiness?) on any (Larry's) terms.*

Someone whispered in the back row. A ripple of laughter passed down the other rows. The back row swayed as punches and elbows in the ribs were abruptly exchanged. It was last year all over again. "Now stop that," Faith said. "This is too important to be fooling and punching. Stop it, do you hear me?" The back row swayed again, as more blows were distributed. Father Carey hurried up the aisle and softly rebuked the offenders. Faith sighed, and a damp miasma of hopelessness enveloped her. It was not just their color, she told herself. It was the utter leaden boredom of the subject, as presented in this same catechism she had herself memorized fifteen years ago. Esther and Margaret, of course, did not agree. They had been blank-eyed with shock when Faith suggested that if Jesus had relied on the Baltimore catechism, the little ones might have crucified him on the spot.

But Faith had spent too much time in classrooms with black-robed nuns pacing the teaching platform while the unlucky victims stood and stumbled through the catechism recitations. Sister Agnes, fat and red-faced, demanding every word, every comma, exactly as it was in the catechism, while the big yardstick waved ominously. If a boy missed, he got it on the hand. A girl had to write out the answer a hundred times. Sister Lamburder, better known as Lambaster, in the second grade, smashing Marilyn Delmar in the face when she panicked and was unable to answer with her usual perfection. No, that was the strangest, most ironic part of your conundrum. This malaise over the religion of your birth was not created by Larry Donahue. It was already there, a disgusted, sometimes querulous voice, thanks to Faith's *experience* in Catholic schools that were supposed to create fervent devotion, whole-souled commitment. But Faith declined to go that last momentous mile and declare, with Larry, *by their fruits ye shall know them.* That opened up too many appalling possibilities. Instead Faith fled almost frantically toward other explanations, even the possibility that it was Faith, not Catholicism, that was infected with metaphysical sickness. Margaret Connolly, after all, had sat in those same classrooms, seeing the same brutality and stupidity and she was untouched, untainted by doubt's contagion.

Gradually, Faith became almost grateful for the chance to teach catechism today. As she read the first few questions and answers she felt an almost exalted reassurance, a resurgence of belief.

*Who is God?*
*God is the creator of Heaven and Earth.*
*Where is God?*
*God is everywhere.*
*Why did God make me?*
*God made me to know Him and to love Him and to serve Him in this world and to be happy with Him forever in the next.*

Fundamentals. Take those answers away and the world was a dry chip spinning through emptiness. Was that what you recoiled from facing, Faith, the enormity of what Larry's answer meant? Fear. It was as simple and primitive as childhood tears in the dark room. Remember that frantic night, after seeing *Dracula,* when you had insisted on a light, and Mother, serenely indifferent to emotions as always, had refused? The Judge had come home at 3 or 4 A.M., also as usual, and heard you crying. For over an hour he had sat on the edge of the bed, his big hard arm around you, teasing you out of your terror. Was that the day the angry transference began, the birth of Faith, the rebel against all Mother's cloying goodness, the worshipper of Father's rough, loud mockery? God, God, God, it was like a gigantic spider web in which they were all enmeshed from birth. Impossible to stand back and look at it. Only the mind, held at arm's length like a vanity mirror, caught glimpses that seemed to say something, and probably meant nothing.

Back and forth her voice went, over those first fundamental questions, making the boys recite them, as tomboy Faith had been forced to recite them at their age, twisting truth (fear?) into the mind like a mechanic building a machine. It seemed especially monstrous in this church, constructing this necessity to be humble, forgiving, into these minds, when their black skin required something totally opposite, an infusion of courage, not submission, pride, not humility. The language of the weak, Larry called it. Suddenly she hated these monologue answers, possibly even hated God for inflicting them on her.

The catechism slipped from Faith's numb fingers. She heard her voice saying, "That's all for today." Father Carey looked unhappy. He glanced at his watch, hinting that Faith knew as well as he did that there were still ten minutes left in the hour. "They're so restless on the first day, Father. I think we ought to give them a break."

The boys swarmed out of the church into the playground beside it. There was no school attached to the church. They all went to public schools. That was why they needed catechists each week. Father Carey and Faith stood on the steps, watching them charge around the black asphalt in pursuit of a basketball.

"Your father is Judge Kilpatrick, isn't he?" Father Carey asked.

"Yes."

"Where would it be best to write him a letter?"

"To the Supreme Court, at the capital. Or right here in town, to our house." Feeling guilty about the catechism, Faith added: "Is it anything I can help with?"

"Well. It's a political matter. The son of one of the parishioners. He was arrested a few months ago. Maybe you heard something about it? His name is Andy Barton."

"Something to do with an election?"

"They claim he bribed an election officer in the primary last June. He had been making speeches against the organization. He's been sentenced to five years in jail. Awfully severe, in my opinion. I—was hoping I could persuade your father to reduce the sentence when it comes up on appeal this fall. He's not a bad kid really. I'm afraid the whole thing is political."

Faith scribbled the Kilpatrick home address on a page of her notebook and ripped it out. "Write him here. Tell him you talked to me about it. Tell him I think the sentence ought to be suspended."

On the bus back to school, Esther set Faith's teeth on edge with a half hour of gushing about "one little pickaninny" asking her this question about God and another one asking her that question about Jesus. Faith tried not to think about her brother spending a lifetime listening to this driveling voice, and looked out the window as the trolley skirted the crumbling edges of Nighttown and finally headed for the white semi-suburbs on the city's fringe. Suddenly she heard Esther's bland nasal voice asking Margaret a question that recaptured her attention.

"Do you think it's a sin to kiss a boy?"

Margaret was looking puzzled, and a little appalled. In a flash of bitter prescience, Faith anticipated Esther's next words. "This summer Jim—Faith's brother—kissed me several times. I didn't kiss him back. But I wanted him to kiss me. So you see, I did will it in a way."

It was a marvelous ploy. Esther was simultaneously salving her conscience, scoring on Faith, and matching Margaret's romance with a bigger and better one. All three filled Faith with intense loathing. This was Esther at her worst. This kind of discussion was the favorite sport of her theological clique at school. In previous years, of course, and for most of them still, this particular problem was purely theoretical. It was undoubtedly an enormous triumph for Esther to have a real man to talk about.

"It doesn't seem—serious enough," Margaret said.

"Father Malone doesn't feel that way," Esther said. "He agrees with those moral theologians who maintain that any act of impurity is a mortal sin."

"What utter tripe," Faith snapped.

"I haven't told it in confession," Esther rattled on. "I understand if you have a real doubt—"

"Esther," Faith said, "are you trying to tell me something?"

"What do you mean?" Esther said archly.

"Are you and Jim engaged?"

"Well, not literally. But we have—an understanding."

"You both have my sympathy," Faith said.

"We wouldn't expect anything better from you, my dear," Esther clawed back. She took a deep breath and in a tone of one who has reposed a confidence, turned to Margaret. "Are you serious about Dick Thornton?"

"Esther, really," Margaret said. "I've only gone out with him four or five times."

"I know how you feel. I've got the same problem with Jim and my—vocation."

Faith, for once in her life, was speechless. Margaret murmured, "Oh, I didn't know you—"

"Oh, yes," Esther said. "I've been thinking about it for almost a year now. At first I thought I was more suited for the literary life, but as Father Malone has pointed out, it's such a sordid world, you know—bohemians, sexual liaisons, perversions—and a religious vocation can actually be a source of discipline for a creative talent. It can purify it, strengthen it. That's what Thomas Merton says.

"But then I keep thinking would that be fair to Jim? I've developed a deep, really deep affection for him. I've even written a poem about it."

"Come live with me and be my lug?" Faith asked.

Esther ignored her. "Has Dick shown any interest in the church?"

"No," Margaret said.

"There's an excellent book by Karl Adam, *The Spirit of Catholicism.* Why don't you buy him a copy for Christmas?"

"Thank you, I'll—keep that in mind," Margaret said.

Esther beamed, suffused with her usual self-satisfaction. But Faith, with her acute sensitivity to emotional nuances, caught the emptiness in Margaret's voice. She had absolutely no intention of giving Dick Thornton a book about Catholicism. They were sitting in the long rear seat of the rattling trolley with Margaret in the middle. For a flickering moment, her eyes met Faith's, and there was a cautionary, almost conspiratorial look exchanged.

Margaret said nothing until they reached the privacy of their own room. With a vehemence that took Faith by complete surprise, she threw her catechetical teacher's manual on the desk and said, "Honestly, your sister-in-law-to-be—"

"God forbid."

"When she started telling me to send Dick that book, it suddenly hit me how totally different Dick was. I'd no more give him a book like that. He's—"

She groped for a word.

"Mature?" Faith suggested.

"Yes," Margaret said eagerly. "I suddenly realized, listening to Esther, that whole horrible day—the tea dance—was my fault. Really my fault. In a sneaky sort of way, I was trying to convert him."

"Thank God you're giving up that idea," Faith said.

"I'm not sure I'm giving it up," Margaret said hastily. "I mean—we've got to talk about it sometime. But—dragging him around the school, visiting the chapel—listening to Esther I suddenly realized it was all *unfair*. Almost an insult to Dick's intelligence. Trying to trick him into it."

Faith limited herself to a murmur of assent. If for a moment Margaret thought she was being manipulated or pushed into this opinion, there would be an instant reaction in the opposite direction. But it was difficult to keep still. She almost wanted to shout the exultant news that Margaret Connolly had taken a stride toward freedom. She could hardly wait to tell a certain cynic named Lawrence Donahue.

A half hour later, Faith was struggling to make sense out of *Cymbeline* when Margaret returned her to the present century. "By the way," she said, "would you and Larry like to come to the party for Dwight Slocum?"

"I would say offhand we need two things—an invitation—and a reconciliation."

"I'll ask Dick to see what he can do about the invitation."

For the next ten days Faith kept her discriminating eyes and ears on Margaret. There *was* a change, a small shift toward that other Margaret in whose existence Faith half humorously believed, that second self trapped within the formal, shy, obedient Margaret. This secret, independent spirit spoke now, at least occasionally, grumbling at the utter dullness of scholastic philosophy, exhibiting a wider tolerance for Faith's outrageous opinions on this and other subjects, even urging on Faith a rapprochement with Larry Donahue, with the serene remark, "If I can get along with Dick—"

There were, of course, moments of retreat. Faith saw one, in vivid detail, the day she and Margaret were hurrying across the campus to an after-lunch class. "Margaret," a voice called, "I've been waiting to hear from you." Margaret turned to confront Father Denton Malone. The sight of him had a catastrophic impact. Margaret's whole appearance seemed to change before Faith's eyes. The supple mouth lost some of its firmness, the high-cheeked, delicately boned structure of her face seemed suddenly gaunt, the eyes withdrawn and clouded. Her voice had a haunted quality. "Oh, Father, I'm sorry, I—"

"Don't you think it's about time for a talk?" Father Malone said, exuding the toothy joviality that instantly made Faith's nerves go taut.

"I've been—so busy, Father."

"Of course. Of course," Father Malone said, "but let's not let it go too long. After all, this is—the year of decision, isn't it?"

"Yes," Margaret said. "I've been—praying about it, Father, very hard."

"Good. Good," Father Malone said. "I have no doubt about the answer myself."

"We're late, Meg," Faith said. "Excuse us, Father."

They left Father Malone standing there, vaguely frowning, and resumed their rush to class. "You've got to disappoint him," Faith said as they raced up the stairs.

"That's hardly the point," Margaret snapped, and stalked ahead of Faith down the hall, as if she wanted to avoid contamination.

Faith's first reaction was fury. She spent the period telling herself how ridiculous it was to become involved in this mythic use of a symbolic Margaret. It was simply one of Larry's more diabolical fantasies. What was his original thesis? The well of loneliness bit. Maybe you are just a little queer, Faith dear, because you have this Electra thing with your father, and terrified by your own repressed female libido, you yearn to escape by switching sexes. Margaret, the quintessence of submissive femininity, brings out the lesbian in you. Yes, no doubt about it, Larry Donahue was fun to be around. All by himself, he was the answer to peace of mind and peace of soul.

For the rest of the week Faith saw Margaret through a glaze of icy neutrality. At times she was not sure whether the vision was produced by her own feelings or a change in Margaret. There was something about their whole environment which made it practically impossible to draw a line between the subjective and the objective. The world in which they moved was so intensely feminine, full of condensed, potentially explosive emotions, there were times when Faith felt a kind of pressure enveloping her, like a diver with the bends. Then more than ever she yearned to escape from this insanely artificial, hopelessly unreal world where she was learning nothing, where every day seemed only more loss, more erosion, more slippage down the blank face of something into a void.

Was it just sex? Or was it, as Larry claimed, a combination of the sexual and the metaphysical? He was very strong on the importance of metaphysical influences. Nausea, Jean Paul Sartre's fundamental reaction to life, was the first, the primary step. He had taught her to experience it, acutely. More and more she wondered if he was really awakening her to something she had always recognized. Then, in gusts of terror, she wondered if he had not invented it, injected it into her spiritual bloodstream, as part of his plan to possess her totally.

Purity, that was what Larry wanted. The absolute. A totality of nausea, or of love. With no reservations, no diminutions. No stopping, while Icarus soars aloft, to notice a horse scratching his behind against a tree, no, only the thereness of the flight, the essence of the ecstasy. You never believed in such a possibility before. Realist, you faced the mirror and dismissed romantic love. But there was always the temptation, the yearning. *That* explained Margaret more than anything. She embodied a kind of purity, a possible absolute. She could, if she only awakened to the possibility, achieve this love, this special, timeless living; and Faith, metaphysical voyeur, wanted to be close enough to savor it. Sickening. Now you know, perhaps, a little of what troubles Margaret. There is a kind of terror in perfectionism, of any kind.

But if you believe . . .

If you believe that Christ has called us to follow him, that God through Christ supplies the grace to create this miraculous spiritual symmetry, why do you play the enemy? Why are you the voice that echoes, in a tentative whisper, Larry's angry no? There is only one answer. The state of your soul, my dear girl, is not faith but doubt, a supposedly alarming condition. A thousand difficulties do not constitute a doubt, said Cardinal Newman. A thousand difficulties constitute a thousand doubts, said Lawrence Donahue. But Margaret? If faith is as real as her mother's possessive smile, Father

Malone's soothing voice, why is there this thin wavering line of resistance? Is it because, faith, no matter how much we talk about it, is only one tiny step away from doubt? The substance of things not seen, that was St. Paul's line. But invisibility is so close to non-existence. Even Margaret, the personification of faith (or at least the persona), is infected. So you are both on the pendulum of doubt, Faith thought, looking up from her Shakespeare to study Margaret's impeccable profile, as she bowed her head beside her lamp. But I am farther down, very close to the end, so I experience the really brutal swings, while you get only a gentle sway or two. Yet even that much turbulence is disturbing to someone who is taunted by a dream of inhuman perfection. For a moment Faith felt so sorry for Margaret she almost wept. Then the anger (self-hatred?) returned as the pendulum swung sickeningly back in the other direction.

You know so little, you are so absurdly ignorant. What would you do, what would you feel, if you knew what I know?

# Chapter Eight

Bong, bong, bong. Three o'clock by the automatic chimes in the chapel tower, donated through the generosity of grateful alumnae. With a groan, Father Denton Malone kicked off the covers and struggled into the bathrobe he had draped over the chair beside his bed. This insomnia was becoming a very bad habit. Out in the kitchen he poured himself a glass of milk and added a double shot of Canadian Club to it. Mother's eggnog without the egg. Guaranteed to produce slumber. He sipped the liquor-laced milk and the very taste brought Mother swimming back to him over the years. He could see the round, intense face in the lamplight beside his bed, clutching the old red bathrobe around her. *Denton, I can't sleep. I hate to wake you, but it does me good to talk.*

So he would listen, drowsy head propped against the headboard, while she reminisced about her girlhood days and her dozens of beaus and what had become of them all. Tragedy seemed to have claimed most of them. One had "turned to stone," in her inimitable phrase—the victim of chronic arthritis; another had died in World War I; a third had taken to drink. Some, of course, were successful. There was Dr. Wilson Langley, the city's leading dentist, and Brian Mahoney, president of the Board of Education. All of them much more successful than Tom Malone, and healthier too. Who would think that a mailman could die of heart trouble at the age of thirty-nine? Exercise was supposed to be good for the heart. But thank

God for his pension, and for his son, who was all the things his father had never been. Intelligent, warm, oh, my little sweetheart, what would I do without you? Hugs and kisses, sometimes tears; then, *Finish this now,* and the unforgettable taste of love and liquor carrying him back.

All very touching, but Mother, as she grew older, began drinking her instant eggnogs in the morning and in the afternoon. She began to make less and less sense when Denton came home from school. Her conversation was one long monologue about all the men she knew who had wanted to marry her, and she had turned them down for that idiot Tom Malone. Then she began complaining in even wilder terms about telephone calls from these men, asking her to meet them in hotel rooms. Of course there were no calls. The doctor and the parish priest agreed it was a tragic case of alcoholic deterioration, and with the help of the local ward leader, Mother was placed in the county asylum.

What a terrible day that was, when those two burly ambulance attendants took Mother away, weeping and protesting against the obscene things she was sure they were going to do to her. A sad terrible day. But that good priest, Father James McMahon, was there. Without him, what would have happened to you? There were no close relatives. But you had won a scholarship at St. Francis Prep. A little finagling with the ward leader had persuaded the county hospital to carve enough money off Mother's pension to finance a boarding-out arrangement with the brother of Father McMahon's housekeeper. Good, hard-working people, first generation Irish. He drove a bus, she ran a switchboard at the Medical Center. They had married too late to have children, and at first they tried to be parents to him. But he had nothing in common with Mickey Murphy, whose idea of a good time was a baseball game, or better, if a traveling Irish team was in town, Gaelic football. He had held himself consciously (almost severely, he reproached himself now) aloof from them, buoyed by his friendship with Father McMahon and, more important, with Father Shallow.

This big, burly native of Rochester had become dean of St. Francis only the year before. He swiftly created a new atmosphere at the school, which had tended to be a place where the city's well-to-do Catholics sent their spoiled sons, more for the prestige of it than the education. Father Shallow had ruthlessly expelled the more dissolute examples of this tendency, handed out scholarships by the dozens to the city's poor and browbeat tens of thousands out of the alumni to pay for them. A man of enormous energy, he had demonstrated an astonishing ability to run the school and simultaneously involve himself in the individual lives of his boys. Denton Malone, fatherless, now motherless, had inevitably attracted his special attention.

How he still treasured those hours he had spent after school in the smoke-filled office with that big oblong face cocked engagingly to the right, the quizzical smile playing nervously as Denton talked about his temptations. No doubt because of his mother's breakdown, he had developed a terrible fear of sexual sin. He began to dread the thought of even touching himself while urinating and he would delay going for incredible lengths of time, until his body was racked by explosive pain. Father Shallow had brought him back from this brink of madness, or so it seemed to him then, gently, quietly, firmly, exuding a massive confidence in distinguishing between right and wrong, creating an aura of special power that still made him grow warm with gratitude when he thought of it. Then came that momentous day in sophomore year when Father Shallow had leaned forward, stubbed out his last cigarette of the afternoon and said in that husky knowing voice: *Denton, I think you have a vocation.* A blurring of the room, a great buzzing in the back of his head that had almost overwhelmed him. Could it be true? The idea had filled him with awe.

What happened next was more confusing—a feud between his original mentor, Father McMahon, and Father Shallow. "He thinks he's getting you for the Jesuits, does he," Father McMahon growled when he heard the news of Father Shallow's pronouncement. For two years the tug of war had lasted, blatant on Father McMahon's side, more subtle on Father Shallow's side. It had been a flattering experience, too flattering, Father Malone ruefully saw now. Father McMahon had tempted him with dreams of power in his home city. The fatherless boy, the teacher's pet whom so many boys had sneered at and tormented, would one day walk these streets with authority in his hands and on his lips. *You can be Archbishop of this diocese, boy, before you're through. I guarantee it. You've got the brains and the energy. With me on your side . . .*

The Archbishop and Father McMahon had been in the seminary together. It did not occur to Denton Malone then that the Archbishop had failed to make his old seminary pal even a monsignor,

nor did he stop to think what Father Shallow had gently tried to point out to him—the intellectual world of the Jesuits was far more attuned to his talents. Alas, instead, young Denton made a typically adolescent decision. Father Shallow would have the honor of creating his priesthood, Father McMahon the honor of guiding it. He would enter the diocesan seminary. Long before he emerged from that dreary prison, he realized he had boarded a potential treadmill to spiritual and intellectual oblivion. The poetry he wrote was totally unappreciated by his classmates. The little reputation he won in the Catholic magazines went unnoticed, except for a handful of cultured women in the city to whom he distributed his books. Worse, the entire strategy of his career had gone sour. He had hated the dull monotony of parish work, especially among the Puerto Ricans of the city's South End, and had written numerous letters to the chancery office begging for reassignment. That same disastrous year, Father McMahon died. Not that it mattered. Young Father Malone had realized by now that his spiritual godfather was a cipher. His true spiritual father, the man he had ignored in that last arrogant adolescent year at St. Francis, was Father Shallow.

The tower clock bonged half past three. Father Malone wandered out of the kitchen into his study, the half glass of eggnog still in his hand. He dropped into his swivel chair and flicked on the desk lamp. The light bounced off the littered desk top and glowed against the pictures on the desk. Mother in her wedding dress beside that husky, bright-eyed stranger, Tom Malone.

On the opposite side of the desk in an elaborate gold frame, Father Shallow, standing beside him on ordination day. At least you have tried to repair the damage of those first years. When the Archbishop transferred you out here to Mount St. Monica's (in exasperation, you were privately told) you embraced the job with joyous eagerness and vowed to imitate Father Shallow's example. No man on the eastern seaboard had produced more vocations than Father Shallow. That, once the school had been revitalized, had been his dominant interest. It was, he once explained to Father Malone, why he had brought the children of the poor and the middle class into the school. The rich gave nothing back to the church or to God. Only the poor, and the almost poor, as he sometimes wryly called the middle class, were grateful for the little they had. Once a family passed a certain point in public prestige or worldly goods—in this materialistic society the two were almost synonymous—they lost interest in the things of the spirit. The Kilpatricks and the Cudahys were good examples. Could anything be more negative than their daughters' attitude toward holiness? Of course, there was Mrs. Kilpatrick, a truly noble woman. And she had succeeded in passing her piety on to her daughter Theresa. Landing that one had been almost unbelievably easy. Hardly more than a pat on the head and a word or two of encouragement and she was in the convent. The fact that her father and sister refused to come to her profession as a novice spoke for itself.

Father Malone sipped his instant eggnog and brooded for a moment on the vagaries of the world and the flesh. Father Shallow at the height of his career (he was getting old now) had produced an average of ten vocations a year from a graduating class of less than a hundred. High school was, of course, a happy hunting ground compared to college. Most vocations were planted at thirteen, cultivated carefully by a dedicated few until sixteen or seventeen and then harvested into the seminaries. From colleges, the numbers were tragically fewer, a mournful commentary on what a more extended exposure to a materialistic culture did to the Catholic soul. Nevertheless, working in admittedly fallow soil, in the last six years Father Malone had achieved a staggering average of twelve a year.

Only those, alas, who understood and appreciated the vocation apostolate realized the immensity of his achievement. It was no accident. He had a network of careful contacts with similarly minded nuns and priests in the high schools throughout the state. They passed on to him the names of those, like Theresa Kilpatrick, who had toyed with the decision and seemingly abandoned it. It had proved amazingly easy to reawaken in freshman year the yearning for the peace and fulfillment of a marriage to Christ. The loneliness and uncertainty of the first out-of-home experience predisposed so many souls to seek a new and more profound sense of belonging.

But the Archbishop, that plodding, prudent, maddeningly obtuse man, had remained immune to Father Malone's enthusiasm. From his desk drawer he took out a carbon copy of his twenty-page memorandum, A Plan for A Bureau of Vocations at the Archdiocesan Level. It was a detailed, painstakingly thought-out diagram for quintupling the vocational harvest in the Archdiocese within the next five years. Special vocational counsellors were to be appointed for each Catholic school, beginning with the eighth grades of the grammar schools. They would have training in the theology and psychology of vocations, as well as constant communication through the bureau and at quarterly conferences.

This bureau was to be a seed planted here and imitated in other dioceses until it was a national organization drawing on the immense educational resources of the American Catholic Church, with the same goal, to quintuple the harvest of souls for Christ. Naturally, the man in charge would be Denton Malone. But the Archbishop, with a truly marvelous insensitivity to the Church's real needs, had ignored the document. He was still inclined to remember Father Malone with severity because of his unenthusiasm for parish work. So the "Plan" had mouldered in some chancery file for over a year now, while Father Malone frantically tried to make points with the Archbishop by sparkling at such things as the recent conference on the Catholic family.

The telephone rang. Not again. The midnight mocker. Who else could it be? He picked it up and there was that familiar rasping, slightly drunken voice in his ear. "Hello, Father. How are things going?"

He hung up. A minute later, the phone rang again. With a groan he picked it up again. The same voice, the same mocking question. "Listen," Father Malone said, "I don't know what you do. But I'm teaching five classes tomorrow."

"I'm working my eight hours, Father. I just thought I'd call you to find out how things are going with you and Margaret Connolly. Have you landed her yet?"

"I don't think of it that way."

"Oh, I know, I know. But that's the name of the game, isn't it? She's like one of those big beautiful marlin out there dancing on the hook and you've got to play her until you get her up to the boat. Then whammo, the spiritual gaff underneath the chin, and haul her aboard."

"You are so hopelessly disgusting, I can't believe you have ever been a Catholic."

"Father, how could I know this much without the experience? I've got an Irish name, a drunken Irish father, and an Irish mother who goes to communion every Sunday. I give her all the credit for revealing unto me the precious truth that what you're selling is a lot of shit. For fifteen years she's been praying day and night to get the old man off the sauce. And what's happened? He drinks more than ever."

"God works in mysterious ways."

"So mysterious, Father, that you get the impression He isn't working at all. But let's not debate theology. Tell me how you're making out with Margaret. Do you think you can stop that Protestant from getting his hot hands on her?"

"I told you—"

"Oh, I know. You don't think of it that way. But that's the contest, Father. You versus this fine, clean-cut, honest, hard-working model of Protestant America. I can't wait to see who's going to win."

"What did you say your name was?"

"Father. I'm not that dumb. You can't get me to blurt out what you want to hear. Not that it would matter, for me. But I'm going with one of Margaret's classmates. I know your type. You'd crucify her if you could connect us."

"I haven't the slightest doubt that Margaret has a vocation," Father Malone said icily. "Nor do I have the slightest doubt that God's grace will prevail in her soul. Unless she yields to an unspeakable temptation, which would cut her off from that grace."

"Oh, don't worry about that, Father. I'm coaching this guy. He isn't going to yield to any temptation. That would be made to order for your technique. Loaded with guilt, the ex-virgin flees to her confessor. And what does he tell her? There is only one way you can expiate this sin, Margaret. No, Father, he's going to beat you at your own game. He's going to be purer than pure, the very model of the Christian gentleman."

"I wish I could believe that. Then I would worry less about Margaret's ultimate decision."

"Actually, Father, you're the one I worry about. Doesn't it get you sometimes, out there surrounded by all that snatch? Up to your eyeballs in it, for Christ's sake. Have you ever thought about how it would feel, lying there on top of something like Margaret? She's got a rich hairy one, Father—"

He hung up. Pinpoints of sweat burned in his palms. Stigmata? Ha. What spiritual arrogance. It was the third time the midnight mocker had called. He obviously knew a great deal about Margaret Connolly and Mount St. Monica's. A vicious, twisted soul, almost preternatural in his ability to torment. Father Malone gulped the last of his instant eggnog and gagged. It was warm. Preternatural, that vicious voice. Even supernatural?

Was it possible? Satan himself was attempting to destroy the man who had created a plan that could make the Church triumphant in America and in the whole world. Quintupled vocations would reap, in the next generation, a twenty-five-fold harvest, and the power, a voice speaking on Christ's behalf, that this godless nation and confused Communist-racked world would find irresistible. Perhaps it was Satan himself, or one of his agents (again beware of spiritual arrogance) attempting to torment you into that old adolescent frenzy when you saw everything connected with the body as evil, dirty, menacing. Satan had a habit of overreaching himself. Could there be a better example of it than the suggestion the voice had just made about Margaret Connolly?

If there was one girl among the twenty or thirty he was currently counseling, about whom the mere thought of lust was absurd, it was Margaret. True, she was a beautiful girl. But there was a perfection about her beauty, a kind of armor in the humility and tranquility she so habitually displayed that made it psychologically impossible to think of her lustfully.

Not so Gloria Cochran, with her bright-red lipstick always so heavily and tastelessly applied, the bulging breasts on the thick body beneath the slatternly sweater, the habit of crossing and uncrossing her legs. Lust was not impossible there, it was even probable, if we accept Freud's explanation that dreams are wish fulfillments. That hideous dream of a week ago in which you watched a police *dog* take Gloria from behind, while she grovelled and squealed with pleasure and you slavered above them, the mad priest, peeing at last on the unrepenting obscene consummation. Oh, Lord, Lord, forgive us even our involuntary trespasses, this vile body which we could not hope to overcome without your grace.

Bong, bong, bong, bong, went the tower chimes. Father Malone's eyes drooped. Pavlovian. When insomnia struck, it never seemed to last more than an hour. Drowsily he fell into bed, telling himself he must call Margaret Connolly's mother tomorrow to find out what was happening between Margaret and this Protestant she had met at the beach. Mrs. Connolly was wholeheartedly on his side, and the good fisherman used all the resources he could find. For a moment, he was staring awake, remembering the midnight mocker's vicious description of his vocation work. But what was wrong with being a fisherman? Our Lord himself used the phrase. Surely He could have no objection to one of His faithful servants becoming a fisher of women?

# Chapter Nine

"Have you heard from Larry?"

Margaret's innocent, offhand tone made the words doubly maddening.

"No, why should I?" Faith said.

"Dick called to tell me what time he was picking me up. He said he was sure he could get Larry an invitation. The whole world's invited for the great Dwight Slocum's birthday."

"Thanks, but—I really can't decide whether I want to see him," Faith said. "Or meet the great Dwight Slocum."

"Oh." Margaret frowned at the Shakespeare textbook on her desk. "Is it my fault? I mean—I don't like Larry but that's no reason—"

Faith began to laugh. Margaret looked puzzled at first, then a little angry. "What—?"

"I'm sorry," Faith said, "I'm a little more hysterical than usual tonight. I'm sitting here worrying about you, and you're sitting there worrying about me."

"Oh," Margaret said as she smiled a little ruefully. "Well. We are friends, aren't we? In a way, it's nice."

"And in another way, it's idiotic."

"Yes," Margaret said, "I guess it is."

They went back to their books.

A day drifted by in dull equilibrium. Would Larry call? Do you want him to call? Neither question was answerable. The pendulum had stopped moving. Movement was up to him now. But every time the hall telephone rang, Faith felt the harsh, old-fashioned jangle penetrate her body like a blade. At ten o'clock, another ring, then the almost inaudible footsteps of Eileen Becker, who answered every call. Having no sex life of her own, she was the voyeur personified. Someday, no doubt, she would write a smashing novel about them all and make millions on it. Then, her tiny rap on the door, her mouse-voice squeaking, "Faith. For you."

Walking down the familiar hall with its damp splotched brown walls and scuffed dull-red linoleum, Faith was suddenly, terrifyingly displaced. She watched herself, fragile and afraid, walking toward the menacing old-fashioned black telephone, the receiver perched on top of it like an absurd hat, the empty claw beneath it, the mouthpiece an indignant snout. It was the head of an obscene, devouring animal and Faith walked toward it, blindly, numbly like the maiden to the Minotaur.

*Jesus, get a grip on yourself.* She felt the receiver's dull warmth in her sweaty hand. "Hello," said her hollow voice.

"Hello," Larry said. "How goes it, Mrs. Stotesworth?"

"I think you've got the wrong number."

"Aren't you the little genius responsible for my invitation to the party of the year?"

"Not really."

"I hate indirection. If you wanted to go out with me, why didn't you just call me up and say so?"

"Because I didn't want to go out with you. How's that for openers?"

"It wasn't your idea?"

"It was Margaret's idea."

"Margaret doesn't have ideas."

"I hate to break it to you, but you're really not as clever as you think you are."

"I've always been willing to concede that possibility. If you'd make a few concessions, maybe we'd get somewhere."

"It's what you want to get, not where, that bothers me."

"How many times do I have to tell you, wit is no substitute for intelligence?"

"Once more is my limit."

"I take it you want to go to this Wasp orgy?"

"Not desperately."

"It'll be boring. They're the most boring people in the world."

"But they're such fun to name-drop. Besides, I think you're chicken."

"Prove that accusation, please."

"They intimidate *me*. And you're much more déclassé."

"Not bad. Not bad. That almost hurt."

"I took lessons from a master this summer."

"Lucky girl. Do you really want to go to this thing?"

"I haven't been invited. I'm waiting for an invitation."

"Okay, we'll go. Late."

"Your gallantry is overwhelming. From what tradition of courtliness would you say that form of address derives? Late Spenserian?"

"Early Dreiser."

"Do you want me to come home, or will you risk contamination by coming out here?"

"Come home," he said. "The old jalopy has given up. To be more precise, my father missed the last six payments and they took it back."

"Oh."

"But you won't mind riding trolleys. It does royalty good to mingle with the people occasionally."

"That's why I first started going out with you."

"And look how much you've learned. I'll see you around eight."

He hung up and left Faith standing there in the dim hall, the dead earpiece in her hand. She put it back on its claw and walked slowly down the hall to her room. What was there about him? Physically he was not attractive. That had worried you in your more involuted moments of self-analysis. Did you deliberately select someone six or seven times less handsome than Dick Thornton to reduce the obvious temptation? And why was the temptation obvious? Because belief once weakened, what did stand between you and your animal desires? Oh, *Jesus,* you are trapped into that kind of thinking by this dreadful school. You know, without any need to explain it, that if you believed in absolutely nothing, no God, simply void, even Camus' outrageous Absurdity, you would still retain your dignity as a person. What kind of dignity would be left if you crawled in bed with every Dick Thornton you saw? The idea was repulsive, ridiculous. But in the murky world of the mind, where certainties dissolved, there still lingered the possibility that the other threat was true. No not true, but simply possible, yes, that was the terrifying part of self-consciousness. Without it, we would go contentedly about the business of being fairly intelligent animals, rutting in the spring and summer, dozing away the winter in a cave, eating, sleeping, loving without this nagging, questioning, fearful voice pondering the infinite variety of choices that this miner's lamp in the skull creates for us. Roosevelt said there was nothing to fear but fear itself. But he was speaking as an economist. At twenty, this personal fear, this dread of becoming something that creates revulsion in the mind, is not so easily dismissed.

In the room, Margaret looked up from her books with an almost sly, inquiring expression. "That was Mr. Donahue," Faith said. "You've gotten him an invitation to the party of the year, and he hates me for it."

"I don't understand," Margaret said.

"I wish I didn't," Faith said. "Anyway, we're going eventually. But don't count on seeing me. I think he plans on arriving as late as possible, in the hope that everyone will be stoned by then and he'll be able to stand there in magnificent sobriety and despise them all."

"I won't be stoned," Margaret said.

"You don't count. I mean the Wasps. It's strange, but they really terrify Larry. Even more than I do."

"*You* terrify him?"

"I arouse something in him, and it isn't sexual passion."

"Oh, Faith," Margaret scoffed.

"No one has the slightest interest in my metaphysical insights. The trouble is I don't believe them myself."

In the morning, Margaret professed disappointment that they were not going to double-date. But it was an automatic, not very intense regret. The peculiar serenity created by the absurdities of Esther Sugrue was still in charge. Or was it the simple, uncomplicated happiness of seeing Dick Thornton again? Yes, Faith, of course, that was it. When it comes to uncomplicated happiness, you are a real ignoramus.

Two days later, Faith stepped from the warmth of her father's Cadillac, thanked chauffeur Eddie Dombrowski as elaborately as if he had volunteered to pick her up on his own time, and fled up the steps into more comfortable warmth, that familiar world of home that now balanced precariously between menace and happiness in her mind. Only Minnie, their enormous Negro maid, greeted her. "Your mother, she at a Lady of Charity meeting with th' Archbishop. Your father, he say he be home for dinner as soon as he finish sendin' another dozen niggers to the 'lectric chair." Minnie emitted one of her deep interior chuckles that sounded like Mount Vesuvius trying to explode. "That man, he such a tease. He never send any black men to the 'lectric chair if he can help it. Why, just last month he save one. A poor boy that got hisself railroaded by a crooked judge and jury."

"Really," Faith said, a little shaken to discover Minnie knew more about the decisions of Chief Justice Kilpatrick than his daughter did.

Looming out of the darkness on the stairs was brother Jim. "I wonder how much he got paid for that one?" he said in his most patronizing tone.

"What you mean get paid?" Minnie said indignantly. "How could some poor black boy pay any money, a boy never had ten dollars in his pocket in his whole life?"

"There's got to be an angle in it somewhere."

"I think that's terrible. Saying things like that about yo' own father. Don't you, Miss Faith?"

"I'm not surprised at anything he says." Faith seized her suitcase and trudged up the stairs past Jim.

"What brings you home?"

"A date."

*"Moi aussi."*

Faith looked down at him from the top of the stairs. In the half-light, he looked both strong and weak. The bulky shoulders, the solid torso, and shadowy uncertainty of his face. "I thought I saw Esther getting on the trolley."

"I'm giving her a miniature this weekend."

"Oh, no."

She stormed into her room and flung the suitcase on the bed. Jim was in the doorway a second later, shouting furiously: "I didn't ask you for an opinion."

"You're getting one anyway. She's a creep. She'll make your life miserable."

"She has a genuine, exciting mind."

"Exciting to whom? Sister Concepta, maybe. What have they done to you at that school? Sometimes I think they've performed a frontal lobotomy and replaced your brain with a textbook on scholastic philosophy."

"We are in school to acquire wisdom, aren't we?"

"If that's true, which I doubt in the first place, we're going to the wrong schools."

"Are you sleeping with Larry Donahue?"

The question was beautifully timed. Caught completely off guard, Faith's first reaction was shame. She felt her face grow hot. "If I am, it's none of your business."

"I'm trying to find some explanation for the obvious fact that you have lost your faith."

"You think that's why people lose their faith? Because they start sleeping around? And then they have to rationalize it?"

"It's a common pattern. Sin cuts us off from grace, and when grace goes, wisdom seldom lingers very long."

Faith beat her fists on her suitcase in total frustration. "Jim, can't you see that is tripe? Utter, godawful tripe?"

He looked at her, genuinely dismayed. Whether it was in her mind or in his eyes she was not sure, but Faith suddenly saw memories. Dialogue from that first postwar summer when she had been the bratty but still beloved little sister, worshipping her hero brother with his forty-one missions over Germany. Older images from those golden, almost imaginary prewar summers, playing their favorite make-believe costume game in the attic, with rain drumming on the roof. The Good Old Days, they had called it, and the Judge had entered enthusiastically, at times almost passionately, into the insane fun of recreating the years 1900 to 1913. Jim had been the Handsome Fellow, she the Maiden Sister. There had been a kind of crazy but proud and confident love between them in those days, a childish exaltation, almost a frenzy, a kind of creature born of the Judge's energy and joy. Now you know (no, not really) the source of that joy.

Slipping away (no, please, Jim) those memories, never more than a sheen, a momentary patina of caring on his face as the orthodox mouth resolves itself, the metaphysical eyes narrow. "You have lost your faith. I consider that a very important—may I say even a tragic —event."

"If you say so, Jim, it must be true."

Matching him, sneer for sneer. God, how sick. She began unpacking her suitcase.

"It's not really so surprising when we consider the kind of spiritual atmosphere the head of the family creates. I was discussing it with Esther the other day. A metaphor based on the Mystical Body. If the head of a family declines to cooperate with God's grace, isn't it logical to suppose that for a while at least, his children will experience an acute deprivation? Not total, but—"

"He has a mistress. Do you know that?"

"What?"

Slowly Jim reached out with his right hand and steadied himself on the carved newel of Faith's bed.

"A mistress," she repeated. "For the past fifteen years."

Moral, spiritual, every other kind of superiority had vanished from her brother's face. It was an intensely satisfying sight.

"Who told you?"

"Larry. Apparently everyone in the city knows but us."

"That can't be true."

"All right. A lot of people know."

"Jesus," he said, his head bowed, as if she had struck him an actual blow. "Poor Mother. How could he? I knew he had no morals when it came to politics. No one in this rotten city does. But this—is totally unforgivable."

"It rocked me at first. But is it really so—unforgivable? Take a good look at Mother some one of these days. She isn't exactly what you'd call sexy."

"You foul-mouthed bitch."

There was movement, a flash like an explosion (or her idea of an explosion), and she was crouched against the wall, an intense brightness expanding and contracting around her eyes, and a pain on her face that seemed simultaneously hot and excruciatingly cold. "Oh, oh," she said, struggling erect, filled with hatred.

He was over her, huge, gathering her against him before she could move. She breathed the sweaty male stink of him. What was the couplet she had written for the school paper last year? *Possessed of supernatural powers/at Saint Jerome's they scorn all showers.* "Jesus, Faith, I'm sorry. I—"

"Let me go!" She kicked and smashed at him, tore loose from that scarifying maleness, sobbing, "You hurt me, you hurt me." Yet she knew at the same time it was precisely what she had deserved, he had only returned hurt for hurt. For a moment she loathed this endless self-knowing, this insight into insight. "I hate you," she raged. "I hate everything and everyone in this whole rotten family. Get out of my room before I start throwing things, before I try to kill you with something." She snatched up a nail file and brandished it histrionically, without the slightest intention of using it.

Jim stalked out, giving the door a titanic slam. Faith fled into the bathroom to put a cold washcloth on her battered face and study the damage in the mirror. It still hurt, but it was not turning black and blue. Holding her washcloth to the damaged area with one hand, she tried to read Joyce's *Dubliners*. Were they really Irish in that same stupid, hopelessly futile way, trapped in petty lives, petty politics, hopeless memories of defeat and lost love? She recognized how intensely satisfying it was to think so. It suffused the mind with a sweet-sour sadness that ridiculed every variety of hope. But was it true?

Until this summer she had never really examined her life as part of a larger life, a world. Amazing, now, this lack of social introspection, this blasé acceptance of father, mother, city, church as given, as natural and unassailable as the state's geography. It was not that she had been a vegetable, immune from introspection, but all her self-examination had been in the narrow, moral world of the confessional. It involved nothing larger than the state of Faith's petty personal soul. Strange, but the fate of that white inconstant blur (the image she carried from catechism days) was no longer so frantically important. To understand, once and for all, who they *were*—Judge, mother, brother, Larry, Faith, Margaret—seemed far more urgent.

The dinner bell tinkled, and she heard her mother calling: "Faith, Faith dear?" Down the stairs she went, while Mother smiled benignly at her. "How are you, my dear? I just had the most delightful tea with the Archbishop. He said the most *comp*limentary things about your school."

"How nice," Faith said, realizing with a twist of inner pain that she spoke to this woman the way a parent handled an overtalkative child.

"He said you gave him the feeling that the next generation might well see the triumph of the Church in America. Isn't that marvelous?"

"Absolutely."

The Judge and Jim were already at the table, silently pondering their soup. Mother sat down and repeated the Archbishop's message. "Of course, he includes your school too, Jim. He takes for granted that the Jesuits are producing their usual crop of geniuses."

"I wish I was so sure of that," Jim said. "Frankly, St. Jerome's strikes me as one big swamp of spiritual apathy."

"What the hell does that mean?" growled the Judge.

"We've been trying to organize a cell of Young Christian Students. It's hard to find ten people really interested in committing themselves."

"What, exactly, are Young Christian Students?"

"They derive from the Catholic worker movement in France. They use the cell technique just like the Communists. The goal is to apply Christian principles at all levels of society."

"Isn't that exciting?" Mother said.

"Sounds ridiculous," said the Judge.

"I wouldn't expect you to understand it," Jim said icily.

The Judge's jungle of gray eyebrows contracted and expanded ominously. "Why not?"

"Because you're not interested in the moral and social dimensions of Christianity."

"Maybe I don't think it has any," the Judge said. "Not since Thomas Jefferson wrote the Declaration of Independence."

"Please," said Mother. "I hope you're not going to start arguing about religion. Remember, the last time it brought on the worst attack of my angina . . ."

"What else did the Archbishop have to say?" the Judge asked.

"Well, he could hardly stop talking about the check for the Cathedral. I must say it took my breath away. I had no idea you'd gone over a million dollars again."

The Judge chuckled contentedly. "When we do something, we do it right."

"He says it means the Cathedral will have the finest statuary and stained glass in the country. He's so grateful."

"I didn't even know you were raising money," Faith said.

"We just passed the hat inside the organization," the Judge said. "There was nothing to it."

"You were the chairman?"

"As usual."

Faith felt slightly dizzy for a moment. Reality was simply too confusing. Here was a man who did not believe in the Catholic Church, if his actions meant anything, raising a million dollars to perpetuate it. She almost wanted to shout why, but it would have started a new argument. So she said nothing while the Judge buttered a roll, took a bite, and answered her silent cry as if he had read her mind.

"It's good politics."

"Come now," said Jim. "You're not suggesting the Archbishop is involved—"

"Of course not. He's just there when we need him. Like three years ago, when the new constitution came up for a vote. Don't you remember, they read a pastoral letter in all the churches, telling Catholics to vote against it?"

"There was good reason for that," Jim said fervently. "As I understood it, they were going to force priests to break the seal of the confessional. And they wanted the power to tax church schools—"

"They also had the power to force public officials to testify about their personal finances. That was the one we couldn't tolerate."

"Were the others true—about the church schools and the confessional?" Faith asked.

The Judge smiled momentarily at the roll in his hand. "Well, let's say they were theoretical constructions, based on a close reading of the proposed constitution by a prominent judge."

"Named James Kilpatrick?"

"Please," the Judge said, stuffing the rest of the roll into his mouth. "You know how modest I am." He swallowed the roll and presto, there were the false teeth jutting over his lower lip, while the Mortimer Snerd voice said: "Yethir, we put one over on them hayseeds that time."

Faith laughed, and Mother smiled automatically, only dimly understanding the performance. "Oh, Daddy," she said. She refused to stop using that childish name. Brother Jim managed to force a smile, a feat which was, all things considered, almost miraculous. As for Faith, the racking sound of her own laughter was suddenly unbearable. Why, why, and where had the happiness gone? With no warning to herself or anyone else, she burst into tears.

The Judge was aghast. "For God's sake, what's the matter? Everywhere I go these days women start bawling."

Faith flung her napkin into the half-finished soup and fled upstairs to her room. There she decided her tears were ridiculous and stopped crying instantly. She threw herself on the bed and stared intently at the blank plaster ceiling, rehearsing a conversation she might have with her father if he came in to find out what was wrong with her.

*How's Margaret Halloran?*

*What do you know about her?*

*I'd like to meet her.*

*Who told you?*

*Never mind. Why can't I meet her?*

Absurdity. You would never say one word. You would go on playing the laugh-it-up game with him until death. Those words would destroy the last sad shreds of that laughter, and you could not bear to lose them. You were trapped between past and future and only Lawrence Donahue knew it. There was no one else who could bear the knowledge without destroying either you or the Judge. She fell asleep on this despairing conclusion and awoke at midnight, chilled and stiff, to realize with rueful disappointment that the Judge had not even bothered to visit. The next morning, she stayed in bed until 11 A.M., listlessly flipping the pages of Nietzsche's *Thus Spake Zarathustra,* which Larry had given her. It struck her as windy breast-beating. She was in no mood to believe in supermen.

Downstairs, she was dismayed to find the Judge still eating breakfast, surrounded by his mail. "I knocked on your door last night on my way out," he said. "No answer."

"I was asleep."

"What the hell is eating you? I know what's wrong with your brother. His brain has been softened by sanctifying grace. But I thought you were all right."

"I am all right," Faith said, fingering the glass of orange juice Minnie deposited in front of her.

"I'm not so sure after last night. I'm even less sure this morning." He picked up a piece of stationery covered with large, loose scrawls. "Here's a letter from some bleeding heart priest you're mixed up with, telling me that you think I ought to reduce his jiggaboo parishioner's sentence."

"What?" Faith said blankly.

"Caa-ree is his name," the Judge said, giving it a Southern roll.

"Oh, him. I teach catechism at his church." She floundered through the rest of the explanation while the Judge's eyebrows bristled. "I just thought it sounded like—an unjust sentence."

"Is that so?" the Judge said testily. "You just took Father Carey's word for it? You didn't bother to come home and ask me or someone else who might just happen to know something about it?"

"No," Faith said, her face flushing. She could not remember when he had ever talked to her this way.

"Well, for your information, I consider bribing an election officer a pretty serious offense."

"In this city?"

"In this city or any city," the Judge roared. "Sure, they pulled a lot of rough stuff in the downtown wards in the old days but we don't need it any more. And we won't stand for it. This punk Barton is out on bail telling everybody the judge who sentenced him is a fraud. Next week he's coming up on appeal to me, and I'm sustaining that five-year sentence. Tell that to Father Carey."

The Judge was practically shouting. For a moment Faith wondered if this was a new kind of teasing. But he was unmistakably serious.

"I'm not trying to tell you what to do," she snapped. "If he's guilty you can give him the works as far as I'm concerned. I'm not interested in politics."

"No," said the Judge, gathering his scattered mail. "But you're damn interested in getting a dress for the big party down at Stapleton's tonight. You're damn interested in a ride home in the Cadillac instead of taking that lousy trolley. You're interested in having Minnie around to pick up your pajamas. Where the hell do you think all this comes from?"

"Politics?" Faith asked dazedly. "But you're the Chief Justice—"

Abruptly, the Judge's anger vanished. He had finished stacking his mail. He tapped the letters together like a deck of playing cards and riffled them with his thumb. "To hell with it," he said. "It's too complicated. Maybe it isn't worth explaining in the first place. I never really wanted you to understand it. It's just that sometimes—"

He tapped the letters again. "Ah, the hell with it."

He heaved himself to his full majestic height and gave Faith a smile that was just a little forced. "I'm in a bad mood. I was up till three A.M. listening to a bunch of blatherskites tell lies about World War One." His big hand came down on the back of her neck with a paternal squeeze. "Have a good time at that party tonight. Who's taking you?"

"Larry Donahue."

"Oh Christ. Well, we've argued enough for one morning. Just remember. You'll never get me to walk up the aisle to give you away to that sourball."

"How can I forget it?" Faith said. "It's the third time you've told me."

To her considerable relief, the Judge was not home when Larry arrived that night. After six weeks of separation, she tried to see him with a stranger's eyes. But it was impossible. The thin, tough face struck her the same emotional blow somewhere vaguely above the solar plexus. It was a street urchin's face, elongated to fit a man's head without changing the defiant bitterness of the eyes, the angry disappointment of the mouth. The rest of him only heightened the essential image. The cheap overcoat and the even cheaper shirt, the awful scrambled blue and green one-dollar tie were a kind of uniform that Larry wore with belligerent pride. Her preplanned defenses crumpled at the sight of it.

Mother was no help. She was in one of her more asinine moods. "I'm so *glad* to see Faith going out with a nice Irish-Catholic boy," she said. "At lunch yesterday with the Archbishop, Mrs. Connolly went on and on about Margaret going out with that Protestant fellow. She's *all* upset about it."

"He's not a very good Protestant," Larry said wryly. "Maybe Margaret will convert him."

"That's *exactly* what the Archbishop said," Mother cooed, with a giggle. "He said he'd make it a special intention for one of his Masses this week. Isn't that wonderful?"

"Wonderful," Larry echoed.

They suffered through a long description of Mother's only visit to the Stapleton mansion, some ten years ago when the elder Mrs. Stapleton was still living and invited Mother along with a half-dozen other local Lady Bountifuls to take tea. "It's such a *beautiful* house. I hate to think of you people jitterbugging in it."

"Don't worry, we won't," Faith said. "Mr. Donahue doesn't believe in dancing. He considers it a form of public humiliation."

Outside on the street, in the chilly November darkness, Larry said, "Do you really want to go to this goddamn thing?"

Instantly Faith knew that she had never really expected to go. Or was it the sight of him in those cheap clothes that made the impossibility blatant?

"I don't really care," she lied.

"Sure you do," he said. "You're dressed to the nines."

"How sweet of you to notice."

"How much did it cost?"

"What?"

"The dress."

"None of your damn business."

She stood there shivering while he lit a cigarette. She was a breath away from saying good night when he spoke. "I'm sorry," he said. "I've had a bad day."

"What happened?"

"I saw a good friend of mine get beaten up. Andy Barton. Do you know who he is?"

"I've heard of him."

"He tried to speak down in Washington Park. The cops were laying for him. It was terrible. They knocked all his teeth out. Broke his nose. Then they arrested him."

"God." The wind seemed to snatch the word out of her mouth and send it spinning past him, unheard.

"You don't believe me, do you?"

"I believe you."

"But you don't give a damn."

"Take me to him. Show me."

"Now?" For the first time he sounded defensive.

"Is he still in jail?"

"No. We bailed him out. But he's not exactly in the mood for curiosity seekers."

"Can't you think up a better way to describe me? Or is the whole story a phony?"

"Okay. Let's go."

They hailed a passing cab and after considerable argument persuaded the driver to take them to an address deep in Nighttown. Down a winding street barely wide enough for one-way traffic they crept to a row of sagging brownstones. They went up the stairs, thick with a musky aroma, mingled with cooking odors and an occasional whiff of urine. A thick-bodied Negro woman with a bandanna on her head, looking like Aunt Jemima's daughter, answered Larry's knock.

"Who are you?"

"Donahue. Larry Donahue."

"Oh yes. Andy's bad. Very bad. The doctor says there might be a concussion. His teeth—" Great tears welled in her eyes.

She spoke with scarcely a trace of Southern accent. Are you noticing this, Faith wondered, to avoid thinking about anything more important? Larry introduced Faith in a stricken voice and asked if they could say "just a word" to Barton.

The sister hesitated, then nodded. They followed her down a hall into a small bedroom. A thin, black-skinned Negro lay on a cot in the corner. His head was wrapped in bandages. There were strips of cotton across his gums, and two strips of adhesive on the bridge of his nose. There was a great broken bruise on his cheekbone, beneath his right eye.

"Andy," Larry said, "I just wanted to make sure you were—okay."

Barton nodded slowly. His eyes were clouded. He pointed to his mouth and muttered something through the cotton. It sounded like, "This will cost them money."

"You bet it will, Andy," Larry said. "This is Faith Kilpatrick, the Judge's daughter. She heard about what happened. She asked to come down and tell you she's on your side. Isn't that right, Faith?"

"Yes," Faith said woodenly.

Barton snatched the cotton out of his mouth. Through gaping, bloody gums he snarled, "What about her old man? Will that son of a bitch be on my side next week?"

"The hell with him," Larry said. "We've got to start with the people our age. If we can reach them, who cares about the old farts?"

"Yeah, sure, Larry," Barton shrilled. "You don't have to worry about five years in the pen. Where the hell were you when those clubs started swinging this afternoon?"

"I was hiding under a bush," Larry snapped. "Would it make you feel any better to see me wearing bandages?"

"Maybe it would," Barton snarled. "Maybe it'd make me stop wondering if I'm just another nigger playing patsy for a white hustler."

"You're in pain, Andy," Larry said. "Let's not talk about it now."

"Yeah," Barton said. He stared at the bloody cotton in his hand, then flung it on the floor. "Where's some clean cotton, for Christ's sake?"

The sister came rushing in with a roll of cotton in her hand and began cutting fresh strips. "You'd better go," she said.

"Good night, Andy. I'm really sorry," Larry said.

Andy Barton turned his face to the wall.

Down on the street Larry said, "Let's walk."

They walked for what seemed like hours along totally unfamiliar streets, with the white towers of the city's Medical Center looming through the night on the hill above them. Larry talked and Faith listened as usual. But the tone was different. The mockery, the accusation that had made Faith almost hate him at times, was gone. There was a kind of grief, even guilt in his voice, a new personal dimension. He admitted that making Andy Barton a political gadfly was his idea. He had written his speeches for him, collected clandestine money from anti-organization politicians to back him, bucked him up when he lost his nerve, which he did frequently. "And all the time I knew it was going to turn out this way. I knew they'd cream him. It was necessary. You can't bring down any political system without first creating some martyrs. But I thought I could do it without getting involved emotionally. I didn't realize it would tear my guts out. That's why I didn't want to go see him tonight. I couldn't face him. You saw what I did, I had to lie about you. That faked him off me. For the first time I really wonder if I've got what it takes."

"For what?" Faith asked, suddenly panicky at the way he was affecting her emotions. The spasms of pity she had felt for his poverty had been extinguished by his consistently outrageous manner. Now immense quantities of new pity seemed to be flooding her body and mind.

"To create, to build," Larry said, "to purify this garbage heap somehow. To do it, you have to be ruthless. You can't let your emotions get involved with individuals. To achieve that kind of equilibrium I believe you've got to have a really profound emotional relationship with someone, a kind of perfect rapport. That's why this summer I asked you . . . Well, you know what I asked."

"But what about my emotions?" Faith said. "I'm not supposed to feel anything? Any regret for what I'm giving up? God, the Church, now my father?"

"Of course you'll feel it. Why the hell do you think I chose you? The more you regret what you're giving up, the deeper your commitment to me. Jesus was right about a few things, you know. It's all paradox. The more you give up, the more you treasure what you've given it up for. The greatest sinners make the greatest saints. And vice versa, but He left that one out."

"But, Larry, why does it have to be this way?"

"Because people like you and I can't be happy any other way. Jesus again, the lukewarm. Vomit. That's the kind of people we are. We have to reach for the heights, Faith. Otherwise it isn't worth reaching at all."

"Are they heights—or depths?"

"It's all relative," Larry said.

The almost-winter wind whipped down the street into their faces. Faith shivered again, not sure whether it was his words, or the weather. Here she was, in the heart of the City of Man, but who was her escort? A savior or a destroyer, a twentieth-century Christ or a thirteenth-century Satan? Or simply a very confused, angry, unhappy young man?

"I wish—I wish I could go all the way with you, Larry," she said, "but I don't see the *necessity*."

"Not even after tonight? Not after seeing that black face dripping blood? Those cops belong to your father, you know, just as much as they belong to Dave Shea."

"They don't! He wouldn't beat up anybody. He'd laugh them out of town first. That's where you keep going wrong, Larry. You try to make everything fit your generalizations and it doesn't—people don't."

"They do, but it just takes time—too much time, I guess—for people like you to see it."

They walked in silence for almost a block. "The next time you see the Judge," Larry said, "ask him about Barton. I bet he breaks up telling you what the cops did to him today. When you've got almost absolute power, beating up people who don't matter can be pretty funny."

Faith said nothing.

"Are you scared to ask him?"

"Yes," she said. "But it isn't a fair test. If he knew how I felt about it, he'd take it more seriously. I mean, I could argue with him and he would admit it was wrong."

"Sure, he'd put on an act."

"It wouldn't be an act! He doesn't really believe in beating people up but—"

"He's a cynic. That's his real tragedy. He's got the brains of an idealist and the soul of a cynic."

"He's not a cynic. In the complete, absolute philosophic sense."

"Okay, let's give him an eighty-twenty split. Eighty percent of the time he's a cynic, twenty percent he's on the level. That's not exactly a passing mark."

*Oh, damn you. Why did I go out with you? I think life is some-*

*thing to be enjoyed, not judged, analyzed, idealized, sacrificed. Yet there's no escaping you, no escaping the terrifying sensation that you are right and I am wrong.*

They stood on the corner opposite the Medical Center and she stared up at the huge blank, windowed slab of concrete until it became a hot, wavering blur. Any moment you are going to start bawling like an idiot. That is unacceptable. Desperately, she tried to change the subject. "I wonder if Margaret's enjoying herself."

"Where?"

"At the party. The one that you were supposed to take me to, about three hours ago."

"Oh yeah," Larry said sourly. "She's probably standing in a corner saying her rosary. Either that or she ran home after Dwight Slocum goosed her."

"Wouldn't you be shocked if she was having a wonderful time?"

"Not really. Anything is possible when you've got her looks. But it wouldn't make any difference. When you get back to Mount St. Monica's, you'll see the real Margaret all over again."

"How do you know which one is real?" Faith said fiercely. "Where do you get off being so damn sure of everything?"

"There's a motel, what's it called, The Wagon Wheel? About a mile from your main gate, just off the expressway. If I'm wrong, I'll meet you there on the night of your choice and take you to the best restaurant in the state—your pick. If I'm right, I decide what we'll do."

"That would save a lot of gas, wouldn't it?" Faith said.

"Bet?" Larry said.

"Bet," Faith snapped. "Now take me home."

Ten minutes later, she slumped against the inner door of the silent, empty house and felt angry but authentic fear clutch at her. Ridiculous, you didn't really mean it. It didn't make sense to convert Margaret into this all-powerful symbol. But wouldn't it be wonderful if you won? Up the stairs Faith trudged, and the words in her mind were a kind of scrambled prayer. Don't stand in a corner, Margaret. Don't let Dwight Slocum upset you. I'm depending on you to hold what is left of my fragile little declaration of independence together. I know it makes no sense. You have no connection whatsoever with Judge James Kilpatrick and Andy Barton of the bleeding gums and Larry Donahue, my prince of darkness. But maybe, as the prince has often pointed out, everything is part of everything, if we wait long enough to see the invisible threads. And I want to see them. I want to see them before I can believe.

Faster and faster she went up the stairs till she was racing fear herself into the bedroom. Seize the old battered suitcase, fling books, underwear into it, call a taxi. The last trolley out to Mount St. Monica left the carbarns in twenty minutes. A scribbled note for Mother, *Gone back to school—studying to do.* Another scribbled note for Father, left on his pillow. Would he find it there? Sick thought. *It's not Barton's fault. It was all Larry's idea.* Then downstairs, to shiver on the darkened porch until the taxi beeped and you began the long ride back to school, while the voice inside you simultaneously whispered, *This is crazy.* But life itself was suddenly crazy, from every conceivable point of view, after so many complacent years, when every event seemed to have a cause, and every cause was good. Now all the causes, the faces, the whole city, seemed swallowed in inexplicable chilling darkness and Faith had to find new ways to save—or perhaps to find—her soul.

# Chapter Ten

Sitting beside Dick in his car, Margaret had only half listened as he discussed Dwight Slocum, his fiancée Paula Stapleton, and the other guests they could expect to meet at the party. The names *Slocum, Stapleton* produced a numbing effect on her nerves. This was a more formidable challenge than the Catholic enclave at the beach. Her glimpse of it on the night of the Yacht Club dance had been anything but reassuring. At the Kilpatricks' she had been surrounded and even exalted by that delicious sense of acceptance, of happy camaraderie. More and more, the thought that she was entering a hostile world tonight began to obscure the pleasure of being with Dick again.

"They all sound so—rich," Margaret said. "I've never met many best families."

"They haven't met you either," Dick said.

He told her about Dwight and Paula. "It's an unlikely combination, if you take away the money. Paula's up to her ears in charity drives and social work. She was magna cum laude at Vassar. Most of Dwight's donations are tips to headwaiters—and he hasn't opened a book of his own volition in his entire life. I guess it's just the money. When you've got as much as the Slocums and the Stapletons, there isn't anybody else you can marry."

"I don't think I'll like Dwight."

"Yes, you will. He's a big friendly ape," Dick said. She was surprised by the sudden sharpness in his voice.

A few moments later they rolled up the circular driveway to the Stapleton mansion. Margaret had passed the place a hundred times, but she had never ventured inside the big iron gates as some of the more daring boys in her neighborhood liked to do. Armed guards roamed the property at night and any intruder was guaranteed a good chase. The house bordered an immense park which the Stapletons had given to the city a century ago. Past illuminated flower beds and a lovely fountain, they drove to the house itself, a white-columned colonial mansion with high vaulted windows on the first and second floors. The front door was sheltered by a wooden portico. Beneath it an old-fashioned coach light glistened. A Negro servant in livery opened the car door and another Negro stepped out of the darkness and replaced Dick at the wheel.

They walked into the front hall and Margaret gazed up at a lovely curving stairway with a balustrade so delicate it seemed almost traced on air. Great bunches of flowers stood in huge Chinese vases. Another servant took their coats and directed them "to the front parlor." They strolled down a long panelled hall toward a room already jammed with people.

A tall girl with dark-brown hair greeted them at the door. She was wearing a black jersey afternoon dress. The padded hips, the straightened skirt, with extended side slits, and the big wing collar were direct from the latest Paris showings. The strand of pearls at her throat was equally authentic. "Richard, it's so good to see you." She beamed.

"Hello, Paula," Dick said, and introduced Margaret Connolly to Paula Stapleton.

"Welcome," Paula said. "Any friend of Dick's and all that."

"Where's the terrible tycoon?" Dick said.

"Oh, in there being moody," Paula said. "You know how he is when he finds more than three people in a room."

They moved into the crowd. Couples swirled past them, greeting Dick. Margaret nodded, smiled hello and tried in vain to remember names and faces. Dick plowed ahead, obviously looking for Dwight. Suddenly their path was barred by a tiny dark girl with wide penetrating eyes and a tight determined mouth.

"Hello, Dick," she said.

"Hello, Vicky," Dick said, and reminded Margaret that she had met Victoria Sand at the Yacht Club dance.

"I bet you go to college," she said with a bitter smile.

"Yes," Margaret said.

"How delightfully girlish. What do you study?"

"English literature," Margaret said more cautiously.

"How gorgeous. Have you read Moravia?"

"No, I'm afraid not."

"You simply must," Victoria murmured.

For some strange reason Dick stood paralyzed, watching them. To Margaret's relief, Paula Stapleton reappeared through the crowd and seized Dick by the arm. "He's crouched in the far corner," she said, "and he won't come out until he sees you."

Paula led them into the corner where Dwight Slocum stood talking with another couple. He was a remarkable looking young man, almost too handsome, with wavy dark hair and a wide arrogant mouth. He had a superb build, broad shoulders tapering down to a slim athlete's waist. He was not exactly crouching, but he did look rather morose.

"Smile," Dick said. "This is supposed to be good for you."

"Richard," Dwight said, "a fellow human being. How did you get by the guards? My beloved here has gone to all kinds of trouble to make sure no one but a certified zombie gets into this party."

"Margaret," Dick said, "this is Dwight Slocum. He's a little strange but we try to make allowances."

Dwight's eyes started with Margaret's face and worked their way down to her shoes. It made her feel that she was on appraisal. "You are at least twice as beautiful as this clod said you were. Where have you been all his life?"

Paula groaned. "Listen to him. Would he ever say anything like that to me? Not that you don't deserve it, Margaret."

"I love your dress," Margaret said.

"Did you hear that, Li'l Abner?" Paula said, poking Dwight. "Margaret likes my dress."

"Come on, Margaret," Dwight said. "You're with friends. Tell the truth."

"He wanted to come in dungarees," Paula said.

"Hell, whose birthday is it anyway? I called her up last night and told her I was wearing an old athletic sweater. She nearly melted the phone right out of my hand."

"When are you going to face the fact that civilization is here to stay?" Dick said.

"Darling," Paula said, "if the pain becomes unbearable, you can always catch the night plane to Las Vegas."

"Come with me and it's a deal," Dwight said.

"I'm enjoying myself right here," Paula said.

There was too much tension in Paula's voice, too much mockery on Dwight's face to dismiss the exchange as offhand banter. Sensing this, Margaret found Dick's laugh hollow and almost tasteless. *These people are not happy*. Why do you find that a comforting thought, Margaret?

"What do you say, Margaret, do you want to come instead?" Dwight asked. "Ever been to Las Vegas?"

"No," Margaret said, flustered, and a little angry. "I'm afraid–"

Her mind closed down in complete panic. Dick came to her rescue. "Sorry, Dwight," he said casually, "she's got to get back to school."

"Oh," Paula said, "what school?"

"Mount St. Monica's," Margaret said.

"A Catholic?" Dwight said.

"Is there a law against it?" Dick said.

"Hell no," Dwight said, "it's just that–"

"It's just that you can't stand one of your friends doing something you wouldn't do," Paula said.

"Oh no," Dwight said, "here comes the maturity lecture. It so happens, Miss Stapleton, I like Catholics. Especially Italian Catholics. They have the right attitude towards life–eat, drink, and make love, and do it again tomorrow."

"Would you like to see the rest of the house, Margaret?" Paula asked, deliberately turning away from Dwight. "It's going to be given to the state in another six months."

"Go ahead, Margaret," Dwight sneered, "and don't forget to look impressed."

The moment they were alone in the hall, Paula apologized for Dwight. "He doesn't mean to be so boorish, at least that's what I keep telling myself."

"Oh," Margaret lied, "I thought he was just trying to be funny."

Paula gave her a skeptical smile and began the tour. They wandered through a dining room that seated thirty beneath a huge crystal chandelier, a library with row upon row of leather-bound books reaching up into a shadowed ceiling of elaborate scrollwork, innumerable sitting rooms and parlors with portraits staring down from the walls. Everywhere there were flowers, deep Oriental carpets and mementos of what Paula called Stapletonia—ship models, pictures of factories, weaving machines, railroad trains. It was all so totally different from the Connollys' six rooms on DeVore Street that Margaret was able to accept it without a trace of awe or amazement. It was only difficult to realize Paula thought of it as home.

"I'm going to hate to see this house closed," she said.

"Why are you closing it?"

"It costs too much." She smiled ruefully. "The Stapletons aren't quite as rich as everyone thinks they are. Not since 1929 anyway."

"It's hard to give up—anything you get used to, I suppose."

Does that include states of mind and soul as well as houses, Margaret? Is that what you are doing now, walking through this house making polite conversation with Paula Stapleton? Are you leaving a way of thinking about yourself, humble Margaret, polite, earnest, shy? Is that person disappearing every time you let Dick Thornton take your hand and lead you another step into his different world? If Dwight Slocum was typical of this world, you did not want to go much further.

"How do you like Mount St. Monica?" Paula was saying. "I have a cousin there. Dolores Talbot."

"She's in my class. We eat at the same table."

"Dolores seems to hate it, but then she's always been hard to please."

"I love it."

"Where did you meet Dick?"

"At the shore. This summer."

They were approaching the party again. "I like Dick very much," Paula said. "He's a good influence on Dwight. One of the few."

"You don't include yourself?" Margaret said, forcing a smile.

"I'm afraid not. Dwight and I have had this running argument for years. He wants me to love, honor, and obey him every time he feels like packing up and zooming off on a safari to Tanganyika or a big weekend in Honolulu. But a family means home to me, and home means a place one stays in. If we'd settled it, I might have been able to—keep this place."

"I'm—sorry," Margaret said, for want of a better choice of words. She was embarrassed by the intensity in Paula's voice.

"I've always dreamed of having a big family," Paula said. "I'm an only child."

"I am too," Margaret said.

It was both startling and confusing. Here was this Protestant girl talking about having a big family. Wasn't she supposed to be a passionate advocate of birth control?

"I think four children is the very least you should have, if you can afford them, don't you?"

"Yes," Margaret said. That ominous phrase, *if you can afford them,* was the giveaway. She felt more comfortable again. Paula Stapleton did believe in birth control after all. She did not have the Catholic's faith that God would somehow provide for the children He sent everyone. Puzzling, these Protestants, they seemed so reasonable, but there was always the twisted philosophy of secularism and heresy distorting their thinking. What else explained this girl's attraction to Dwight Slocum?

The rest of the party was pleasant in a harmless way. Margaret found little time or opportunity to worry about what to say. Everyone was too busy saying lively and interesting things to her. Finding Dick in some sort of masculine conclave with Dwight, she wandered idly around the room, stopping to admire an occasional painting or piece of small statuary. Every time she stopped she found herself talking to a man. They were all charming, amusing, and very interested in taking her to dinner. She began to get tired of pointing out Dick Thornton as her escort for the evening.

Oddest of all was an extremely mannered fellow in a suit with a foreign cut. He handed her a glass of champagne and said: "I just told myself I am going to talk to that girl—I'm going to *force* myself to do it—even though we don't have a thing in common."

"How can you be so sure?" Margaret said.

"Extraordinarily beautiful people never have anything in common with me. I am a worshipper at the shrine of beauty—always from a distance. Take my sixth cousin, Dolores Talbot, who has just told me everything I should know about you. I have pursued her with an absolutely mad passion since the age of eight, and she's never given me a backward glance."

Dolores sauntered over, shimmeringly beautiful in a gray faille cocktail dress, cut much too low for Margaret's taste. "He's an utter, total liar, Margaret. I've panted after him for years—or at least after his money—but now I find out he doesn't really have any. It's been my greatest disappointment. Incidentally, this *is* my cousin, Raymond Snodgrass."

"See her wince at the mere mention of that name. I'm defeated before I begin. I've yet to find a woman who wants to change her name to Snodgrass," Raymond said.

"I don't think it's such a terrible name," Margaret said.

"Ah." Raymond stood on his tiptoes, beaming. "Come to dinner with me and I will tell you all about the Snodgrasses. They are a brilliant bunch. They have managed to get themselves killed in every major battle of history. Hastings, Agincourt, Bunker Hill, Waterloo, Bull Run—the Snodgrasses got it in the neck every time."

"How did *you* get here?" Dolores asked.

"We have always made it a point to sire progeny before leaving for the field of battle."

"I knew there was a reason why my guardian angel stopped me from playing in the attic with you after we reached puberty," Dolores said.

"Will you come to dinner and learn the fascinating history of the Snodgrasses? Please disregard all the remarks this *demimondaine* is making against my character."

"I couldn't possibly," Margaret said. "I have a date already."

"Go away," Dolores said, and pushed Raymond back into the crowd. She smiled at Margaret. "I see you've been having a good time."

"I guess I am."

"Thrust and parry. It's really fun if you take it in the right spirit. Most of them are harmless."

"Yes," Margaret said, lagging several dozen feet behind Dolores' meaning.

"But not all of them. Here comes one that isn't."

"Isn't what?" Dwight Slocum said, casually putting his arm around Dolores' waist.

"Harmless. I am warning Margaret here of the perils of local society."

"And that includes me?"

"It *is* you, practically."

"I'm flattered," Dwight said, grinning. "Just for that I'll take you out tomorrow night."

"I'm still a mere schoolgirl. Saturday is my night out."

"Next Saturday then."

"It's taken. For the next ten weeks."

Dolores smiled sweetly, but again Margaret sensed an undercurrent of seriousness in the exchange.

"It's got to happen someday between you and me," Dwight said. "You know that, don't you?"

"No. Mother never told me about the powers of hypnotism. Or is it voodoo? Is that what you're studying on your next world tour?"

"You know what I'd like to do to this one?" Dwight said to Margaret.

Margaret saw an answer was unnecessary.

"In the trophy room, that's where she belongs. The head right up there on the wall. And I'll sit there and say, 'Yes, I got that one on the Parkway, in late November.' "

Dolores calmly pushed up his sleeve and bit him on the forearm. "Remember, the female is more deadly," she said.

"Hey," said Paula, strolling up to them. "That's private property."

"It's neither private nor proper," Dolores said. "You have my sympathy, cousin."

She wandered into the crowd, leaving Margaret alone with Dwight and Paula. "I would just like to know one thing," Dwight said. "Where did old Thornton find you?"

"At the beach. This summer."

"He never brought you down to the Yacht Club? That proves the bastard doesn't trust me."

"Dwight," Paula said, gouging him in the ribs with her elbow.

"Excuse my French," Dwight said. "I forgot I was talking to a convent girl."

Dick appeared and casually took Margaret's hand. "What's going on?" he said. "Or is this a private brawl?"

"I said a naughty word to your convent girl here and our friend, Miss Purina, almost fractured one of my ribs with her elbow."

It was basic in Margaret's credo that you tried to like everyone you met. Christian charity demanded the effort. Most of the time she succeeded. She liked Paula Stapleton, and even that silly Raymond Snodgrass and Dolores Talbot, different though she was in her attitudes and style. But Dwight Slocum was testing her spiritual forebearance to the breaking point. More and more he became the personification of everything she had heard and read about the world of the secular rich. She sensed a kind of evil emanating from this man. She wanted intensely to get away from him as soon as possible.

Yet she stood there and listened in mute amazement as Dick treated Dwight with mocking contempt. "Apologize to her, you big baboon, or I'll be forced to challenge you."

Dwight liked that. He roared with laughter and pounded Dick on the back. "What'll it be, law books at twenty paces?"

"Maybe if I hit you between the eyes with Prosser on torts, some of it would get into your thick skull," Dick said.

"Listen," Dwight said, "how about you and this Irish beauty coming to dinner some night at the country house? You can chaperone me and Paula. I've been trying to get her out there alone for about a century, and she keeps saying no."

"I'll be glad to come. All you have to do is put a certain decoration on this finger," Paula said, holding up her left hand.

"You know I'm going to do that eventually," Dwight said.

"I've only been waiting twelve months. You now have exactly sixty more days to make up your little mind."

"What the hell? Do you hear that, Thornton, I'm being served with an ultimatum. Give me some legal advice quick."

"I understand Sears Roebuck is selling diamonds. You can pay for them on time."

"What the hell kind of advice is that? Sometimes I think you're really a Jew, Thornton, with no opinions of your own. Strictly for sale."

"A good lawyer gives his client the right advice, even when he doesn't want to hear it."

"This has got to be your fault, Margaret," Dwight said. "He had a nice, small bachelor-type mind the last time I saw him."

"Listen, you phony Warbucks," Dick said, "for once listen to something besides the echo of your own voice in that big head of yours."

Dwight stopped laughing. "You're very funny tonight, Richard," he said.

"We try, we try," Dick said.

"Why don't you stay and have dinner here after everyone clears out?" Paula said.

"Sorry," Dick said, "this girl has to get back before eleven or Mother Superior gives her forty lashes."

"You have my deepest sympathy, Thornton," Dwight said. He turned his back on them and headed for the bar.

"I'm so glad you could come, Dick," Paula said, "and you too, Margaret."

She was so polite, composed, serene. How in the world did she stand Dwight Slocum? Margaret wondered as she listened to Dick telling Paula they had had a great time.

They drove away through the crisp fall darkness and stopped for supper at a restaurant on the highway about halfway to school. "Want a drink?" Dick said.

"Just ginger ale."

"No liquor for convent girls?"

"Now you're sounding like Dwight." She was shocked by the angry accusation in her voice.

Dick looked embarrassed. "You'll meet him some other night and he'll be completely charming."

"I find that hard to believe."

"Take my word for it," Dick said.

The waiter rescued them from this imminent confrontation. Margaret felt both annoyed and depressed. It was silly to argue about Dwight Slocum when the rest of the day had been so enjoyable. "In spite of Mr. Slocum, I had a good time."

"They're a pretty good bunch," Dick said. "I had a good time too. Watching you."

"What was I doing?"

"Acting a lot more like the girl I met at the beach. Getting out of that school is good for you, Miss Connolly."

"Now you're being silly."

"I am not being silly," he said. "It is a very profound observation on my part. It's going to cost me a lot of dough in suppers and gasoline."

They arrived back at Mount St. Monica's gates a little after ten. Dick did not drive all the way up to the illuminated main entrance. He stopped just outside the woods and switched off his lights. "Let's not rush," he said. "It's a beautiful night."

They got out of the car and stood beside it. The first clear cold of fall was in the air. The trees stood hushed. There was almost no wind. Above them the stars glittered in a moonless sky.

"Reminds me of that first night—on the beach," Dick said, looking up at the sky.

"Yes," Margaret said. "I love the country. When I was little, *Heidi* was my favorite book."

"I know what you mean," Dick said. "I was so crazy about the sea, I was going to be a commercial fisherman."

Silence for a moment. Then he took her hand. "I'm sorry about

Dwight. I feel pretty much the same way you do about him. About all those people, for that matter. I mean—I know how you feel—out of it—because I've gone through it. I felt that way for a long time. But you can't let it beat you down. You have to learn to use these people. Even people like Dwight. Without letting them touch you in any essential way."

Amazing, how deeply these words moved her. She did not understand what he meant, really, by "touching you in any essential way." In fact, her mind flinched from the words. But the thought that here for the first time was someone who shared her persistent sense of loneliness, of dislocation, made Margaret both enormously joyous and enormously sad.

"I understand," she lied. "I understand."

Gently, without an iota of resistance from her (in fact, the sense of *not happening* was so strong, she was like a spectator watching) and simultaneously *knowing, feeling, thinking* his lips against her mouth, her lips, her cheek untrembling, passive against his harder, harsher skin. Suddenly her arms circled his neck and she returned the kiss, her body against him, her eyes on the distant stars. His hand in her hair, all condensed in a moment that was trying to *speak:* what?

Then Esther Sugrue's words caromed through her mind. *I didn't will it, I didn't.* Margaret drew back in astonished confusion. What did that thought have to do with what was happening?

Dick took her hand. "I think we'd better go in."

They walked up the curving path to Sacré Coeur in silence. What had *happened?* What were those words just beyond the reach of her mind, yet also as distant as the stars? She could not think. Her body was full of nothing but soft warmth.

The outer door jerked open and stolid Sister Agnes Marie, the dean of Mount St. Monica, stepped out. She smiled briefly at them. "Well, Margaret," she said, "I hope when you stay out till the last minute it's a sign that you've had a very good time."

"I did, Sister," she said.

She introduced Dick to Sister Agnes Marie. They exchanged a remark or two about what a gorgeous night it was. Then Dick said, "Good night, Meg."

It was the first time he had called her that since they said goodbye at Paradise Beach. The dreadful memories of the tea dance vanished. "Good night, Dick," she said.

How hopelessly inadequate those words were. They did not carry even a tiny fraction of the meaning she suddenly yearned to hear in them. But what was the meaning? What was the precious, difficult, yet somehow joyous phrase or sentence or paragraph you wanted to say? You don't know. You don't know. What a stupid girl you are.

In the quiet empty room (thank God, Faith was home for the weekend) Margaret sank into the Morris chair by the window. Desperately she struggled to control the slippery, sliding chaotic world of her mind. It was like the picture "One Million B.C.," primeval, murky fumes and absurd mysterious islands in a sea of bubbling lava.

*Stop.* It was only one kiss, Margaret, and one kiss hardly meant you were in love. No, love was much more serious. But still a kiss was an act. It went beyond words, it was hard to believe how far beyond words it went. You really did not know how far until it happened. You were incredibly ignorant. But that was your secret. No one knew how incredibly ignorant Margaret Connolly was. Not even Faith. Certainly not all those sophisticated friends of Dick Thornton who seemed to accept Margaret Connolly because of the way she looked.

In the lamplight, Margaret could see her reflection in the window. Listen to me, you out there. Stop looking so solemn. Someone in your position needs a sense of humor. Learn to laugh at yourself a little. No. Still not a smile. Well, you may be right. Your situation may be terribly, terribly dangerous, and you are too stupid to know it. You may be in a state of suspended animation, which will suddenly cease—and crash, you will find yourself flat on the cold, cold earth, wide awake. Maybe not, too. Maybe it's a permanent condition. Maybe everyone—even those brilliant, charming people at the party—is out there with you in dark, uncharted space, groping toward some sort of permanent living place.

"For God's sake."

Faith's normally boisterous voice was a whisper. She closed the door with maximum care and tiptoed over to her bed. Margaret smiled indifferently at her roommate. "I thought you were home for the weekend."

"I decided to come back," Faith whispered. "I couldn't wait to find out if Dwight Slocum had succeeded in raping you."

"Oh, don't be silly. He's just a little crazy, that's all. That's what Dick says."

"What else did Dick say—and do?"

Margaret hesitated and looked away, toward the girl in the dark window. "He . . . kissed me."

"At last it's happened."

"No," Margaret said. "Don't you remember the time that horrible Kelly boy kissed me in freshman year?"

"And you ran upstairs and threw up. Almost on me."

"This was different. Completely different."

"Come on, tell me everything."

"I had a wonderful time," Margaret said, still avoiding Faith's eyes. "It was a good party. I was surprised—they weren't Catholics —but I didn't have any trouble talking to them—"

"Come on, tell in *detail,*" Faith said.

*Why not? She wanted to tell someone.* In a moment she was giving Faith practically verbatim transcripts of her talks with Paula Stapleton and Dwight Slocum, Victoria Sand and one or two other guests. "Honestly, Faith," Margaret was saying, "I was so amazed—"

Faith was holding up her hand. *Click, click, click, click* came down the hall toward them—the rosary beads of the prefect. The penalty for staying up after hours was eight demerits.

"Get in bed. Don't undress," Faith hissed. "Quick." She switched off the desk lamp and leaped under her own covers. Margaret stumbled across the darkened room and fell into her bed.

A second later, the nun shoved the door open without knocking and stepped across the threshold. "I heard voices in here," she said, and shot her flashlight toward Faith. It was Sister Mary Benedict, one of the school's less pleasant prefects.

"Maybe you're becoming a mystic, Sister," Faith said.

Sister Mary Benedict laughed dryly. "I'd like to think so," she said. "For your sakes as well as my own."

The light played abruptly over Margaret. She kept her face in the pillow and did not move. "Was Miss Connolly too tired to take the spread off her bed?" Sister Mary Benedict asked.

"That's exactly what happened, Sister," Faith said. "She's all worn out from trying to take the spread off herself. She has the biggest one in the whole school, you know . . ."

Sister Mary Benedict laughed again in her mirthless way. "Well, wake her up and tell her to take it off," she said. "Before you go to sleep."

"Yes, Sister," Faith said solemnly.

"All right. And then go to sleep. Hear?"

"Yes, Sister."

The footsteps receded down the hall. Faith lit her bed lamp and threw a blanket over it. Margaret still had not moved. Faith bounded over and gave her a wallop across the behind.

"Get up, Miss Spread of the Year," she said.

Margaret got up quickly and hurried to the closet and got her pajamas. "She might come back," she said as she undressed. "Put out the light."

"She won't come back. Relax."

"How do *you* know?" Margaret whispered angrily. She was suddenly angry at everyone—Dick, Faith, herself. The aura was gone. The girl outside the window had vanished.

"I've made a study of the habits of hall prefects. Only an atomic explosion brings them back."

Margaret buttoned her pajamas and turned off the light. "Good night," she said.

"I'm not sleepy," Faith complained. "I want to hear what else happened."

"It'll keep till morning."

Faith gave an annoyed grunt. She rolled over in her bed and was still. Margaret moved restlessly. No position was comfortable. She even tried lying on her stomach, Faith's favorite position, but nothing worked. Then she became aware of the thoughts that were filtering through her concentration on sleep. *A sin. You took pleasure in it. You're not married and you'll never marry him. The next time it will be two, no, ten kisses, and the next time . . .*

"Faith. Do you think it's a sin?" She was startled by the sepulchral sound of her own voice.

"What's a sin?" Faith said, almost equally sepulchral in the darkness.

"Kissing someone like that."

"No," Faith said.

"It didn't feel like a sin," Margaret said, "but the religion book says it is—to kiss someone carnally."

"Are you in love with Dick?"

"I don't know."

"You act like you are."

"You can't just—decide something like that. What difference does it make anyway?"

"All the difference in the world."

"I don't see how love makes any difference at all."

"I take it back," Faith said. "If you were in love you couldn't say that."

Margaret slept poorly. She repeatedly saw herself and Faith and Father Malone in a church that was decorated for a wedding. But there was no bridegroom or crowd of well-wishers. Father Malone kept glaring down at Faith and shouting: "She is married to God." Margaret herself said nothing. All she could think about was the girl outside the window who had had a very serious accident and was in a hospital. Dick Thornton was with her—and that meant he was not coming to this wedding service. It made her furious.

The shrill clang of the alarm clock scattered these berserk images. Margaret sat up and stared sleepily around the suddenly unfamiliar room. The windows were gray, with a thin coat of frost on them. Opposite, Faith sat up in her bed and grimaced at her. For the hundredth time Margaret marveled at the childlike quality of her expression, unmasked in half sleep from any artificial emotion.

"Happy birthday, sourpuss," Faith said.

"Oh, I thought you'd forget."

"Do you think we're all like you around here? Some of us have emotions."

"I have emotions."

"You're twenty-one. Does that mean anything to you on this dismal October morning?"

Faith hopped across the freezing floor to the closet for her slippers. She consistently forgot to leave them under the bed.

"No," Margaret said, "why should it?"

"That's what I mean about emotions," Faith said from the closet.

"What should it mean?"

"If you don't know," Faith said, "it won't do me any good to tell you."

"Oh, you're being stupid again."

Margaret frowned at the clock. "We're going to be late for Mass."

"Did you tell Dick today was your birthday?"

Still sleepy, Margaret spoke without thinking. "No. I was afraid to, I guess."

They washed and dressed at the usual frantic pace and were in the church by five of eight. Father Malone said the Mass in his familiar solemn, stately fashion. It was one of the things Margaret liked most about him. So many priests dashed through the liturgy, apparently thinking they were doing the congregation a favor. More than once Margaret had heard her pastor, Monsignor O'Sullivan, say to her mother, "Well, I got you girls out of there in seventeen minutes this morning. You can't beat that." Father Malone made you feel that every movement, every prayer was profoundly important.

Margaret finished her seat-checking and sat down beside Faith as Father Malone finished reading the Gospel in Latin and walked slowly to the small pulpit at the altar rail. He paused for a moment, shuffling some papers, then placing both hands on the lectern said, "The subject I want to discuss with you today, my dear girls, has nothing to do with this Sunday's Gospel. But it has a great deal to do with the salvation of your immortal souls."

Margaret was still arranging her missal when he said these opening words. She looked up, automatically. Where they sat, in the first pews, with the rest of the senior class, Father Malone was almost close enough to reach out and touch them. She had never seen him so stern. He looked a foot taller than usual, in the raised pulpit. Now he leaned on one elbow, as he often did in class, but there was an aggressive quality in the motion. "The subject I want to discuss is the Sixth Commandment and its violation here at Mount St. Monica."

There was another long pause as these words slowly sank into his audience, causing a long uneasy ripple of movement.

Beside her Margaret heard Faith mutter, "Oh, for God's sake." Then Father Malone was speaking again. "You would not suppose that the Sixth Commandment is being violated here, of all places, would you? Thirty miles away, in the city, it is a common practice, such violation, so common no one thinks very much about it. But here, on these sanctified grounds, dedicated to the Queen of Virgins, the Mother of God, it *is* shocking. And we *are* going to think about it!

"I am sure many of you have adjusted your consciences nicely to this violation. Just as you have to shorts and slacks and two-piece bathing suits. But adjustment does not carry any weight in the eyes of God. And it will not carry any weight in the eyes of those of us who are entrusted with the care of your immortal souls!

"A chance observer who wandered onto this campus on a Saturday night, thinking that it would be a pleasant place for a solitary ramble, would be the most surprised person in the world. For wherever he went, he would find young people, Mount St. Monica's girls and their escorts, in parked cars, on benches, yes, in the very shadows of the main entrance, saying good night for a half and three-quarters of an hour.

"Necking! That's what they call it, my dear girls, in the more sophisticated communities. It is a pastime that young Americans play at by the hour, I am told. And apparently the habits of this godless country of ours have penetrated even this sanctuary of truth and grace."

He waited a moment and leaned forward dramatically.

"Well, it is a sin! That is what I am going to drive home to you this morning, my dear young women. *It is a sin!* No matter what you call it, saying good night, necking, a party pastime, it is still a sin. Almighty God did not give you those bodies, temples of the Holy Ghost, to be playthings for some young wiseacre's leisure. He gave them to you to be used according to His will!

"You yourselves, each of you (and I could not begin to express my shock at discovering just who, how many, make a habit of this), know in your hearts that it is a sin, that you are defiling yourselves.

"And I am warning you now," Father Malone went on, his voice rising, "that I have discussed this situation with Mother President, and she has assured me that she will not tolerate it, and that any offender will be ipso facto expelled. A physician would not allow a patient under his care to willfully and maliciously destroy his health—so we who are entrusted with the health of your souls will not sit idly by and watch you destroy yourselves spiritually. I will not raise a little finger to help a girl who is expelled for this offense. And no one else will. Let this be a warning!

"And let each of you, now, before this sacred altar, vow to the Blessed Mother that you will never commit this sin again, and promise to confess it, at the earliest opportunity, if you have it on your souls.

"The Gospel for today."

Margaret rose numbly and stood while he read the story of the woman with an issue of blood. Suddenly she found herself arguing angrily with Father Malone. No matter how many times she kissed Dick, she did not commit a sin. But it was only a tiny flicker of defiance and it went out like a wet match. She stood alone, empty, forlorn. How could she resist this clear warning from God? How could she deny the impact of it on her soul?

Up in the room after breakfast, Faith sat morosely in the Morris chair and stared out the window. Margaret flipped the pages of an English book. The gray overcast sky persisted. She could feel scraps of raw cold wind filtering through the loose windowpane. Neither spoke for about ten minutes.

"Do you think he did it on purpose?" Faith finally said.

"Don't be silly."

"Do you think he's above it?"

"Please don't talk like that." Margaret's voice sounded mournful in her own ears. "I don't want to argue about it."

"You should talk about it. He's obviously got you all worked up."

"I'm going to confess it," Margaret said. "There's nothing else I can do."

Faith groaned. "Don't go to him, Meg. Try some other priest."

"Why? Confession is a sacrament. The priest's personality doesn't have anything to do with it."

"It has plenty to do with it."

"It doesn't. Honestly, you'd think sometimes you never went to a Catholic school."

"I wish I never did."

"There's confession today after benediction," Margaret said. "I'm going."

Faith flung herself down on her bed. After about ten minutes of silence, she said. "Confess it to me. I guarantee absolution."

"I don't see anything funny about it, Faith."

If Margaret was just a little pleased to find herself resisting Faith so majestically, the emotion vanished swiftly as she contemplated the prospect of confessing to Father Malone. It would have been difficult to confess a sin of impurity to any priest, but to Father Malone, who so often spoke with admiration of her character, her spiritual gifts, it would be doubly agonizing. For a moment she felt a dull resentment against Dick Thornton and his insistent pursuit. But it was unfair to blame Dick for something which to him meant no more than holding hands. If you have a higher moral standard, Margaret, it is up to you to impose it. You could not expect him to read your mind, much less your religion book.

At noon there was another ordeal—a birthday visit from Mother with presents and a solid hour of conversation about cousins and neighbors and Mrs. Kilpatrick's latest benefit. Margaret's birthday present was a five-volume commentary on St. Thomas Aquinas called *A Companion to the Summa.*

"Father Malone suggested it," Mother said. "I tried to read one *paragraph* and I got a headache. He said you'd love it."

"I'm sure I will, Mother."

"Your father said he thought you'd rather have a new party dress now that you're in *high society*. But I told him I knew my daughter and she'd much rather have these." She gave the books an authoritative pat.

"Of course, Mother," Margaret said.

She was barely listening. In her mind she was three hours ahead, watching Father Malone bow and chant his way through the stately ritual of benediction while off to the left the dark, silent confessional brooded. There would be only a handful of girls at benediction. It was not compulsory. Afterward, even fewer would go to confession. As few as possible, Margaret hoped. There was a nasty tradition in the school that Sunday confession was provided for those who had been seduced on Saturday night.

"I told him you were the last person in the world to be impressed by going to a party at the Stapletons'. But it must have been *fascinating*. Tell me all about it."

Mother listened greedily while Margaret gave her a flat and barren narration of her evening.

"Oh, I can't wait to tell Mrs. Loughran," she said, "but I still don't see how this Thornton boy is part of that crowd. After all, he doesn't have any money, does he?"

"No," Margaret said, and suddenly found herself tempted to add in a tone of fierce rebuke, *but he will.*

She stifled the impulse and let Mother chatter on for another twenty minutes, then got rid of her by announcing an urgent need to study. Up in her room she did nothing but stare out the window at the wintry sky while Faith dozed on the bed. Three o'clock finally came, and with it, the incense, the hymns of benediction, Father Malone in gold robes holding up the glittering monstrance with the white Host at its center, the symbol of Christ, Son of God, sun of the spiritual universe. Then it was over and she waited in the silent church with only three other girls, all freshmen, while Father Malone shed his robes and walked swiftly down the aisle to the waiting confessional.

Margaret entered the upright coffin-like box, closed the door behind her and waited in the darkness while Father Malone settled himself on the other side of the wooden wall. Finally, he drew back the screen on the small eye-level window. Margaret leaned toward the wire netting and in a tense hurried voice whispered into the darkness: "Bless me, Father, for I have sinned since my last confession which was one week ago . . ."

She stopped, her throat constricted with dread.

There was a heavy shifting sound in the darkness on the other side of the window.

"Yes, Margaret, go on."

"I—was late for Mass once."

"How late? Seriously?"

"No. Just a few minutes."

"Where was the priest?"

"He was at the Epistle."

"Don't let lateness ever become a habit, Margaret."

"No, Father."

"All right, go on."

"I lied once."

"How?"

"I told one of the Sisters I didn't know where my roommate was when I did—know."

"Where was she?"

"Playing bridge in another room."

"Why did you do that?"

"Because she's—my best friend."

"Margaret, you have rare gifts, a rare chance for sanctity, don't endanger it for anyone."

"Yes, Father."

"All right, go on."

"I—" Margaret forced the words out. "Committed an impure act last night."

"You what?" Father Malone's voice rose not in volume but in intensity.

"I com—committed—"

Suddenly the darkness swirled in front of Margaret's eyes as if it had been stirred by a giant spoon. Her mind raced weirdly back across fifteen years to her first confession when her brain had gone utterly blank and she had not been able to remember a single one of the six sins she had so carefully rehearsed for three previous weeks. The same thing was happening now.

"Margaret, are you all right?"

"Yes, I will be—in a second."

"Margaret, there are other girls waiting."

"Father . . . I want to confess this. I want to terribly. But I want to see you and talk to you about it. I'm so—mixed up."

"All right, Margaret. All right. Suppose you just confess it now and we'll talk about it later. Let's see. How about tonight at five thirty?"

"Yes. Yes, Father."

A great surge of relief made Margaret's body feel almost weightless. She would not have to answer questions now. It was impossible to answer questions here in the darkness where the answers had to be brief and literal, and for days after you were haunted by the fear that you had not told the whole truth and were not really forgiven.

"Now go ahead with your confession, Margaret."

"I've been dating a boy. Last night when we were saying good night he kissed me. We kissed—I mean—"

Father Malone sighed. Then after a moment of unbearable silence he asked, "Is there anything else?"

"No, Father."

"All right. For your penance say three decades of the rosary. Now make an act of contrition and I'll give you absolution."

He began to mutter the Latin words for absolution. Margaret's tight throat made her voice slightly hoarse; the sound somehow interfered with her desperate effort to understand and mean every word of the act of contrition.

"Oh my God, I am heartily sorry for having offended Thee, and I detest all my sins, not only because I dread the loss of Heaven and the pains of Hell, but most of all because they offend Thee, my God, Who are all good and worthy of all my love. I firmly resolve with the help of Thy Grace to confess my sins, do penance and amend my life. Amen."

"All right. I'll see you at five thirty."

"Yes, Father."

Blundering out of the confessional into the dim church, Margaret almost collided with one of the freshmen. She brushed past her and hurried up the narrow side aisle to the altar, where she knelt before a blue-robed, blank-faced statue of the Blessed Virgin to say her penance.

A half-hour later, her knees aching and her brain slightly numb, Margaret wandered morosely across the campus into the woods. Stripped and tattered after their last burst of October glory, the trees seemed to suit her mood.

"Good afternoon, Margaret."

Sister Agnes Marie, the dean of Mount St. Monica, was coming toward her down a side path. Beside her, tall and frozen-eyed, stalked Sister Mary Benedict.

"Good afternoon, Sister," she said.

"I haven't seen you since school opened. Did you have a good summer?" Sister Agnes Marie said.

"Yes," Margaret said. "I spent three weeks with Faith Kilpatrick at Paradise Beach."

"Ah," Sister Agnes Marie said, her stolid face coming alive, "I love that place. I spent all my high school summers down there."

"I hope you had some time to think, Margaret," Sister Mary Benedict said.

"I beg your pardon, Sister?"

"Think. About your vocation."

"Oh. I—I thought about it, Sister."

"I wonder if this is the time, much less the place, for such difficult questions," Sister Agnes Marie said mildly. "For one thing I find it almost impossible to think clearly about a vocation when the preceding topic has been Paradise Beach."

"It is quite a contrast, Sister," Margaret said.

"How is your roommate Faith? Still denouncing our system of education?"

"I'm—afraid so, Sister," Margaret said, trying to conceal her bewilderment. How did Sister Agnes Marie know so much about the personal lives of everyone in the school? She constantly amazed girls by asking them about spiritual problems, boy friends, conflicts with parents and teachers.

"I've always been rather puzzled," Sister Mary Benedict said, "why Margaret chose that girl as a roommate."

"There may be more to Margaret than meets the eye," Sister Agnes Marie said playfully. "Beneath that docile, serene exterior she may be thinking very, very naughty thoughts."

"Not really, Sister."

"I don't think so either," Sister Agnes Marie said.

Back in the room Margaret found Faith paging through *A Companion to the Summa.* "Who gave you this garbage?" she said.

"My mother."

"At Father Malone's suggestion?"

"Yes."

"Did he give you absolution?"

"Yes."

"Congratulations."

Margaret immersed herself in Shakespeare's *Coriolanus* until five fifteen. Then she silently put on her coat and walked to the door.

"Where are you going?"

"To see Father Malone."

"Oh. It's that sort of treatment."

Was it true? You are getting part of a carefully worked out formula designed to make you say and do and think what Father Malone wanted? Were others, such as Sister Agnes Marie and Sister Mary Benedict, part of the plot? The mere idea was ridiculous. Margaret Connolly simply was not worth thc trouble.

"He's just worried about me, that's all."

"Worried about losing a good prospect."

Margaret slammed the door, hard. It was the best possible answer. But outside in the gloomy twilight, her bravado dwindled. She walked slowly toward the small white chaplain's cottage, desperately wishing there was some way to avoid this meeting. It would be so much easier if she could settle the upheaval in her mind alone. It was the first time she had ever felt this desire to be alone, to think her own thoughts in silence. It was a new wish, and not an easy one to realize because until now she had allowed other people to help her decide so many things.

She hesitated at the foot of the uneven wooden steps. Much too late to retreat—if you really wanted to retreat. What was there to fear, really? You are under God's guidance, and this man is God's spokesman here, in these vital formative years of your life. One, two, three, four steps and you are on the porch, ringing the bell.

"Hello, Margaret," said Father Malone's cheerful voice. She knew that did not necessarily mean he was cheerful. He often used that voice when he came into class in one of his black moods. He opened the door and stood there smiling at her beneath the bare bulb. The harsh downward light broke his face into odd disconnected patches of flesh and darkness. It made his smile look disconcertingly crafty. An illusion, of course. Margaret usually liked Father Malone very much when he smiled. He was a handsome man; too handsome to be real, according to Faith.

"Good evening, Father. I'm sorry I'm late."

"Perfectly all right, perfectly all right. Come in."

She followed him down the hall into the study. The fluorescent desk lamp was the only illumination in the big square room. Margaret waited while he preceded her once more, and dropped into the swivel chair behind the desk.

"Sit down, Margaret. And happy birthday."

"Thank you, Father."

Margaret sat down in the straight chair beside the desk, which was, as usual, covered with a confusion of books, papers and magazines. Rising above the debris was a silver-framed picture of Father Malone's mother. It was a wedding picture—something that always struck Margaret as somehow sad and touchingly sweet.

"How's your mother, Margaret?" he said as she sat down. "As cheerful and charming as ever?"

"Oh—yes, she's fine, thank you," Margaret said.

Father Malone looked away and fiddled abstractedly with a cigarette lighter while she adjusted her skirt. Then he swiveled slowly in her direction again. "She sounded a little tired the last time I talked with her on the phone. Or worried."

"I don't know why she should be tired. She hasn't had you to dinner in a long while now."

If Faith had said it, that would have been a joke. But Margaret simply could not match her manner to her intention. There was no playful impudence in her voice. The tone was flat and almost unpleasant. What was wrong?

Father Malone smiled briefly. "Your mother's a wonderful cook. But you don't follow in her footsteps, do you?"

For a moment Margaret remembered, with just a trace of annoyance, the night she had cooked dinner for her father, the words of his compliment, *You'll make some man a good wife someday.* But to be honest, steak and home-fried potatoes was the only meal she would dare to tackle. "I'm afraid not, Father," Margaret said, studying her hands.

"Nothing to worry about. It's undoubtedly a sign that you have other . . . less worldly gifts."

There was a moment of silence in which Margaret realized that she was expected to say something, but could find no words.

"Which brings us," Father Malone said, leaning forward and placing both arms on his desk, "to what we want to talk about tonight."

Margaret could not meet his eyes. "Yes, Father."

"I was extremely shocked by your confession this afternoon, Margaret. But I was not surprised."

"I—don't know what you mean, Father."

"Do you know why I preached that sermon this morning, Margaret?"

"I . . . have no idea, Father."

"Because of you, Margaret. Your mother told me about you . . . and this fellow. It pains me to admit it, but I watched from my study window and saw you necking with him. I said to myself, If this can happen to Margaret, what about the rest of the girls?"

Margaret kept her eyes on her hands, clenched knots. Now he would tell her how disgusting she was, how seriously she had sinned. She waited, her body rigid with shame.

But Father Malone's voice was amazingly gentle: "Tell me what happened, from the beginning, Margaret."

"Well—I was saying good night to Dick, and he kissed me. We held it—a long time. It made me feel—strange." She looked up pleadingly. "But that's all, really."

"Did you try to persuade him in any way?"

"No, Father."

"Did you try to stop him?"

Margaret lowered her head. "No, Father, I didn't."

"Did his tongue invade your mouth?"

"No, Father."

"Did his hands explore any part of your body?"

"No, absolutely not, Father!"

Father Malone leaned back in his swivel chair. He seemed relieved—like a doctor who had finished the difficult part of an examination.

"You don't mind my smoking, do you?"

"No, Father."

He slipped a cigarette out of a half-empty pack, plucked a large silver lighter from a pile of papers and lit up. There was a dry sucking sound as he took the long deep first pull. Margaret had heard the sound a hundred times before and still, something in her mind or body—she did not know which—recoiled from it. What followed was equally familiar; Father Malone unhooked the top button of his cassock and threw his round white collar on the desk. Then he leaned back in the swivel chair again, tilted his head a little to one side and said:

"Margaret, I've tried to talk to you about this fellow, but you don't seem to want to cooperate."

"I'm sorry, Father. I just didn't see any reason to make a fuss about him."

"But now you do."

Margaret met his eyes. "No, Father," she said. "I still don't."

Father Malone slouched in his chair and regarded her with mild disappointment. "Now, Margaret," he said, in a soft, quietly patient voice, "tell me in your own words why you're going out with this fellow."

"Well . . . because I enjoy his company, I suppose."

Father Malone nodded and rolled his eyes to one side. Margaret gathered she had given the expected wrong answer. He leaned back in his chair again and took another long sucking pull on the cigarette. Then he shoved the chair away from the desk and walked around and past her.

In the middle of the room, he turned and looked at her. "We've had a lot of talks over the past few years, haven't we, Margaret?"

"Yes, Father."

"I think we discussed pretty thoroughly how . . . our bodies desire things our souls despise, didn't we?"

"Yes, Father."

Margaret felt her face and neck and arms grow hot. They had not really discussed it thoroughly. Father Malone had confined himself to general statements. Remarks like: *Sexual desire can be sublimated, Margaret.* Or: *Our bodies have appetites but that does not mean we have to satisfy them.* But he became so agitated when he attacked the subject, pacing up and down, staring fixedly away from Margaret, he communicated an acute unease to her.

Father Malone stared at the picture of his mother on his desk. "Our animal desires, Margaret, are always with us."

"Yes, Father."

"Now this young fellow, he's very handsome, isn't he? Sort of the opposite of me, right?"

He laughed heavily, but Margaret was unable to force a smile. "I suppose you'd . . . say he's handsome, Father."

Father Malone's face grew solemn. He came back to the desk to crush out his cigarette. He spoke as the acrid smoke swirled in Margaret's face, making her eyes water.

"I've told you again and again, Margaret. You have rare gifts. A rare chance for sanctity."

Margaret shook her head and slowly raised her eyes to meet his.

"It's hard to believe," she said. "I never think of myself that way."

"That's one of the most beautiful signs. You're perfectly humble."

Again he waited for a response. But Margaret could find nothing to say. Father Malone lit another cigarette.

"Sanctity is a goal, a destination, Margaret. We must race for it. There are obstacles in our path. Obstacles within us. Around us. People around us, for instance."

He took a deep pull on the cigarette and exhaled slowly.

"You met this fellow with—through your roommate, Faith Kilpatrick, didn't you?"

Margaret's hands clasped and unclasped. She shifted in her chair. "I'm sorry, Father. We've talked about Faith before. We make good roommates."

"How can you say that, Margaret, after what's happened?"

"It's true, Father. We get along so—"

He stepped back a little. "Can't you see I am only thinking of your spiritual welfare, Margaret?"

"I know you are, Father. But—"

"You can't change roommates now. It's too late for that. But you *can* stop outside associations with Faith Kilpatrick and her friends—and you *can* stop seeing this fellow. Will you promise to do that, now?"

Margaret had to struggle for breath to speak. "You mean write him a note or call him and tell him I can't see him again? Father, that would be terribly unfair to him. He doesn't have the slightest consciousness that he's done anything wrong. It would be—insulting. He'd think I was idiotic. I have to see him at least once more, or perhaps twice, so I could talk over with him why it isn't going to work out."

Father Malone's expression was not happy.

"It didn't seem so terrible when it happened, Father. Only when I thought about it later. But it won't happen again, Father, now that I know. I really didn't know before, really."

Father Malone walked slowly around the other end of the desk.

He dropped into the swivel chair with a jarring thud and leaned forward until both his elbows were on the desk.

"Margaret. We *must* grasp this subject if we are to progress spiritually. We must not be deceived by our *animal desires.*"

"But, Father. I can't see what this has to do with—"

"It does, Margaret. Will you take my word for it?"

Margaret half-shook her head. "I want to understand . . ."

"We have to pray for grace, Margaret. To endure, to ignore these desires. I have them. Every human being has them. Why do you think this fellow is going out with you?"

Margaret's mind went blank with dread. She did not know why, and she did not want to know why. Not yet. Not so soon.

"Why? Tell me in your own words, Margaret."

"He—he—enjoys my company, I suppose."

"No, Margaret, no. Because he *desires* you."

Margaret twisted her head away. "Please, Father."

"I'm sorry if I've shocked you, Margaret. The world is a vile place. I pray constantly that you can pass through it without being soiled."

"I want to, Father."

"Then perhaps, on this day—on your twenty-first birthday—you can come to a decision?"

Margaret sat quietly, letting the word *decision* enfold her like a clammy blanket. She had known, of course, that this word was going to be used before the talk ended. She had known it and wanted to avoid it. But knowledge, there in the confessional, with that overpowering dread gripping her mind, was not enough. Numbly, Margaret bowed her head, a helplessness, almost a despair seizing her. It was her fault, her fault from the beginning. It was she who had come to Father Malone on an evening not unlike this three years ago and told him about her befuddled mixture of piety and ignorance, which she had "hoped" was a vocation.

He had been wise and kind, then. And of course he was being wise and kind now. Perhaps a little impatient, but justifiably so. Three years of waiting and praying had passed, and Margaret Connolly was no closer to being certain, one way or another. Finally she looked up at him, half afraid to read the expression on his face. To her relief, he still was not angry.

"You're a mature woman now, Margaret. You know your own mind. Or you should."

"Father, I'm trying—I really am. But—"

"But what, Margaret?"

"It's . . . confusing, Father. I want to be *sure*. And there are so many things I don't know—that I'd thought I'd know when I got to my last year in college."

"You've learned all the essential truths, Margaret," Father Malone said. "Or you will have by the end of this year."

"If I could only feel the certainty inside. Hear God calling me."

"You can if you listen, Margaret," Father Malone said, his voice regaining some of its early softness. "If you don't let carnal distractions interfere."

He looked at his watch. "All right. You have to get to supper. Will you promise me now, Margaret, that you'll stop going out with this fellow?"

For a moment Margaret thought she had misheard him. Hadn't she just answered that question? Why was he asking it again? Only when she tried to answer did she realize she could not refuse him. She could not say no again.

"All right, Father," she said, meekly lowering her eyes.

"Good!" Father Malone said, jolting back in his chair. "And let's talk about it some more, shall we?"

"All right, Father."

A whirring dizziness blurred Margaret's eyes as she stood up. She rested her hand on the edge of the desk; the words were almost involuntary:

"Father," she said. "Did I commit a mortal sin?"

Father Malone looked down at his mother's picture as if the answer were mysteriously concealed on her lips. "There are many theologians," he said solemnly, "who consider every sin of impurity to be a mortal sin. Fundamentally I am in agreement with them. But I hope . . . your case is an exception, Margaret. For your sake." He looked up at her. "Of course, if you continue to associate with him, knowing he is an occasion of sin—"

"I see, Father," Margaret said.

"Margaret," he said, as she reached the door. "Just a little advice. Talk to your mother. She's terribly upset about this fellow."

Margaret ate supper in an exhausted daze. The conversation buzzed around her, but only occasional words penetrated the weariness that seemed to envelop her like gelatin. To her dismay, her tablemates produced a birthday cake for dessert. By that time she was feeling physically ill. She excused herself after a perfunctory nibble and fled to her room. Faith came in a few minutes later and began teasing her for being a party poop.

"I'm sorry," Margaret said. "I just feel—so awful. Father Malone made me promise—to stop seeing Dick."

"And you said yes?"

Margaret nodded. "There wasn't—any way out of it, Faith. He is—my spiritual adviser."

Faith stood in the center of the room looking wrathful. Margaret braced herself for a diatribe. But instead of flinging emotion at her, Faith seemed, if Margaret could read her expression, to make a bitter inner decision that had nothing to do with Father Malone.

"That does it," Faith said. "That really does it."

She seized her coat and with a slam of the door was gone. Margaret was alone in the silent room. She sat motionless for a long time, her mind blank, a gray sadness pervading her body. She got up and sat on the windowsill, staring out at the star-flecked autumn sky. At last she returned to her desk and casually, as if she did not want even herself to be a witness, pulled out the top drawer. The snapshot was under several sheets of loose-leaf paper. She had glanced at it a dozen times since Judge Kilpatrick had given it to her. But now she studied it intensely. Dick's smile was mysterious. It was not broad and blatantly cheerful, it was more an expression which involved his entire face. Somehow, the more she studied it, the sadder it became. There was something veiled about his eyes, which were not looking directly into the camera, but away from her, and slightly downward. An accident of timing, of course. It was only a snapshot, Margaret. But why did it seem to say, in a subtle weary whisper: *Why are you afraid to love me?*

She slammed the drawer and tried to read Shakespeare. It was impossible. She finally gave up and went to bed. She slept poorly. Faith came in very late and woke her up. Margaret lay staring up at the darkened ceiling for hours, her mind full of images. Dick walking across the beach toward her. Dick stepping out of the waves gleaming wet. Dick in a white evening jacket beneath the technicolor glow of the dance-floor lights. When the morning alarm clanged in her ear, she was so tired it took her an extra ten minutes to struggle out of bed. She was almost dressed when she noticed Faith was still under the covers.

"Faith, we're late. It's seven forty-five."

"I'm not going."

"You'll lose all your late permissions."

"I'll sneak out."

"Stop talking like an idiot."

Faith sat up in bed. She had obviously been awake for some time. "I'm not going today, tomorrow, or the next day, including Sunday. I'm never going into a Catholic church again. I have had it."

"Faith–"

"What happened to you in that confessional yesterday finished the last little flickering afterglow of belief in me, Meg."

"Faith, you're being ridiculous. What happens between me and Father Malone–"

"Yes, yes, I know. It's your business," Faith said. "But it isn't just your business. Meg. A person doesn't live with someone for three years without getting involved with them–without caring about them. Not if you're human."

By now it was seven fifty-five. Margaret could argue no longer. Leaving Faith stubbornly submerged beneath her blankets, Margaret hurried through a chill drizzle to the chapel, where Sister Mary Benedict handed her a seating list. "Another minute and you'd have had to mark yourself late, Margaret," she said with her grim smile.

Esther Sugrue was already checking her side of the chapel. Margaret could see Faith's empty space in the first row of Esther's section. No doubt Esther would take intense pleasure in recording her future sister-in-law's absence.

Margaret finished checking her rows of fuzzy-eyed, scraggly-headed worshippers and knelt down in the first pew. Father Malone had his back to them, reciting the prayers of the Epistle. The green and white chasuble with the white cross down the center suddenly took on a menacing, armored appearance. What was happening in your life, Margaret? Faith was becoming serious. A pun, an unfunny pun. Faith *was* serious and faith has always been serious. But now that word has a different, more somber ring. How can you escape this welter of conflicting hopes and desires?

You know the answer to that, Margaret. Sadly, through a mist of tears, she saw the uplifted face of the girl in the painting, summoned by Christ to a life of sacrifice and prayer. How simple, how tranquil that world would be, compared to this unruly, uncertain tangle of emotions. *Send me wisdom and strength, O Lord,* she prayed. *Send me certainty, but above all knowledge. Help me to know.*

Then, behind her closed eyes, the image of the girl dissolved, and there was Dick, with the same soft, somehow hurt eyes that Christ had in the painting. What was he asking her to do? *He desires you.* Father Malone's words caromed through her mind. She shook her head. No, no, it wasn't true. He needed her. In some strange, uncertain, unspoken way he needed her. Remember those words on the beach? *There are times when everybody needs—*

Oh, you are trapped, Margaret, trapped between his needing and Christ's calling. You must let God supply the answer.

# Chapter Eleven

*Dawn.* In the twin bed on the other side of the room, Bill Connolly's wife issued a series of remarkable snores and snorts. Once those started, there was no further hope of sleep. He put both feet on the cold wooden floor beneath his bed, found his slippers and with a habit that was almost instinct his hand simultaneously plucked his bathrobe from the bedpost. Out the door with only a tiny click, then a pause in the hall to see if the sleeping beauty awoke. Amazing how someone who could make so much noise in her sleep was wide awake the moment a door closed too hard or lock clicked too sharply. Wide awake and yelling about it for the rest of the day.

In the kitchen, he put on the coffeepot and sat there, half asleep, letting the aroma carry him back. It never failed. Suddenly the kitchen was no longer empty. There was his father, that taut, reflective man, sitting there in his shirt, minus the high celluloid collar that he would put on moments before he departed for school. His long, lean, sensitive face would grow sharp as he looked down the table at his three offspring and questioned them on their lessons for the day. No wonder Martin Connolly's children got high marks. They always had to pass two examinations, one from their father, and one from the school. Then he would snap on his collar, shrug on his tight brown coat with the leather patches on the elbows, and, briefcase in hand, stride into the morning.

A schoolteacher, yet a tremendously important man, in his own small way. He was the first Catholic appointed to the city school system. He had won the job on merit, too, scoring the highest mark in the history of the civil service examination. Politics had helped, finally, of course. Martin Connolly had had to go to court to force the Board of Education to hire him, and his fellow Irish had backed him with angry truculence.

What a difference that job had made in their lives! William and his brother and sister had been abruptly transferred from St. Bridget's Parochial School to P.S. 13. Only years later did his mother tell him the behind-the-scenes story of his father's tense conferences with Monsignor O'Boyle at St. Bridget's. At one point the Monsignor threatened him with excommunication and read aloud the clause from canon law specifying that Catholics must educate their children in Catholic schools, under pain of mortal sin. Martin Connolly finally ended the argument by challenging the Monsignor to get him a job teaching in a Catholic school at the same salary he was getting from the public school system. Naturally, no such job existed, and the Monsignor capitulated.

Yes, what a difference. Going to school with Protestants. The only Catholic in the class. What did they call him that first year? Shanty. Shanty Connolly. He had been a kind of celebrity in the neighborhood. His old friends from St. Bridget's waited, almost breathlessly, for horns to grow out of his forehead. When nothing happened, they were disappointed. Not that a few of the characters in P.S. 13 didn't deserve to wear horns. That big thug, Oscar Dirksen, for instance, the one who liked to grab your book bag and drop it down the stairwell from the third floor. But he had strictly obeyed his father's injunction and treated Dirksen and his friends with silent contempt. "Never fight a hoodlum," Martin Connolly was fond of saying, "it puts you on his level." It was good advice, practically as well as morally. Dirksen outweighed skinny, studious William Connolly by forty pounds. But one day, after Dirksen had thrown his book bag down the stairwell three times, William Connolly had sought the help of his ex-classmate from St. Bridget's, Jimmie Kilpatrick. Jimmie and his friends had cheerfully agreed to whale hell out of Dirksen, and William Connolly's book bag was troubled no more.

"Retain your dignity, and you will win the sympathy of the best people." That was another of Martin Connolly's dictums. Again, it was only a half truth. The best people had done practically nothing to stop Oscar Dirksen. They were as intimidated by his hulking frame and guttural bellow as everybody else. But over the years at P.S. 13 and at George Washington High School, Bill Connolly did acquire a few Protestant friends. Fred Berlin, who shared his enthusiasm for Altsheler's books on the Civil War. Frank Pell, who shared his adolescent enthusiasm for surf-fishing.

Silent Frank, killed in World War I. They would spend a whole weekend together at the shore without exchanging more than ten words. But even silence can be a teacher. For William Connolly, the Protestants were never "them." They were simply people, as assorted and confusing and occasionally as intimidating to a shy man as the Irish or the Italians or the Germans or any other group. In fact, if he had to make a choice—and come to think of it, he had made a choice—Bill Connolly preferred the Protestants. Perhaps he was simply more comfortable with them, perhaps it was the impossibility of wholeheartedly joining the Irish, his natural companions, because in this city, as in so many other cities, they had combined politics, piety and larceny so intricately, you had to accept it all or nothing.

Although Martin Connolly always voted the Democratic ticket and never said a word against an Irish candidate in public, in his home he often bitterly denounced them. "Politics is the art of selling your soul piece by piece," he used to say. "Get into work where you owe nothing to any man." Of course, he owed a good deal to those Irish ward bosses who had put the screws on the Board of Education. But when Martin Connolly was uttering a dictum, he preferred not to think about petty details. His wife was inclined to remind him that they existed, however, especially when he began criticizing Irish politicians. Her father had been a district leader, one of the thousands of corporals who toiled in the political army, getting out the neighborhood vote each election day. "Where would you be without the likes of Poppa and his friends?" she would ask, elevating her father to the ranks of the party's sachems. "Where would they have been without me?" he would demand triumphantly. "I didn't need them. I would have won my case," he invariably insisted. "And we'd still be paying off the lawyer's bill," was her inevitable retort.

How silly, and just a little sad, it all seemed now. Yet in 1910 it had been charged with marvelous drama—a drama that Martin Connolly took too seriously. He drove himself to achieve an impossible perfection in the teaching of high school English. He fretted over the clods who declined to appreciate Shakespeare, he struggled to produce prose stylists among those who would never write anything more demanding than a business letter or a note to the milkman. Bill Connolly was certain that he would have worked as hard, even if the Board of Education had not maintained a hostile scrutiny over the years. He was determined to prove, not merely to himself, but to the students and their parents, that his hiring had been on merit and had nothing to do with political pressure. He saw himself fighting for the dignity of the Irish race. No, that was too grandiose. Perhaps it was just his own dignity. But there *was* an acute consciousness of being Irish and Catholic that made the scrutiny unbearable. His widow never stopped lamenting that the revengeful Protestants had killed him. Secretly, she had never approved of the daring experiment. She would have been happier if he had worked out his days in the teller's cage at the First National Bank.

Looking back, now, Bill Connolly could see how this revulsion of feeling had affected him. Defeated by fate, his mother had lapsed into negative dictums: "Don't stick your neck out. No one will ever thank you for it." Or the even more destructive: "Remember, the most important thing in life is your health, not your career." He could see her now, withered and increasingly bitter, standing beside the stove stirring the morning porridge. Amazing, how much more you can see, when you look back down the tunnel of thirty years.

Yet why blame her for your incarceration at Stapleton Talbot? You had read enough novels by now to analyze your own character pretty well. It had been a logical job, for a man interested in the law. But in a subtle way, it had also been a ruinous choice. Was that part of your plan too? No, don't rate yourself any lower than necessary. That was part of the process. Seeing the quality of the law they practiced, talking with these men, accumulating in innumerable words, phrases, tones, gestures the quality of minds that were truly educated, bred a kind of despair in him that perfectly complemented his inborn lassitude. He was a dreamer like his mother, and perhaps she knew it, with that peasant wisdom women so often possess. She encouraged his lassitude under the guise of security, measuring his eminence as managing clerk of Stapleton Talbot by the $1200 a year his father had earned in the classroom. The hours were long, the work demanding—more demanding in many ways than the pressure that had killed his father. Yet, she convinced herself, simply because it was different, that it was better.

Bill Connolly poured himself a cup of coffee and stared into its inky depths for a moment. Women. Men. He knew his mother and his father were wrong about him, about a thousand other things. His mother's life had been so totally limited by the boundaries of church and home, it was almost criminal to accuse her of ignorance, and a kind of charity to attribute wisdom to anything she said. His father was, of course, a far more experienced person but he too had a fatal narrowness to his thrust at life. His dictums were worthless, like all generalizations, and yet he clung to them because they were the essence of his schoolmaster's trade. He was in many ways a kind of failed priest, with the stern, distant manner of the priests of his day. No toothy charm-boy mannerisms, such as Father Denton Malone had perfected. Advice was given in a tone—often in a roar—of command. But they stood on such narrow ground, tightrope walkers with insecurity lapping at their feet, they could not afford to trip the light fantastic. They needed all their strength to combat the enemies, both real and imaginary, that immediately confronted them, Often, as in his father's case, the strength, physical or emotional, was inadequate. Was that what you sensed, looking down at Martin Connolly's shrunken corpse in the coffin? Perhaps.

You tried to overcome it. There was no other explanation (you knew now) for your choice of a wife. The big woman who ran the hospital ward in which Mother had died was incredibly energetic. She presided magisterially over ward maids and orderlies and student nurses, bathed, rubbed and bandaged forty sick and dying patients twelve hours a day, and then was ready to dance until dawn. He had charmed her with his wry humor, with his offhand dropping of big names from Stapleton-Talbot, with his obviously superior education. He was not troubled by her shamefaced confession that she had never read a book in her life, except for her school texts. He was not looking for erudition, he was seeking energy. Yet, when he finally possessed it, both in that total way in the darkness of the bedroom and in the morning and evening light, it had turned out to be a futile, undifferentiated, meaningless energy that never penetrated him, as he had penetrated her. Gradually, he had come to see her as a character in a novel he happened to be living instead of reading. Even without his novels, he would not have been especially surprised to find his marriage unhappy. He had never heard marriage spoken of in terms that made happiness a legitimate expectation. Marriage was an inevitability which one accepted, if the priesthood did not beckon. Alas, he understood now that there was a third alternative, bachelorhood, which he should have chosen.

But by that time, Margaret had arrived. A new dimension had entered his life, a love that was intense and simple because it was unflawed by his too knowing, critical mind. Whenever he felt depressed, he would pull himself out of it by remembering Margaret as a baby. Dreamy, she had been, with those wide, dark incredible eyes staring into space for hours. Her mother had panicked, thought she was retarded. He had tried to defend her. It was a Connolly trait, this placid, peaceful silence. His mother had had it. Night after night in the little kitchen of their tenement she would sit by the window, staring out at the roofs on the next block, until darkness descended. Once he had asked her what she was thinking about. She had been amazed by the question. "Why nothing," she said, "nothing at all."

Ironic, that Margaret was also the source of so many of his marital woes. That agonizing birth, the screams. At first, it was impossible to blame his wife when she bought twin beds and refused him his sexual privileges. He had rarely asked for them more than three or four times a month. But it was his right after all, even the Church said so. Then she had found a priest who assured her that abstinence was highly praised by the Church in certain situations. If she was incapable of having more children, if the possibility literally threatened her life. Here she had the advantage of her supposedly superior medical knowledge. She ipso facto declared that her life was threatened, and hence her decision was not only permissible but justified.

Not without resentment, he agreed. Because by then he was under attack on another far more sensitive front. Margaret meant his wife gave up her job. The pleasant, rather careless comfort of two salaries, which enabled them to drive a Ford, vacation in places like Atlantic City, vanished. Beneath the humdrum routine of motherhood, her energy festered into a massive discontent. She began telling her friends that he was being robbed by his bloodsucking Protestant employers. When he tried to defend his job as one that at least suited his talents, she would urge him to go into politics. When he in turn tried to explain that he had no gift for the art of double-talk, like Jim Kilpatrick, she went back to her Protestant bloodsucker refrain.

It was hopeless. Soon her resentment destroyed her respect for his superior intelligence. If he was "so smart," always reading books and magazines, why couldn't he make more money? Around and around in this vicious whirlpool they went, while resentment muddled his mind and hardened his body. Once a month, he sat in the bathtub, simultaneously praying to God to forgive him and imagining behind his closed eyes one of the young secretaries at the office, a different one each month, standing there in the steamy bathroom naked before him, while he masturbated.

Relief and revenge—and sin. Again and again he went to confession, communion, praying for help to control this despicable spirit that raged inside him. Sometimes, when he looked at Margaret, he was seized by an awful terror, that she would suffer, that she would pay the price of his perversity. The thought made him take a sudden swallow of scalding coffee. The acute pain it caused in his throat and chest made him somehow feel better. He would do anything, suffer anything. God could not be so cruel.

He heard his wife's heavy step in the bedroom. Next came the usual bathroom sounds. He poured her a glass of orange juice and a cup of coffee, and was seated at the table again, when she came massively down the hall toward him.

"When did you get up?"

"About six."

"And you've just been sitting here?"

"Is there anything wrong with that?"

"Did I say there was?"

She downed her orange juice like a longshoreman, in one gulp.

"What time did you get in last night?"

"About midnight. A very big case."

"As usual."

"I know."

"I stayed up to tell you some good news. I finally decided it would wait until morning."

"What?"

"Margaret has promised Father Malone to stop seeing that Protestant boy."

"Oh."

"Don't you think it's good news?"

Her bulk seemed to move across the table toward him. He stared first at her stubborn chin, all but swallowed by the folds of fat on her neck, and then his eyes dropped lower, to the bulging breasts.

"I—I suppose so."

Dear God, was that the punishment? The crucifixion of Margaret's happiness in the name of this ignorant woman's piety and Father Malone's ambition? Perhaps, perhaps. It would be his punishment too. Who suffers more exquisitely than the man who understands everything, who sees into every face with the insight of the novelist, but lacks the courage or strength or power or perhaps simply the energy to act?

# Chapter Twelve

*He's going to kiss you and there is nothing in the world you can do to stop him.*

*You can stop him. But how can you explain it without sounding like the world's biggest fool?*

*The arm on your shoulder turning you to him so effortlessly. You don't want to stop him.*

*There is too much strength in that arm, can't you see that, God, Father Malone, Margaret?*

*They all disagree, even sensible Margaret, watching your performance as always with a jaundiced eye.*

*You said something about a promise? What was it? He kissed you anyway. You see how helpless I am. You see how strong he is. There is nothing I can do, absolutely nothing.*

*Except one thing.*

*Oh, that was wrong, Margaret. You kissed him back with all your strength, with all your heart. "There," you said in defiance of God, Father Malone and sensible Margaret. How much do you think one human being can stand?*

Dazedly Margaret found herself staring into Sister Agnes Marie's smiling face. The lights of the rotunda glared above them.

"He's terribly handsome, Margaret," Sister Agnes Marie said.

"Yes."

"I'm glad you found someone like him," Sister Agnes Marie went quietly on. "You always looked so—out of place with those boys you've dated other years."

Margaret nodded mechanically. She had never been sure how she should act with this plump, soft-voiced woman. Though Sister Agnes Marie was rarely stern, she was also not friendly. When it came to personal relations, she maintained a careful distance between herself and individual students. Besides, her official position had always intimidated Margaret. But for a moment, alone with her in the quiet rotunda, Sister Agnes Marie seemed to invite a confidence.

"He's not a Catholic, Sister. That—bothers me."

"Yes, that is a problem," Sister Agnes Marie said.

She said it so mildly, in a manner that was almost offhand. Margaret had expected a warning, perhaps even a lecture. She murmured good night and made her way up the long flights to the third floor of the dormitory. Faith was sitting in the Morris chair reading a novel.

Margaret sat down on the bed. Rain spattered against the window. "I didn't tell him again," she said.

"Tell him what?"

"That I couldn't—see him."

"Congratulations," Faith said. "That's your third strike."

"It was just—impossible."

"What are you going to do now, write him a letter instead?"

"I don't know."

They went to bed. The next morning was Sunday, and once more Margaret left Faith beneath the covers and trudged to church. For six weeks now Faith had persisted in her stubborn revolt. But to Margaret's bafflement—and no doubt to Esther Sugrue's, who had made several probing remarks in the dining hall—there had been no response from the dean's office. Faith struggled to explain this to herself and Margaret. "Aggie," as she called Sister Agnes Marie, was probably hoping she would come back voluntarily. She was trying to avoid a confrontation with Mrs. Kilpatrick, who had, after all, raised thousands of dollars for the school, of which she was proud to call herself an alumna. "With a mother like mine, you can't even get thrown out of this rotten dump," Faith raged.

Always, unspoken, behind Faith's intransigence was her accusation. There were times when Margaret found herself intensely resenting the idea that it was in any way her fault. At other moments, she felt overwhelmed by an absolute, undeniable guilt. She had promised to stop seeing Dick, a promise that made no sense, really. But a promise given in return for absolution of a sin. Not a mortal sin, but a sin nevertheless, and one that could become mortal, perhaps already had become mortal thanks to those kisses which he had taken so effortlessly last night.

Margaret found Faith's defiance especially trying on Sunday, when missing Mass was a mortal sin. At the consecration of the Mass, Margaret raised her eyes and caught a glimpse of the Host as Father Malone raised it, changed now in the daily miracle of transubstantiation from bread to the body of Christ. When the communion bells rang, Margaret shut her missal and bowed her head to pray: "O Lord, I am not worthy that Thou should enter into my house. Say but the word and my soul shall be healed."

When she raised her eyes again, Father Malone was meeting the first of the communicants as they reached the marble rail. Margaret joined them a few moments later and received the Host on her dry, parched tongue. Once more she knelt in her pew and felt the wafer dissolve slowly, and slide down her throat into her body. Christ entering her body. Christ, who was God.

*O Lord, please tell me what I should do.*

Should she tell Dick when he called this week that she could never see him again? Or was Faith right, was this the ultimate cowardice? Had she committed a mortal sin by kissing Dick again with such angry fervor?

Margaret shuddered. Had she already violated that purity of mind and soul that was essential if she was to remain open to the continued flow of grace from God? How could she hope to hear God's message if the channel of communication was clogged by sin? Yet the thought of confessing another sin to Father Malone was too overwhelming. Instead, she pleaded her ignorance, her helplessness to God himself. *Forgive me. Forgive me.*

As the Mass droned to a close, a weary depression possessed her. All her thoughts and feelings seemed to impel her toward giving up Dick forever. But a tremendous, wordless force within her cried no. Watching Father Malone as he knelt to say the final prayers at the foot of the altar, Margaret realized that she had not thought or prayed about her vocation for the better part of a month. That would simplify everything, a decision there. It would solve Dick and all these worries about sinful Margaret. She bowed her head quickly as the girls crowded into the aisle on the way to breakfast.

*I still don't know, dear Lord. Help me make a decision soon.*

Back in the room she and Faith made desultory small talk interspersed by long, uneasy silences. Ruefully, Margaret had to admit that Faith's Mass strike had had its intended effect. It had forced Margaret to think of herself and Dick in a larger, more alarming way. She might have surrendered easily to Father Malone if there was nothing more at stake than her own small future (yes, it is small; doesn't humility force you to see it that way?). But day after day, as Faith maintained her sullen brooding refusal, Margaret became accustomed to thinking of her crisis as something more than personal. It was not just a question of *my* soul, *my* salvation, *my* vocation, any more. The *my, my, my,* which was the standard concern of her fellow students. They were all that way, wrapped in their little cocoons, playing out their little personal dramas with childish temptations and silly theological debates, failing to see that they were also figures in a larger landscape, symbols, examples of a whole way of life that could be judged by other people such as Larry Donahue and Dick Thornton, judged and found wanting.

But what to do about it? Talking to Faith was hopeless. Margaret had made one or two feeble attempts. Faith did not want to talk. She wanted action. She wanted Margaret Connolly to go see Father Malone and tell him that she was defying him and his cleverly imposed promise. But that was something Margaret Connolly lacked the strength to do.

Oh, it was not mere cowardice, it was wisdom, too. Margaret knew she would not stand a chance against him in open argument. Within five minutes, he would have her more firmly convinced, or at least admitting firmer convictions. But Margaret already knew Faith's answer to this plea. Twenty-one years old, Margaret, twenty-one years old, an adult, and you can't defend yourself, express your convictions and feelings. Why, Margaret, why?

After another lunch and an afternoon in the room, during which she and Faith did not exchange a word, Margaret could stand it no longer and flung on her coat for a walk in the woods. It was a raw December day with a knifing wind moaning through the trees. Margaret plunged her chin into her coat collar and trudged along morosely. It was hopeless. Tonight she would have to sit down and write Dick a letter, telling him she could not see him again. Why? Because I have made a promise in confession. Why did you make a promise? Because a priest talked me into it. No, it was too incredibly stupid. She could not tell him the truth. It would have to be one of those elaborately worded letters about the possibility of her vocation, the pressure of study and the need for reflection, which would leave him wondering what personal blunder he had made.

*Idiocy, idiocy.*

"Good afternoon, Margaret."

Sister Agnes Marie was standing quietly on a bypath to the right, a somber apparition in black and white against the background of the woods' wintry desolation.

"Oh—Sister," Margaret said.

Sister Agnes Marie smiled in that slow, faintly rueful way that reminded Margaret of her father. She had a firm mouth, which was in perfect harmony with her steady gray eyes. Beneath the nun's coif, it was almost a man's face—only the slender feminine nose rescued it from ugliness. "I didn't mean to scare you," she said.

"You—didn't. I was just thinking—"

"A healthy sign. I wish I saw more of it around here."

Sister Agnes Marie fell in step beside her. "I've been thinking, too, Margaret. Thinking about asking you why Faith Kilpatrick has stopped going to church."

Margaret kept walking but she was no longer alive. She was a zombie, pacing numbly down the frozen path in the gray air. "I—don't know," she mumbled. "It's—very complicated."

"Come now, Margaret," Sister Agnes Marie said in the same measured voice. "You must know. I have a feeling it involves you, somehow."

"It's—complicated, Sister."

"I'm not the most intelligent human being in the world, Margaret, but I will do my best to follow you. Try to explain it."

It poured out then, the whole story of Father Malone, confession, her promise, Dick, Larry Donahue, a jumble of uncertain emotions and guarded words and half-concealed anger which Margaret was sure this silent, listening woman walking beside her, head down, square shoulders hunched beneath the thick wool shawl, must consider the supreme combination of adolescent stupidity and naïveté.

"Father Malone made you promise to stop seeing this young man?"

Margaret nodded.

Sister Agnes Marie trudged twenty steps in silence. "That seems rather extreme, Margaret, when all you've done is kiss him."

"Father considers him—an occasion of sin for me."

"That's rather ridiculous."

A burst of wind swept a few leftover autumn leaves down the path ahead of them. Margaret felt giddy. Cautiously she let her eyes stray to the face of the woman beside her. The features were composed, seemingly emotionless.

"It has something to do—I'm afraid—with my vocation."

"Oh." Sister Agnes Marie's eyebrows moved. "You have a vocation?"

"No, Sister. I mean—I'm not sure. Father's been counseling me on it. I suppose that's why he's especially severe about things like—kissing."

"How absurd."

Margaret floundered. What was there to say? She took her favorite refuge, silence.

They went almost a hundred yards before Sister Agnes Marie spoke again. "What makes you think you might have a vocation, Margaret?"

Margaret hastily explained how the idea had come to her during her senior retreat in high school.

"The priest no doubt spent a good deal of time talking about vocations?"

"Yes—he did," Margaret said. "He preached four or five sermons on it."

"Had you thought about it before this retreat?"

"Never in a really serious personal way. I was more interested in going to college."

"And you've been thinking about this vocation for three years now—without making a decision?"

"Yes, Sister. I keep praying but somehow I don't feel I'm strong enough—or good enough. Worthy, I guess you'd call it."

"That's silly too," Sister Agnes Marie said.

"That's what Father Malone tells me. He says I have extraordinary gifts. But I don't know—"

"He said that?"

"Yes."

"What a frightening thing to tell someone."

"I wasn't—frightened, Sister."

"You should have been."

Another hundred yards of silence. "I don't know what to say, Margaret. I've probably said too much already. I don't want to scandalize you about Father Malone. He's an earnest, dedicated young priest. But I don't agree with his attitude toward vocations. As far as I am concerned, the whole thing is a mystery. No one really knows why a person makes the decision, and another person, who seems to love Christ just as much, chooses to stay in the world. I couldn't tell you why I did it, except that at the time it seemed absolutely necessary to me. It should come out of your life, Margaret, a flowing. This is what I think. I could be wrong. It contradicts many of the stories we have about the saints, like Ignatius and Francis, but I frankly think they are more pious writing than truth. The idea to serve Christ didn't come at them like a bolt from above; it had been working in them for a long time. I'm sure of it."

"It would seem—logical," Margaret said. She would have preferred to say nothing, but Sister Agnes Marie had vanished within herself again. The heavy face was almost somnolent. She might have been a sleepwalker.

"One thing you should understand, Margaret. There is joy in the religious life, but you have to fight for it. The first happiness fades rather quickly, and after that a vocation becomes the most terrible gamble in the world, a gamble that you can love someone invisible, someone who flees before you like a shadow, who can give you moments of terrible joy and then abandon you when you need Him most. Those who fail, who lose hope, play it safe. They try to settle for a kind of plateau when they have committed themselves to climbing a precipice. A lot of them end up clinging to a little shelf of vanity or bitterness. You've seen them in our classrooms, in the parish pulpits. They're unpleasant, blundering people. They probably die trying to figure out what went wrong."

"You make it sound—formidable, Sister."

"It is formidable. I'm not saying it's beyond you, Margaret. You are a superior woman. But I think you deserve the whole truth about the choice."

"I—appreciate it. Really, Sister." Margaret felt tears come to her eyes, and for a moment the path blurred. It was astonishing. No one had ever spoken this way to her before. No one—except Faith Kilpatrick.

More silence while the wind howled and the leaves skittered. Then Sister Agnes Marie said, "If I were you, I would write Father Malone a note telling him that you don't feel that it is fair or wise to hold you to this promise."

"Yes, Sister."

"As for Faith Kilpatrick, do your best to keep your life separate from hers, Margaret, no matter how hard she tries to intrude herself on you. People like Faith have very difficult spiritual problems. You'd have none at all if people would let you alone. I'm more like Faith so I can envy your simplicity, Margaret, which is probably what Faith does more than anything else."

"I don't feel—very simple. Nothing does lately."

"Maybe that's a good thing. You're getting an education here in spite of some people's efforts to prevent it."

This was such a startling remark, Margaret again took refuge in silence. Sister Agnes Marie's face seemed to descend from solemn to somber. "Yes," she said again. "Let me talk with Faith, when the right time comes. We will probably have to wait for a while. Even then, there may be nothing we can do."

Sister Agnes Marie no longer seemed to be concentrating on the subject. Her eyes were searching the trees. "Where are they?" she said. "They've never missed an appointment before."

Suddenly the air was thick with beating wings, and a flock of sparrows came swooping out of the sky to dart and dip above their heads. "You'd better synchronize your watches," Sister Agnes Marie said to them. "I can't afford to waste my time on you." While she spoke she reached beneath her dark robes and brought out a huge handful of bread crumbs. She flung most of them up in the air, and the birds came rushing down for them. The rest she held in her small stubby hand, and one bird after another came fluttering up for a peck. "Don't be afraid of Margaret," Sister Agnes Marie said. "She won't hurt you." But the advice was ignored. They flitted in and out of her hand with nervous haste.

"Oh dear, I'm afraid you'd better go, Margaret," Sister Agnes Marie said. "It's almost time for your supper, anyway."

"Yes. Thank you—for everything, Sister."

Margaret might as well not have spoken. Smiling and whispering and beckoning, Sister Agnes Marie was completely absorbed in her birds. The last thing Margaret saw, when she looked back before the path curved away, was the stocky figure in black, with the creatures of the air whirling above her head.

Up in the room, Margaret found Faith Kilpatrick face down on her bed, crying quietly and steadily. Margaret asked her what was wrong. It was a foolish question which Faith did not immediately answer. She finally murmured something into her pillow and lurched to a sitting position to give Margaret a red-eyed stare. "Where've you been?"

"Walking."

"Exercise. That's what I need."

"Faith. Please talk to someone."

"Who would that be—around here?"

"Sister Agnes Marie, maybe."

"Aggie? I'd rather talk to an IBM machine. I'd get more emotional response."

"I don't know whether that's true. I just talked with her. She advised me to—disregard the promise."

Faith was impressed, but tried not to show it. "I'm glad you finally realized someone else has a brain, besides Father Malone." She slid off the bed and sat down morosely at her desk. "However, I'm afraid my problems are a little more complex."

"I still think she could help you."

Faith shook her head. "No, I've thought about it all week. One thing I wanted to say to you, Meg, is how sorry I am that I blamed you. That was stupid, petty—all the names you want to call it. This has been coming on me for a long time. I honestly think the best thing that could happen would be for me to get thrown out of this school. That would end it, for good. Then I could do some intelligent thinking about the other things that are driving me crazy, like Larry Donahue."

"You're still seeing him?"

"Yes. On his terms."

Margaret shook her head. "If you get thrown out of here now, Faith, you'll never go to church again. You'll lose your faith completely."

Faith laughed mirthlessly. "You—really do care about my poor little soul, don't you?"

Margaret looked out the window to the woods where Sister Agnes Marie was probably still communing with her birds. "You are my best friend."

"I—appreciate it," Faith said, and left the room hurriedly, no doubt to avoid another crying fit.

The solitude gave Margaret time to think about her astonishing conversation with Sister Agnes Marie. While it had lasted Sister

Agnes seemed to be assuming responsibility for all Margaret's decisions—the promise, the vocation, Faith. Now Margaret realized that her enigmatic counsellor had assumed very little. Sister Agnes Marie obviously preferred to remain outside Margaret's relationship to Father Malone. She had no jurisdiction there, and Father Malone could accuse her of interfering in a delicate spiritual problem. She was clearly relying on Margaret's discretion to say nothing about their talk in the woods. She had quietly passed on to Margaret the unpleasant task of announcing to Father Malone that the promise was to be disregarded.

*If I were you, I would write Father Malone a note.*

But you are not me, Sister, and you probably do not recoil from such a difficult assignment in my timid fashion. Margaret meditated on the dull landscape, constructing the future of the argument: Father Malone receives letter, summons victim again, smiles, bemoans, persuades—and Margaret Connolly walks out of his study, once more vowed to abstain forever from that occasion of sin known as Richard C. Thornton. It was hopeless, the letter was a waste of time.

In the hall, the telephone rang.

It was Dick. Margaret knew it, instantly.

She sat motionless at the desk, like a trapped animal, while Eileen Becker answered the insistent bell. A moment later the footsteps came down the hall, and the hand knocked on the door. "Margaret, phone," said the familiar voice.

She walked woodenly down the hall and picked up the dangling receiver of the old-fashioned wall phone. "I am the local publisher of our state university law review," Dick said. "Would you like a subscription?"

"I never read immoral literature," Margaret said.

"This isn't immoral, it's just dull. God, is it dull. How are you?"

"Dull."

"Then why am I wasting my money on you?"

"I haven't the foggiest notion."

"You have no feminine instincts, that is your problem. You don't know when a man needs to be soothed, complimented."

"How was this edition of the law review?"

"Brilliant. I expect letters of bewildered admiration from the entire Supreme Court."

"What a frightening thought."

"Good God, you sound like Faith Kilpatrick. Where is the docile, obedient girl I met on the sands of Paradise Beach?"

"I'm in a difficult mood. Even we quiet types have difficult moods."

"I like it. Stay that way until next Saturday."

There it was, the invitation you knew was coming. But why hesitate? Hasn't everything you've already said been an acceptance? Could you possibly reverse yourself now, and say, with total solemnity, *Dick, I can never see you again?* Not if you want to consider yourself a normal human being, Margaret. So say the only words: "What time?"

"The usual."

"Where are we going?"

"No place special. There must be a decent movie playing somewhere."

"That sounds relaxing."

"I'll see you."

Now the trick was to get back into the room without really thinking. Hold your mind as if it were a piece of ice floating in a brimming bowl, Margaret. Do not let it slop in either direction, walk carefully down the middle of the hall and into the room and take out a piece of paper and your pen and sit down and write:

Dear Father Malone:

I have discussed the promise I made to you with another person, whose spiritual advice I value highly. This person does not feel it is a good way to solve my problem, or reach a decision. I feel the same way. It would be far better if I went ahead and saw Dick regularly, until I decide how I feel about him, and what he may or may not mean to me. You can depend on me morally, Father. I am sure you know that. I appreciate your deep concern for my spiritual welfare, which led you to suggest the promise. But I honestly feel I must work this out in my own way.

Sincerely,
MARGARET

Done. Now, address it, seal it, and take it downstairs and leave it at the switchboard, where Father Malone would pick it up when he came back to school tonight. Now back upstairs, and you can collapse, Margaret, have your hysterics, your nervous fit, or whatever. She sat on the edge of her bed in the empty room and watched dusk darken the windowpane. At first all she felt was a general numbness, as if she had just narrowly escaped falling from a great height. As this ebbed, something amazing began to happen. Not hysterics or nerves, but a slow, steady elation. You did it, Margaret. You brave silly Margaret, you are not quite as humble and quiet and helpless as everyone, including you, thinks you are. Maybe Faith is partially right (you cannot dare concede more than that); maybe there is another Margaret, someone slightly stronger and more daring than the docile, pious girl you have known so long.

She shivered. The room was suddenly cold. She put on a sweater and picked up her English textbook. Not so fast, my dear. It was only a small change, a shift in emphasis. No matter what happened, you will never lose that deep, steady devotion to Jesus Christ which is the foundation of your life. Don't even use words like *pious,* Margaret, as if they were vices instead of virtues. Change all you want, Margaret, but you cannot and will not change your faith.

*Watch over me, O Lord, and protect me.*

# Chapter Thirteen

"May it please the court, I would like to request his Honuh's permission for a stay of six weeks in regard to the petition in re Andrew Bahton."

"Why?" asked Judge Kilpatrick, brushing dandruff off his black-robed shoulders.

"There is a possibility that we may be able to acquire new evidence, yoh Honuh."

Judge Kilpatrick stared down at Leroy Brown's glistening black head. A fly couldn't land on that boogie's conked skull without breaking his leg, he thought. Oh, you prejudiced bastard, just because he says *yoh*. At least he doesn't commit felonious assault on the basic principles of the English language like too many of the Irish and Italian lawyers that grace—or better disgrace—this Supreme Court room.

"The court will grant the stay on one condition. That the prisoner cease and desist forthwith from his utterly reprehensible attacks on the character of the judge who sentenced him, and the jury who found him guilty."

"I can assure yoh Honuh that these attacks will cease forthwith. The defendant has undergone a radical transformation of his thinkin' processes, yoh Honuh. He truly regrets his earlier conduct, which was due to youth and an unfortunate misunderstanding of his legal situation."

Amazing what a nightstick in the teeth can do, the Judge thought. Maybe that was still the best political answer. Maybe Dave Shea had been right all along. It was you who had taught him the importance of respectability, of controlling courts and rigging juries to harass and demoralize political enemies. It made for such beautiful political copy—to be able to bellow that word *indictment,* or even better, *convicted.* Yes, James, that is the essential irony here. You have constructed your own exquisite Hobson's choice, and the only thing you can do is stall for time.

"The stay is granted. The court will entertain a renewal of the petition on February fifth."

With a rap of his gavel the Judge ended the morning session. "Counsellor," he said, "I'd like to see you in my chambers."

Minutes later he was handing Leroy Brown a Scotch and soda and mixing one for himself, and simultaneously snarling, "Now, listen to me, Leroy. You've got six weeks to cool that kid off. Otherwise I'm going to put him away for five years. Understand? Five years."

Brown almost dropped his glass. "Jes-us Christ, you can't get away with that, Judge," he gasped.

"You know goddamn well we can get *away* with it," the Judge said. "But that doesn't mean I think it's a smart thing to do. It's what the Big Guy wants."

Brown took a large gulp of his Scotch and soda and went ten agitated paces up the crimson carpet, and turned around, like a sentry walking his post. "Jim," he said, "it's a bum rap."

"You know that's irrelevant."

"Goddamn it," Brown said. "Ah'm not tryin' to tell you guys how to run things, but how much shit does he think people can eat?"

"As much as he can get away with cramming down their throats. He's gotten away with it for forty years. Do you have any ideas on how to stop him?"

Leroy Brown blinked. He obviously could not quite believe what he had just heard. Neither, for a moment, could Chief Justice James Kilpatrick. The moment the words were heard, understood, and then absorbed in all their possible meanings, the current of blunt honesty which the Judge had created between them short-circuited. Habits of years reasserted themselves, with repulsive nakedness.

"Me?" said Leroy, furrowing his brown brow and swishing his drink. "Me? Ah got no suggestions. Ah'm no fink. Ah got no beefs against the organization."

"Neither have I," said the Judge, while a voice forty years back in his mind's darkness shouted *liar,* and the echo rebounded crazily down the jigsaw-puzzle veins of his cortex.

"But you got to be reasonable," Brown said. "You got to realize that people react to things. Even Negro people."

"Why the hell didn't that occur to your idiot client? Did he think the Big Man wasn't going to react? When has anybody ever said one word against City Hall and gotten away with it?"

"It's a new generation, Jim. These kids won't stand for the old Gestapo stuff."

"They'll stand for it. Their heads aren't any harder than ours were. The've got relatives on the pad, just like we have. They can be scared shitless by calls in the middle of the night—"

"Yeah, ah suppose so." Leroy Brown's voice was toneless—the pale, neutral sound of the realist, the man who has accepted the cards life dealt him, the ruthless city, his Irish masters, his own mediocrity. And you, James? You were bolder. You roared your defiance at conventional thinking. But behind the scenes, didn't you strike the same bland pose? Just bold enough to win the awed admiration of a few close friends, your mistress and your daughter, but not so bold that anything substantial was risked.

*Jesus Christ, shut up,* the Judge told his mirror voice with its mocking, ancient echoes. "Keep his nose clean for six weeks, and maybe, just maybe, we can talk Big Dave out of it," the Judge said. "Here's what I want you to do. Get together thirty or forty important Negroes. Ministers, doctors, the works. Get them to sign a letter, an absolutely confidential letter, which only you and I will see. I'll take it to Shea."

"Me?" Leroy Brown said. "What happens to me if the word goes down to the Hall that ah'm organizin' people? Look, Jim, ah want to see this kid get off the hook. But not at mah expense."

"All right," the Judge said. "Keep his goddamn nose clean and I'll see what I can do for him, on my own."

"Thanks, Jim," Leroy Brown said. "Thanks a lot. I really think it's fo the best. . . ."

Alone in his chambers, the Judge had another Scotch and soda. For a moment he felt almost sorry for the Negroes in Nighttown. They were never going to get out of those crummy tenements with people like Leroy Brown for leaders. But that was not his worry. The

Judge's clerk, Eddie Logan, came in looking rabbit-eyed, as usual. Politics forced him to take his clerks from the state's only Catholic law school. He hadn't gotten a decent one since the war. This kid was a typical 4F who went to Mass and communion every morning, and had asthma attacks every time his mother breathed on him. Maybe next year, when more veterans started graduating from law school, he would get someone decent. But he doubted it. Why would anyone with brains and the G.I. Bill waste his money on that third-rate diploma mill the Archbishop had set up in the thirties to protect Catholic lawyers from communism? Maybe next year he would defy prudence and take on a sharp young kid like Dick Thornton for his clerk. Maybe Jake O'Connor. Somebody you could talk to man to man, an impossibility with this overgrown altar boy.

The telephone rang. "Answer it, will you, Eddie," the Judge said.

"Chief Justice Kilpatrick's chambers," said Logan sweetly.

"I'm not here," said the Judge.

"What?" said Eddie, rattled. Without covering the phone he turned and said, "It's City Hall. The deputy mayor."

"Oh, for Christ's sake," the Judge growled, and snatched the phone.

"Hello, Judge," said Johnny Kenellen in his all too familiar downtown rasp. "What's the word on Barton?"

"I granted him a six weeks' stay."

"You *what?*"

"With a guarantee. An absolute guarantee that he keeps his mouth shut."

"We can do that with a nightstick, for Christ's sake. We want him *outa* here."

"You run City Hall, I'll run this court."

He slammed down the phone. In ten seconds it rang again. "Listen," Kenellen said, "I think you'd better get the hell down here tomorrow morning."

"Shove it, Johnny, will you? The whole fucking thing. Bend over and shove it."

"It's got nuthin' to do with the boogie. It's another matta."

"What?"

"Personal. A membeh of your family. I don't wanna discuss it on the phone."

"If you have done or said anything to one of my kids, so help me Christ I'll—"

"Nobody's done or said anything. Not from here. But I can't say the same for the person involved."

"I'll see you in two hours."

"Ain't you sitting?"

"It's cancelled. I'll see you in two hours. This better be important."

"I think it is. For you, anyway."

The Judge stormed past the astonished Logan, roaring orders to get his car, cancel the afternoon's cases, and put them on next week's docket. Downstairs, in front of the gray marble Supreme Court building, he paced up and down, frantically trying to decide what Kenellen knew. Was it Jim, mixing politics with his idiotic Young Christian Students? Or one of his goddamn in-laws caught with his hand in the till? That could be it. He personally would not trust Bernie Brophy any farther than he could drop-kick him. But the way Kenellen said *family* made it sound somehow closer and more ominous. The old lady? Impossible, she doesn't have the brains to make a political remark, much less a move that would excite City Hall. Faith—and that skinny shit, Larry Donahue? His old man was a drunken Republican and you had overheard Larry talking in omnious adolescent tones about the organization. But only a few weeks ago you had stood there in the dining room looking down at Faith's gamin face as the pouting mouth bitterly inflicted the words: *I'm not interested in politics.* Why had the words infuriated you, then? Now you are clutching at them as if they were your last best hope. Get a grip on your goddamn nerves. The whole thing is probably one more stupid ploy the Big Guy cooked up over his prunes, to guarantee getting his way in this Barton mess.

But he couldn't get a grip on his nerves or his temper. He snarled at chauffeur Eddie Dombrowski about the five-minute delay, and all the way across the long, flat center of the state he kept growling for speed and more speed.

"Jesus Christ, Judge," Eddie gasped, "we just hit ninety-five passin' them last two trucks."

"Hit a hundred the next time."

A state policeman stopped them. The Judge roared about a family emergency and the goggle-eyed cop formed up in front of them and, siren howling, sent drivers scurrying up on the shoulder as they blazed the last fifty miles in what had to be record time.

"Take down that cop's number," the Judge told Eddie Dombrowski. "I'm going to write a personal letter to the superintendent and get him a promotion."

In the city, Eddie turned on his horn and went zooming through red lights, over the top of the hill and down to City Hall. Up the flights of marble stairs the Judge charged, ignoring the sliver of pain that ran out of his chest and down his arm. Without so much as a look at the startled secretaries, he barged through the mighty oak doors into the anteroom of the mayor's office, where Kenellen sat behind a polished mahogany desk ten sizes too big for him. He almost fell over backwards in his chair at the shock of the Judge's appearance. "Jesus Christ," he said, "did you come by rocket? It's only an hour since I called."

"Give me the story," the Judge said.

"Sit down, for Christ's sake," Kenellen said. The Judge had seldom seen him so jittery. "I don't like this any more than you do."

"I wish I could believe that."

"Jesus Christ." Kenellen's withered fist of a face suddenly screwed into a grimace that seemed almost sincere. "You think I enjoy being a goddamn hatchet man twenty-four hours a day? Do you think I asked for this job? Somebody's got to keep the animals in their goddamn cages. The big shot don't do it any more. He's too busy talkin' to the President or some goddamn flea-bitten Southern Senator who's invitin' him down to his plantation."

"Okay, Johnny, you're a fucking martyr," the Judge said. "Cut the stalling. Give it to me."

"I wish I never heard it," Kenellen said. "But as a friend—we don't get along so good, but, hell, we're in this together—as a friend I thought you ought to know."

"What, for Christ's sake?" the Judge roared.

"You know that turnpike motel out near Holland Township? The Wagon Wheel?"

"Sure."

"Well, we got a guy on the pad there. He clues us on the action—there's a lot of it. An awful lot of guys take broads there, you'd be amazed."

"Yeah, yeah."

"We got a concealed camera in the wall behind the desk. All the clerk has to do is step on a button and it takes pictures as they're signing in. Well, I got this picture three days ago that really upset me."

From the center drawer of his desk, Kenellen extracted a brown envelope. His stubby, horny fingers fumbled momentarily with the clasp on the back, and then it was open, and from it slid almost obscenely a single rectangular black and white photograph, the shiny kind of blowups they had handed out by the dozen when they announced James Kilpatrick's appointment as Chief Justice. Wordlessly Kenellen handed it to him, and the Judge stared down at a picture of Faith Kilpatrick—eyes lowered, those long, beautiful lashes she had inherited from him strangely visible, a plaintive, almost mournful droop to the puckish mouth that had laughed up at him with such abandon in other years, one hand clutching the front of her dirty, half-open raincoat. Beside her, face saturnine, the hooded reptilian eyes on the register, was Larry Donahue. His hair, as usual, stood out at erratic, irregular angles. The same repulsive gutter-face, suffused now with snide self-satisfaction. The ragged Woolworth shirt, the cheap tie, the corduroy jacket, completed the degradation.

The Judge was voiceless. He heard someone whispering *Jesus Christ, Jesus Christ,* but it was not him, it was a stranger who stood beside him, smashing a pair of brass knuckles into his rib cage. He heard Kenellen's flat obscene twang. "Like I say, it ain't a political matta. It ain't somethin' I really wanna know about."

How could it happen? How could a man's world come apart like a child's toy just because he saw a picture? The thing in his hand was lethal, and maybe the pain in his chest was lethal and maybe that was the perfect answer to everything. *Jesus, stop.* All your life you have performed on a tightrope while creatures like Kenellen clawed at you from one side, and your virgin wife stuck her dainty fingers in your eyes, and the snobs at Stapleton Talbot clubbed you with their degrees and pedigrees, and your moron in-laws sucked your veins and the idiot clergy infected your conscience and you are still here, still sane, still on the tightrope. Don't quit now.

"The negative," the Judge said. "Give me the negative."

"I'm sorry," Kenellen said, reaching for the brown envelope.

The Judge ripped it away from him and plunged his hand into it. Empty. "Give me that negative, you little prick," the Judge said, "or I'll kill you. I mean it."

"I can't—"

The Judge picked Johnny Kenellen up out of his swivel chair and threw him against the wall. His head cracked against the hard oak panelling and he slid to the floor in a dazed heap, the steel-rimmed glasses popping off one ear to dangle underneath his chin.

"GIVE ME THE NEGATIVE!"

Cowering like a trapped rabbit, Kenellen screamed, "The mayor's got it. It's on his desk."

Judge Kilpatrick swung open the second set of oaken doors. Dave Shea sat behind his desk, the long, lean, dour face fixed in a savage glare of disapproval. "On his desk," Kenellen's voice squawked through the intercom. "Mayor, shall I call the cops?"

"Give me that negative, Dave."

Shea held it out to him. "Take it. What do I want with the goddamn thing? Do you think I want the city to know my Chief Justice lives like a pig and so does the rest of his family?"

"I live like a man," the Judge said, snatching the negative.

"You live like a goddamn pig," the mayor sneered. "How do you think your kids are going to turn out? Why the hell are you surprised? Do you think I don't know about you and that slut of a schoolteacher you've been screwing for fifteen years? I used to think you were Mr. Brains. But not any more."

"You miserable hypocritical old son of a bitch," the Judge roared. "You've stolen forty million dollars out of this town and you've never given a cent of it to anybody. You're a goddamn lousy dictatorial Irish miser."

"Nobody talks like that to Shea," the mayor roared.

He was on his feet, coming across the room at him, those old iron fists doubled. Jesus, remember Barney Cronin, the first police commissioner, six foot four, this monster kicked him in the crotch and he was dead six months later. The Judge turned his head, eyes groping in the shadows for a weapon, a bookend, even a book. The brutal bastard was capable of murder. Suddenly through the gloom a massive man came hurtling toward them at incredible speed and planted himself between Shea and the Judge. Bill O'Brien, summoned by Kenellen. There was the little ferret, with his Pinocchio eyes and needle nose, peering through the door. The Judge almost laughed at the mad irony of it. Thanks to the lump on his own head, Kenellen thought that Mayor Shea needed protection from this judicial madman. Magnificently the Judge rose to the occasion. "Get out of the way, Bill. Let him come. We'll settle this goddamn thing his way."

Simultaneously Shea was roaring, "Get out of my way, you clodhopping shitkicker. Nobody says what that son of a bitch just said to me and gets away with it."

"Jesus Christ," thundered Bill O'Brien, and the walls shook. " 'Tis a solemn oath I've sworn to keep the peace and I'm not going to break it, no matter if you've all gone crazy."

"Have it your way, Bill," said the Judge, and strolled casually toward the door. Over his shoulder, he kept an eye on Dave Shea, all but invisible except for the top of the bulky bald head above Bill O'Brien's big shoulder.

The gutter voice bellowed: "I'll make you sorry you said that for the rest of your life, you rotten stinking goddamn ingrate. I'll have you impeached and indicted before sundown tomorrow. I'll run that whore of yours out of this city and you and your cocksucking family right after them."

"Fuck you," the Judge roared. "You lay a hand on anything I care about and I'll put you in the pen for the next hundred years." Then in a more normal voice, he added, "I didn't ask for this fight, Dave. If you kept your mouth shut, we'd still be friends."

Life seemed to be repeating itself, like a berserk movie that insisted on running the same reels again and again. You were walking past the same gaping secretaries, down the same marble stairs, drenched in sweat, the same fist driving a hole through your rib cage. Was that buckling sensation in the knees fear? Or something even more alarming? He looked down at the picture, still clutched in his hand, and a huge nausea engulfed him. He almost vomited on the scrubbed marble steps, a very fitting gesture, but not especially dignified.

A blast of freezing wind hit him as he came out the door. He shuddered, and clutched for the iron scrollwork railing as he came down the last flight of steps. Twice, as he walked through the little park in front of City Hall, past the World War I victory monument stained green with pigeon shit, he had to stop and lean against the fence. His breath came in slow, shallow gasps, and the brass fist in his chest had turned into a ball of molten lead. Eddie Dombrowski leaped out as he approached the car. "Jesus Christ, what happened, chief? You're white as a goddamn sheet."

"Nothing. Nothing," the Judge said. "Take me home. No wait—take me to 1301 Boulevard."

Home was the wrong place. It was the stranger-wife's house, thick with claustrophobia. With menace. Those pictures on the wall, a glance at one of them could kill. He needed—oh, Christ, what did he need? A shot of spiritual adrenalin? As the big car growled up the hill into the city's heights, the Judge stared dully out at the gray sagging housefronts, at the littered lots, the grime-covered factories, and prayed. The first prayer he had said in thirty years. *Whoever you are, whatever you are, help me or at least help her.*

"When do you want me?" Eddie Dombrowski said. The Judge realized they had been parked in front of 1301 for at least five minutes.

"I don't," he said. "Leave it here. I'll see you tomorrow."

"You sure you're okay?" Eddie said. "You still look like you swallowed shit."

"I have," the Judge said. "I'll see you tomorrow, Eddie."

Up in the creaking elevator he rode to the familiar apartment, stripped off his sweat-soaked clothes and collapsed into the oversized double bed. He lay there for a half hour, thinking of nothing, while the nausea rose and fell inside him with every breath. Gradually, like a tidal flood, it began to recede, leaving behind the slimy debris of fact. He stumbled out of bed and into the living room, where he mixed himself a triple Scotch and soda and chugged it. He still had the picture in his hand. Was the goddamn thing grafted onto his fingers? Had he even put it down when he was undressing? He pondered his daughter's mournful puppet face, then Larry Donahue's lean ratchet features. If it was with someone else, someone decent, would you care? Dick Thornton, Jake O'Connor? A guy with some class, a future? Yes. Goddamn it, yes. All these years of giving things Irish the horselaugh, and it was still there in your marrow, that mean, cruel morality that exploded so easily into rage. In the guts, you are still Dave Shea with his repulsive apostrophes to clean living. Face it, that is why you are here in this apartment, waiting for a wife who is not your wife. You could not take the other route, the call-girl-New York-weekend route. Now can you rise like Kraken from the mud and breathe fire on your daughter?

Yes, goddamn it, yes. That is part of the game, the double-faced, triple-imaged game we call living. Everyone wears more than one face. It is absolutely necessary in order to survive . . .

"Jim, what's the matter—are you all right?"

Margaret stood over him. "You look—"

The soft sweet scent of her perfume, the womanness of her wide tender eyes. The Judge almost wept. "Trouble," he said. "Trouble. I've got to talk about it."

Jesus Christ, any minute you are going to become a crying drunk.

With an immense effort, he sat up and began talking in a normal voice. Margaret poured herself a drink and sat opposite him, and his eyes moved pleasurably up those long spectacular legs as he told her what had happened in City Hall. Her face sagged, first with disbelief, then with horror. She reached out for the picture and studied it for a long mournful moment.

"He may come after you," the Judge said. "If he does, I'll make him regret it. Oh, will I make him regret it."

"How?"

"I know a few things . . ."

His voice trailed off. You know *everything,* but would anyone believe you if you told it? Would anyone particularly appreciate hearing how you helped a thug like Shea—that was the best name for him—a barrel-chested, brass-voiced, iron-nerved Irish thug—steal $40 million, corrupt the city and the state? Not really. Face it, Jim, you are Dr. Frankenstein, and your monster is out of control.

"Don't worry about me," Margaret said. "I can take care of myself. But Faith—"

"I'll go see him," the Judge said. "I'll go see that little twerp. His name is Donahue. I'll take along a blackjack."

"Jim, don't be ridiculous."

That calm, even voice, the steady eyes. She was angelic. She had to be, no creature of flesh and blood could stand this close to the dissolving chaos inside you without being infected by the collapse. Cling to it, Jim, cling to her calm, your peaceful piece—oh, you dirty bastard.

"You're right. I am being ridiculous. Who should I talk to? Faith? Somehow I can't face it."

"Both, or neither. But first, calm down. Have another drink and I'll get some supper."

"I couldn't eat a thing."

"You can, and you will. You look terrible."

"I feel terrible."

She took the glass out of his hand. "Instead of another drink, take a bath."

A few minutes later, flat on his back in the warm womby tub, the

Judge felt like a different person. Freer, somehow purified by the simple sensation of water on his weary flesh. Was death like this, a floating nothingness in a world of light? His fingers explored his chest. The pain was gone but it felt vaguely tender. Was that bad? What the hell do you know about heart disease? Goddamn it, are you trying to consciously destroy the good idea of yourself you have labored to construct over so many years, the man who thinks, plans, knows what he's doing? Drying himself, he pondered his big flabby body in the mirror. The shoulders were as solid and meaty as ever, but from there to the thighs it was a disaster area. A bulge of fat around the belly, and the ass twice oversize, the whole trunk encased in suet. A little repulsive. Maybe Sister Alice Joseph had something when she warned them every day in the eighth grade against the "dirty, filthy sins of the flesh." He was calmer now, but as he pulled on his underwear, hiked up his pants and stepped into the cooler air of the dining room, he felt depressed. Weights seemed suddenly to hang from his shoulders.

Jesus Christ, why shouldn't you be depressed? You have lost something precious, that mystical faith that Jim Kilpatrick was at least smart enough to have his cake and eat it twice. Throughout dinner, Margaret tried to get his mind off the subject. She earnestly discussed the latest collection of idiot remarks from her slow learners, began telling him about her latest literary enthusiasm, an obscure Czech named Kafka. It was pathetic, and finally irritating. Did she really think she had that much power over him? He picked at the beef bourguignonne, largely to keep her happy, and finally snapped, "I couldn't care less what some screwball Czech thinks."

Tears glistened in her eyes. "I hate to say it, but it upsets me to see you so upset."

"What should I do, smile? My daughter's getting laid by a two-bit birdbrain."

"Is he really? I can't believe, from what you've told me about Faith, that she would go to bed with a birdbrain."

"He's an obnoxious, antagonistic little shit."

"To you maybe. But to her?"

"I know exactly what he's done. He's made her feel guilty, sorry for him because she lives in a decent house and has good clothes on her back and a father who works at a job."

"Is that so bad, feeling sorry for someone? You have to start out feeling something. Love has to start somewhere. In fact, I think a person goes through a whole series of emotions before she reaches love. Admiration, then some pity."

"Don't be ridiculous," the Judge snarled. "When did you ever feel sorry for me?"

Her face was a study in shock, then in pain, but her voice remained calm. "When I saw how unhappy you were."

"I never asked you to feel sorry for me. Not once! The idea repels me."

The Watcher, the voice from the murky past, instantly contradicted him. *That is a lousy lie.* "You never asked in so many words," Margaret said, her voice tightening, "but there was something sad about a man who had so much to offer to a woman, and no woman."

"That is your opinion," the Judge snarled. "I wasn't looking for it."

Again the Watcher's voice. *Oh, you lousy liar.*

"Oh. What were you looking for, just a—good piece?"

"Right. It was so good I decided to keep it around for fifteen years."

Slowly, quietly, Margaret pushed back her chair, laid her napkin beside her half-finished dinner and walked into the kitchen. The Judge sat there like a bewildered Samson in the wreckage. Completely berserk, he pounded the table and dragged down the last few tottering walls.

"If there was any pity involved anywhere, it was on my side. I couldn't resist rescuing a born spinster from her fate."

Silence as the last bits and pieces of his private temple, the house of refuge he had constructed so carefully over the years, joined the rest in the dust. He flailed at the debris. "When I want your opinion on any other aspect of my life I'll ask for it. What I do in this apartment has nothing whatsoever to do with my attitude toward my children, or even my wife. It's separate, completely separate."

The appalled Watcher could only whisper: *You insane, hopeless bastard.*

Silence. Silence in the ruins. An image out of the past swelled behind the Judge's eyes. He was at another table forty-five years ago, thirteen years old, listening to another Irishman, big Jim Kilpatrick, thick of neck and thick of head, pounding the table in a drunken temper and roaring brainless denunciations at his son and wife. There he was sitting opposite him, the beery sweat running off his low furrowed forehead and the voice, oh Jesus, the voice. *The bitch of the wurrld. A man can't take a drop of drink without the voice or worse the look from the bitch of the wurrld.* Later, in bed, the sound of his mother's weeping, every gasp and sob, through the cardboard tenement walls. After forty-five years of running, are you back where you started?

"Please go home."

A voice from the silent kitchen. A voice that spoke words that summoned something worse than silence: nothingness. He suddenly felt that he was a thousand feet below the surface of the earth or sea, breathing pressurized claustrophobic air. It seemed to thicken around him, until he was moving with the elaborate motions of a swimmer or a dancer as he walked from the dining room into the bedroom, put on his still damp shirt, tied his tie, shrugged on his coat and overcoat and walked into the living room, to recover the picture. As he picked it up, it seemed to pulse in his hands like a time bomb. He held it by the tip of two fingers, at the end of his slack, dangling arm as he struggled back through the impossible air to the door. *What happened?* he wondered dazedly, like a survivor of an explosion.

"Margaret," he said. "Margaret. I'm sorry."

Silence. What else did you expect from ruins?

For hours he drove aimlessly around the city. Stopping for red lights, accelerating, braking, turning, these minimum functions were the only actions he was able to perform. Their simplicity, their automatism, were a kind of therapy. The black steel shell of the Cadillac, a symbol of power and prestige, was a kind of womb in which he crouched for protection. *You have to begin again, Jimmy boy, from the beginning.* Where did it go wrong, where was the first wrong turn made? Coming out of Mother feetfirst maybe? Christ, how the old lady complained about her breech-birth boy for the next twenty years. No, seriously, maybe it was the day old man Brophy, Lord rest his crooked soul, hired you to tutor his son Bernie, so the birdbrain could get into Georgetown. Sitting there in that overstuffed, overdecorated, lace-curtained living room, stuffing Latin verbs into Bernie's empty skull, maybe that was when you decided you rated that carpeted, satiny, gold-wallpapered, grand-pianoed splendor more than the whole goddamn tribe of Brophys. Or maybe it was the first day you met Dave Shea, the new mayor by a whisker-thin margin, and saw the same kind of beetling brow and bullneck that spelled father, but this time the roaring voice, the iron handshake were magically combined with cash. *I need young guys like you, guys with brains. We're gonna run this town.* Then out of his pocket came that astonishing wad, with the thousand-dollar bills on the outside. *That's what this is all about,* roared the fathering voice. *It's time the Irish made some of it.*

Oh, forget it. You can't drive back through time and turn right where you turned left. All you can do is drive around and around now, while the city grinds past you into the appalling future.

Toward midnight he felt better. Not good. As if all the blood had been sucked from his body, or his nerves deadened by some semi-lethal gas, he was able to make a leaden lunge toward movement. He double-parked the car and telephoned Larry Donahue from a corner bar. The father, Bill Donahue, drunk as usual, slurred out the message that Larry was working at the paper. The Judge found him there. "This is Jim Kilpatrick, Faith's father. I want to talk to you."

"What about?"

"About something I don't care to discuss on a goddamn party line, with half the city desk listening in."

"I'm here till midnight."

"I'll meet you in front of the building."

Fifteen minutes later, Larry opened the door of the darkened car and got in beside him. "What's up?" he said. The words were cocky, but the voice was not.

"This is what's up." The Judge switched on the overhead light and took the picture off the dashboard and handed it to him.

Larry's narrow, hollow-cheeked face went through several descending transformations, from self-confidence to something very close to fear. "Where did you get it?" he finally asked.

"Johnny Kenellen gave it to me. At City Hall."

"You guys think of everything, don't you?" There was a kind of rueful awe in the words. "What do you do, have a detective watching her all the time? Or watching me? Tapping my phone?"

"Sonny boy, you've got a hell of a lot to learn. You're not important enough to get your phone tapped. They wouldn't waste a detective on you either. And I wouldn't let one of Dave Shea's plug-uglies shadow my daughter even if her life was in danger."

"Then what's the answer to this?"

"There's a camera right up there in the wall behind the desk clerk. You and every other swordsman from the city get a mug shot free of charge when you visit the Wagon Wheel Motel. If they steer you to the right room, I understand the whole performance gets filmed. You were lucky. You weren't important enough."

"Jesus Christ. What a city."

"Save the sociological commentary for some other time and place. I'm here to talk to you about my daughter. How in Christ did you get her into bed? It sure as hell isn't with sex appeal."

A small smile flitted across Larry's bitter mouth. "Thanks."

"How?"

"Why do you want to know, Judge?"

"Because I suspect it has something to do with me and I want to be able to give her straight answers to your crummy, rotten lies."

Again the smile. "What if I told the truth, Judge?"

"About what?"

"About you and that schoolteacher. Margaret Halloran?"

"What do you know about her?"

"I know she's your mistress."

"Prove it."

"She has an apartment out on the Parkway someplace. You pay the rent. Or most of it."

"Prove it."

"I don't have to prove it. It's common knowledge."

"You snotty little rat." He wanted to smash this snide face against the windshield until it was a bloody blob. But what good would that do?

"Isn't it true, Judge?"

"Assuming that it is, would I admit it to you? Again assuming, did it ever occur to you that maybe a man, even a big shot, wants something more out of life than a good quick lay? Maybe what he's doing has something to do with the word *love.* A shit like you naturally wouldn't know anything about that."

"Maybe you're assuming too goddamn much, Judge."

"You don't love her. You don't love anything. All you want to do is score. On me, on her, on life. Because you got dealt a lousy opening hand. Jesus Christ, so you got a drunk for a father. I had one too but it didn't turn me into a sick, vicious neurotic like you."

A nerve twitched in the sallow cheek. "We all have to do the best we can with that opening hand, Judge. Mine didn't have a joker in it."

"It sure as hell had a jack of clubs."

"Maybe, just maybe, I love Faith. Maybe she loves me. I've got to say *maybe,* Judge, because what I've seen, what I've gone through, makes it almost impossible for me to love anyone. That isn't true about Faith. She's full of love. Maybe you deserve some credit for that. I don't know. Maybe I started out like you say I did, just wanting to score. But she's changed that."

"Jesus Christ, you mean I'm liable to get you for a son-in-law?"

Silence. Your talent for destructive remarks has never been more brilliantly displayed than it has tonight, James.

"Are you going to keep seeing her?"

"I guess that's up to you."

"It's up to her. What kind of an ignoramus do you think I am? Just because one part of me wants to throw up at the thought of you in bed with her, that doesn't mean I think you can tell people who to love, or who not to love."

"Are you going to tell her about this?" Larry picked up the picture and dropped it again on the seat between them.

"I don't know. I don't think so. I hope you don't."

"I believe in absolute frankness, Judge."

"Then you're an absolute idiot. Absolute frankness with women guarantees absolute disaster. Stop and *think* about it for a minute, will you, for Christ's sake? You're scoring, you're performing. You wouldn't care if they filmed it in technicolor and ran it as a short in the movie theaters. She's giving herself, opening herself, risking."

The nausea came on again, with the pain in the chest. It was too much, the images were unbearable.

"I'm learning something, Judge," Larry said. He looked straight ahead into the darkened windshield. "About you, maybe about life."

"It's about time."

"I'm only twenty-three, Judge."

"I knew that much at twenty-three."

"Maybe you learn one thing and you don't learn another thing. I know you can't play games with a punk like Dave Shea. You didn't know that, did you?"

The narrow face turned and cut into you. This kid is tougher, cooler, smarter than you have been willing to admit. Answer him, truth for truth. Do it for Faith. Maybe it will help.

"No," the Judge said, "I didn't."

"I don't know whether Faith even wants to see me again," Larry said. "It wasn't the greatest thing in the world. It was the first time for both of us."

"Good Christ," the Judge said.

"Jesuit education, Judge. It guarantees essential ignorance. That's what I can't figure out. You all knew so much at twenty-one. Then you turn around and send your kids to Catholic schools, where they learn nothing. Or worse than nothing."

"The women did that. We didn't."

"Why didn't you stop them, for Christ's sake?" Larry said. His voice trembled again.

"Because you have to live with them. You have to live with so goddamn many things."

Silence. But perhaps in a blind, unfathomable way, something good has happened, there has been a small blundering advance in the scheme of things. Two people have spoken the truth to each other. For two, perhaps three full minutes. A remarkable event.

"Can I drive you home?"

"No thanks. I'm going downtown for a few drinks. I hate to get home before the Old Man goes to bed."

The Judge nodded and switched off the overhead light. The door closed with its familiar hollow thump, and Larry Donahue was gone. The Judge sat in the darkness, feeling strangely comforted. Nothing has been accomplished. You have not saved your daughter from further assault and yet . . .

He drove swiftly down the Parkway to the familiar apartment. Up in the creaking elevator once more, the ascent into the ruins of happiness. He opened the door and found himself face to face with Beatrice Halloran. The incredible beaked nose and owl eyes, the fright wig of graying hair, the yellow-toothed hag's mouth. "What the hell are you doing here?" he snarled.

"I'm here at the invitation of my sister. She called me up hysterical over your brutality. It is ending like I always predicted it would end, with you treating her like a common streetwalker."

"Where is she?"

"She's sleeping. I gave her a sedative."

Down the hall he charged, while behind him the hag's voice screamed, "Don't you dare go in that bedroom." Into the dark overheated room he stormed, crashing the door against the side wall. Margaret struggled up on one elbow and said groggily, "What—"

"Margaret, I had to come back and tell you—I didn't mean one of those goddamn things I said. I talked to Larry Donahue. It's okay. I think they love each other. Or at least they're trying."

She fell back onto the pillow and her head moved slowly back and forth. "It's too late," she said wanly. "You can't take back—"

"Margaret, it wasn't me. I was out of my mind. I—"

"Too late," she moaned, and rolled away from him, into the blank darkness against the wall.

In the doorway, Beatrice Halloran's hulking outline loomed. "If you dare to touch her I will call the police."

"I'll see you tomorrow, Margaret," the Judge said. "Tomorrow?"

# Chapter Fourteen

It was a gray unpleasant day in late December. Rain swept in icy gusts across the highway, at times overwhelming the windshield wipers. The weather was a perfect match for Dick Thornton's mood. A gray uneasiness permeated his flesh. Life seemed to be moving in a kind of nightmare slow motion, resisting, even mocking, his pretensions and illusions of speed. He was finding the last year of law school dull. It was not the fault of the school or the subject matter. He had simply been going to school too long.

There were other more personal worries. Dwight Slocum had suddenly developed an extraordinary interest in Victoria Sand, thus proving Vicky had by no means wasted her night aboard the Slocum Special. She had pursued Dwight down to the campus and enrolled for another year of graduate study at the university theater department. There was an alliance which, if it was ever consummated, would reduce to zero Richard Thornton's influence in the Slocum panorama.

Dwight's love life was not the only worry. He was also displaying a total indifference to the realities of law school life. He had yet to open a book and was barely attending classes. Last year Dick had gotten him through with a massive final week of tutoring. But there was at least a foundation of information on which to build that house of cardboard knowledge. This year it looked like there would be nothing—and the comprehensive three-year exam was a brute.

It was important for Dwight to get through law school. It might help resolve that strange war of nerves he played with his father. Thus far Dwight had done little to convince the old man that he was "morally or intellectually qualified" to assume control of Slocum Industries. You remember that phrase very well, don't you, Richard? It was from a letter the old man had written to Dwight during his first year in law school, when he had almost been expelled for getting caught with a girl in his room. "My responsibility," the letter had continued in small, precise handwritten script, "is to the hundreds of executives who have given their lives to this business, to the thousands of workmen who have done likewise. Don't presume my affection for you will ever displace that responsibility." A tough old bastard, Dwight Slocum, Senior. You had to be tough and hard to make it big in the United States of America. But his son Dwight had toughened only his body, not his mind and spirit. You cannot complain about that too much, Richard. That very softness, that inability to take life seriously, is your opportunity as well as your distress.

But Margaret. The more wearisome and messy life elsewhere grew, the more grateful you became for Margaret. She was an island of calm and reassurance. Admit it, with each date you looked forward to seeing her a little more. At the same time you kept a careful check on your feelings. You were not going to fall headfirst into another orgy of wishful emotion. She was a lovely relief from harassment and anxiety. But problems remained. Doubts had yet to be dispelled.

There was the religious uncertainty—or to put it more exactly, Margaret's vocation. He had not mentioned it since their nearly disastrous argument. He had scrupulously followed Larry Donahue's advice and avoided the subject of religion whenever possible. It was good advice. With each date he could see a slow subtle change in Margaret's feelings.

And your own feelings, Richard? What if you get very, very close and then lose her? He shook his head. Sometimes he wondered if she really was good for him. With all the perfection she potentially had, she was almost too entangled with her religion. He told himself, for the twenty-third or -fourth time, that he did not object to women being religious. It came naturally to them and only pseudo-intellectuals, like Victoria Sand, rejected it, at their peril.

But it was easier to make the general statement than it was to cope with the particular intrusion of this religious spirit. The other night, after that art show for the benefit of a Paula Stapleton charity, you had taken her to the Garden Square Hotel for dinner. While you were recoiling from the prices on the menu, you heard her saying, "I wish—you weren't so involved with Dwight Slocum."

"So do I, sometimes," Dick said. "But I think I can do it and still save my soul."

"What do you mean by *that?*"

"My integrity, self-respect—you name it."

"Oh."

"The world isn't run according to moral principles, Miss Connolly. You just find yourself—in situations and do the best you can."

"You don't think people are responsible for what they do?"

"I think they're responsible as *hell,* if you'll excuse the expression. But there are times when you have to compromise on—nonessentials. I've gotten drunk with Dwight, for instance. I don't believe in getting drunk. I think it's a waste of time, energy. But Dwight likes you to get drunk with him, every so often."

Margaret frowned. "Isn't it possible that if you give in too much on small things, eventually the bigger things—"

A shake of the head. You were absolutely confident, Richard, listening to your proud, definite, "No."

Margaret sighed. "I'm going to worry, anyway."

He smiled. "Which Margaret is talking now? The on- or off-campus version?"

"Let's not start that silly game again."

"I need to know whether I am being stamped approved—or rejected for moral turpitude."

"Neither Margaret feels qualified—to judge."

From that sticky confrontation, they had moved without warning to the most remarkable personal communion.

"You may convert me yet," he had said, "when I compare your attitude toward life to my grandmother's."

"Is she religious?"

"She's the original hard-shell hellfire Baptist. When my father was practically starving in 1930, he asked for some help. She wouldn't even let him in the house until he took the pledge."

"So . . . you think religious people are hypocrites."

"Most of them," Dick said. "They use religion like stilts, to look down on people."

"What . . . about me?"

Dick laughed. "You should know by now you break all the rules. I don't try to understand you."

"Because you think women are stupid, I suppose, or some masculine cliché like that!"

"Nope. You're just unique. Resign yourself to it."

Margaret blushed slightly. "You're trying to make me conceited," she said. "Then I'll be as bad as you."

"Why not?" Dick said. "Am I that bad? You need a little conceit anyway. Just a little."

"My mother was always very careful to keep me from being conceited."

"She did too good a job."

Margaret was silent for a moment. "It's funny," she said, looking down. "I was unhappy too—growing up."

"Why?"

"My mother and father used to argue all the time. Terribly."

"Your father doesn't look like the arguing type."

"He isn't. It used to make me feel awful. My mother always blamed him for not making enough money."

"Do you?"

"No, that isn't the only thing important about a father."

With almost inexplicable eagerness, Margaret began talking about her past. She told him about her anguished shyness with boys during her gawky high school days, the embarrassment of never having enough money until her mother went back to nursing, part time, a secret that the family still maintained with almost incomprehensible shame. But she carefully avoided the one topic that he wanted most to hear—how she became involved with this priest and her so-called vocation. It first annoyed, then saddened him that there was still, after so many months, this forbidden preserve between them. It made it easier for him to give her a selective version of his past. He talked candidly about his father's financial and emotional collapse during the Depression, the family's retreat to Paradise Beach, the departure of his mother. But nothing, absolutely nothing about his visit to her, and its enormous impact on him.

Yet he knew, with absolute certainty that this was the single most important experience in his life. The knowing drove into him and became almost a need to share it with this girl as a pledge of his inner commitment. But he could not speak. He was trapped by that earlier commitment to silence, to waiting for her to speak. To tell the whole truth about his mother and the aftermath would plunge them into a discussion of morality and religion that would inevitably become an argument. Instead of a bond, the secret could become a crude, immediate cause for rejection. Yet he did not believe that was possible, as he looked into Margaret's sad, lovely face.

Jesus, what *do* you believe, Richard? he heard himself asking. Where do you stand between relief and belief, insight and option? Accept what this girl can give you, now. Accept it as the best she can offer, this much of her inner self, which she has obviously never shared with another person.

Maybe sex explained it all. His mind drifted back to the sunlight of the first day on the beach, the physical impact of the moment as he looked down at Margaret on the blanket. Would there ever be a day when you knelt beside her and unbuttoned the shoulder straps, pulled the bathing suit slowly down . . .

*No.*

He swung into the outside lane and zoomed past a string of weekend drivers. Sex would come. But if it was at the wrong time it could destroy everything. He understood perfectly that his ability to control himself stood as a solemn vow between them. He was proud of the confidence with which he made that vow.

He was getting anxious to meet this priest, Father Malone, whom Margaret mentioned so often. He had tried to discover from Margaret what role this man played in her daily life, but she had been reluctant and evasive. Finally she said:

"He's . . . my confessor."

"What's that, if you'll excuse my ignorance?"

"The person—the priest—you confess your sins to. The spiritual writers advise you to . . . have a regular one. One you go to all the time."

"Do you go to him very often?"

"Every week."

"Every week!" He had been astonished. "What sins do you have to confess every week?"

"Catholics never discuss their confessions. . . ."

"I mean, how do you have any? What sins do you commit?"

Margaret smiled. "Do you think I'm so saintly?"

"I don't think you're committing any sins."

"We all have imperfections we try to overcome. It helps to confess them."

He told himself to forget it. But he could not stop. "It's the damnedest thing I ever heard," he said. "You *can't* have any sins to confess."

"Oh Dick, you don't understand it! Why are we arguing about it? There's sanctifying grace you get from it too. It's a sacrament."

"I thought you only got sanctifying grace when you were converted."

"You get grace every minute of your life," Margaret said. "There are two kinds, actual grace and sanctifying grace. The most important kind is sanctifying."

"What does it do?"

"It . . . strengthens your will. It brings you closer to God. You can't live without grace. You need it every second. To lead a good moral life."

"Am I getting it?"

"You? I don't know."

"How can I be getting it if I don't even believe in it?"

"I don't know." She looked nervously away from him. "I told you before . . . you mix me up."

"You'd say I was leading a good moral life, wouldn't you?"

"From what I know of it," she said tensely.

"I think I can guarantee you it's reasonably good." His tone was a little sharp at the hint of doubt.

She said nothing.

"Then how can I be leading this good moral life without this grace you say everyone needs?"

"I told you I don't know!" She turned to him, and the words came in a rush of anger and remonstration. "Do you like to make me feel stupid? I don't know everything about theology. There are priests who can answer that question, if you want to go ask them. Just because I can't answer it doesn't mean there is no answer. Why do you argue with me about it?"

"I was looking for an answer."

"I haven't got it!"

"All right. Let's forget about it then."

Little by little, from this and other exchanges, he began to get an idea of how deeply this religious faith was entrenched in Margaret's mind. He visualized her as a little girl, memorizing her catechism, studying her Bible History, repeating it all year after year, as she grew, until in high school "catechism" became "religion" and she memorized more intricate and authoritative dogma, to recite, write in tests and examinations, meditate on, as she prepared for confession each week. And always believing it intensely, in her quiet, inner self. Giving herself to what she believed was good, to what she ought to do. There was something in this very depth and strength of her feelings that attracted him. If once she agreed to love him, he knew she would never again hesitate. It would be permanent and strong and true.

He abruptly withdrew from this thought. For the moment she was worth the trouble. Anything beyond that was dangerous imagination.

She was waiting for him in the rotunda, talking with Faith. Margaret was wearing a dark-green suit. He liked her in suits. The New Look accentuated the long slender lines of her figure. She looked sleek and composed and her smile was bright.

"What sort of party are you taking this girl to?" Faith said sternly. "I represent Mother President and we have to consider the moral tone of any party before we expose one of our girls to it."

"A Christmas party," Dick said.

"Oh my goodness," Faith gasped, "you can't be serious. Christmas parties are totally immoral. They derive their inspiration from a pagan, secular approach to life. Don't you know that enjoying yourself is against the moral law?"

"I'm sorry, Sister," Margaret said solemnly, "but as I told you, the young man who is taking me is something of an autocrat. He never gives me a chance to select my entertainment."

"My advice is to refuse his attentions in the future, absolutely. Any youth who would take one of our girls to a Christmas party is certainly of low moral caliber."

"It's my personality and bank account that attract, Sister," Dick said.

"That's perfectly legitimate," Faith said. "What we expect our girls to do is find someone with an attractive bank account and a nice personality *as well as* high moral caliber."

"I'm sure she's looked," Dick said, "but she isn't getting any younger and this is the best she could do."

"Oh," Faith said, clapping her hand to her forehead, "how can I explain to Mother President?"

"Oh, shut up," Margaret said good-naturedly.

"I hear you've resumed diplomatic relations with Mr. Donahue."

"Diplomatic he's not," Faith said.

"I'm giving you credit for the diplomacy."

"Thanks," Faith said.

The expressway's yellow lights came on as they swung into the gleaming concrete lanes. The rain had subsided into a mean, sloppy winter drizzle.

"Does Faith ever say much about Larry?"

"No."

"But she is seeing him?"

"Unfortunately."

"Why unfortunately?"

"He doesn't do her any good. She just gets more bitter and morose. Today—was the first time I've seen her even trying to be cheerful in a good month."

"Larry scares me, too," Dick said. "It seems like you Catholics can't take the Church—or leave it."

"It goes deep," Margaret said, "when you're born into it."

Was there a faintly mournful note in her voice, or were you just wishing it into your ears? He switched the conversation to Dwight Slocum's Christmas party. He had planned to tell her why they were arriving late and leaving early. Or to put it more bluntly, why they were going at all. But would she understand, much less approve of the notion of a command performance?

For a moment he wanted to tell her the whole truth about Dwight. But his nerve failed him. He was still not sure whether she might suddenly identify him with Dwight's philosophy of life.

In the city they drove down side streets where house windows were aglow with blue and red and green Christmas trees and candles and illuminated wreaths, and along shopping streets where the merchants were using low fidelity records and megaphones to herald the birth of the newborn king. The scratchy hymns blared in the distance created by the car's closed windows; a few hardy shoppers trudged along the wet sidewalks, their arms rigid with shopping bags, their heads bowed against the drizzle.

"There aren't nearly as many X-mas signs this year," Margaret said.

"You don't like them?"

"Christmas is Christ's birthday. Doesn't it seem wrong to take

His name out of the word? Last year some girls from school launched a big campaign here in the city, went around to every merchant with an X-mas sign. Jim Kilpatrick and some fellows from St. Jerome's worked with them."

"Did you?"

"No—I'm not the crusading type."

"Did Faith?"

"No—she laughed at them. She kept saying things like 'Let's put Christ back in Santa Claus too.' It made for awful arguments at the dinner table."

"I'm inclined to agree with Faith."

"As usual."

"Not as usual. But I don't think you can make people religious by advertising, or putting 'In God We Trust' on a coin."

"Every little bit helps—that's what Esther Sugrue says."

"She's a jerk, if I ever saw one."

"Does that mean I'm a jerk, if I agree with her?"

"Absolutely."

She turned toward him with an abrupt, angry movement of her head, but before she could speak he started to laugh. "Every time I look at you, I say to myself, why don't I go out with Esther Sugrue? You're practically twins—and Esther's got more money."

"I thought we were having a serious discussion."

"I'm not in the mood for it. We're going to a party. Anyway, does it really matter whether we agree on browbeating merchants to take the *X* out of X-mas?"

"It would make me feel better if we did," Margaret said.

"Feel better about what?"

"Us going out—so much."

"Let's not think about us for a while. Let's just *be* us. You can't think and be something at the same time."

She said nothing. The windshield wipers clicked busily. The wheels sloshed through giant puddles created by the city's antique sewage system. From elation he began to spiral down into annoyance, even disgust. It was really not very good. They could go from repartee to theology in the space of a single breath, and after theology there was always the taste of ashes. Maybe he was the one who should start thinking about "us."

He swung off the street onto a gravel drive, and around the first loop of a very sharp oval there were lights and voices and music.

Dwight Slocum's Christmas parties were famous, and rain or blizzard, they could expect a packed house. A butler carrying an extra large umbrella ran out and opened Margaret's door. A man in a slicker and sou'wester hood opened the door on Dick's side, and in a moment they were standing in the foyer of the Slocum mansion.

Dick had been here a dozen times, but he still marveled at the graceful curve of the marble staircase, with its massive golden banister. The high tiled ceilings, the intricate arabesques on the great polished doors were still as impressive as they had been in the years just after the Spanish American War, when the first Slocum had profiteered his pile.

They were directed through doors which opened with an explosion of gaiety. The ballroom was jammed; the cocktail drinkers formed a haphazard circle around the jiving dancers in the center. Later, the party would spread all over the house, and then the real swinging would begin. Mr. and Mrs. Slocum had long made it a point to be in Florida when Dwight gave his parties. Dick also planned to be elsewhere when the orgy became general. That was really what he had wanted to explain to Margaret on the way over, but the silly argument over X-mas had distracted him. Who knows, he thought in his sudden gloom, we might stay. He stood slightly behind Margaret in the doorway, letting his eyes move speculatively over her.

No, Richard. No.

"Hey." Dwight was crunching his way toward them through the crowd, spilling drinks and drinkers in all directions. "I thought you two lovebirds were chickening out on me," he shouted, although he was barely five feet away from them now. He took Margaret's hands and said: "Gotta have some nice people here, along with all the slobs."

"Speak for yourself, Tiger," someone yelled from behind him.

"Oops," Dwight said. He pointed up toward the ceiling and then kissed Margaret full on the mouth with a bear hug that almost lifted her off her feet.

"Mistletoe," he said, setting her down. He pointed up towards the ceiling again. The whole thing was a mass of Christmas greenery. "I got mistletoe hanging from every square inch of that ceiling," he said. "You're not going to be safe anywhere tonight."

Dwight was drunker than Dick expected him to be at this hour.

That was not a good sign. Margaret was obviously in a state of shock from the kiss.

"But according to the way I play the game," Dick said, "no seconds."

"Oh—a dog in the manger?" Dwight laughed uproariously at his own humor. "The trouble with you, Thornton, is you're so damned independent. I like independent people—but not so independent that they've always got to remind me of it every time they open their mouths."

"It's kind of an American trait," Dick said.

"Oh, for Christ's sake, let's have a drink on *that,*" Dwight said, dragging them both toward the bar. "Old Thornton's challenging me to an I'm-a-better-American-than-you duel. Did you hear that, Margaret? When did your ancestors come over?"

"Only about eighty years ago," Margaret said.

"That's what I mean. It *proves* you're better. The longer you stay in a country, the more you stink it up. That's clearly proved by the Slocums, right?" He poked his finger into Dick's chest.

"Where's Paula?" Margaret said brightly.

"Paula? Paula who?"

"Why don't you get yourself some nice strong coffee?" Dick said.

"You mean Paula what's her name? Paula-the-girl-that-I-was-almost-engaged-to?"

"Yes," said Margaret, in a much more subdued voice. Dick suddenly realized that over the last months she and Paula Stapleton had become rather friendly. Temperamentally they had much in common; Paula was earnest, reserved, fond of discussing Life.

Dwight took the ring out of his pocket and stared at it. "I sent this to her the other day. She sent it right back. What do you think it means?"

"I think it means you ought to stick to coffee for several months," Dick said. "Possibly years."

"You know what's wrong with you, Thornton? You are too—true—blue." Dwight beamed at Margaret. "Now if I can say that, I can't be as polluted as he implies, wouldn't you agree?"

"I'm afraid I don't qualify as a judge," Margaret said.

"Too—true—blue." He drew a large square with his hands. "A goddamn true-blue square."

He handed them drinks from the bar. They stood there, pressed together by mutual embarrassment, like a married couple, and listened helplessly while Dwight ripped Paula Stapleton into bits of mangled bone. It was amazing. That cool, impersonal girl had the brute hooked; he was thrashing in agony before their eyes, like a huge maddened shark. It was mostly bleeding ego; no one had ever turned down a reasonable offer from Dwight Slocum before, and more than a few, operating on blind hope, had accepted highly unreasonable offers.

Dwight managed to down two Scotches in the course of his harangue. He now seized Margaret's hand and insisted that she have her first dance with him. "Remember what I said about that mistletoe," Dick said. "I don't want to have to slug you in the middle of your own party."

"Go square yourself, old true blue," Dwight said, with a not entirely pleasant grin.

Margaret disappeared when Dwight turned his massive back to Dick, and they moved onto the dance floor. He grabbed another drink and was trying to keep his eyes on them when Dolores Talbot tapped him on the shoulder. "Dance with me," she said. "My date just collapsed and undertaking isn't my line."

Dolores was wearing a shimmering silver cocktail dress, a bold return to the flapper style. She stood there smiling, certain he would obey. Years were behind that smile; you sensed, instantly, how infallible it had become.

"Who's your date?" he said, moving out onto the floor with her.

"Billy Bridge."

"He's been telling everyone in the state he's going to marry you."

"When he was drunk or sober?"

"It's hard to tell with Billy."

"It doesn't matter. Either way he's wrong. I was watching you and Dwight. Paula sent back the ring?"

"I didn't think beautiful women gossiped."

"Fascinating news."

"Are you thinking of making a reconnaissance?"

"Me? No, Dwight and I understand each other too well. We're both monsters."

It startled him, because he had been thinking of Dwight in precisely that term. "I've never seen your kind of monster before. Where do they grow you?"

"Oh, we look all right. I mean psychologically. *Spoiled* is the highly inadequate word used by people who don't really understand the condition. And only those who have the condition understand it."

"How about me? Do I make the club?"

"Oh, no. You're much too self-disciplined. A monster is someone who does things only because he wants to do them, when he wants to do them."

"That's Dwight all right."

"That's right, all Dwight."

They both laughed. "Let me know when you want to do those things. I'll be glad to help."

"Oh, *no.* Not sex. I mean just *doing* it. That's really dull, for a monster."

"Why?"

"Monsters are perverse. They want to destroy themselves. And someone else, who's somewhat innocent, with them, of course."

"Now you're making me nervous about Margaret. She's dancing with Dwight."

"I wouldn't worry. Margaret's so innocent she doesn't even know Dwight's a monster. And that takes half the fun out of monstering."

"I still think you and Dwight would make a great team."

"No. He needs Paula. A true victim."

Dick twisted his head to scan the dance floor and saw not a sign of Dwight's bulky eminence. The music stopped and Billy Bridge came staggering through the dancers like a moth homing in on the glitter of Dolores Talbot's dress. Billy was almost as rich as Dwight Slocum, but unfortunately was a total slob.

"Hi-hi-hiding on me," he said, hiccuping in Dolores' face. "I was just catching forty winks."

He left Dolores smiling patiently at her ossified love-slave, and went in search of Margaret. He found her in the far corner of the room, in solemn conversation with Dwight. He had her trapped in the angle of the wall, so that if she had wanted to get away, she would have had to knock him down. But the conversation seemed remarkably genuine; only when he saw Dick did Dwight begin clowning. "What the hell have you done to this girl? She's trying to make me *think,* for God's sake. That could be dangerous."

"For you, or her?"

"For the whole room. It might be like unleashing atomic energy, without the lead shields."

"Rust would be more like it. Clogging the air—"

"Listen to the brain," Dwight said. He put his arm around Dick. "You're so goddamn smart, Thornton, you're stupid. You know that?"

"Let's dance," Dick said to Margaret. "I didn't come here to philosophize."

Dwight got the message. He wheeled and strode toward the bar. Out on the floor, Dick said: "What were you telling him—to put the Christ back in X-mas?"

"I was telling him to grow up—"

"That's asking a hell of a lot. For Dwight."

"Oh, I think that's silly. Treating him as if he were unique, just because he's rich."

"Not just because he's rich. You've got to spend some time with him before you realize certain things about him—"

"What?"

Tell her about the prostitute in Mexico City, screaming through the streets after him, the fag with his face punched out of shape in New York? No, because you were there, Richard, you were the guilty spectator or at least bystander, and guilt by association would be all Margaret Connolly needed. "It doesn't really matter, does it? Let's say he's got a mean streak which comes out at unexpected moments."

"Who doesn't?" Margaret said cheerfully.

Oh, you are so goddamn sure of all your judgments, Miss Connolly. Suddenly Miss Connolly you are so goddamn sure of everything. Is this a monster that I see before me in unlovely outline, another all-knowing bitch, convinced of her infallibility just because the mirror says she is beautiful?

Hey, hey, hey, hold onto *your* judgment, Richard. You are letting Dwight Slocum turn you into a premature sourpuss. But the temptation was still there. Wouldn't it be lovely to shatter this confidence, not with a word, but with an act, strip away false knowledge with a tug of the zipper? Have a drink, Richard. Have a couple of drinks.

The band had switched to jazz. The throbbing, wailing music wound through the confusion. Dwight came dancing by with Vicky Sand. She gave Margaret one of her more malevolent looks. "Let's double-cut," Dwight said. "Just like old dancing-school days."

Your old dancing-school days, Dwight, not mine. But there was nothing he could do about it. Silently, with a faded smile and eyes that he hoped were saying: *You son of a bitch,* he accepted Vicky's small moist hand.

"She's lovely," she said, as they moved off, and Dwight whirled Margaret away in a Fred Astaire movement he had invented on the spot. "Is she good in bed?"

"Not as good as you," he said.

"We were only rehearsing, dear. It takes months of practice to really do the big scene."

"Who's in rehearsal now, Dwight?"

"He doesn't need any rehearsal. There's a real man."

She looked past Dick at what may or may not have been Dwight in the distance. It would be stupid to turn around, and even more stupid to deny that Vicky was incapable of making him wince. Old stupidity, old emotion, which, alas, in this case were one and the same.

"How are things in the theater department?"

"I wouldn't know. I'm doing other things."

"I bet they miss you—at rehearsals."

"I wouldn't be surprised."

She looked up at him defiantly, but he caught a flicker of fear in her eyes. There was a line running from the corner of Vicky's mouth to the jawbone, a line where before there had been smooth flesh. And another furrow just above her nose, where before there had been mocking serenity. Age, Vicky. Even twenty-five is old in your profession. You can't go back to the theater department next year. The freshmen are making filthy jokes about you, and it's suddenly a strain, pretending wisdom and culture you never had.

Maybe she caught the reflection in his eyes or sensed the small tingle of pity that momentarily shivered his nerves. Her mood abruptly changed. "I don't know why I came to this stupid party," she said. "I knew I was going to see you, and that isn't good for me. You ought to be proud of that, Richard. You're the only one who's ever caused withdrawal symptoms."

"Not a whole year later," he said.

"Eight months later."

"Still hard to believe."

"Oh, for Christ's sake, I haven't been a goddammed *nun.* But I thought you'd like to know. Not even Dwight cured them."

"I'm sorry."

"Oh *Christ.*" Vicky stopped dancing. Her eyes were glistening with apparently genuine tears. "I'm going to get really stinko."

She pushed her way through the dancers towards the bar.

*Not a bad idea, stinko.* He struggled past more dancers on his way to a smaller bar, on the opposite side of the room, and downed a double Scotch. It made him feel a little better. But it did not obliterate the suddenly overwhelming sense of *wrong*. It had come on him at other parties, without Vicky's help. He was *wrong* at this party, exchanging chatter with the local heiresses and scions, *wrong* pretending that he was going to walk around a house like this someday as owner and conqueror, *wrong* that he was trying to create himself, so to speak, out of the ruins left by his father and a dozen more mediocre forebears, *wrong* that he could create a wife tailored to his specifications by altering Margaret Connolly's mind or Vicky Sand's morals, *wrong*. He was small-town, and proved it in his inability to deal out contempt and venom to Vicky, to give her exactly what she had given him when he had accused her of infidelity, like the wounded lover in a *True Romance*. He saw himself married to Sally Flagg or some other high school classmate, the vestryman of the local church, the big man on the local school board. *Christ!* That was wrong, too. If you are born in a trap, it is better to go down fighting your way out. If this was wrong, this Slocum-generated glitter, so was Paradise Beach.

He had another double Scotch. Maybe the trouble was Margaret Connolly. She did not fit into either scheme. She was ready to turn on Slocum & Company and denounce them as totally as she now seemed to be accepting them. The curious moralism that lay behind all her reactions suddenly infuriated him. Why? Because it slumbered just a little farther back, in the shadowy genesis of your emotions too, Richard? Did she make you realize that you have never really been able to kick that fervent devotion to Jesus that was the big emotion of your adolescence? That goddamn hymn-singing choirboy still haunts you, doesn't he? Nothing the smart-ass professors told you in Comparative Religion, all your tricky books on Biblical criticism, can erase the *fact,* yes, fact, those feelings, those hymns you sang with fervor in every word. *Jesus loves me, Jesus loves me. Jesus!* Was that why you wanted Margaret Connolly? By playing yourself off against her, you were proving once and for all that the choirboy was really dead? And, instead, every time you saw her, his ghost became a little more active? Yes, life was full of those paradoxes. What seems perfectly logical in the brain works out in a totally opposite way in the hypothalamus. Maybe Vicky was better, maybe you can screw that choirboy to death, yet. *Screw the choirboy!* What a great title for a novel. Richard Thornton, the personification—or the idiotification—of the American Dream.

"What the hell are you laughing at, Rover Boy?"

It was Dwight, handing him another very dark drink. A triple Scotch, if taste could tell. Dwight was very drunk. And you're another, Richard. "I'm laughing at my own brilliant, unique humor," he said. "Why in Christ's name did you stick me with Vicky Sand?"

"I thought it'd be good for a laugh. Or a lay."

"Your lack of tact is equaled only by your lack of wit."

Dwight shrugged. "You can't be getting very much from the Queen of Virgins upstairs."

*Upstairs?* The implication somehow failed to penetrate his befogged brain. "I hate to upset the first principle of your philosophy but—"

Dwight belched and rammed a finger into his chest. "Stay away from the Catholics. At least that kind of Catholic. Undress her and you'll find a pair of rosary beads knotted into a goddamn chastity belt. It's a waste of time, kid."

"What you call a waste of time—"

"On the other hand, I get a certain amount of bitch from her. You know sometimes that type can talk a great line about God and country and all the time they're thinking, why doesn't this jerk lead me to the nearest bedroom?"

"Look, Dad, this girl's different—"

"How the hell do you know? You haven't gotten close enough to find out."

"I've gotten as close as I want to get—"

"When are you high I.Q.'s going to stop lying to yourselves? Your goddamn principles. You and Paula. Close ranks. Or legs, that's your goddamn motto. Christ. She's upstairs right now—"

*Upstairs.* "Who's upstairs? Paula?"

"Paula? That'll be the goddamn day. Watch her, I think she's a dike, I really do. Really do." Dwight found two more drinks. "I think maybe she goes for your little virgin, Richard." Dwight threw a massive arm around his shoulder. "Richard. She's upstairs right now, stretched out on that bed, and all you got to do is arrange the furniture. Throw away the key. You can have the whole goddamn weekend. I'll see to it."

"Margaret? Upstairs. Have you—"

"I haven't done a goddamn *thing*. I talked her into taking champagne, and she got dizzy. You know—she must've had all of two-and-a-half sips. I asked her, she want to lie down, and she said yes. The way she moved it going up the stairs made me think—kid—but I couldn't do it to my old buddy. I want to give him the chance—I don't think you've ever had a real cherry, pal, have you? This one could be great, she's got a ripe one. First they're scared and it *hurts,* and then they're begging you to stick it in again, just once more—"

"Where is she?"

"Upstairs. In the green bedroom—"

He was on the stairs, the great marble stairs, stairway to grandeur, his stairs, someday, *yeah*. Good Christ, you know what Dwight is doing now. You know what he wants, and what Dwight wants Dwight must get, or Dwight is disappointed. *Yeah*. Be a man, my son. You son of a bitch, Dwight, you son of a bitch. You shouldn't have finished that last drink, you drunken son of a bitch, with your lousy principles. You know what Dwight wants. If he does not get it, you know you are out of the charmed circle, sent to the rear of the line, Dwight knows. And why shouldn't Dwight get what he wants? Doesn't everybody with ten million bucks get what he wants? Isn't that the goddamn basic premise of American democracy? Isn't that what everybody goddamn wants, until his guts ache, ten million goddamn simple dollars so he can act like Dwight? But not you, Richard. You would be dispensing wisdom and largesse with your ten million. But of course you've got to get it first and it's hard seeing you get it without Dwight.

What do you know, the green room? The green within the gilt on the door's wainscoting announced to all and sundry that this was the green room. The in-between room. The in-between-the-sheets room. He turned the gold handle of the door. She woke up, she locked it, she's no fool, she went home. No. The door swung open, and lying there on the huge round bed in the center of the green and gold room was Margaret Connolly with her eyes closed.

For a long time he stood just inside the door, watching her breathe. Rose and fell rose and fell rose and fell. Those lovely breasts. She was perfectly relaxed, perfectly at peace. Her dress was neatly tucked beneath her legs, her hands by her side. Except for the breathing, she might have been dead. He walked around the bed once, twice, three times, examining the remains like a burlesque detective. She was dead—dead to the world; no, look at that face, a tiny trace of a smile on those contented lips, innocence.

You want everyone like Vicky, the prices all figured in advance, your prices?

Yes, goddamn it, a man wants his world on his terms. But you, of course, are willing to settle for Dwight's terms? No, Dwight's terms just happen to coincide with yours at certain points, and the main point is that you are tired of innocence, tired of adjusting the world to Margaret Connolly's absurd preconceptions; yes, tired of taking the credit and letting the cash go. Be a man, my son.

In the distance, crockery crashed against a wall or floor. A girl laughed, shrilly, over and over again. A male voice shouted sweatily. The party was moving upstairs. He went back to the door and turned the gold key in the lock. Innocence. He sat down on a French Provincial chair beside the door and studied Margaret Connolly's face from a distance. Innocence. Not stupidity. It was not a stupid face. It was open, unscarred. None of those little lines which Vicky wore from her innumerable rehearsals.

That lovely neck, the firm flesh still faintly tan from the Paradise sun, the long, somewhat angular body, marvelous legs, breasts, thighs; it was all there, waiting. There really should be a tape recorder, a movie camera, so Dwight can get the full story. There might be one or both, somewhere. Dwight thinks that way. It didn't matter. He was going to reverse the process. He was going to leave Dwight and Margaret Connolly both wondering what hit them.

You drunken liar. In two weeks, when Dwight whistles, you'll come running. But Margaret won't whistle. She won't sleep so soundly, with that little superior smile for the ways of the world, either. Those lovely lashes will be damp most of the time. Think of it, Thornton, you can say proudly when you add up your life's accomplishments, I once went out with a girl who trusted me absolutely, you know I think the crazy kid even loved me, until I taught her the big lesson. Let me tell you, she was a smarter, wiser, sicker girl when I got through with her. And you know, the funny thing is, that girl never even said thank you. She never showed me one tiny shred of gratitude for all I taught her about life.

Yeah, yeah, yeah, Thornton. Life, life, life. From somewhere above them, there was a heavy crash, which might have been a falling body. Out in the hall he heard a girl say, "Please, I'm feeling *sick.*" Margaret stirred on the bed. She turned slightly, burrowing one shoulder into the pillows. A small frown passed over her face. How dare you annoy me, world. I'm Margaret Connolly, and I have you all figured out. Thomas Aquinas told me what to do about you.

He walked over to the bed and sat down beside her. Quietly he let his fingers move along her arm. She stirred uneasily again. He leaned forward and kissed her. Somewhere inside his body there was a physical response, but he felt nothing. His nerves might have been encased in lead. Still asleep. He kissed her again. Her eyelids fluttered uncertainly, and then she put both arms around him and kissed him back.

He sat there in a kind of paralysis, as she clung to him through a haze of semi-sleep. "Oh Dick, Dick," she murmured. "Oh—" The arms fell away, and she dropped back on the pillows. "Dick," she said, puzzled but totally unalarmed. "I was dreaming, I—"

She laughed softly. "But it wasn't a dream."

Smiling now. "All I do is compromise myself with you. And you never say a *word.*"

"It's part of the plan."

She looked around. "Where are we? I remember getting awfully dizzy, Dwight insisted I sample his twelve-year-old champagne. He—scared me, he was so drunk—I didn't faint, did I?"

"No, you just passed out, like a lady, after you reached the bed."

"I can't help it if that stuff makes me so sleepy. I'm not a hardened souse like you. What time is it?"

"Ten thirty."

She got up and went over to a multi-mirrored dressing table and began combing her hair. It was incredible. She was so goddamn trusting you'd think he was castrated. It was not an act. It was natural.

But listen dear, the door is locked, we're not going home for a while. Why don't you go in the bathroom and take off your clothes like a good girl? I don't want to rip anything. It was easy to say and perhaps even easier to do. You can surrender from disgust as quickly as you can from desire. Wasn't that what he was doing, with Dwight? I'll play your sick game, just to show you I can play it, and goodbye. The same principle here. Naked in the bed of love, teeth bared in unlovely revulsion, but who cares about the expression on the face? Below the face there is no expression.

You care. In Christ's name or in nobody's name, you care. You care, you care, you *care*. It doesn't matter who else cares, or doesn't care. Whether Dwight Slocum sneers or applauds, Vicky Sand laughs or cries, Larry Donahue denounces or deplores. You care. So let's go home.

A great hand pounded on the door. "Everybody happy in there?" Dwight roared.

Dick sat down on the bed. Margaret looked over her shoulder at him. Dwight pounded again. "Hey, little boy blue. Are you blowing that horn?"

Get lost, Slocum, lost in hell. I am going to sit on the side of this bed until dawn, if necessary, before I answer you. But Margaret, before he could speak or stop her, walked over and unlocked the door.

"You look happy," he heard Dwight say.

"Why shouldn't I be?" Margaret said.

A nasty laugh and Dwight was swaying over him, an open bottle of champagne in one hand and his other arm around Vicky Sand. "Well, for Christ's sake, look at him. The big-time operator. Now we know where he isn't big."

"Oh, I could have told you that a year ago," Vicky said.

Dwight thought this was very funny. He almost choked on his champagne. There was equally wild laughter from a growing crowd in the doorway. Familiar faces, all of them, from Yacht Club and college days. The young rich, young friends, Richard, all part of that highly complex apparatus that was going to produce your fortune.

"Are you happy, Richard?" Dwight said, prodding him with his foot.

"Of course I'm happy," he said, without looking up.

"You don't look it."

"He's just tired," Margaret said.

"Things are never what they seem. That's the first principle of philosophy," Dick said.

"Yeah," Dwight sneered. "You look like a man, for instance, but—"

He came off the bed and punched Dwight Slocum in the mouth.

He knocked him loose from his champagne bottle, and from Vicky, and sent him staggering over a small French Provincial couch, flat on his back on his expensive pale-green bedroom rug. He heard Margaret give a little cry, and Vicky and the doorway crowd a gurgle of unbelief, but his eyes were on Dwight.

Dwight came up and crouched there on one knee for a moment, a great lithe animal, absorbing his anger. A small line of blood dribbled from one corner of his mouth. Then, without a word, he came at Dick. It could not really be called a fight. Dwight had been intercollegiate heavyweight champion. One big fist caught Dick in the ear as his own right hand bounced harmlessly off Dwight's weaving head. Explosions then, one just above the waistline, the other in the face, flinging him backward into a soft sea of darkness, and thump the rug, face down, as he rolled off the bed.

From a far, far distance he heard Dwight ask: "We spill all the champagne?"

Vicky: "No."

"Good. Let's go play some real games."

Cold darkness on his face. A washcloth. A wish-cloth. What do you wish, now, Richard, now that Slocum and his ten million have vanished into the far, far distance? Wish, wish, wish. Her face, in a halo of dark glittering haze, and the room, the famous room where Richard Thornton became a man or stopped becoming one. Take your choice. Don't ask him to pay his money, because he has none. Just take his choice.

He was on his feet now, staggering carefully into the bathroom. Put your head under the cold faucet, real man, and fling the freezing water in your face. There you are in the mirror, with a tremendous black and blue bruise on your right cheek. He touched it gingerly with a towel. It hurt. In the bedroom, Margaret was standing by the dressing table.

"Don't look so sad," he said. "It's really kind of funny."

"But—why? Why did you do it? He could have killed you."

For a moment, through the ringing inside his head, he heard a mocking, secret voice, laughing. *She doesn't even know what happened. You don't even get any white points in her doomsday book. But if you really told her, if she really knew why Dwight sent you upstairs, she would run back to her convent forever, clutching this proof of the world's bestiality. And you are committed now, committed to stopping that brainless monstrous surrender. So say noth-*

*ing, just shake your head again, while down the hall a man laughs drunkenly and a girl screams, half frolic, half fright. Grab her hand and get her out of here.*

"Take a good look," he said on the way down the stairs. "We won't be back."

"That's fine with me."

"You know—it's fine with me too."

Then why the sinking, dooming sensation, Richard? Why, along with the ache in your jaw and the ringing in your head, is there that voice again, laughing, laughing, laughing?

# Chapter Fifteen

Margaret stood in the crowded church unsmiling.

Standing, yes, wherever there was standing you were there.

Standing so alone and not alone, Margaret.

Standing with him beside the rumpled bed among the overturned furniture.

Standing while the words spoken, the blows struck, resound in your mind like the crash of thunder.

All the walking, kneeling, sleeping, eating, praying, thinking you have done in the last month, all the answers you have scribbled on examination papers, the words you exchanged with Faith Kilpatrick and Dolores Talbot and Esther Sugrue, and you were still in that silent room with those words, those blows, while meanings flopped and twisted in your body like fish in the bottom of a boat. And other meanings crept through your brain with the stealthy ugliness of the crab.

Was it?

Did it mean he loved you?

What did that mean?

But why didn't he speak?

You had stood there, eyes blurred, body and mind chaotic. It was hard to see any expression on his bruised, swollen face. But something awoke in the silence of that moment when you faced each other. Yes, that is what traps you in that room, Margaret, roots you to the floor there like one of those nymphs turned into statues or trees by disgruntled gods.

And now standing. Oh, yes, standing in a church. There was Father Malone in a green chasuble on the altar, between the two tall candles. Your spiritual adviser. To the right and left, big banks of vigil lights flickered in the gray, early morning light. Each one, she knew, represented a prayer, ignited by one of the 355 other girls who stood around her in the chapel. One of them was yours, a flickering temporary prayer wavering like Margaret herself before the Blessed Sacrament, while she sat in class or walked the halls and lawns of Mount St. Monica asking herself so many questions.

Why didn't Dick say something? Why didn't he explain everything? Because he assumed you understood. Because he assumed he was dealing with intelligence, not stupidity, with a woman of the world. Because he assumed there were certain things that did not have to be said.

And you, Margaret, are you too proud to admit your ignorance, too cowardly to confess your fear, too frozen to take the one step toward him which might release the words you hunger to hear—and also dread?

Yes, dread. Face it, Margaret, in that room a secret conception took place. You acknowledged for the first time the possibility of a new Margaret, the dream girl, the witty, bold companion who slumbered inside that other simpleton, sensible Margaret, frozen there in the amber silence. Was she growing inside your body even now? Would the birth be as brutal and bloody and agonizing as your own? Strange, how you keep thinking about Mother's favorite story, those forty-eight hours of agony in which she labored to bring you forth. The worst two days of her life. You know every step of that messy, repulsive story, from the enema that began it to the Caesarean operation that finally ended it. Yet, in spite of that fear, you find yourself dreaming in the most ridiculous, grandiose way about this new Margaret, what she might (will?) be like. The opposite of sensible Margaret, reckless and uncaring? No silence for her; on the contrary, a perpetual babble of witty dialogue and profound discussion, about life, its meaning, its purpose, its destination. Yes, a person born with a zeal, even a passion for equality in her blood. She will be bold (but not crude) with men, simple, direct, casual. She will talk to them as she might talk to a brother, yet she will retain, within this remodeled exterior, the same intense devotion to Christian values, yes, the same profound love for Jesus and his Mother. But it would be blended with strength, confidence born of . . . what? Don't flinch from it, Margaret, accept it, exult in it. Born of the fact that someone *loves* you. Amazing, remarkable, impossible, incredible fact. You, this tongue-tied, awkward mediocrity, this flighty, frightened semi-person, loved for what you were, but even more for what you could become, this new Margaret who would someday flower out of the old, like the butterfly out of the awkward squishy caterpillar.

*Ite, Missa est,* intoned Father Malone.

The words were like a stone thudding against Margaret's body. Absurd, you stupid girl; you have daydreamed away the Mass without so much as a prayer, living in this fantasy world, gorging yourself on make-believe when there was not a word, not even a gesture really, to prove that love was there. No, there was simply interest. Interest that was neither defined nor committed. Why should Dick go beyond that when he has seen your inability to cope with the Dwight Slocums of the world, your obvious preference for being alone with him, instead of joining that sophisticated crowd with their parties and their inside jokes. You were glad to see him turn his back on Dwight Slocum, because you sensed evil (No—who are you to be so profound, Margaret?—just grossness, crudeness, but that was enough). You even saw it for a while as a turning in your direction, a sense, somehow (God knows you have done precious little talking about them) that your values, the truths of faith, were superior. But that too is absurd, as if you could really compete with Dwight and his cabin cruisers and sports cars and mansions.

At breakfast, Faith sat before the scrambled eggs, moody and silent as usual. She still refused to go to church, and Sister Agnes Marie, for some mysterious reason, continued to permit her to get away with it unpunished. Would the new Margaret end like this, full of bitter revolt against the religion of her birth?

No, no, no. There would always be the soft, sweet peace of meditative prayer in the twilit chapel, the deep rush of emotion as the communion Host touched her lips. Those things were real, and the new Margaret could never change them.

Walking with these thoughts, Margaret almost forgot where she was going until she entered the classroom and saw Father Malone at his desk, cheerfully greeting his favorites. He had said very little to Margaret about Dick since the day she had written him the note.

Instead, their weekly conferences were severely limited to discussing in the loftiest terms the quest for spiritual perfection. He had given her the autobiography of that model of humility, St. Theresa of Lisieux, the Little Flower, and they had discussed her approach to spirituality almost exhaustively. The little way, the constant referral to God of all disappointments, frustrations, problems, was deeply touching.

The class opened with the usual prayer and they settled down to hear Father Malone outline the next section of their course in theology. They would begin with the creation of the universe. From there they would cover the spirit world—angels, the origin of man, the transgression of Adam, the problem of evil, the last things of man—judgment, hell, purgatory, the last things of the human race—the general resurrection, the general judgment and the communion of saints. Their textbook was written by a Jesuit who was a former teacher of Father Malone's. He considered it a masterpiece and constantly referred to the author as "our theologian."

Father Malone began by reading the thesis which was in capital letters at the top of the page: "THE WORLD WAS CREATED BY GOD ALONE, NOT FROM ETERNITY BUT SIMULTANEOUSLY WITH THE BEGINNING OF TIME." The important terms in this thesis were analyzed and explained. Next came a consideration of the "adversaries." Father Malone picked up the textbook: "Let's see what our theologian tells us. 'Materialists, evolutionists, positivists and some others hold the unestablished theory of self-existent primitive matter requiring no Creator from which all things are made or evolved . . . Pantheists, with whom may be classified theosophists, hold in varying degrees the theory that the assemblage of finite things or beings in some way is God. Agnostics and the various followers of the chance theory who represent the universe and all it contains as the result of chance or who, with other atheists, deny the Divine revelation contend that the origin of the world cannot be determined.'

"And now we come to the most important point," Father Malone continued. "You will see on page fifty-nine the theological note: 'This thesis in all its parts is *Of Faith.*' "

Faith Kilpatrick's hand went up. "I thought we were supposed to study the creation of the world this term in Natural Theology."

"You will," Father Malone said. "But in Natural Theology you will study it only from the viewpoint of human reason. Here you are studying what we know of creation from the theological or divine viewpoint."

"It sounds like the same thing to me. For instance, you're asserting that the world began at a certain point in time. There are a tremendous number of scientists who believe this is simply not true. The steady state theory of the universe is most respectable in scientific circles."

"You will find in Natural Theology," Father Malone said, "among the proofs of St. Thomas Aquinas that it is impossible to have an infinite series of causes. There must be a first cause."

"That is simply not true," Faith said. "Thirty years ago Bertrand Russell demonstrated mathematically that an infinite series is possible."

Father Malone's good mood was crumbling rapidly. "Miss Kilpatrick," he said, "I am not here to debate philosophy with you. I am here to teach you theology."

"In other words, even if philosophically we come to the conclusion that the world is eternal, we have to believe it was created because the Church says so."

"Miss Kilpatrick, the hostile tone which you are injecting into this class is unnecessary, unwelcome and unwholesome. You are here in this class to listen, to open your mind to the mind of the Church, not to question, argue, bicker. Theology is a science in which you have no competence whatsoever, and I might add that by attempting to raise the old canard of opposition between the teachings of religion and natural science you are about fifty years behind the times."

Margaret closed her eyes and prayed that Faith would say nothing, but this was a foolish hope. "Maybe the canard is not as dead as you think, Father," she said, "but I'm more interested in pointing out that we are told to think for ourselves in one class and accept things on faith in another class—the same things. Doesn't that strike you as rather absurd?"

Father Malone strode down the class until he was only a few feet from Faith's chair. "*You* strike me as rather absurd, Miss Kilpatrick, opposing your childish mind to the mind of the Catholic Church. Two thousand years of wisdom is wrong and Faith Kilpatrick is right. Is that what we are all supposed to believe?"

"I think my objection deserves an explanation," Faith said.

"Is it an objection—or a vicious attempt to disturb the faith of your fellow students? An attempt to create unhealthy doubt where none existed?"

"I'm not particularly interested in what you call it, Father."

"Now you are being impertinent. I think perhaps the best thing for you to do, Miss Kilpatrick, is memorize the proof of the thesis which you will see on pages fifty-nine and sixty. I want you to memorize both pages and recite it for us in the next class. Understand?"

"Yes, Father."

Margaret stared down at the vast quotations from the Fourth Lateran Council, the Vatican Council, the Ecumenical Council of Florence, the passages from Genesis and the New Testament. The thought of memorizing them all, word for word, made her head ache.

Poor Faith. Still trying to use Mount St. Monica as proof that the Catholic Church was the untrue faith. Father Malone, of course, played right into her hands. He was not the only teacher at Mount St. Monica with a low toleration for disagreement. As Faith loved to point out, it was so easy to lapse into infallibility when you taught in clerical robes. But even if most of the teachers followed this formula, what did it prove? Mount St. Monica was only one school, dominated by the cold impersonal old woman they called Mother President.

What happened here proved nothing about the entire Catholic Church. No school was perfect. There were probably teachers at Wellesley and Smith who were equally intolerant with those who disagreed, who cut down the class disrupter with the same cruel sarcasm. The tragedy here was that the performance involved the prestige, the value, the image of the Roman Catholic Church and thereby affected the deepest, most profound feelings of the human soul.

Up in their room after lunch, Margaret watched Faith plunge once more into a book entitled *Modern German Existentialism.* Day after day, Faith spent her time reading books like this on evolution, philosophy, comparative religion, ignoring her friends, preferring the gloomy solitude of the room or solitary walks in the winter woods.

"I'm worried about you," Margaret said.

"Why?"

"I haven't heard you laugh in four months."

"Maybe I've decided life isn't a laughing matter."

"I don't think it is either. But—"

Faith threw her book aside and sprawled back on the bed. "Why don't I go to confession and get it over with?" she said, staring up at the ceiling. "I want to. That's the hell of it, Meg. I want to. But Larry told me to expect that. You can't turn off Catholicism like water coming out of a spigot. It takes time to kill it."

Another kind of newness, Margaret. This was not the voice of the teen-ager, the impudent, mocking girl. This was a woman speaking. Margaret found it even more difficult to answer her, because Faith had yielded to her persuasion and gone to see Sister Agnes Marie. She had in turn sent her to see a priest named Lewis, the pastor of the church in the nearby village of Weston. She had gone back several times, ruefully admitting that he was an "improvement" on Father Malone. But it had not stopped her from carrying on her savage spiritual struggle, which she acted out in class and in the dormitory, to the growing dismay of her friends.

There were times when Margaret intensely resented Faith's use of her as a symbol in this struggle. But there were other times when she felt curiously grateful. In some strange, illogical way, she felt relieved of the responsibility of making the final enormously difficult decision about Dick and her vocation. Then Faith's struggle for what she called freedom became by an impossible reverse, her struggle too. If Faith failed, Margaret would have her answer. If she succeeded—No, it was too ridiculous. You are thinking like that reckless creature, New Margaret.

Suddenly Margaret remembered with an unpleasant sensation in her stomach that she was scheduled to see Father Malone for another conference today. This time, would Dick be the subject? Sitting in other classes, listening to the familiar voices of the teachers discoursing on English literature and scholastic philosophy, she looked out at the clear winter sunshine and once more imagined herself sitting calmly in Father Malone's study, two adults discussing a perfectly ordinary situation. Something that happened thousands of times all over the country every year, a Protestant boy and a Catholic girl interested in each other—not madly in love but exploring the possibility of love. There was nothing to get excited about. My faith is not in danger. "Can't you see that, Father? Dick respects my beliefs and I respect his beliefs." Oh, it was perfectly simple, there was absolutely nothing to worry about.

By three o'clock the day had turned gloomy. Dark snow-clouds scudded across the lowering sky as Margaret crossed the brown lawn to the chaplain's cottage. As she neared the steps, a whisper of old anxiety stirred in her body. She banished it by walking a little faster. There was *nothing* to worry about.

Father Malone greeted her at the door with his brightest smile. The shadows in the doorway left his face vaguely undefined. It made Margaret uncomfortable, but once more she stifled the feeling and followed him into the dim disordered study. "What strange weather," he said. "If it gets any darker we'll have to set the clocks ahead."

"Yes," Margaret said as she sat down in the familiar chair.

"I've always liked the twilight," Father Malone said, still looking out the window at the deepening gloom. "I think it's the most spiritual part of the day, don't you?"

"I don't think I've ever thought about it that way, Father."

"I've been working on a poem about it. Would you like to hear it?"

"I'd love to."

He walked over to the desk and picked up a piece of paper. "It's called 'Twilight.' Not the greatest title, I might change it.

"In this gray hour when the wind falls and
    the dun sky thickens
There is a sudden mystery in the gull's call
    A paradox that quickens.
In the great gloom of the sky's face
    A single star
Salutes the secret of His kindled grace
    The flame afar."

"That's lovely, Father," Margaret said.

"It's only the first stanza," he said, "but you get the idea."

"It's a wonderful thought."

"Yes. The flame afar." He pushed his swivel chair away from the desk and looked out across the darkening lawn. "The flame afar. That's the trouble. It's been afar, Margaret, for two thousand years. Two thousand years of war and disaster and human failure. Because human beings have never had the faith to reach up and seize that flame, Margaret, and bring it down to earth. That's what Christ wants us all to do. Bring the flame of His grace boldly down to earth.

Use it to burn away every trace of deceit and corruption and lust."

"I know, Father."

"You could do it, Margaret, perhaps better than anyone I know. You have the unique gift of moving people, simply by being yourself. Someone like me—I have to write poems, preach sermons, scribble articles. And even then I don't reach them. Do you know I get discouraged sometimes, Margaret?"

"No—I didn't, Father."

She was suddenly very uneasy. He had never talked to her this way before.

"I get discouraged. Every priest does. But those of us who see more, who have an opportunity to see more—I think maybe we get more discouraged. I'm speaking to you very personally, Margaret."

"I—appreciate it, Father."

"Do you realize how few there are like you, Margaret? People who are truly good? Oh, I don't mean to disparage the moral lives of the majority of the class. They are all good girls—largely because their parents and teachers have arranged a way of life for them that keeps temptations to a minimum. But how many of them really aspire? How many of them reach up to bring that flame down to earth? How many of them try to make charity a rule, a beacon in their own lives? You know they are very few, Margaret."

"I suppose so, Father."

"That's why—this change in you has been especially discouraging to me, Margaret."

"What change, Father?"

"Well, not a change. I know you haven't changed your faith, your spiritual intentions, your goodness. But you have—shall we say, deserted the very highest counsels of perfection in your association with this Thornton fellow. I don't pretend to be infallible, God knows, but I am your spiritual director, and with the soundest reasons in the world, I advised you not to continue seeing him, and you refused to take my advice. That's what I mean by change. It makes me wonder if there's not another, more unpleasant change in the future."

"There isn't, Father," Margaret said. "I don't intend to change in any way."

"Who did you discuss this with—who gave you other advice?"

"I'd really rather not say, Father."

"Well, yes, of course," he said, picking up a paper weight and letting it drop with a small *bump* on the desk. "I shouldn't have asked you that. I'm actually glad you did talk it over with someone else. I'm sure that in general they confirmed the prudence of the advice I gave you, at least?"

"Oh yes, Father."

"Well, I'm glad you feel there won't be any change, Margaret. That's very important."

His face was deep in shadow now. She could only see light on the top of his forehead, the tip of his nose, and center of his chin. It made his words somehow more penetrating. With a tiny flicker of panic, Margaret realized how much they had already penetrated. Desperately, she summoned another reserve of calm, probably her last.

"Let me admit that you are very important to me, *personally,* Margaret. I see you as a woman with this unique gift, this ability to make grace *visible.* This is an enormous potential for good that I want to win for Christ, Margaret. I sit here trying to tell you about the glories of the religious life, when all I can think about is what a failure I am. How far I fall short of the kind of perfection, the kind of shadowing forth of grace, that I should possess. The mere fact that I have to talk so much is proof of my inadequacy, Margaret. But you—as a religious, you wouldn't have to say anything. It would shine out of you—the meaning of the power and the majesty of Christ's love. That flame afar."

"I—can't believe it, Father. If I only could—"

Margaret heard the tremor in her voice and knew serious trouble was not far ahead.

"The flame afar, Margaret. You could achieve wonderful things for Christ and His Church if only you would cooperate with the grace that's in you. Think of the gratitude, the gifts you would receive from a grateful Christ, and His Mother. Can anything else approach that kind of happiness? That kind of achievement?"

"No, Father—no. But—"

Margaret heard her voice, flat and emotionless. Suddenly there were tears in her eyes. Oh, let me alone, you there, in the almost darkness, you voice with no face, let me alone, don't make me say that I don't want to serve Christ, that I don't want to love Him, that I prefer loving a person I can see, feel, touch, kiss. Don't make me despise myself for this choice, which I haven't chosen, and may not choose, if my prayers are only answered. Let me alone, Father, let me alone. The tears clogged her throat, and she struggled to swallow them, but it was impossible. A moment later it was out, the first choking sob.

"Margaret! What's wrong?"

He turned on the light. The white glare came up on his face, wide-eyed and dismayed, even frightened. It turned the window black and she saw them both there, suspended in the outer darkness. Together, even out there. Even the other Margaret out there is trapped by you, Father, haunted by your voice. She tried to stop them but the sobs came repeatedly now, great strangling gasps that shook her whole body.

"Margaret–"

She shook her head, trying to explain it was all right, it was not his fault. But she could not get out a single word. Only sobs. "Let me get you some water," Father Malone said, and hurried into the rear of the house. He came back in a moment and held out a glass to her. She forced some water down and the sobs slowed. In a moment she was breathing normally again, but her eyes still streamed.

"I am trying–Father," she said. "Believe me. But it's hard–terribly hard."

"I realize that, Margaret. That's why I'm so anxious to help you."

"I appreciate it, Father. I appreciate it tremendously."

Oh, why didn't she have Faith's gift of saying exactly what she thought? Because charity did not permit that. Charity made it necessary to lie. There's a puzzle, Margaret, but mild compared to The Puzzle. She stood up and tried to force a smile.

"Can I go now?"

"Yes, of course. I think perhaps–you've been studying too hard, Margaret. Why don't you–take a little vacation next weekend? Go see a movie or two."

They were walking down the long hall to the door. "No, Father, really. There's nothing wrong that a–good decision wouldn't cure."

He laughed. "I'm sure it's a lot closer than you realize, Margaret. God's grace is a very sudden, as well as a very mysterious thing."

"I know, Father."

"I'll remember you in all my Masses this week, Margaret."

"Thank you."

For a moment he stood there on the porch, an oblong black figure with a smile and nothing else on his face. Margaret turned, and he vanished into the larger darkness. So simple, now you see him, now you don't. Wouldn't it be nice if you could turn your head this way or that way and make people disappear, Margaret? Beware, that could be one of New Margaret's several dangerous illusions. Perhaps, in her worldly way, she was as stupid as Old Margaret with her sensible cautions. Perhaps it is time to perform a psychological abortion on this creature. Perhaps she was, ultimately, a temptation sent by the devil to lure away the Margaret whom Father Malone had just described so beautifully. If this power, this shining forth truly belonged to her, could she callously refuse it to Christ's service? Perhaps that moment, standing in the jumbled room, was just a moment, the silence simply silence. Walking through the darkness, Margaret began to cry again, not racking sobs, but a quiet mournful flow.

# Chapter Sixteen

It was not quite dawn. Sister Agnes Marie was awake as usual. She lay quietly on the thick, unyielding plank of solid oak that was her bed and listened intently for the first faint twitter of her friends, the sparrows, who nested in the eaves of the building, just above her window. *Sleepyheads,* she thought finally when there was no sound forthcoming. She placed her feet on the linoleum and felt the dead, penetrating cold numb them almost instantly. Was there pleasure in that pain? No, satisfaction perhaps, the satisfaction of the athlete who has trained his body to obey, for a purpose.

Sister Agnes Marie turned on the desk lamp on the small table behind her bed and padded across the icy room. The cheap thermometer on the wall by the window read 10 degrees above zero. She broke the skim of ice in the white porcelain bowl and bathed her face and neck in the freezing water. Again there was that momentary sensation, coursing downward now, through her body, a kind of pain that was also (words mean so little) a sort of pleasure. She knew by heart the passage from St. John of the Cross. *Unreasonable people . . . undervalue submission and obedience, which is the penance of the reason and judgment, and therefore a more acceptable and sweet sacrifice unto God than all the acts of bodily penance. Bodily penance, which is nothing more than a suffering of the body and might as well be imposed on animals is full of imperfections when the penance of the will is neglected, for many undertake it merely because they like it, and for the sweetness which they find in it.*

A hard saying, but who can dispute the Master? She would admit the word *satisfaction* to describe her feelings, but not pride. No, pride was not possible because so many of the things that happened in Sister Agnes Marie's mind and body were beyond the power of choice. She could take no pride in her achievements (again the word was barren) so there was no need to worry about her reaction to the momentary displeasure (a better word, how easy it is in the language of the spirit to turn words inside out) of icy floor, freezing water.

She knelt in the center of the room, still wearing only her long woolen nightgown, stretched out her arms and began her morning prayers. In the semidarkened room, her mind drifted like a toy boat on a black, utterly calm pond. For a moment a gust of terror assailed her, like a current of Arctic air. How much longer could she endure this agonizing sense of loss, this miserable sense of emptiness that made her body as empty and dry as a withered pod? At first she had thought, no doubt like so many other fools, that the knowledge, the words from St. John, would be enough. *This love, in general, is not felt at first, but only the dryness and emptiness of which I am speaking; and then, instead of love, which is afterwards enkindled, what the soul feels in the dryness and emptiness of its faculties is a general painful anxiety about God, and a certain painful misgiving that it is not serving Him.*

The dark night of the senses was behind her. The dark night of the spirit was beginning. Or so you hoped, my daring one. How terribly you were tempted last night to return to that inner sweetness, that exquisite garden by the sea, where you walked hand in hand with Christ for so many years. You are remembering, even now, like a glutton barred from a banquet, that moment when it first began, in the quiet, empty midday church at Paradise Beach. Ironic name in your present state. But not ironic, or tawdry then, as you gazed at the white altar and the red flickering sanctuary lamp with the small gold crucifix suspended above it. *Suffer the little children to come unto me.* Christ's words had whispered their way through your mind and body, again and again. Suddenly there was a sense of condensation, pressure, as if giant arms were enfolding you. The pressure penetrated your whole body, and once inside, it seemed to reverse itself and begin to expand outward again. An enormous lifting sensation that for a moment was frightening, and then there was the inner bursting, as if a unique, exquisite chemical had been smuggled inside your body and exploded into a gas that absorbed the expanding force and finally became a liquid that suffused your brain and blood with fiery sweetness. *Suffer the little children to come unto me.* The words themselves were like clear, delicious water flowing around you, splashing against your parched, trembling lips. You had stumbled into the street, bewildered but not afraid. For the rest of the day you saw a different world. Never had the beach looked so fantastically white. You could see each individual grain of sand in your cupped palm. The waves seemed to break in slow motion and roll toward the beach in soundless, spotless purity. The sun was an immense exalted disc in a sky painted by Giotto. Children's laughter, even older voices were muted music. Father's thrice-told tales of his medical school days became delightfully amusing at dinner, and his scowling drillmaster's face, complete with Prussian moustaches, became bathed in essential kindness. Mother's drab, whining triteness took on the radiance of humble devotion.

Could it happen again? It could and it did. Cautiously, she had gone to Father Nathaniel Lewis, the chaplain of Mount St. Monica, and he had suggested reading St. John of the Cross. At first, she had been bored and disappointed by the romantic imagery of the *Ascent of Mount Carmel.* The English translations at least struck her as verbose and turgid. Then, almost as an afterthought, she had picked up that slimmest of all his books, *The Dark Night of the Soul.* In an hour, her life had changed forever. The spiritual challenge was incomparably greater than any of her childishly heroic dreams, in which she so often pictured herself accepting Mother's fate, marrying an essentially unlovable man and transcending her distaste for him by the sheer power of God's grace, bearing ten children for him without a murmur of complaint (Mother never stopped moaning about her paltry six). No, that was girlish fantasy, easily explained by Freud. St. John was real, summoning her to the noblest, most daring adventure. Promising her that the sweetness she had already tasted was only a hint of the ultimate ecstasy when, purified by the dark night of the senses and the dark night of the spirit, her soul met God's immense, infinite white intensity face to face.

How delicious the poem which began the book had seemed, that day. Mournfully now, she repeated the first stanza.

*In a dark night,*
*With anxious love inflamed,*
*Oh, happy lot!*
*Forth unobserved I went,*
*My house being now at rest.*

Blithely she had skipped through the warnings with which the book was packed. *How narrow is the gate and strait is the way that leadeth to life, and few there are that find it.* Father Lewis, too, had warned her. But she had been suffused with an arrogant sense of power. Her father, no great believer, had urged her to finish college. Then there was Teddy Franklin, who thought he loved her. How many hours he had spent, that last summer on the beach, begging her to reconsider, or at least to wait a year. But she had been majestic, even awesome in her certitude. Poor Teddy had succumbed to complete panic and had begun wondering if he did not have a vocation himself. She had talked him out of that absurdity and swept serenely into the Sisters of the Sacred Heart of Mary.

Father Lewis was the chief reason for entering the order. She had grandly selected him as her spiritual director. Though he never discussed it with her, she sensed he too was a follower of the mystical way. Dear God, was that the first mistake, blundering in my pride into this place, disregarding the advice of Father Lewis and others, that neither the Rule nor the atmosphere encouraged contemplation? Founded specifically for Catholic teaching by an English-born convert, the order was a small, barely disguised imitation of a larger educational order. In spite of the fact that she did her utmost to conceal her talents and begged for an assignment in the poorest parish grammar school, she had been singled out, told to finish college, and planted irrevocably on the faculty of Mount St. Monica, the order's only college.

Her consolation had been the continuing ecstasy of her meditations. Passage after passage in the life of Christ, but especially the healing miracles and the Sermon on the Mount, filled her again with that unique inner flowing. At times the force seemed to lift her into the air, and it was easy to see how earlier ages spawned so many stories of flying saints. They were undoubtedly exaggerations based on the blessed person's attempts to explain their inner experiences.

Oh, listen to that arrogance. The blessed person. Thank God for Father Lewis, who had really read St. John. Without him, you would have wandered forever through those delicious sunlit bypaths with Jesus. Of course, his direction was easy to follow at first. The earlier years of mortification were so simple. Getting rid of the mattress was a delight. Permanently shutting off the radiator was a joke. Praying with arms outstretched was a lark, when the pain could be offered as a direct gift of love to Christ's smiling face. But then, two years ago, as mysteriously and totally as if a flame that had been burning within her had been snuffed out, all thoughts of Jesus had vanished. It was impossible to see Him, or even to feel Him. Worse, the loss had coincided disastrously with her appointment as dean of the college, working directly under Mother Mary Catherine. At first, she had frantically tried to renew her communion with Christ. Night after night she had knelt in the middle of this small room in the darkness, grappling for a touch, even a breath of His love. She pleaded, like a deserted wife. She whined like a punished child. She cajoled, with atrocious logic. She told Him she needed His strength if she was to endure her new proximity to Mother Mary Catherine. The woman was the personification of a religious life organized around action, with nothing but the pale religiosity of the nineteenth century for spiritual substance. A wizened bureaucrat, with no more, and perhaps less, religion than the president of a secular college.

And all the time you knew—and of course Father Lewis had been telling you—that Christ had not deserted you. The inability to meditate, the loss of all sense of Christ's presence, meant only one thing. The night of the spirit had begun. Or had it? St. John himself had almost treacherously buried doubts in the book that was supposed to reassure her.

*It is true that this purgation at first is not continuous in some persons for they are not altogether without sensible sweetness and comfort—their weakness renders their rapid weaning inexpedient—nevertheless, it grows upon them more and more, and the operations of sense diminish; if they are going on to perfection. They however, who are not walking in the way of contemplation, meet with a very different treatment, for the night of aridities is not continuous with them, they are sometimes in it, and sometimes not; they are at one time unable to meditate, and at another able as before. God leads these persons into this night only to try them and to humble them, and to correct their desires, that they may not grow up spiritual gluttons, and not for the purpose of leading them into the way of the spirit, which is contemplation. God does not raise to perfect contemplation everyone that has tried in the way of the spirit, nor even half of them, and He alone knoweth why.*

Was this why your soul drifted back inexorably to that ruined garden where you walked with Christ, that blasted, withered place through which winter winds now howl, and once-flowering trees are shrunken and bare? Are you failing in this, the crucial test, because your faith is not strong enough? Dear God, how can it be strong when I have seen what I have seen? Why do You test me, again and again, with the care of souls, when You know that I cannot care for my own soul? Why do You make me a witness to things which are certain to torment the fragile ladder of faith to which I cling?

*In darkness and in safety*
*By the secret ladder, disguised*
*Oh, happy lot!*
*In darkness and concealment,*
*My house being now at rest.*

Alas Lord, the house of my body is at rest, but the house beneath my feet trembles with the stink of spiritual vomit. I breathe it each day as I walk the halls. Is this the way of love, Lord? Why does the path to the mountaintop run through a sewer?

Be still. Let St. Theresa talk to God that way. She was a Spanish noblewoman and it came naturally to her. You are just another whining middle-class American. You know the way, you know the words.

*Not the most easy but the most difficult.*
*Not the most savoury but the most insipid.*
*Not that which pleases but that which*
*displeases.*
*Not to desire the greatest but the least.*
*Not to desire anything but to desire*
*nothing.*

My body, Lord, desires nothing now. But will the mind, the soul, ever reach the point where it is equally empty, a scoured receptacle into which Your absolute light may at last enter? There is the point where my faith wavers, where hope, my helmet of salvation, falls grotesquely over my eyes. As long as I must walk these halls, I drown in their lives, Lord, in their hungering for happiness which is not happiness, in their pursuit of shadows they call reality. They draw me back, they even tempt me to mock You, to blaspheme the very idea of trusting You. I know temptations must tempt, Lord, but how long can I wait here alone, in the silence?

Nothing.

Sickening. That is very close to despair. You must *wait* for Him to come. Only He knows when you are ready to climb the secret ladder. Only He can help you climb it and realize the words.

*O, guiding night;*
*O, night more lovely than the dawn;*
*O, night that hast united*
*The lover with his beloved,*
*And changed her into her love.*

*Mary Jane Comiskey.*

No, Lord, not her again. Why do You drive me back into those swamps of despair? With the pleading, sobbing voice, with the streaming eyes, *Mother, I didn't want to do it. It was almost rape, Mother. He said he'd kill me.* Mother Mary Catherine, spasmodic, twitching. *You have violated the most precious of all Commandments. You have besmirched the honor of St. Monica.* Expelled three days before graduation. It made no sense. The girl was innocent before God, and even before man. If she'd only kept her mouth shut about her misadventure at the senior ball, but she told her roommate, who in turn told her best friend, who in turn told one of those vicious souls who wrote an anonymous note to Mother President. Innocent, and even if she was guilty, wasn't it incumbent upon those whose lives were supposed to be a witness to Christ's love, to forgive her? But did you speak? Did you denounce that wizened woman as a vicious bureaucrat, a scapegoat seeker? No. The most you dared do was persuade her to disguise the poor girl's sin, and have the student council expel her for drunkenness.

And Mary Jane? What had become of that happy, bumptious, cheerful girl? You do not ask. Perhaps you are afraid. But to ask is to seek a kind of possession, and you know how dangerous that can be.

*In order to enjoy everything*
*You are required to find enjoyment in*
*nothing.*
*In order to possess everything*
*You are required to possess nothing.*

Faith Kilpatrick. Wasn't this a more dangerous kind of possession, the violation of the college's rules in the name of your own vague wisdom? True, St. Theresa broke her Rule when she became convinced, after years of trying to live it, that it was no good. But here you are endangering two souls. What will happen to Margaret Connolly if in Your wisdom, Lord, You allow Faith to dangle in the pit of doubt? Is this why You continue to deny me, Lord? It must be so. I am a miserable sinner in Your eyes. Faith is so much like me, Lord, like the girl I was, full of anger and magnificent dreams of reform.

Forgive me, Your Majesty, but I will endure Your neglect. I will let You watch over Margaret as best You can. You know better than I the dangers of a quiet soul.

Silence.

Sister Agnes Marie saw the pitiful toy balloon of her soul dwindle down to a withered grape. She saw the immensity of her failure and felt the hot tears of anguish on her cheeks. She would never reach it. She was not one of the chosen. She would never be able to say:

*My soul is detached*
*From everything created*
*And raised above itself*
*Into a life delicious*
*Of God alone supported.*

# Chapter Seventeen

"I've just been putting it off too long," Mother said. "I was just saying to your father the other night I've put it off too long. And what do you think, I've been able to get Father Malone too. How's that for killing two birds with one stone?"

Margaret found it hard to match her mother's enthusiasm. She had no desire to be a witness at a meeting that could only be a confrontation. Yet the idea of having Dick to dinner had been as much her own as her mother's. Off and on, over the last several months, Mother had made half-hearted negative comments about Dick, probing little queries about getting serious, that Margaret had conveniently evaded. It was perfectly reasonable for Mother to invite him now, with the "romance," as she no doubt called it, in its seventh month. It was equally reasonable for her to invite Father Malone. Why not give him a chance to meet Dick? Perhaps he would be impressed, might even change his mind about him. Moreover, Dick had been delighted by the invitation and not in the least dismayed by the news that Father Malone was coming too.

"I've been wanting to meet him," he said.

"Why?"

"I've heard a lot about him. From you."

"Really?" Margaret could not recall talking about Father Malone that much.

"He is the source of all your spiritual wisdom, isn't he?"

"He's a very brilliant man," Margaret said, annoyed at the hint of mockery in Dick's tone.

"Maybe I'll learn something."

"Maybe you will."

As the week drifted by, with Faith maintaining her stubborn revolt and the teachers achieving what seemed to Margaret new lows in boredom, her feelings about the dinner fluctuated violently. One day she found herself looking forward to it eagerly, the next day the whole idea filled her mind with a numb dread. How would Dick behave with a priest? Would he begin exchanging insults? She could suddenly see Father Malone's shocked face, her mother sobbing, her father sadly ordering Dick from the house.

By the time Saturday night arrived Margaret was an emotional chaos. Abandoning Mother to hard labor in the kitchen, she retreated to her bedroom. For an hour she walked restlessly up and down the brown carpet, looking at all the room's familiar objects and decorations as if they were strange and mysterious. There, collapsed on a chest in the corner, sat the worn and weary Goo-Goo bear, her favorite childhood toy. Sleep was impossible once without that furry, sadly foolish little thing beside you. How many hours you spent hugging and kissing it, talking earnestly into its blank brown eyes. And on the wall, that smiling picture of Margaret Connolly, the class valedictorian, and grouped around it, framed report cards from high school. Oh, what a bright girl you were, Margaret, the genius of that third-rate school, collecting your 95s and 96s while people like Faith coasted through the expensive private school run, ironically, by the sisters of the same order, and came out knowing so much more than you. Other pictures of a spidery looking twelve-year-old with frightened questioning eyes, a thin seven-year-old in a fluffy First Communion dress with a say-cheese smile on her boyish face. Ghosts of other Margarets. A small retinted picture of her father in World War I uniform which she had specifically requested as a Christmas present a few years ago. Another ghost.

Margaret lay down on the bed. Two words moved restlessly through her mind. *Love* and *beautiful.* What did they mean? Beneath her robe, she felt her body, warm and quiet from the bath. She had idled in the burning water and allowed the pleasure of seeing Dick again to drift lazily in her mind—happiness, as soft and warm and simple as her body, whitely before her in the rectangle of water. But now there were words: *beautiful* and *love. Beautiful* was her body, her. That was what Faith and others had said. She had angrily rejected them. But she could not reject the word.

Impatiently, she flung her robe aside and walked naked to the round mirror above her dressing table. How good the rug felt, underneath her feet! Her memory raced back to sand and warmth, and sunlight. *Beautiful.* Was this beautiful? This her? And if so, what did it mean?

She stood very straight, her legs close together, and felt her body with her eyes. She looked steadily at it, trying to give each part of herself a name: her breasts were full; she was tall; her legs were not heavy, except perhaps her thighs, or should they have such fullness? She moved her hand across her stomach; wasn't there too much flesh? Wasn't she beefy? Fat? Yet her face was not. And her stomach was flat.

How could she tell if she was beautiful? What did she have to judge by? Faith had said it. But she did not trust Faith. She turned away and put on her robe. She lay down on the bed again with her robe open. The cool air felt good on her warm flesh.

When she was sixteen, her Uncle Bart had told her she was beautiful. But her mother had told her she should forget he had ever said it, she should forget all about Bart and his sardonic mouth and impudent eyes. He was no good, she had said. Yet Margaret had never forgotten him.

Bart had invited himself to dinner. There had been an atmosphere of strain throughout the meal. It was his first visit in almost five years.

Her father was working late at the office as usual. Margaret and Bart had gone into the living room while her mother stacked the dishes. He had suddenly cocked his balding head and looked at her as if she were a statue or a painting.

"And how are you liking life, Meggy, now that you're getting old enough to enjoy it?"

Margaret was bewildered by the remark. Bart went on, obviously enjoying the sound of his own words:

"You're going to be a beautiful woman, Meggy. Remember that. Don't throw it away. Use it to get yourself the best in life."

"Bart!" Her mother was standing at the door, the dish towel twisted in her hands. "What are you saying to this child?"

He had turned, his long arms swinging loosely, and given his sister a look of complete contempt.

"Just a little philosophy."

"I don't want her to hear any of your philosophy."

Bart dropped his bantering manner and became intensely serious. "Haven't I got a right to speak to my godchild?"

Margaret was astonished. It was the first time she had ever heard that Bart was her godfather.

"She's *my* daughter," her mother said. "And you've forfeited every right to be anyone's godfather."

"Why? Because I've lived according to the feelings inside me? Because I'd rather have a few years of love with a real woman than a life with a stick-in-the-muck?"

"Get out of this house," her mother had hissed. "Get out or I'll call the police."

"All right." He whirled and gripped Margaret's arms so hard he hurt her. He glared into her eyes, defiant fury twisting his unnaturally thin face. "Don't live her way, Meggy, the sick way, acting like love doesn't exist in this world. It does. It does. Never forget that." He had snatched up his coat and hat and rushed from the house.

Her mother had been almost hysterical. She had ordered Margaret to forget him—forget everything he had said.

She had almost forgotten it. Not for years had she remembered it in such detail. Uncle Bart and his new Protestant wife had moved to the Midwest. Margaret remembered now how she had puzzled over his words, occasionally, in her adolescent years. What did he mean when he said her mother lived without love in her life? It did not make sense. Her mother was full of love for her, for God, for poor people. Why else did she donate so much of her time and energy to charitable causes? Those words were still a puzzle to her.

Margaret shivered and pulled the robe around her as a hint of winter chill penetrated the room's warm air. For the first time she wondered if Bart meant . . . the other meaning of love?

*He desires you.* Father Malone's words. Oh, no, was Uncle Bart that sick to make sex synonymous with love, the *act,* as the dried up, white-haired old priest had called it in the lecture he gave them on their senior high school retreat. *The male organ is inserted in the female organ. Intercourse. He desires you.*

But you do not desire him. You have no passionate hunger for that absurd insertion. You simply fail to see the connection between love and that smelly, bloody, baby-making, pain-creating part of your body. *The curse,* Faith called it, *a girl's trouble* was Mother's favorite description, and you appreciated both of them when those agonizing cramps attacked you, as they did every third or fourth period. What did love have to do with Mother's forty-eight hours in the labor room, the enema, the water bursting, gushing between your legs. The plop, plop of excrement, the hiss of urine, they were all down there and love existed in the heart and mind. It was above, part of God, spirit, beyond the flesh, this smelly sweaty, painful body.

Men, of course, were different. They were casual about smells and sweat. They were unimpressed by pain. (Of course, as Mother pointed out, it was the woman who always put up with the pain.) And men were equipped with that organ, that dangling thing you had seen on statues and in paintings. The male organ. Ugly. But simply because Dick had one, does that prove Father Malone was right? *He desires you.* Where was the proof? Not one word, not one act in seven months. "No." Suddenly, passionately, Margaret brought her fist down on the bed. "No," and again her hand sank deep into the soft mattress. "No."

She began to dress with meticulous care. She was no longer worried about how Dick would behave. She felt detached from him now. Strange, how at moments she felt mysteriously linked with him, almost felt he was her responsibility. Now, for no reason she could understand, the sense of separation was dominant.

Perhaps he would solve everything this evening by making all sorts of ridiculous statements. Perhaps Father Malone would show her, in a few deft exchanges, how fundamentally opposed they were to each other, how fantastic it was to think seriously of attempting to love him.

She stood before the mirror in her slip and faced herself somberly. What if there were difficult feelings? An inclination toward him. A wish. She could overcome them. God would give her the strength.

*No,* cried that other, steadily swelling, ever stronger voice within her. *You must not let that happen, Margaret. Let Father Malone fight for you. But don't help him, Margaret.*

"Margaret! Mr. Thornton is downstairs."

Her mother gave a light tap on the door after she spoke—a strange habit.

Margaret sat down slowly at the dressing table, watching herself in the mirror. The mere knowledge that he was downstairs . . .

A tight dryness was suddenly in her throat; a pressure in her chest and stomach. She clutched her arms about herself, as if she would wrestle the adversary out. But it was not possible. She dropped her arms and began to dress more rapidly.

A few minutes later, wearing a gray knitted dress she knew Dick liked, she walked calmly down the wine-carpeted stairs. He appeared at the door of the living room as she entered the hall.

"Hello," Margaret said. She went quickly to meet him and he took her hand. They stood in the doorway for a moment, and he obviously meditated kissing her. Quickly she walked past him into the room.

"Wow," he said, strolling after her.

"What's that for?"

"You look . . ." He shook his head.

"Horrible?"

"That's right," Dick said, grinning impudently. "I was just afraid to say it."

"I dressed in two minutes flat," Margaret said.

Dick sprawled comfortably on the couch. "Now you may be a lot of things, Miss Connolly, but you're not flat."

"Was there much traffic coming up, Mr. Thornton?"

Margaret blushed. Mother stood stiffly in the doorway. She had certainly heard Dick's last remark.

Dick sprang to his feet with an unabashed smile. "Practically none. And how are you, Mr. Connolly?"

Her father stood behind her mother in the doorway, more or less obscured. He slid by his wife and shook hands, responding, for him, quite warmly.

Margaret could see her mother was nervous, as they sat down, Dick beside her on the couch and her parents in the two large easy chairs.

"Did you know Father Malone, Margaret's theology professor, is coming tonight, Mr. Thornton?"

"Yes, Margaret told me," Dick said. "I'm looking forward to meeting him."

"He's a fascinating man," Mother said. "I heard someone say recently he's one of the finest minds in the diocese."

"Really," Dick said.

"Yes, I must tell that to Father. Remind me, Margaret."

"Oh, he's already a little conceited," Margaret said.

Mother stared at her in alarm. "You're only fooling, aren't you, Meggy dear? If ever I've seen a man who is more—well, almost saintly—" She turned to Dick. "Do you have any members of your family in relig— Oh! I forgot."

Dick passed over it with a smile. "If there were any others, I don't think they'd be in religion. We're not the ministering kind. Too avaricious."

Mother did not smile. "Mr. Connolly has a first cousin who's a Christian Brother," she said. "But that's all we have. Catholics consider it a great honor, you know."

"So do Protestants," Dick said. "I guess people aren't very different, are they?"

Mother studied the pattern in the carpet for a moment.

"Do you get down to the shore much, Mrs. Connolly?" Dick said.

"No, I'm afraid not," Mother said sweetly. "That's where you were brought up, weren't you?"

There was an alarming silence. Before Margaret could think of a new subject, her father cleared his throat and said, "I used to go down there all the time when I was a bachelor. Surf fishing."

Dick turned to him, obviously relieved. "That's before the concessionaires took over," he said. "It was really nice, then, wasn't it?"

"Now all sorts of people from the city are moving down there year round," Mother said. "You'll have more Catholics than Protestants if you don't watch out."

"We've got quite a few now," Dick said. "We get along fine."

The bell rang and Mother rushed out to answer it. In a moment she reappeared with Father Malone. He stood beaming in the doorway as Mr. Connolly and Dick got to their feet. Forgetting she was not in the classroom, Margaret stood up too.

"This is Dick Thornton, Father."

"So this is the young man I've heard so much about," Father Malone said as he gave Dick a vigorous handshake. Her father got a briefer, more perfunctory hello.

"I've heard a lot about you, too," Dick said, smiling. "I guess we start out about even."

"I hope the mistress of the house is feeling as fine as ever."

Mother fluttered her eyes like a schoolgirl. "We're having your favorite dinner tonight, Father."

"All your dinners are my favorites," Father Malone said.

"Oh, Father, you're an awful tease," Mother giggled.

"No," Father Malone said solemnly, "you cook exactly like my mother, God bless her."

Margaret looked away, vaguely embarrassed. Father Malone never failed to pay a tribute to his mother with every visit. There was a silence as he sat down in one of the big square easy chairs. It made him look diminutive, with only the tips of his polished shoes touching the floor. *Like a little boy,* Margaret found herself thinking. A polite little boy with his eager, smiling face and bright innocent eyes.

"Now what were we talking about?" he said. "Don't let me interrupt anything."

"We were talking about the shore," Mother said. "About how many Catholics are moving down from the city."

"You might wind up converting us all," Dick said with a cheerful grin.

"I doubt that very much," Father Malone said solemnly. "I've traveled around this country a good bit. I've never met more bigoted people than I have met in those shore towns of our own state."

Dick looked baffled. "Really? You might get that reaction from a few of the old people like my grandmother. They still kind of see horns sprouting out of a priest's head. But most of the people my age, or my father's age, don't feel that way. I went to school with Catholics. There were at least a dozen of them in my graduating class."

"But what kind of Catholics were they?" Father Malone said.

"I—I don't know," Dick said. "They went to church. Everybody in town did, just about."

"A Catholic who grows up in that kind of environment without any opportunity for a Catholic education—is little more than a slightly disguised Protestant."

"Well, to be honest with you," Dick said, "I never have been able to see that much difference between a good churchgoing Protestant and a practicing Catholic."

"Of course you wouldn't," Father Malone said triumphantly.

"I would say offhand," her father said in his quiet monotone, "I agree with Dick. There really isn't much difference."

"Oh, what do you know about it," Mother said. "You've never gone to a Catholic *college* where the really profound understanding of Catholicism is taught."

"Precisely, Mr. Connolly," Father Malone said.

"Well—" Margaret watched her father polish his glasses. "That's true, I suppose."

"Where did you go to college, Mr. Thornton?"

"The state university."

Father Malone spread his hands wide in a hopeless gesture. "You won't see any genuine Catholics there either. Just the other day I was talking to the priest who's been stuck with the Newman Club down there. Absolutely hopeless, he tells me. He feels like a man trying to dam the Mississippi River single handed. In the first place there's hardly one Catholic in fifty on the campus who even belongs to the Newman Club. And even they are completely swamped by the irreligious amoral atmosphere."

"I don't think it's any worse than the rest of the country, Father," Dick said.

"And what do you think of the rest of the country?" Father Malone asked, eyebrows raised.

"It seems pretty religious to me. About sixty percent of the people go to church regularly according to some survey I read."

"And you think sixty is a passing mark?"

Margaret held her breath. Dick studied his hands for a moment. "Well," he said, in the same relaxed friendly way, "I don't think statistics like that mean very much anyway. There's no doubt in my mind that this country is religiously involved. There's a sense of being under God even though different people see different meanings in the phrase. That's the way it is at the university too. People are religiously involved. They take it pretty seriously. Some of them wind up changing their beliefs, but I never saw any evidence that it was all in one direction—toward atheism."

"How about the Communist influence?" Father Malone said softly.

"What about it?"

"It's pretty strong, isn't it?"

"That's funny," Dick said, smiling. "My father has asked me the same question. How does an idea like that get around? In all the years I've been there I don't think I've met more than five or six Communists."

"How many do you need to poison the atmosphere?" Father Malone said. "We only needed one Alger Hiss to betray our secrets."

"The ones I saw were students," Dick said, a little sharply. "Kids go off half-cocked, you know."

"Maybe you have trouble telling the difference between a liberal and a Communist," Father Malone said.

"I don't think so," Dick said. "I like liberals. They make you think even when you don't agree with them."

Father Malone laughed briefly. "Pink or red, it's all the same. Right, Mr. Connolly?"

Her father made a noise that might have been assent or just an attempt to clear his throat.

"What did you say, dear?" Mother said.

"Of course," her father said. "Of course."

"Yes," Father Malone said, "liberals are what happen when you let religion leak out of an educational system."

Margaret felt her face grow hot. Now it would happen. Dick could not possibly keep his temper. He would stand up and declare Father Malone seven varieties of idiot rolled into one. But it did not happen. Dick remained perfectly calm, smiling.

"In their own way," he said, "liberals are about the most religious people I've ever met."

Mother sprang to her feet. "My goodness," she said, "it's seven forty-five. The roast will be falling apart. Come on, everyone." She hurried out to the kitchen.

Father Malone turned expectantly to Margaret and Dick and her father. They got up and followed him into the dining room. Mother was busily setting large steaming dishes on the table.

"It's all right," she said. "Thank goodness I was cooking it on retained heat."

They sat down and Father Malone scrutinized the laden table with glowing eyes. "I'm afraid I'm going to gain weight tonight," he said.

"Would you say grace, Father?" Mother said.

"Certainly."

While Father Malone said the brief prayer Margaret bowed her head but kept her eyes on Dick. He remained silent, head unbowed. But he could hardly be expected to recite the Catholic version of grace.

They began with tomato juice; then cream-of-chicken soup. At first Margaret thought Father Malone would take up the "liberals" again, but he was too absorbed in the food. He praised the soup lavishly.

Margaret cleared off the soup plates, and her father stood up to carve the roast. "Oh, Daddy," Mother said, "let Father do it." She smiled a little nervously at Dick. "Father loves to do little homey things like carving, and he never has a chance."

Father Malone smiled and said he would be delighted. Margaret had watched this scene enacted several times before, and it always gave her an uneasy feeling. Her father yielded the knife and fork with a rather unhappy look. He slid his chair back, and Father Malone stepped in between him and the table and went to work. He carved badly, chopping more than he sliced. But he did obviously enjoy it.

Mother was busy filling the plates as Father Malone carved, and when he sat down again, he faced a staggering dish, all but invisible beneath a heap of roast beef, potatoes, beets, and a coating of thick brown gravy. He made a startled face and raised his eyes slowly to his hostess, with the beginning of a knowing smile. Mother was waiting for him with a pleased, eager expression on her face. She dropped her eyes coyly as Father Malone wagged his finger.

"Mrs. Connolly," he said. "You know you shouldn't. How can I ever lose weight if you do this to me?"

Mother raised her eyes with a girlish appeal. "Now, Father," she said. "It's good for you."

"I'll be big as a house, if you keep this up."

He laughed immediately to make sure Mother knew he was only fooling. Then, with ritualistic solemnity, he took a slice of roast beef, divided it in half and chewed it vigorously. His expression grew exalted. "Unbelievable. Unbelievably good."

Mother giggled delightedly. "Oh, I'm so glad," she said. "I was really worried . . ."

There was very little conversation for the first ten minutes. Then Mother filled Father Malone's plate with a second helping of everything, and he became more talkative. He paid most of his attention to Mother, though he tried by glances and side remarks to include Margaret in the conversation. He discussed food at great length, criticizing and praising a number of restaurants in the city.

Mother began asking him about a saint that a friend of hers had recommended for neuralgia. She was not sure of his name. Father Malone ran through a long list of minor saints, but none of them was the right one. He went on to discuss other saints who were specialists in various diseases, asking Margaret occasionally if she knew this one or that one.

Suddenly Margaret realized that they were leaving Dick out, totally, absolutely. Over and over they were saying to him, we are different, completely different from you. We are interested in different things. Here is a world you cannot hope to understand or accept. Frantically Margaret groped for a subject which would bring him back into the conversation.

Mother and Father Malone began discussing the tragic case of Cardinal Mindzenty, tortured into confessing crimes against the state by the Hungarian Communists, and sentenced to life imprisonment. The Catholic papers were full of protests and editorials about it. "Perhaps you read my essay on it in the paper," Father Malone said, " 'It Can Happen Here.' I got a very nice letter from Louis Budenz, complimenting me on it."

"It was wonderful," Mother said. "That reminds me. I was talking just the other day to Mrs. Kilpatrick. She wondered if you could persuade Mr. Budenz to come here and give us one of his lecture courses on communism."

"He's very expensive," Father Malone said.

"I'm sure Mrs. Kilpatrick could raise the money. She's a genius at fund-raising."

"As a would-be lawyer, I must say I'm a little dubious about Mr. Budenz," Dick said.

Who *was* Louis Budenz? All the professional anti-Communists who wrote for the Catholic press were a kind of blur in Margaret's mind. The whole growing crusade against communism did not have much meaning here in this city, with its vast majority of Catholics. Yet it was pursued and preached from the pulpit and in the diocesan paper and in Catholic magazines with repetitive fury.

"Why do you say that?" Father Malone asked Dick, with undisguised hostility.

"I didn't think too much of his testimony at the trial of the Communist Party leaders. He remembered too much, too easily. But he could never remember convincing details under cross-examination."

"I've met him," Father Malone said, "and I think he is one of the finest, most dedicated Americans I have ever met."

Dick shrugged, unimpressed. "I wish he had a better memory."

"Well! I hope everyone's ready for dessert!" Mother said.

In another moment, she was displaying a huge coconut cream pie and giving everyone a generous slice. Margaret halved hers, and her mother protested. "What are you doing? You love this pie."

"But I don't love the calories in it," Margaret said.

"Oh, you're fat already," her mother said.

"Mrs. Connolly," Dick said banteringly, "I consider that a slur on my taste."

Father Malone gave Dick a look which let him know the remark was definitely unappreciated. Dick caught it but refused to let it intimidate him. Father Malone was forced to retreat into ecstasies over the pie and request a second piece to prove his sincerity.

There was a silence until Father Malone had finished his pie. He leaned back, gave a satisfied groan and began to stir his coffee. They waited while he put his words in order.

"Tell me, Mr. Thornton," he finally said. "What sort of philosophy do they teach down at the university?"

"Just about every kind, I guess."

"Huh." Father Malone took a sip of coffee and peered at Dick over the cup, as if he were certain he was going to lie. "Which one did you take?"

"I'm afraid I'm not much of a philosopher, Father," Dick said. "I majored in economics."

"You mean you took *none?*"

"Well, I read some of this fellow, Kierkegaard. He seemed pretty good—in spots."

Father Malone again grunted contemptuously. "He's getting to be quite a fad, isn't he?"

Dick nodded. Margaret had heard Kierkegaard lumped in with a dozen other existentialist philosophers in class, but she knew nothing about him, beyond the fact that he was a Protestant.

"Well, don't you have a philosophy?" Father Malone said. "It's difficult for me to think of a man without one. Every Catholic college graduate has a complete and thorough grasp of the truth—"

Dick smiled—Margaret was not sure at what. "I'm afraid I'm still working one out."

Father Malone grunted contemptuously again. "It seems to me a man should have one by the time he graduates from college. If he doesn't know all the answers then . . ."

"I thought college is where you lose your preconceptions." Dick's tone was still unserious. He was not arguing. "Didn't William James . . . or somebody say that?"

"Oh, the pragmatist," Father Malone said. "I *thought* you got plenty of him down there."

"I read his *Varieties of Religious Experience,"* Dick said. "Very interesting book."

"This is all Greek to me," Mother said, "but I think it's awfully interesting."

"If you think that whatever you *want* is right," Father Malone said, "what have you got to *restrain* you?"

"I don't understand, sir," Dick said.

"Isn't that what the pragmatists teach—whatever you want—?"

"I think it's a little more complicated than that," Dick said.

"It's what it boils down to," Father Malone said. "What have you got to restrain you?"

"I'm afraid I still don't understand," Dick said.

For a fleeting moment, his eyes met Margaret's. He asked her a wordless question and returned his attention to Father Malone.

"I wouldn't let a daughter of mine go out with a pragmatist," Father Malone said. "What has he got to control himself? What motive?"

Margaret blushed. For a moment Dick looked completely astounded. But he retained his composure and said easily, "I'm glad I'm not a pragmatist, if they stand that low in the public eye."

There was a long silence. Mother suggested they leave the dishes just where they were and adjourn to the living room.

No sooner were they seated than Father Malone started again. "You say you go to state law school, Mr. Thornton?"

"That's right."

"I'll bet you get a lot of pragmatism in your law down there."

"I honestly haven't noticed any."

"Underlying, I mean. Your mind is probably full of it."

"I somehow doubt that," Dick said. "I know pretty much what's in my mind."

"It's a vicious philosophy," Father Malone said.

"Frankly," Dick said, with a friendly smile, "I never realized it before. But from the way you describe it, most pragmatists should be in cages. It makes me wonder if most of them aren't already."

Father Malone made an exasperated noise. "I can't understand it," he said. "You must have *some* philosophy."

"I suppose I have," Dick said. "But I don't know what you'd call it. I don't like labels. They're misleading . . ."

"A rose by any other name," Father Malone sighed.

"A rose is a rose is a rose," Dick said. He smiled at Mother, but she missed the remark completely.

*Why don't you answer him?* The words broke into her mind so sharply Margaret started in her chair, afraid that she had actually spoken them. Why don't you refute him? Is it because you can't? At that moment Dick looked at her, and she thought there was a pleading or at least a confused expression on his face. Enormous sorrow overwhelmed Margaret. He simply did not understand the nature of this interrogation. Suddenly he seemed to recede before her eyes, dwindling into a somehow smaller, sadder person, sitting perhaps a hundred yards away in an immensely large room. Oh, Dick, Dick, said a mournful voice from somewhere deep in her body. New Margaret speaking, still unborn but articulate.

There was only one thing to do, rescue him from a situation that was completely beyond his depth. It was her responsibility really. He was her guest as well as her friend and there was no need to humiliate him completely, as Father Malone seemed bent on doing.

"It seems to me—" Father Malone began.

"Mother," Margaret said, standing up. "Why don't we turn on the television for a while . . . ?"

"That's a good idea," her father said.

Did he know too? Was he, as usual, ignored in his objections?

"Why . . . Meggy," Mother said confusedly. "There really isn't anything on . . ."

"Oh, there must be *something,*" Margaret said. She walked over to the television set. The guide for the week was conveniently on top of it.

"Why, *One for the Money* is on," Margaret said. "That's your favorite program, isn't it, Mother?"

"Well, it is one of them," Mother said.

"I'll get it—only take a second," her father said. He jumped up and began adjusting the dials.

Margaret turned to Dick. He was watching her with intent, speculative eyes. "Dick," she said. "Could you drive me back to school tonight?"

"Meggy! It's only Saturday—" her mother cried.

"I know it, Mother," Margaret said patiently. "But I have a lot of studying to do."

"Sure," Dick said. "We'd better get a fairly early start."

"Now wait," Father Malone said. "There's absolutely no reason why Dick should go so far out of his way. I've got my car and I'm going straight back, Margaret . . ."

"Oh, it's not that much out of the way," Dick said. "I'm used to the road by now."

No one smiled.

"It would take you at least two extra hours—just driving," Father Malone said.

Margaret caught the innuendo and flushed angrily. Dick missed it. "I really don't mind it," he said. "Really."

"But it *would* be so much easier to let her go with Father. Don't *you* think so, Daddy. . . ?"

"I suppose so . . ."

"We ought to get going soon," Father Malone said. "I'm saying seven o'clock Mass for the Sisters, God bless 'em."

"Yes, well why not right now?" Mother said. "I'm sure, Father, you don't have any interest in this *silly* program."

"Oh, it's a lot of fun," Father Malone said. "I watch it often. But you're right about going."

Margaret struggled to control an almost intolerable rage. How could they be so utterly, callously cruel? She stared dazedly at her parents and Father Malone, as they discussed the memorable moments in *One for the Money.* The answer throbbed dully deep in her body. They did not realize it was cruel. It was simply one more way of letting Dick know that she belonged to them, not him; that he was the stranger, the outsider, who would never be welcome. Margaret glanced guiltily at Dick, almost dreading what she might see in his eyes. But his eyes were blanks to her, his face expressionless, neither angry nor sad. In her mind, New Margaret whispered the words that Old Margaret did not speak: *I have to go with him, Dick. Please understand. It would upset my mother and father. It would suggest all kinds of horrible things to them.*

"Are you ready to go, Margaret?" Father Malone asked.

"I'll get my coat," she said. "I have my bag almost packed . . ."

It was a clear cold night. She said goodbye to Dick on the front porch, glad of the darkness which did not permit her to see his face. He said he was leaving right after them—Father Malone's car was blocking his car in the driveway. Beside them Mother chattered to Father Malone about the weather, and how she intended to go to bed early, after cooking such a big dinner.

Father Malone drove slowly, his hands clutching opposite sides of the wheel. The car was a new one—a Chrysler which, technically at least, belonged to the College of Mount St. Monica. Neither spoke for the first few minutes. Margaret was tense, certain of what the topic would be. Painfully she reviewed the last hours, seeing more and more clearly how arranged the entire evening had been. But the knowledge bred in her, not anger but a kind of despair. The tension had worn her physically, and yielding to Father Malone on the small matter of the drive back to school was like a lever in her spirit, turning her feelings toward a weary wish to surrender.

She made no attempt to argue when Father Malone, safely out on the turnpike, relaxed at the wheel, slid down a little in the seat and chuckled loudly.

"That's a very unusual young man, Margaret. He doesn't even *have* a philosophy."

She said nothing.

"It makes it rather obvious, don't you think?"

"Obvious—how, Father?"

"Why—it's out of the question for you, Margaret. Anyone who's had as much education—real education—a thorough grounding in philosophy."

"But—I've often discussed ideas with him, Father," Margaret said with a half-hearted stubborness. "He has a very philosophic mind—he can discuss almost anything. Really."

"Well . . ." Father Malone said benignly, "perhaps he has a knack of impressing someone your age, Margaret, who hasn't had a chance to thoroughly digest the philosophy you've learned."

"Perhaps, Father," Margaret said.

"He's also an awfully nice young man. I mean, clean-cut, good-natured. I can see why you enjoy being with him, Margaret. In fact, I really don't see any harm in your continuing to go out with him."

"Really, Father?" Margaret said, dazedly.

"Yes," Father Malone said. "Perhaps you can give him what he obviously needs, a genuine, solid religious faith, a comprehensive philosophy of life."

"Do you really think I could, Father?" Margaret said. "I mean—the few times I've tried to bring it up with him, we've had some rather nasty arguments. So we've just—mostly avoided the subject."

"It isn't easy to reach people like him. He's a little egotistic, if I may say so. But there is one way you could reach him, on a really fundamental level, one way you could show him how much your faith means, Margaret."

"Yes?" Margaret said, hearing her voice slip, with her feelings, into another downward spiral.

"If you gave yourself to Christ, Margaret. Think of the impact this would have on him. He cares about you, I can see that. Just think of how that would hit him, Margaret."

"Yes. Yes," Margaret said, "I suppose it would. But that isn't—a really adequate reason to—"

"No, of course not. The fundamental decision has to come from you, Margaret, from your own willingness to dedicate yourself to Christ."

In her mind Margaret saw the black highway unreeling behind the car, mile after mile, and Dick moving along it in the opposite direction, in his own car. The two of them, speeding endlessly away into a black, blank night. The stars, those same moonless stars stared down. She felt tears trickling down her cheeks. Then, above the tires' hum, her own voice: "Maybe you're right, Father, maybe you're right."

# Chapter Eighteen

*Click,* the icy iron bar slid back into place and Faith Kilpatrick was on the inside of Mount St. Monica's massive fence, and Larry Donahue was on the outside. Behind him the car purred on the road, like an obedient waiting animal. How many dozens of other lovers had met here, Faith wondered, passing on the secret of the removable bar since the day some enterprising Monican or her boyfriend had sawed it loose.

She reached through the bars, touched Larry's gloved hand.

"I love you," she said. "Isn't that a ridiculous thing to say—when we're sexually incompatible?"

"How many times do I have to tell you—it wasn't us, it was that rotten motel."

"You're sweet."

"There's someplace else we could try. When you're ready. Over the state line into Dover. The place is full of big old-fashioned rooming houses, with crazy double beds."

"I've got to go. They turn out the library lights at ten o'clock, and they lock the front doors at ten fifteen."

"That's what I like about Catholic schools, they have such confidence in their ability to teach the Ten Commandments."

"The sixth is the one that worries them."

"Listen, stay away from Father Lewis. Promise?"

"That's cowardly."

"It's realistic."

"Good night."

She fled down the squishy path, while the March wind howled through the bare trees. It had been their best, their most serious evening, since their disaster in the motel. She had blamed herself, wholly, morbidly, for that clumsy, fumbling failure, in spite of Larry's attempts to share the guilt and displace a little of it on the seedy surroundings. There had not been a second invitation. Instead, Larry seemed to switch from lover to spiritual coach, a transformation she found anything but pleasant. He gave her books to read, told her that it would take time to eliminate Catholicism from her blood and brain. "You're like an addict that's been hooked on a drug. You've got to expect some cold-turkey experiences before it's over."

Then, tonight, Faith had told him about her visits to Father Nathaniel Lewis, her talks with Sister Agnes Marie. Larry had disapproved, violently, angrily. But his anger had a reaching, wanting quality in it that had moved her deeply. She did not know how or why, but the glass wall behind which he thought and felt seemed to vanish, and they were able to talk and argue in a new, no less intense but far more open way.

For the first time she had tried to free herself from the tangle of emotion about Margaret. "Sometimes I think it really is almost—evil, playing that kind of game with her. I haven't mentioned it for weeks now."

To her surprise Larry declined to agree. He said Margaret still fascinated him, although he was obviously a little embarrassed to admit it. "The whole thing is a sort of theological drama. The good girl has asked God for guidance. What will she get for an answer?"

"Does that make Dick the devil's advocate?"

"No. He's in the play too, though I doubt if he'd admit it to himself, much less to you or me. He's straining himself to be absolutely indifferent to what Margaret believes. That's part of the democratic faith. But I suspect there's a hell of a lot of hostility way down deep."

"And you feel—this is going to come out eventually?"

"It's bound to come out if Margaret keeps playing the sanctified virgin."

"Then that's another reason why the whole thing is a little sick," Faith said.

"Sure," Larry said savagely, "you'd rather go back to Pius XII-type generalizations that have no application to anything anywhere. If we're going to think at all, I insist that we think about real people. About their lives and our lives."

"But the church just *isn't* as totally hopelessly bad as you say it is."

"I never said it was totally bad, in that sense. Sure there are good people in it, like your wise old owl, Father Lewis, shrewd psychologists like Sister Agnes Marie. I'm saying that you can't use them to argue away the Archbishop McGuires and Father Malones. Their preponderance invalidates the divine claim. Why can't you see that? If you're divinely inspired, impregnated with grace, the bride of Christ, you should be giving birth to children that bear the stamp. The evidence is all on the other side. They are no more divine than the Loyal Order of Moose. But they go on screwing up people's lives, telling them how to live and die, as if they were divine. We have to get all that garbage out of our minds and start all over again with American premises."

Was he right? It didn't matter, another, warmer voice whispered inside Faith. Not the Watcher voice, the cold-eyed impersonal intellect, but a hot voice, an I-sound, a Faith-favoring voice. He loved you. And you would love him, with your body as you loved him now in your mind. It had to happen, it had to come true, and the terms, those ridiculous intellectual abstractions which they kept debating, were really irrelevant.

Behind her on the road, she could hear Larry's car pulling away. It was damp and dark in the woods. Partly because it was cold, partly because it was creepy, Faith started to run. She was just picking up speed when she collided violently with another human being. Flat on her back in the mud, she blinked into the white beam of a flashlight. "I thought it was you," Father Denton Malone said. "Get up."

"Where's your badge, Father?" Faith said.

"I don't need one."

"Do you make a habit of playing policeman?"

"Only when I see people sneaking out the back door of the library three nights in a row."

"Who'd ever think you'd waste your time staring out your bedroom window?" Faith said.

"What were you doing out there?"

By now Faith was on her feet, trying to brush the mud off her coat. She glared into the interrogating flashlight. "Seeing a man."

"Why?"

"Why? Why the hell do you think? I'm in love with him."

"Were you having sexual intercourse with him in that car?"

"None of your goddamn business."

A half hour later, Faith Kilpatrick sat on a straight-back chair in the office of Sister Agnes Marie. On the other side of the room Sister Agnes sat at her desk like a stone statue. Was she meditating? Was she so close to God that she was totally indifferent to the trivial trials of mere mortals? She had remained expressionless while Father Malone told his triumphant story of pursuit and capture and announced his intention of informing Mother President forthwith.

Sister Agnes Marie took off her glasses and rubbed her eyes with the tips of her fingers. The telephone rang. She listened for a moment, then said, "Yes, Mother," and motioned to Faith to follow her. They went down the corridor past the dark, empty offices of the school's administration to a set of large, dark-oak double doors at the end.

"You go in there," Sister Agnes Marie said.

For all the bravado she was attempting to muster, Faith felt distinctly dismayed when Sister Agnes Marie closed the door from the outside, leaving her alone in the office of the president of Mount St. Monica.

A thick dark-blue rug ran from wall to wall, and matching drapes hung from three tall windows opposite the door. Hand-carved Jacobean chairs lined the wall. At the far end of the room, before a wide bay window, a massive mahogany desk gleamed in the lamplight. Mother Mary Catherine sat behind the desk in a carved armchair, her eyes ominously bright in her small wrinkled face. Standing with folded arms to the right of the desk was Father Denton Malone.

Mother Catherine did not invite Faith to sit down, nor did she waste any time in preliminaries. "According to my information," she said, "you are guilty of violating one of the school's fundamental rules. As well as the most important commandment of God. Do you know what I'm talking about?"

"Yes, Mother," Faith said. "But save the lecture, will you please? It isn't a commandment of God to me. I stopped going to Mass about three months ago. Just expel me and get it over with."

Mother Mary Catherine's eyes widened. She leaned forward, her mouth working. "You—you admit it. You want me to be forced to tell this vile story to your dear sainted mother?"

"I don't care what you tell her."

Mother Mary Catherine's voice came out in a short strangled screech. "Well, I care. She happens to be a personal friend of mine. As well as a devoted, dedicated alumna of this school. This will break her heart."

"I don't think she's got a heart, Mother," Faith said. "I think it dissolved in holy water or sanctifying grace or something, a long time ago."

"Just a minute, Mother," said Father Malone, "no matter what you think of this girl's mother I see no reason why you should endure this kind of insolence."

He took two steps forward, and now he was in the foreground and Mother Catherine seemed to recede to almost doll-like status in her big carved armchair. "I sense an evil spirit in this girl, Mother. And what especially disturbs me is the fact that she is rooming with Margaret Connolly, a girl with a vocation. It is not at all uncommon for the devil to attempt to destroy such souls with the cooperation of decadents like this girl."

Father Malone's arm shot out and his finger pointed ominously. "Tell me, under pain of damnation, for I believe your very soul is at stake, have you ever touched Margaret Connolly or attempted to lure her into certain postures or positions when she was dressing or undressing in your room?"

Fire. In the body and in the mind, a raging consuming blaze, through which the room was a humming haze. In the distance Faith heard her own voice whispering, "Goddamn you, goddamn your sick, rotten, twisted soul."

"You hear that, Mother, is that the voice of a Catholic college girl or the voice of Satan speaking?"

Mother Catherine's button eyes merely stared. She was speechless with fright, or horror, perhaps both. *This was ludicrous. Why don't you laugh?* But no laughter came to Faith's dry, trembling lips.

Abruptly there was a crucifix in Father Malone's hand, a black cross with a silver Christ twisted on it. "See," Father Malone shrilled, "she cannot face the cross. I know too much about the operation of malignant spirits like yours. Tell the truth. Aren't you waiting, praying for the chance to destroy Margaret Connolly's purity by seducing her into an unnatural act? Was that man in the car part of your plot? Is he the one who calls me in the night? Is he perhaps Satan himself?"

In the motel, the fumbling failure of love. Margaret in a bathing suit, wet, gleaming from the sea. Drowsy, the long limbs stretched beside you on the blanket. Larry, your prince of darkness. Was it true? Terror raced like insane electricity through Faith's body. "Please," she heard herself whispering to Mother Mary Catherine's withered doll's face, "please, it was never intentional. Nothing of the sort. I'm not—"

"Admit it. Admit it now so we can get you out of this school without a moment's delay," Father Malone shouted.

"Stop it!"

Sister Agnes Marie stood in the rear of the room, just inside the big double doors, a small island of calm in a hurricane of hysteria. Never was Faith so grateful for the sight of another human being.

"I am here, Mother," she said, "because you accidentally left your intercom open on your desk. I could not help overhearing what was happening. These kind of scenes can only damage your health, Mother. Moreover, if I may say so, I think Father Malone is exaggerating the seriousness of this girl's spiritual condition. She is in a state of mortal sin and perhaps in danger of losing her soul. And she undoubtedly deserves expulsion for tonight's escapade. But I have found no evidence of satanic possession."

"Perhaps you're not as experienced in such matters—" Father Malone began.

"If you wish to make a formal accusation, Father," said Sister Agnes Marie, her voice rising from its usual soft solemnity, "I believe canon law requires an investigation to be conducted by a trained exorcist, appointed by the Bishop. I need hardly point out the kind of publicity this would give the school."

"I think you are quite right, Sister," said Mother Mary Catherine. "I'm glad you came in. Much as I appreciate Father Malone's zeal, such matters are best conducted in private. Miss Kilpatrick, I wish to see your father here in this office as soon as possible. I cannot see any alternative solution to your case but expulsion. But I wish to discuss it with him first."

Faith followed Sister Agnes Marie down the hall and into her office.

"Sit down."

Faith sat.

"Would you like to talk about this in any way?"

The empty, almost toneless voice, so neutral, so accepting.

"I would only like to tell you—I wasn't doing anything immoral."

"I'm glad to hear that. Is this the young man who has disturbed your life so thoroughly?"

"Yes."

"You've made quite a sacrifice on his behalf. I hope he's impressed."

"He won't be."

"From what you tell me about him, I would diagnose his spiritual health as rather poor. I see you flinching. It's a pity you've learned to think of the word *spiritual* as synonymous with doctrine or obedience. It has to do with all aspects of the soul."

"I think it's a little late for explanations, Sister."

"Yes, I'm afraid it is. You will have to learn from experience. I'm only afraid it will be unpleasant."

"Let it," Faith said fiercely. "Anything is preferable to this state of suspended animation."

Sister Agnes Marie nodded. A ghost of a smile twitched across her lips. "I felt the same way when I was a student."

"Then why did you—"

"Somehow, Faith, you must accept the fact that the world is large enough to permit different people to make different choices. None of them are necessarily wrong."

"Do you think Margaret Connolly should go into the convent?"

Sister Agnes Marie sighed. "You still don't understand. Whether I think so or not is utterly unimportant. The only thing that matters is what happens in Margaret's soul."

"How beautiful that tolerance is, Sister. Wouldn't it be wonderful if everyone adopted it?"

"Yes, wouldn't it," said Sister Agnes Marie.

# Chapter Nineteen

Your problem, Judge James Kilpatrick thought morosely to himself, on a damp and gloomy April Saturday, is ridiculous for a man of fifty-eight. You are frustrated. For almost three months now, Margaret Halloran had refused to let him enter her apartment. She had changed the locks on the doors. His only consolation was that she had also barred her sister Beatrice. If he wanted to see Margaret, all he had to do was invite her to dinner. She was perfectly willing to talk to him, even to let him kiss her hello and goodbye. But the marriage (admit it, you thought of it that way too) was over, unless a real marriage began.

There was no point in rehashing the old arguments that had persuaded her, fifteen years ago, to become his offstage wife. Then they had meant something. He was still the Corporation Counsel, directly under Dave Shea's iron thumb. Now, as Chief Justice of the Supreme Court, the domination was so much more tenuous, it was impossible to justify his hesitation. The argument, as far as Margaret Halloran was concerned, was brutally clear. It was fifteen years later, he was Chief Justice in a modern state where the best people got divorced. Even the current Republican governor had one to his credit, ten years back.

It was impossible to explain that no one ever escaped from Dave Shea, that there was enough incriminating evidence in City Hall files to send Judge James Kilpatrick to jail forever. It was even more impossible to explain that a divorce would ruin him as the ornament of the organization, in the full flower of its respectability.

After thirty-five years, there was no longer any need to steal blatantly, or break heads and wreck polling places to pile up the votes. The organization had the county and the city tied up. The Church was mute; the papers slavishly obedient. So why not respectability Irish-Catholic style? Dave Shea gave a hundred-thousand-dollar altar to his parish church, and the Judge cranked up a cool million for the Archbishop's Cathedral. But how could a divorced man be the toastmaster at the Friendly Sons of St. Patrick's annual dinner? Or serve on the executive board of the county Holy Name Society? Or address the police and firemen's communion breakfasts? At least 60 percent of his value to Dave Shea would vanish if Judge James Kilpatrick got divorced and remarried. That meant trouble—even more than he was already having with Dave Shea.

The Judge sighed, looked out his study window at the drizzle and went back to studying the latest exchange of briefs on the Barton case. The prosecution argument was so good it was obvious that Shea had hired some of the best attorneys in the state to get him what he wanted. They boldly called for sustaining the sentence and cited a half-dozen examples from other states, in which appeals courts had followed similar policies. But no one had done it in this state, in this century. He picked up Leroy Brown's rebuttal, praying that some dark angel had inspired him to surpass mediocrity for once.

A knock on the door. There stood his daughter, Faith, looking forlorn. "Can I see you for a few minutes?"

"Sure. What the hell's the matter? You look like you've been dating Dracula. Not that he wouldn't be an improvement over Larry Donahue—"

She smiled wanly and sat down on the edge of the easy chair opposite him. "I'm getting expelled," she said.

"For what?"

"For seeing Larry one night—without permission. But what they'll probably tell you is—something worse. A lot worse."

*"What,* for Christ's sake?"

"They said—I'm perverted. That I have this unnatural interest in Margaret." Tears began trickling down the pugnacious gamin face. The Judge could only stare in horror. "The awful thing is—I'm not sure they aren't right."

"Goddamn it, don't let them infect you," he roared. "You've got to fight them off. Look what they did to Theresa."

"What should I do, quit?"

"Quit? And pour four thousand dollars down the drain? Like hell you'll quit. You'll graduate from that dump or I'll burn it down."

Faith begged him to be quiet. Another bellow and Mother would be all over them. He acknowledged the wisdom of that point and slammed the study door. "Now tell me the whole story slowly."

He listened, with a patience that astonished even him, as his daughter told him the story of her capture, the star chamber proceedings in Mother President's office, topped by the idiot chaplain's accusation of lesbianism. Then the explanation doubled back to Larry Donahue and his metaphysical approach to romance, omitting, of course, the scene at the Wagon Wheel Motel, and the scenes at other motels which had no doubt occurred regularly since then. Somehow—the process was not very clear—the idea of leaving the Catholic Church and joining forces with this screwball reformer had gotten entangled with Margaret Connolly and Dick Thornton, an exercise in adolescent logic in which the Judge declined to participate. But he pretended to understand it all thoroughly.

"Okay," he said, "I can get you out of it."

"How?"

"Never mind."

"I want to know. I have a right to know."

The Judge lit a cigarette. "Okay," he said. "Step one. I go see Eddie O'Connell, the Vicar General of the diocese. I've done him a couple of favors, like getting his bird-brained brother on the Court of Errors and Appeals. 'Eddie,' I'll say, 'I'm calling one in.' "

"Calling what in?"

"A favor. He owes me a big one and he knows it. He'll put the squeeze on Mother Mary Catherine, while I'm working on her from the opposite direction."

*"How?"*

"I don't know. I'll think of something. I'll threaten to sue her for a million dollars, for defaming your character."

Faith almost smiled. "I like that. One other thing. Can you get rid of that chaplain? You told me how he whined and wheedled his way out of that Puerto Rican parish. Send him back there."

"That's a little harder. That's asking two for one. But I'll see what we can do."

He lit a cigarette and put the Barton briefs back in their folder. "Now I'll ask you to do me a favor."

"What?" The question was superfluous. She knew what was coming. Maybe that was why you loved her so much. She was so damn smart.

"Stop seeing Larry Donahue."

A thoroughly predictable shake of the red head, the stubborn chin out, the impudent troubled mouth pouting the way she did when he scolded her at two. "No, I've got to solve that my own way. On my own terms. If that's the deal, let's forget the whole thing. I'd rather be expelled."

"Who said it was the deal?" he roared. "I'm only telling you what I want, not what I expect to get. If you think I'm going to let a couple of neurotic celibates call my daughter a lesbian and get away with it, you're not half as smart as I thought you were."

To his delight she managed a smile. "I was hoping it would make you mad."

"Mad? Mad is right. Mad as hell. Now get out of here and let me go to work on this thing."

Fifteen minutes later he was in Eddie O'Connell's room at the Cathedral rectory. Eddie greeted him in his usual wild Irish style. "Mother of God, here he is with the scales of Justice in his hand. Whatever the charge is, I plead *nolle contendere.*" In his undershirt, Eddie looked more like a bouncer than a Vicar General. The weight lifter's muscles in his barrel chest bulged through the cotton. The Judge was sure he had the right man. Eddie was as mean and tough as he looked—the Archbishop's abominable no-man. While he poured a drink from a bottle of Ballantine's best, they discussed the possibility of making his brother-in-law a state highway commissioner. Before Eddie was through, he was going to have more relatives on the pad than Dave Shea himself. Two Scotches later, the Judge gave him Faith's story.

For a moment Eddie looked severe. "You're sure Faith's all right?"

"Sure I'm sure. You know how kids are. They all go through this sort of thing. She's as good a Catholic as I am."

"So what do you want me to do?"

"I want you to call up this old bitch, Mother Catherine."

"Yes," said Eddie, obviously accepting the designation.

"While I'm there in her office. The timing has got to be perfect. I want you to tell her you're launching an investigation into Mount St. Monica because you've heard that lesbianism is running rampant in the place."

Eddie laughed until the tears squeezed out of his small, bloodshot drinker's eyes. His round red face turned burnt orange, he thought it was so funny. "I'll do it," he said, "just to see what she says."

Then, with that disconcerting habit the clergy had, he suddenly became serious. "We've had a hell of a lot of complaints about her in the last few years. She's expelled one or two kids just before graduation, each year. Daughter of one of my sister's best friends, Mary Jane Comiskey, last year. For something that happened at the senior prom. You know, anyone with a little sympathy would look the other way." Eddie shook his head. "She could use a little shaking up."

"While you're at it, get rid of that chaplain too. He's a real loser."

Eddie groaned and scratched his balding head. "An empire builder. You know the type. He's always got a plan for a new program. For him to run. I worry about him. He's got crack-up written all over him."

"Well, let him do it someplace else where he won't take a half-dozen kids with him."

Eddie nodded grimly. For a moment the Judge felt sorry for him and all the others, sucked into this huge impersonal soul-saving machine in their teens, and now trying to make it to the finish line without a woman's love, with the booze always there on the dresser, while neurotic women and unbalanced curates crawled over and around them. No wonder the good ones got tough and cold. There was no other way to make it.

The Judge held out his hand. "Thanks for the booze, Eddie," he said. "I haven't tasted such good Scotch since 1939. I'll be there at two o'clock tomorrow."

"I'm synchronizing it right now," Eddie said, checking the gold watch on his wrist. "And listen, Jim. You will speak to Shea about the brother-in-law?"

"Absolutely."

No point in telling Eddie that Dave Shea was not speaking to Jim Kilpatrick. The Judge had granted Andrew Barton another six weeks' stay, hoping Big Dave would cool down enough to consider clemency the better part of political wisdom. But Mayor Shea never seemed to be at his desk when Judge James Kilpatrick called. Nor was he ever at home in his mansion on the Parkway, nor even long distance in his Palm Springs, Florida, palace. A letter, containing an oblique apology, went unanswered. So here you were, coming up against another Barton hearing next week, with no more delays left in the law books.

Precisely at two o'clock the following day, Sunday, the Judge rolled up Mount St. Monica's curving main drive through the woods and along the edge of the huge open lawn. Whatever else she was, old Mother Catherine was a hell of a good real estate woman. She'd obviously grabbed off what could have been the best golf course in the state. Faith, looking subdued in her gray skirt and dark-blue blazer, was waiting for him on the front steps of the main building. "Get in the car," the Judge said.

"I'm supposed to come with you," Faith said.

"Get in the car," the Judge said.

"I just want to make sure of one thing. Don't even mention Margaret's name. I don't want that old bat to take it out on her, if she can't get me."

"What the hell kind of a lawyer do you think I am?" the Judge snapped. "Get in the goddamn car."

Down the corridor he strode to the double doors of Mother Catherine's office. They reminded him of City Hall, and he meditated for a moment on the similarity between the organization's power structure and the Church. Shea was the Pope, stealing for himself and his family just about as much as the average pontiff hooked for his clan of spaghetti benders. The ward leaders were the bishops, the district leaders the monsignors and pastors, and then there were the Cardinals, the honorary bishops, the Papal Knights, who corresponded to judges, commissioners of various sorts and the big party contributors. So here comes the careless cardinal, he thought, rapping on the door.

"Come in," said a steely voice.

The room was almost as big as the mayor's office, and it had the same phony oversized carved furniture. The little nun behind the gigantic desk looked shrunken, like a diseased ten-year-old playing at being Mother Superior.

"Where is your daughter, Judge Kilpatrick?"

"She's out in the car. What you and I have to discuss, Mother, is not for her tender ears."

"I have no reason to believe her ears are tender, Judge Kilpatrick."

"What you believe is beside the point, Mother. I am here to tell you things, not listen to you."

"My dear Judge," said Mother Catherine, rising to her full four feet eleven inches, "if you think you can exercise any of your political pull, as you call it, in this school, you can leave immediately and take your daughter with you. Our interview is terminated."

"Our interview is just beginning, Mother," the Judge said.

The two of them stood there for almost a full minute. Mother Catherine finally sat down. The Judge lit a cigarette. "Mother," he said, "you are in very serious trouble."

"*I* am in serious trouble?"

"Your school, I assume, is as close to you as, well—my daughter is to me."

"It is a heartwarming comparison. No doubt there is some truth in it."

"You have opened a Pandora's box, Mother, which threatens to destroy your school."

Again Mother Catherine was on her feet. "Such allegations are—"

"Lesbianism, Mother. Rampant lesbianism. You accused my daughter of this filthy sin. As a good lawyer, to answer this charge I have made a careful investigation of the school. It was very simple to do. There are at least forty girls here who are daughters of prominent Democratic politicians. These girls talked freely. They tell a frightening story, Mother. Rampant lesbianism, encouraged inadvertently by the sex-obsessed lectures of your chaplain, Father Malone."

From the briefcase in his lap the Judge drew out a sheaf of legal papers. "I have here depositions from thirty girls testifying to attempted lesbian assaults in the last year alone. Several of them involve nuns, members of your faculty."

"Give them to me. I dare you."

"Oh no," said the Judge, calmly slipping the papers back into the briefcase. "The only place you'll hear these stories, Mother, is in a court of law. I intend to sue you, Mother, in my daughter's name for defiling her reputation."

"I dare you," Mother screeched. "I—"

The telephone rang. She snatched the receiver out of its cradle as if it were the neck of a rebellious freshman and shrilled, "Yes?"

Eddie O'Connell's basso voice on the other end of the line spoke rapidly. "Oh, Monsignor O'Connell," Mother said in an entirely new tone. Consternation swiftly replaced the rage that had screwed her wrinkled little face into a fist.

"Monsignor!"

"You've been misinformed!"

"My girls!"

"Monsignor, I can't believe it! For thirty-eight years I've done nothing but think about this school day and night. To have it end this way, it's appalling, simply too appalling."

From somewhere beneath her robes Mother extracted a large white handkerchief and blew her nose vigorously.

"I beg you, Monsignor, give us a chance to rectify this situation before you take any formal action. I can tell you right now one of the difficulties. Father Denton Malone, the chaplain. His sermons, Father, are simply sex-obsessed. The man is not spiritually balanced. He's grown worse with every passing year. You know how important the chaplain is in setting the spiritual tone of the school—"

Mother Catherine's eyes rolled erratically past the receiver, toward the Judge. He diplomatically studied the ceiling. There was no point in rubbing it in.

"Thank you, Monsignor. All right, Monsignor. You'll have a full report within a month. And you *can* do something about Father Malone?"

Mother Catherine slowly replaced the phone in the cradle.

"Was that my old friend Eddie O'Connell?" the Judge asked.

"Yes," Mother Catherine said in a voice that was like a stone dropping on the thick blue carpet.

"What a coincidence he should call now. I was telling him about this mess just the other day."

"You are a vicious man, Judge Kilpatrick."

"Not really, Mother. Remember the little comparison about the school and the child? We're both looking for protection now. Can we come to an understanding, like two sensible adults?"

"What do you want?"

"I just want to forget the whole thing, Mother. I don't want to hurt you or your school. I just want my daughter to graduate with absolutely nothing about this on her record."

"Agreed," thudded Mother Catherine.

"Just in case you change your mind, or I get hit by a truck," the Judge said, tapping his briefcase, "these papers will be in my files."

The Judge slung his overcoat over his arm and strolled to the door. Mother Catherine sat at her desk, only the glaring eyes alive in the shrunken face. "Incidentally, Mother, Faith assured me that she didn't do anything more sinful than have a Coke with that fellow the other night. You ought to consider giving them a few more late permissions each week. You can't run this place like a concentration camp forever."

He slammed the door and strolled out to the car. Faith was sitting in the back seat listening with Eddie Dombrowski to a grapefruit-league baseball game. The young face peered up at him from the dim interior. *"Veni, vidi, vici,"* the Judge said.

"So quickly?"

"Nothing to it when you plan your case in advance. Now let me give you some advice. Keep your mouth shut about the whole thing. Pretend it never happened."

Faith climbed out of the car and gave him an enthusiastic squeeze. "You're fantastic," she said, "absolutely fantastic. I don't care what anybody says about you."

"Who's been saying things about me?"

"Oh—certain people."

"His last name begins with D?"

"I want to kiss you," Faith said, and stood on tiptoes to peck him on the cheek.

"Hey," the Judge said, "you're making me look like the original dirty old man. Get the hell back upstairs and do some studying."

Giggling, she ran up the steps, and turned at the top and blew him another kiss. The Judge felt himself go hopelessly soft inside his chest. It was the same thing she used to do at six, when he dropped her off at grammar school on the way downtown. Suddenly he wanted to take her in his arms and tell her an enormous number of things which would guarantee her happiness. Muttering a curse at this idiocy, he blundered into the back of the car and roared at Eddie Dombrowski, "Come on, let's go. Turn off that goddamn game and get me the hell out of this female squirrel cage."

Back home, the Judge found himself confronted by a hysterically weeping wife. Wondering if the best answer wasn't a monastery in Tibet, he asked what was the matter.

"My brother Bernie. I've spent half the afternoon on the telephone with him. They called him down to City Hall Friday. They told him that they were going to indict him for grand larceny."

"So that's how he's been buying a new car every three years."

"It isn't true! He swears it isn't true. He says it's all your fault. They want you to vote on some case about a Negro who's been convicted of something. A Communist agitator. And you won't do it."

"Because it's a frame-up."

"What does that matter, if he's a Communist?"

The immense vacuity of that remark temporarily silenced him. "I haven't made up my mind."

"Well, you'd better make up your mind. Do you want to see your own brother-in-law go to jail for the sake of some Communist? And a Negro at that?"

"Weren't you president of our Catholic Interracial Council last year?" the Judge asked.

"What does that have to do with it?" she screeched.

"Nothing, nothing at all," the Judge said. He looked at his wife and remembered the shrunken face of Mother Mary Catherine. This woman was shrinking too, the face grew more withered every day, the arthritic hands more bony and repulsive. She couldn't get him into bed with her now with a boat hook. Suddenly he saw an idea, the possibility of a possibility which he would not confront now, much less name. But it was there, all part of the same crazy interwoven web of lives and loving in which he was thrashing.

"Let me tell you something," he began shouting. "Let me tell you something once and for all. I don't give a goddamn if Bernie Brophy goes to jail for the next twenty years. I'm through carrying the goddamn Brophies around on my back. Do you get me? And while we're at it, I'm goddamn sick of your phony, sexless piety. You've driven one of your daughters into the convent and you've got the other one so screwed up she's ready to marry an inside-out Jesuit like Larry Donahue. And your son has got all the masculinity of a daffodil."

Screams, sobs, tears. *Clump, clump* down the hall, arthritis temporarily forgotten. A titanic *slam* of the bedroom door. Silence.

Yes, the possibility of a possibility. The possibility of love, the possibility of power? But don't even think about it, Judge. If you think about it you will lose your nerve instantly. Let nonthinking, unthought be your style for the next seven days.

Humming a little tune, the Judge looked at his calendar and began changing his shirt. Where was he going tonight? Oh, yes, the county Holy Name Society dinner. He took out a folder marked "Holy Name Society Jokes," and began thumbing through them. A toastmaster can never use the same gag two years in a row. It was unprofessional. And if you are anything, James, you are a professional.

# Chapter Twenty

"It was so nice to meet you, Mrs. Thornton."

Margaret meant every word of it. But the chopped-out mouth in the granite face failed to achieve even a hint of a smile. Dick's father was the opposite extreme. He seized her hand and hung on to it while a torrent of good-natured flattery poured out. Both reactions only confirmed for Margaret her sharp sense of something wrong. It had persisted from the moment in the living room when Mrs. Thornton had hauled out her family album. Church pictures predominated. Dick singing in the choir, winning medals in Bible study groups, on Sunday school picnics. Perhaps it was simply the basic message of those pictures: *How different we are.*

Margaret had been a little startled by Dick's invitation, but she had finally decided he was simply being polite. Faith had the usual contrary opinion, of course. "Once you start the family visiting bit, the wedding is imminent. Come on, don't you trust me? Have you set the date?" Margaret had scornfully rejected the notion. But the accusation had made her wary, and she had been more than a little nervous on the train coming down. But the afternoon had been a model of polite hospitality, and nothing more. Mrs. Thornton struck Margaret as rather humorless and cold, but that could be explained by the manners of another era. Dick's father, on the other hand, had been delightful, full of funny stories and old-fashioned good humor, almost like a character out of Dickens. But Margaret's dominant impression was the control Dick had exercised over the dinner. Most of the time he had led the conversation, and even when the others were talking, Margaret could sense a certain deference to Dick in their words. It made her feel discouraged about her own family. She had so little control over them.

In the car Dick said, "I hope you weren't too bored."

"I had a wonderful time."

"Come on, you don't have to flatter me."

"I mean it. I thought your father was awfully sweet."

"He's all right for a day but if you go back you'll hear the same stories."

"He's good-natured. I like that in a person."

"I'm not good-natured."

"I didn't say I liked you."

"One more crack like that and you'll walk home. I was worried about my grandmother, but I thought she behaved pretty well."

"Why worried?"

"Your Catholicism horrifies her."

"Oh."

"Don't sound so crestfallen. It doesn't horrify me."

How could she explain that the crestfallen voice was not only a reaction to Mrs. Thornton's hostility, it was a confession Margaret Connolly was making to herself, a confession of the elaborate lies she had constructed to enable herself to believe that this visit meant nothing, was merely polite, when Faith had been right all along. How could she explain to Dick the agonizing fact that she loved this Christ who was calling her as much as she loved him, and whenever she moved toward one or the other, anguish, guilt, a tangle of emotions drove her back in the opposite direction? Any explanation would sound incredibly stupid, unbelievably naïve. How could she have denied, even for a moment, that this was a major step toward a proposal, in Dick's eyes? With lowered head, she could only say, "I'm not going to change, Dick. You're not hoping for that, are you?"

"That's funny," he said, his eyes stilll straight ahead on the highway. "Sometimes I get the feeling you're waiting for me to change."

She said nothing. What could she say? Even her silence said too much.

"I'm not going to change, Meg. I'm not going to become a convert or anything like it."

Don't. Don't. You are summoning Margaret to the altar, oh, yes, to the altar of God, *unto God* who *giveth joy to our youth.* You are summoning her to a sacrifice from which she twists and turns, begging and praying, only to end, as your words make her do now, whimpering, *Not your will but Thine, Lord.*

They drove in silence for another mile. Dick suddenly swung off the highway and crunched up a pebbled road toward the dunes. "You're not in any hurry to get home, are you?" he said.

"Not especially."

"Let's go for a walk on the beach."

Is sensible Margaret afraid? No, sensible Margaret is gone, banished to that wrecked room in a stranger's house. New Margaret says, "That sounds like a lovely idea," and almost weeps as she watches her words tumble lifelessly into the chasm between them.

Get out of the car now, Margaret. Take off your shoes and wiggle your stockinged toes into the sand. Look across the empty littered beach toward the tumbling waves. The afternoon sun was warm but the sand seemed cold.

"Let's hike," Dick said, holding out his hand.

They tramped for what seemed miles without a sign of another human being. There was only sand, gulls, the coarse weed grass waving on the tops of the dunes, the waves plunging endlessly up the beach toward them. They rested at the foot of an almost perpendicular dune and contemplated the glistening sea. "It's like another world," Margaret said, letting her head fall back against the sandy wall.

Dick nodded and fiddled with a long polished piece of driftwood.

"What are you thinking about?" she said.

"About how I—feel so close to you sometimes and so far away other times."

"Yes," she said. "It—bothers me too."

"Down deep you still want—or hope—to convert me, don't you?"

"Don't say it that way, Dick. It's not something I want for—myself. It's something—good. Something that's been—good for me and would be good for you. The grace, the—"

"I appreciate that, Meg," Dick was saying, "your wanting it for me. I try to understand why, too, I really do. But I've got to be honest with myself. If I can't do that, I can't be honest with you or with anyone else. If I became a convert now I'd never know whether I was doing it because I was convinced or because I convinced myself for fear of losing you. I'd never know the answer. I'd never know whether I was fundamentally sincere or fundamentally phony. You wouldn't want me to do that, I know you wouldn't."

"Oh, Dick."

She kissed him. Not waiting to be kissed, but reaching out loving across the void. More wind, more waves, and still they clung to each other and then he broke away and she lay silent in his arms. Oh, Lord, let my silence be a yes, not a no. Let me be honest too. Let me accept him as I accept this kiss, sacredly, lovingly.

His arms crushed her. His lips pressed hers almost to pain, and beyond her closed eyes there was no longer sun on waves and white sand, but some dark primeval continent heaving, struggling like a living person trapped in the grave. Beneath the turgid earth was there still another Margaret, different from the ones you knew, crying out to be uncovered, to be lifted up in his arms? Oh, take me, take me, Dick, take me out of this nightmare world, this tomb in which this secret self, who may be the real Margaret at last, lies buried. Now, Dick, while my eyes are closed and my arms are open.

He stopped. She opened her eyes. There was the sun, the waves, his face. Pain on it. Some sort of suffering. Her body was trembling. Take me, whispered the voice from beneath the earth. But she spoke no words. The earth had not opened. Alas.

They walked back slowly, hand in hand. Midway, Dick said, "May fifteenth is Old Home Weekend at the University. My fraternity is running it this year. I'd like you to come down."

"For the weekend?"

"Yes."

"May fifteenth. That's at the end of our retreat."

"Retreat?"

"The seniors have a retreat at the end of the year."

"What happens?"

"Nothing happens. We just spend a week in prayer and meditation. A visiting priest preaches a series of sermons."

Oh God, the stiff explaining tone is in your voice again. Take it away. Take it away.

"What's the point? You've been praying and meditating and listening to sermons for four years."

"It's a climax—a spiritual climax of our four years."

"Oh. So the weekend is out?"

"No. I'm sure I'll be free. I'd love to come."

It was gone again. What had been created with a kiss had been destroyed with words. How could it happen so quickly, so brutally? There had to be an enemy lurking inside you. Was it sensible Margaret, refusing to yield an inch of the soul to even the voice of new Margaret? *No.* You have to stop thinking that way. There is only one Margaret. If only she were more lovable, likable.

It was twilight when they reached the car. "Let's just sit for a second," Dick said. "I always enjoy this time of day."

They sat down on the sand facing the sea. The waves came on as beautifully as ever, but the water in the dying sunlight changed color, becoming more dark blue and metallic. The wind was cooler and sharper. Margaret shivered as it sprang across the breakers toward them. Dick got a blanket from the back of the car and wrapped it around them.

"I don't know why you want to leave this place to live in the city," Margaret said. "It's so peaceful."

"It's no fun living on clam shells."

"Oh, as usual, you think of money."

"Because I don't have any."

"You're determined to be—happy, aren't you," Margaret said.

"I guess you'd call it that," Dick said.

"That's where we're different," Margaret said. "I never thought of being happy. I didn't expect to be. In this life." She looked up at him. "That sounds funny to you, doesn't it?"

"Nothing you say sounds funny," Dick said. "I just don't think that way."

"I still feel it's—dangerous to depend on being happy," Margaret said. "I think it's—safer to resign yourself to accepting God's will."

"That's where Christianity and I part company," Dick said. "With most people, this resignation idea becomes synonymous with weakness. I just don't think it's compatible with the American attitude toward life. If you've got the brains, go out and get what you can. This doesn't mean you're going to quit if you can't win all the games in sight, but there's nothing wrong with trying for everything."

"But what happens if—you have some really serious disappointment?"

"Like getting killed or dying of cancer? What's the point in thinking about it? Then your worries are over."

Margaret shook her head. "That's not the only kind of disappointment."

"That's the only kind that worries me." Dick picked up a handful of sand and let it drain slowly into his other hand. "Look, Meg," he said. "I don't want you to change your mind, think what I think, I just want you to respect my attitude about different things—if I can show you it makes some sense. Sooner or later we've got to come to some understanding—"

Panic. Far worse than that primitive inferiority reaction you felt when you saw him on this beach, the first day. How fantastically complex life had become since then. "Not now, Dick, please. I still need—more time."

"You're still thinking about—that other idea?"

"Yes."

"Maybe we ought to settle it then. On the weekend. I mean it's kind of sillly to let this drift—indefinitely."

"Yes."

"Let me kiss you again, Meg. Maybe it will help to remember the way it feels when I'm close to you."

He kissed her tenderly, without the angry ferocity.

"Oh, Dick, Dick," she murmured, clinging to him.

"Let's go home," he said.

For the first half hour in the car, practically nothing was said. In the twilight, it was hard to see whether Dick was unhappy, or simply thinking about other things. "Have you decided where you're going to start practicing?" Margaret asked.

"It won't be Stapleton Talbot, I can tell you that," Dick said. "Without Dwight Slocum, I don't have a shot in hell there. But there are plenty of other firms. Don't worry about it."

"I'm sure it will work out. I'm going to make it my special intention at every Mass this week."

"Do that," Dick said. "If it works, I'll become an instant convert."

Another long stretch of silence.

"How's Larry and Faith?" Dick asked. "Still at it?"

"I'm afraid so," Margaret said. "She's still seeing him. She got caught a few weeks ago, sneaking back from a date in the middle of the week, and almost got expelled. Her father got her out of it. She won't talk about it very much."

"It isn't easy, what Larry's asking her to do," Dick said. "But I admire their courage."

"What's so courageous about it?"

"Finding out exactly what they think and feel about life. Putting it on the line, thrashing it out at the risk of splitting up. But if it works, you've got something—real between you."

"Yes, I guess you're right," Margaret said sadly. Was the edge in Dick's voice a hint that he was aware that they had done the exact opposite? Was he blaming himself for the confused, uncertain, unspoken affection in which they still lived? Alas, you are as much to blame, Margaret. Perhaps if you admitted it to him, honesty could miraculously begin.

But before she could speak, her eyes caught the lights of the city in the distance. The lights of home. Somehow they spoke silence to her, and she said nothing until Dick slowed to a stop before the glowing windows of the Connolly house. "Will I see you next Saturday?" he asked.

"I've got to start studying for exams," Margaret pleaded.

"Okay."

Was there bitterness in his voice? She did not want that, no matter what happened.

"I'll be on retreat the whole week after next. I can't study then."

"You're looking forward to this retreat?"

"In a way. It's an opportunity to re-examine your whole spiritual life. That's important."

"It lasts the whole week?"

"Four days really."

"Well, by then you ought to be ready to swing a little."

"Yes," Margaret said.

She heard the old falling sound in her voice. Why, after seven months, was that negative, neuter thing still there? Maybe all Margarets, new, old, unknown, are hopeless. That would mean there is really only one choice.

*O God, tell me what to do.*

She kissed him lightly on the lips. "Good night."

Margaret found her mother and father having milk and cookies in the kitchen. Her father wore his old faded red bathrobe over his pajamas, her mother had her hair up in curlers and there was a dab of cold cream on her nose. She wore a bulky padded blue housecoat.

"Really, Meggy, where have you been? We were so worried. I thought this was an early afternoon dinner," her mother said.

"We went for a long walk on the beach afterwards."

"Alone?"

Margaret tried to match her mother's hard look. But her voice sounded feeble when she said, "Yes."

Her father concentrated on nibbling a cookie. Mother drew a deep sighing breath. "Margaret," she said, "I think it's time we had a serious talk. About this young man. Father Malone was very upset when I told him today that you were visiting his family."

"Why, Mother?"

"Because it makes it sound like you're serious about him, Margaret, and I don't really believe that's true."

"Why not? I mean—don't you think it's possible? Is there something wrong with him, or me?"

"There's nothing wrong with you, Margaret, and I'm not trying to tell you what to do. You know I've done my best to say nothing either way about your going in the convent. But this young man—Dick Thornton—though he's perfectly nice—he's of a different religion, Margaret."

"What do you think, Daddy?" Margaret said.

Bill Connolly was so startled the cookie flittered out of his fingers onto the floor. He picked it up and carefully deposited the pieces in the garbage can and sat down again. "I don't really feel—I'm qualified, Margaret. It's a very complicated thing, marrying someone—from another religion."

"Exactly," Mother said. "All we're concerned about, Margaret, is your happiness. Your happiness in this world, and your eternal happiness. Neither can be separated from your faith. We're afraid you're endangering them both by going out with this man."

While her mother spoke, Margaret's eyes were on her father, hoping her eyes would carry the words she was thinking. *How can you fail me now when I need you so much?* In silence she sat there and listened to her mother's final monstrous words thud solemnly past her. "We want you to stop seeing him, Margaret."

For a long terrible moment there was only silence. Then an incredible thing happened. Looking up at her mother, Margaret saw her dissolve like a face on a motion-picture screen. There was a long moment of total blur, in which the last words echoed wildly:

*Stop Seeing Him. Stop Seeing Him.* Then the familiar blue walls of the kitchen returned. The bulb with the small, silly white shade over it glared down once more. But when Margaret looked up, she no longer saw that hulking familiar woman she called Mother. It was a stranger standing there, repeating the same words with an odd tremor in her voice: "We want you to stop seeing him, Margaret."

Now, now is the time to speak, Margaret thought, with a surge of exultance. Now let New Margaret stand up and proclaim her defiance. Whatever she said, no matter how insulting or outrageous it was, no longer mattered because this woman had no right, no claim to mercy, love or obedience.

But there were no words. Only silence.

A huge, astonishing rage erupted in Margaret's mind. But its target was not Mother, not the accusatory prohibiting stranger, it was Margaret, old and new, Margaret with her absurd, insane dreams of freedom, built around a metaphor, a myth, a game of mental make-believe. Oh, whisper your defiance, New Margaret, you vapid, feckless, cowardly ghost, cry out your absurd pretensions: *I am an American. Freedom is part of my birthright. The freedom to pursue my own happiness in my own way. This is twentieth-century America, not fifteenth-century Spain. I am twenty-one years old, Mother, you have no right to control my life. I will go see Judge Kilpatrick. I will get a legal statement from him barring you from giving me another order. Mother, you are an obscene, gross monster from another age, prehistoric, with your primitive mind and prissy manners.*

Marvelous, all of it, absolutely marvelous. But unspoken. Face it, one last time. New Margaret has no voice. She never will have a voice. If she could not speak today on the beach, how can she speak now, confronted by this mountainous monument of common sense? With a sigh, Margaret spoke the only possible words: "All right, Mother, I'll stop seeing him."

Smiles, confusion. "Well, I didn't think—I didn't think you'd understand so quickly. It just shows how upset I've been. I've forgotten you are my Margaret."

"But I want a chance to explain it all to Dick. He's invited me to a dance at the university the weekend after next. I've already accepted. I'll explain it then."

"Of course. Of course."

The big arms enclose you in their familiar grip. How can you doubt the goodness of this love, Margaret, which has brought you this far, sound in mind and body? You did not doubt it. It was impossible to doubt it. But as she withdrew from Mother's arms, she was startled to discover that the face confronting her still belonged to the stranger. She shook her head, baffled by the complexity of her own self, groping inside her mind and body for a feeling that was familiar. The only one she could find was remorse. There was no longer a current of emotion that linked you to this woman in a simple, total way, like blood flowing down an artery. That bond, once as real as flesh, had been severed by those brutal words just spoken in this kitchen. All there was left was gray, sterile obedience—a limbo world.

"It's for the best, my dearest. It's for the best. Now maybe you can think clearly about your really *big* decision."

Oh, you see tears in my eyes, Mother. You wipe them away with your clumsy hand, thinking they are for my lost love. Perhaps they are. Perhaps they are for that other lost soul, New Margaret, aborted by so many things: words spoken in a car, in a living room, pictures in an album, spasms of prayer and self-reproach, disappointment and confusion. Of course, Mother was surely right, there was no reason now not to make that other decision, the one that would abolish confusion, guarantee peace, tranquility, happiness, here in this life and in eternity.

"Go and get a good night's sleep now."

"Yes, Mother."

Crawl into your bed, Margaret, in the lonely shrouded room of childhood where you said your prayers against the boogie man and hell, and let the tears come. What is the feeling inside you now?

Oh, yes, you remember the day Mother took you to the top of the Empire State Building. You were ten, old enough to know there was no possibility of falling down into that huge shadowy canyon of buildings below, but the mere thought had been an uncontrollable terror and you had begged and screamed until Mother took you down to the street again. Now you are no longer a child and the fear is of another kind of falling.

What, what kind? Somehow, just beyond the streetlight shining in your window, there seemed to be a gigantic abyss into which you were doomed to fall, down, down, for years, like the victim in the *Descent into the Maelstrom,* while you grew older and older and more and more bewildered. *Dick, Dick,* she whispered, that familiar inner voice, *why don't you speak, why don't you stop me?*

Suddenly it was midnight and she and Dick were alone in the car. They had been kissing. She could feel her breath coming slightly quicker and Dick's lips were warm on her cheek. They were parked somewhere on the campus. It was extraordinarily dark, no stars in the sky, no moon. Even the lights which usually illuminated the drive and the entrance to Sacré Coeur were missing. It was cold in the car. She huddled against Dick and a spasm of anxiety shook her. She looked up and her mother was walking in front of the car, dressed in black, a nun's robes, and her wide, square-jawed face was contorted with anger and outrage. Mother proceeded across the front of the car and walked toward them on Dick's side. She was carrying a huge watch. It was at least a foot in diameter, something out of Salvador Dali.

At first she did not seem to see them. She passed by Dick's window and disappeared into the surrounding gloom. Then she reappeared at Margaret's window. She stared at her watch, which read two fifteen, and she seemed to direct most of her rage at the timepiece.

As she walked past the left fender, however, and approached Dick's window again, she saw them. She started back, like a villain in a Punch and Judy show, and peered toward them. Terror raced up through Margaret's body constricting her throat, contorting her lips.

Dick, however, looked at Mother with a mocking smile on his face. "Excuse me," he said to Margaret, and opened the door and got out. Mother stood waiting impatiently, her big chin thrust out, her eyes popping.

She held up the huge watch and pointed to it, gesticulating wildly with her free arm. Margaret, inside the closed car, could hear nothing. Dick looked back at her and winked. She was sure Mother was screaming at him, but he did not seem to be bothered in the least.

Suddenly, Dick tore the watch out of Mother's hand, and holding it up, he punched a hole right through it as if it were papier-maché. He did it effortlessly, in the same spirit of cheerful caprice.

The effect on Mother was devastating. Her face sagged, and her eyes whirled in her head. Dick punched another hole in the watch, and turned and held it up for Margaret to see. Mother's mouth howled, and she rushed at Dick. Effortlessly, he caught her with his right hand and held the watch away from her in his left. Then, as if it was the most natural thing in the world, he began to eat the watch. Starting at the top, he worked across and down the sides, taking huge, obviously pleasurable bites, as if it were a gigantic cookie.

At first, Margaret laughed excitedly. But then, as if the laughter itself was wrong, she stopped abruptly, and another gust of terror overtook her. She could not understand why. It was nameless, reasonless, but it gripped her like a frenzy. It seemed to increase, each time Dick's mouth touched the watch. Again she did not know why. But not knowing only increased the terror. Now Dick had almost completely eaten the watch.

Why was she afraid? she asked herself desperately. Was Mother going to do something awful to Dick? Impossible; Dick still held her at arm's length and she wasn't even able to struggle, so great was her consternation.

Perhaps you are frightened because you want Dick to come back in the car. But you could not let him in. The door did not work. Yes. That must be it. You are locked in and only he knows how to get you out. Maybe he would forget you are here and go away, and you would be locked in here, forever.

He mustn't do that. No, not that. Let him come in through the window, if the door did not work. But she would have to call him and tell him. She tried to call, but the terror was in her breath, choking her voice. She tried again to call but he was absorbed in the watch. He did not even turn his head to look toward her.

"Dick," Margaret sobbed. "Dick, Dick."

Light broke sharply against Margaret's eyes. She felt fingers gently touching her shoulder. She sprang up, trembling. It was her father, flashlight in hand.

"You were having some kind of nightmare, Margaret."

"Oh. Thank you, Daddy."

He turned out the flashlight. Now he was only a disembodied voice in the darkness. "Honey, when two people get married, they make certain arrangements that are very hard to change. That's why —I couldn't help you down there. But I want you to know that as far as I'm concerned that promise you made tonight means nothing. If you want to break it for the sake of your happiness, go ahead. That's the only thing that counts with me—your happiness."

How sad those words were, spoken too late, spoken out of years of weakness. Pity, not courage, was what he awakened in Margaret. She clung to him for a moment there in the darkness, one swift, silent embrace, then let him go.

The next morning Mother could not have been more cheerful. She chattered away about a luncheon bridge for the Marian Society. Mrs. Kilpatrick had made her vice-chairman. The biggest bridge of the year! Margaret found Mother's good humor almost unendurable. It was a relief to get to church and sit through a long boring sermon on the importance of the Legion of Decency. Back home again, Margaret escaped to her room, pleading imminent examinations. She tried to study but it was useless. She ended up staring morosely out the window at the box-like, two-family houses on the other side of the street. There they were, all of them, names and faces you saw every day for years, leading their row lives in their little row houses.

Father Kilane, the priest who had preached her senior high school retreat, had used that description to sum up his opinion of the average American marriage. *Row houses and row lives.* How much more glorious, exciting, dramatic, was a life of sacrifice dedicated to Christ. It had been an irresistible description of a vocation. No less than ten girls had gone into the convent after that retreat. Maybe that was your first mistake, Margaret, not yielding to God's grace when it first came rushing into your soul. Maybe you should have ignored your father's insistence on a college education.

At 2 P.M., Faith Kilpatrick called. "We're driving back to school in about a half hour, want to come?"

"Yes," Margaret said.

Judge Kilpatrick himself was at the wheel. "Margaret," he said, "haven't you eloped with that lifeguard yet?"

"He hasn't asked me," she said.

"I don't know what the hell's the matter with this generation. They've either got too much brains, or not enough."

All the way out to Mount St. Monica, the Judge tormented Faith about Larry Donahue. He assaulted his personality, his politics, his philosophy of life, even his taste in clothes. Faith defended him furiously.

"There is a certain type of Irishman," the Judge said, "who, figuratively speaking, spends his whole life in a hut in the middle of a bog up to his waist in freezing water. Every time he tries to get out and join the human race, he goes ass over teakettle into the goddamn ice water again. That's the Donahues, the whole damn family."

"How do you know so much about the type?"

"I was on my way to being one myself, a long time ago."

"I think—I'm that way, too," Faith said, her voice thick with sudden emotion. "People think I'm like you, always being funny. But inside I'm always closed, tight. I don't feel anything."

"Everybody's that way until they fall in love for the first time. I mean really fall—not like you and Donahue. You're just in love with each other's conversation."

"That's not entirely true," Faith said.

"Oh, hell, I expect him to make passes. I'd be insulted if he didn't. But he really isn't interested in that end of you. His type never is. He just uses it to prove something."

"Maybe I'm inclined to do the same thing."

Margaret closed her eyes. She did not want to look any longer at Faith's tense, angry face. It was simply too much, all this fierce emotion, this complicated thrashing about life and love and happiness. It was impossible to remain perpetually divided between so many opposites. You must simplify things, Margaret, simplify them by a soaring, decisive choice.

The car was winding through the woods inside Mount St. Monica's main gate. It swept out of the trees along the edge of the green lawn. In the distance, the chapel bells began to chime. As they braked to a stop before the main building, through the car window the bell tower of the chapel almost obscured the deep blue of the late afternoon sky. Wasn't that the answer, Margaret? God's voice, filling the heavens for you. Did you need a better answer?

Then the memory of the dream, Dick's disconsolate voice at the beach. *You're still thinking—of that other idea.*

*No. No. No,* whispered the anguished voice of New Margaret, barely audible beneath the clanging bells.

# Chapter Twenty-one

Judge James Kilpatrick was dining with his son. Charming company, his son. He had not said a word since the soup. His wife was taking all her meals in her room, claiming migraine or some other phony illness as usual, but obviously (except to her) punishing him for his outrageous remarks about her relatives.

His only consolation was the hope that the Little Flower's punishment would continue indefinitely. That, in turn, made him think about another less pleasant punishment. He had called Margaret Halloran for dinner and she had coolly declined. A bad sign. What are you going to do about *that* sentence, Judge? It's beginning to look like a life term.

When the coffee arrived, his son suddenly came to life, of sorts. "Are you going to apologize to Mother?"

"For what?"

"For what you said two weeks ago about her family. I gather it was pretty godawful."

"So is her family."

"You did marry for better or for worse."

"I didn't read the fine print in that contract where it said I not only married her, but all her lame-brain relatives. Moreover, when you get ten percent of the better and ninety percent of the worse, you start to wonder about the basic validity of the contract in the first place."

Jim glowered into his coffee cup. "I've always heard it takes two to make a marriage fail."

"And Lincoln said, when you make a bad bargain, squeeze it all the harder. But I'm not Lincoln."

*"That* I know."

"To change the subject, just for the hell of it, are you still stuck on that career in social work?"

He nodded. "After I get my masters degree in philosophy."

"Jim—listen to me, just once. Social work is for indigent widows and spavined spinsters. What the hell is wrong with the law? Take a degree anyway. Even if you never practice a day."

"The law is a sterile, end-in-itself type profession. I want an open-ended, people-oriented profession. That's social work."

"Bullshit."

"What?"

"What you just said is bullshit."

"I don't think so."

"At least with the law you associate with real men. Even if you're fighting them. I don't give a goddamn if you want to be a crusader. Go into politics. Try to turn the goddamn city inside out. With a law degree, if you win the game, you can make some real money—honestly."

Jim shook his head. The Judge found himself grinding his back teeth. "Oh, the hell with it."

He went into the study and switched on the television. The rest of the evening was a blur of dancing bears, cowboys and Indians, overpadded opera stars and situation comedies where father knew least. He went to bed and dreamed about Margaret Halloran. They were alone in the apartment. He began kissing her. Suddenly Negro faces peered through all the paintings on the wall, leering, jeering. Dave Shea's voice roared out of the past, *"Stick with me and you'll get rich."* He woke up aching, rigid with desire, and prowled the house in the dawn.

When Eddie Dombrowski arrived with the car, the Judge was sitting on the front porch, tapping his cane impatiently. He could not wait to get back to work, back to the calm, impersonal language of the law, away from this personal world that seemed to do nothing but soften and then frustrate him, to make a mockery of words like love and happiness. He was even grateful for the two-hour ride across the green center of the state to the capital. The humming tranquility in the back of the car was almost hypnotic. The distance seemed to cleanse him of the weekend's muddle of emotion.

He was barely in his chambers, when clerk Logan stuck his pie face in the door. "Deputy Mayor Kenellen's on the phone."

Jesus. Escape was an illusion. "What the hell do you want?"

"Barton's comin' up tomorrow. I just wanna remind you."

"Where's the Commissar?"

"I don't know."

"Don't be such a pitiful bullshitter. If you don't know where he is, he's not on the planet. I want to talk to him."

"Maybe he'll talk to you. After you deliver."

"I don't deliver unless I talk to him."

"It's your funeral, Jimmy boy. Just remember that."

Sweat. There it was again in the palm of the hands. Knowledge caused it. You knew the kind of leverage Shea had. Even with the Republican governor, he could ruin Chief Justice James Kilpatrick and get one of his own into the vacated catbird seat. He would have to sell off a lot of jobs, but they could afford it.

The court did not sit on Monday. The Judge spent the day studying the Barton case from start to finish. Around four o'clock, he polled his fellow justices. Predictably they were split three and three. The Democrats had all gotten the word from City Hall.

He had just finished taking the count and gone back to rereading Leroy Brown's appeals brief (which was surprisingly good) when the telephone rang once, twice, three times. Pieface Logan must be in the john. The Judge put on a Swedish accent: "Allo, yis bane Yudge Kilpatrick's phune?"

"I'm looking for the Judge," said a confused young voice on the other end of the phone.

"The Yudge? Who's please speaking?"

"Mr. Donahue. Larry Donahue."

"What the hell do you want?" the Judge snapped. "Have you got my daughter pregnant?"

"No. Nothing personal, Judge. I'm just calling you—well, I know this is crazy, but I'm calling you about this Negro kid Barton."

"What the hell do you know about it?"

"Well—it's sort of my fault, Judge. I mean, I feel guilty as hell about the whole thing. I put him up to it. Maybe because I didn't have the guts to do it myself. I hate to see him get the business."

"That's exactly what he's going to get."

"I know. But—I was sort of hoping. At least I thought it wouldn't do any harm to tell you. I mean, I'd almost take the rap for him myself. One other thing, Judge. I haven't touched Faith since the night we talked."

"Jesus Christ, you are a nervy son of a bitch. For not getting my daughter pregnant, I'm supposed to owe you a favor?"

"Okay. I give up."

"Why the hell are you quitting when you're ahead? I'll think about it. I don't want to give the kid the business any more than you do."

He hung up, riffled the Barton papers and muttered: "That Mick could be one hell of a politician some day. If he gets the inside of his head straightened out."

Twenty minutes later, the telephone rang again. His clerk informed him it was someone named Richard Thornton. "I'll talk," growled the Judge.

"Judge," said the familiar voice, "I thought it would be easier to call you than write you a letter. I'm speaking as editor of the law review. The rest of the board wanted to make a formal statement, but I convinced them that a call like this might do more good. It's about the Barton case."

"You think it's a bum rap."

"That's right, Judge."

"Well, so do I. But that has nothing to do with how I'm going to vote on it. For the information of you and the rest of the idealists down at the university, this kind of case is a hell of a lot more complicated than it looks." He paused to light a cigarette, and there was only silence on the other end of the telephone. The Judge got a grip on his nerves and realized how bad he was sounding. "Believe me, Dick, I'm doing everything in my power to get the kid off. And I appreciate your coming to me this way, instead of putting the heat on me in public. Some night down at the beach, when it's over, I'll explain the whole thing in more detail."

"Sure, Judge," Dick said. "But you understand. As editor of the law review, I had to do something."

"You bet I do. And I'll write you a letter to prove you did it."

The phone clicked and the Judge went back to studying the upcoming docket. Suddenly he was seeing the wistful look on Margaret Connolly's face as he drove her back to school last weekend, the mournful note in her voice as she said: *He hasn't asked me.* What was it Faith had told him about Margaret wrestling with a vocation and Larry Donahue playing God with Dick, giving him that phony, inside-out-Jesuit advice that was his dubious specialty. Again the Judge's gorge rose at Larry's arrogant intellectualism. By Christ, he *would* write Dick Thornton a letter. It would tell him to quit playing Larry's pretentious games and get to Margaret before she vanished into the convent, courtesy of that neurotic chaplain and that midget zombie, Mother Mary Catherine, a pair of spooks if he ever saw two. The girl was so much like Margaret Halloran when he first met her. The kind of woman that cries out to be dominated, saved from this idiotic religion of humility and surrender.

Then what happens? You give them self-respect, independence—and the capacity to tell you to go to hell. Life *was* essentially ridiculous.

At five o'clock, the justices gathered in his chambers for cocktails, and then they went out to dinner at the private dining room the Judge always reserved for them on Monday nights. They talked about two dozen innocuous cases involving wills, damages and corporate law, without getting anywhere near the one that was on everybody's mind. Judge Kilpatrick, sitting at the head of the table, looked down the right-hand side at the three Democrats, Bill Mackey, Eddie Condon, and Joe Blaney—three bland, genial mediocrities who had come up from County Prosecutor. On the other side, the three Republicans, Jim Strait, Joe Bright, and Harry Klein, were graduates of the same hard political school. No one would be surprised, or particularly upset, if he voted to uphold Barton's sentence. The Republicans would probably squawk at the impropriety. But once they saw they were outvoted four to three, they would shut up and go on to other things. There was no reason in the world why he shouldn't play the game, except—

The Judge picked up his last glass of wine and drained it. Châteauneuf du Pape '38. An excellent year. It was his third or fourth glass and it seemed to liquify that single word and send it tingling through every cell in his body.

Except.

Except for Faith standing on the top step, blowing him that kiss.

Except for Margaret Halloran, brooding in that lonely apartment.

Except for Larry Donahue, who just might possibly change his mind about life's essential lousiness.

Except for this innocent kid, Barton, and what will be left of him after five years in the state pen.

Except for that tall, broad-shouldered young law clerk named Jim Kilpatrick, that dim distant ghost who dreamed about fighting the interests, as they called the corporations once upon a time, on behalf of the poor.

Except for Dave Shea, that monster you had helped to create, never dreaming he had the power to corrupt an entire state.

Except.

"As for the Barton case, gentlemen," the Judge said, "there is no doubt in my mind that the sentence is excessive and ought to be reduced to eighteen months and suspended."

The jaws of the three Democratic jurists simultaneously sagged. The Republican jaws gaped a little, too. Obviously the word was out everywhere. Dave Shea was a talker. He loved to tell people how he was going to throw his weight around, in advance of throwing it. It made him look more impressive when the knockout punch was delivered precisely on schedule.

"I suppose you want to write the decision, Jim?" asked Republican Strait.

"With your permission."

Heads nodded. He had it. No one wanted to stand up and be counted when Dave Shea was on the warpath. The next twelve hours were a kind of blur. The Judge knocked down four jolts of Benzedrine and stayed up most of the night writing the decision. The telephone rang twice. The first call was from Johnny Kenellen. "Is it true?" he screeched. "Is it true what Blaney told me?"

"I'm writing the decision now," the Judge said.

"You got two choices. Resign quietly and get the hell out of the state. And take your whore with you. Or watch her and every other relative you got on the pad go to jail."

"I'm resigning all right," the Judge roared. "But I'm not getting out of this state. I'm coming back to the city, and I'm going to tie your ass in a sling and throw you into the river. I'll personally defend every goddamn relative and anyone else you go after in court. Tell that to Big Dave. I'm coming back home to get you."

Kenellen laughed hysterically. It was almost a girlish giggle. "You're out of your mind."

"We'll see who's out, Johnny."

The next call was from Shea. "Jim," he said, "how can you do this to me? I can't believe it. I'll make that fucking brother-in-law of yours a commissioner. Just say the word. You can't make me look like a fool in front of the whole organization. Not after all these years."

"Yes, I can."

"You're upset, Jim. You've been drivin' yourself. I know how heavy that docket is. And this thing with your daughter. Postpone the goddamn case and take a rest. Think it over. You can have my place in Florida. All the servants, the works. On the arm."

"Get lost, Dave."

When the Judge finally threw himself down on the couch in his chambers, he couldn't sleep. He had taken too much Benzedrine. At ten o'clock, when he was putting on his robes, he began to feel punchy and took another tablet to clear his mind. But it did not do any good. He sat there waiting for the call from the clerk of the court, trying to hold enough of his mind together to get through the hearing.

The telephone rang. It was Eddie Dinsmore, very excited, very scared. "Jim, for Christ's sake, what's going on? I just got a call from the district attorney. I still can't believe it. He says he's gonna indict your daughter. For illicit intercourse, and the performance of sundry unnatural acts, with a guy named Donahue. He says they got the manager of the Wagon Wheel Motel ready to testify. And they got *pictures,* for Christ sake."

So there it was. As always, Big Dave's timing was perfect. He was a professional poker player. He never showed his ace until everything else was on the table. Why didn't you expect it? He let you take the negative, that brawling day down at City Hall. But there were undoubtedly other pictures, other negatives.

You know why you didn't expect it. Nothing like it had ever been done before. Tough and mean as he was, Shea had never stooped quite this low. A man's family, especially his daughter, had been off limits. But he was stooping now and there was only one answer.

"Tell him he's won, Eddie. Just do me a favor. Go down there and get all the negatives from him, now. And burn them."

"Sure, Jim. And listen. I'm sorry as hell—"

The clerk of the court was knocking on the door. The Judge stumbled to his feet and somehow found his way to the high bench. He stared down at the blur of faces in the courtroom and heard a voice, remarkably like his own, telling them that Andrew Barton was guilty, and for his public contempt of the court and the judge who had sentenced him, his sentence was sustained—the maximum penalty, five years.

Then he was back in his chambers, fighting off paroxysms of rage and humiliation. There is only one thing left to do, now, Jim. You have fallen off that high wire. Pick yourself out of the sawdust and dictate your resignation. No, wait, you cannot even look your secretary in the eye. He took a pen and scrawled:

Dear Governor:

This constitutes my resignation, as of the end of this month of May, 1948.

Sincerely yours,

JAMES KILPATRICK, Chief Justice

There it goes, two years short of the twenty you need for the pension. But there was one thing left for you to do, one good thing that was still in your power. He dialed Margaret Halloran's school.

The clerk who answered the phone tried to tell him that she was in class. "I know she's in class, you goddamn idiot. Get her out. I want to talk to her. This is Chief Justice James Kilpatrick."

Five minutes of waiting and then the breathy voice on the other end of the line. "Yes?"

"I just wanted to tell you—I had to tell you—I'm resigning. I want to marry you. As soon as possible."

"Oh."

"What's the matter, scared?" he mocked.

"You're not teasing?"

"You goddamn women, don't you trust anybody?"

"Can you give me one reason why we should?"

"I'm not teasing. I happen to be deliriously stupidly idiotically in love. Like a goddamn teen-ager. I better warn you in advance that we're not going to have much more money than a couple of teenagers. I'm going to have to open an office and start practicing. I'm still on the list down at City Hall, and that means I can't get back in my old firm."

"Stop fussing over silly details," she said. "You're making me cry. I'll see you for dinner?"

"Yes."

Out to the car, the long boring ride across the state, one last time.

Christ, it was like dying. Dozing, but not really sleeping. The Benzedrine still hitting him. What was that pounding sound? Your heart, stupid. But Benzedrine did that sort of thing. Two good shots of Scotch and you would sleep all afternoon, ready then for the evening.

Only when the air around him suddenly turned acrid with burning garbage did the lowering, dooming, clutching truth seize both his mind and his body. Through the blowing smoke, the city loomed on its hill ahead of them, a gray, ominous, authoritative mass. Suddenly, it seemed to rush toward him, instead of the car moving toward it, looming like a huge breaking wave that shattered against his mind and body with roaring, smashing, brutal reality. It was impossible, insane, idiotic, moronic. A Kamikaze pilot, taking on the entire U.S. Air Force, would have a better chance. They had gotten to you, all of them, the women with their goddamn porous hearts and yielding mouths, they had infested your flesh, and finally your mind, infected your sanity, until you actually thought with a kind of mad purity that what you were doing was clever as well as moral. Fool, fool, fool, with your $8923 in the bank. It was doom you were riding toward, more cruel, destructive humiliation.

Do you think Shea will let you resign without permission? Throw the court to the Republicans? A Republican governor in the statehouse meant a Republican Chief Justice. Do you think Big Dave is going to take that with a smile? Gone, the crucial leverage he had toiled twenty years to create?

Blood, moisture, breath seemed to drain out of his body, until he lay there in the back seat, a dry husk, a papier-maché man that a gust of wind might blow out the window into the path of an oncoming truck. *Jesus, Jesus,* he muttered, and tried to take a deep breath. It was impossible. All he could get down were small shallow gulps of the putrid air. *Me nose is in the city.* He saw Leroy Brown's stricken black face, the staring compromised eyes. He could hear Larry Donahue asking Faith: *What do you think of your Big Hero Father now?* And his son, accusing him with that sour Jesuit mouth: *How much did you get for that one?*

Out of the car he stumbled in front of the big, wide-bellied house, the home of unlove, waving Eddie Dombrowski away for the last time. Up the steps, still no breath, the whole city was claustrophobic now. Where could you go? Where could you run? He could see the obscene charges against Margaret Halloran, recited by one of her favorite black pupils in well-paid (and well-frightened) words. Sickening charges, and Dave Shea bellowing, *I drove him out. Chief Justice of the state and I drove him out. I won't have no man around me who ain't clean.*

*Jesus, Jesus, Jesus.* Up the stairs he dragged himself, and down the hall into the loveless bedroom. As he opened the door, the pain hit him, a massive fist, ten times the punch that Dave Shea could ever deliver, in the middle of his chest. Behind his eyes it flashed like white lightning. Not here, he thought, not in this miserable room. Why here?

He was on the floor. There was a telephone on the other side of the bed. If he could get to it. He crawled. Up on the bed he dragged himself, as if it were an Himalayan peak. As his hand groped out, the pain struck again, a pile driver this time, as if the roof of the house had collapsed on him. He rolled over, crying out, and now the whole city seemed to be crushing him. He was lying at the bottom of the immense coagulated mass of lives, loves, lusts, loss.

Then suddenly, miraculously, he was free. He was out of it, out of the loveless house, the murderous city, the treacherous, breathless body, out and floating in a kind of void, while faces circled him like planets around a sun. There was Faith at ten, wrinkling her nose, laughing at his false-teeth act. There were Margaret Halloran and Margaret Connolly, both aglow with that quintessential innocence that broke and bled a man. Words swept out of his weightless body to float beside them, simple, total words like *want* and *wish* and *hope.*

Then, like stars in a night sky, the faces slowly faded, and one by one, the words, until there was only one glinting blackly in a brilliant void: *Wish.*

# Chapter Twenty-two

Dick Thornton wound the paper into the typewriter and began typing the letter, which he had already written out in longhand. Beneath the sheet of yellow legal-sized paper on which the draft was written, a corner of the white letter of rejection from Stapleton Talbot peered out.

Dear Judge Kilpatrick:

After giving it considerable thought, I've decided to take advantage of your kind offer to recommend me for a position in your former law firm. It will, I think, give me an opportunity to practise a wider variety of law.

The telephone rang. Larry Donahue's voice came murkily over a very bad connection. "Say, Dick. I thought you'd like to know. The Judge is dead."

"Kilpatrick?"

"Yeah. Died of a heart attack today around noon."

"Jesus, that's a shame. How's Faith?"

"Taking it pretty hard, I'm afraid. I only talked to her for a minute. Anyway, I thought you might want to come up for the wake."

"Sure. Sure. When is the funeral?"

"Thursday morning."

"I'll be there Wednesday night. Could I stay with you for a few days? Classes are pretty much over down here. I want to start looking around."

"What happened to Stapleton Talbot?"

"That's a long story."

"You can stay here as long as you want, if you can stand the squalor."

"I can't afford to be choosy."

He hung up and stared at the letter in the typewriter.

Slowly, carefully, you crumple your little psalm of hope into a ragged ball in your fist. Into the city, down those familiar highways that hummed so confidently on other days, to dinner with Larry and then to the wake. "Incidentally," you ask as they crawled through the downtown traffic, "what's this retreat they're having at Mount St. Monica's?"

"It's an annual bit," Larry says, with the inevitable acid smile. "They bring in some priest with a throb in his throat and give them four days of sermons, devotions, the rosary."

"What's the point?"

Larry shrugged, bored by it all. "Spiritual overhauling. And they usually manage to drum up a few vocations. At my senior retreat in prep school about six guys joined the Jesuits. Poor bastards."

But Richard Thornton, the prototypical ex-Protestant, the small-town saint, is not retreating. He is parking the car, listening to Larry's brittle voice discuss the political effects of the Judge's demise, walking the uneven city pavement, and simultaneously crawling in eye-wide horror the sawdust trail, shouting *Jesus Jesus Jesus, I'm coming to Jesus.* How many times had he seen them, grown men, his own father, his own friends, men who had fought through Europe and the Pacific, pledging heart, lungs, eyes, testicles to Jesus? And Margaret? In that murky chapel where she had taken him that first day, Margaret there with the candles and the statues and windows of popeyed saints? He shuddered, swept by a sudden sensation of total loss. Someone is stripping everything away, Richard, every one of your puerile hopes.

Into the funeral home, past the bulky men, topcoats dangling from their arms, beefy women squatting on chairs along the walls, to Faith standing beside the open casket. Poor Faith, sad little clown who has tried so hard to believe in so many things, red-rimmed Pierrette eyes, trembling mouth.

"I'll always remember him best—down at the beach."

Amen to that is the wry unspoken reply. There is a finality about the Judge, crepuscular against the white satin, a rosary he never owned wound through his ivory fingers. Only around the mouth lingers a hint of his quixotic smile.

"Margaret's in the next room with her mother."

The Connollys, mother, father and daughter, mournful in dress and manner. Especially daughter. Subdued, blank-eyed, until eyes meet. "Dick! What—what are you doing here—"

What is that arch glint in Mother's eyes, the total evasion of Father's fumbling hand? Larry, deserter as always, departs with Faith. Sad, so sad the Judge's fate. Twenty words consume that topic. Inevitably: "I'm going to be in town—job interviews. Would you like—"

Margaret, eyes down, trapped between Father's pallid lips and Mother's iron jaw. "I'm sorry, Dick. We can't—get late permissions during the week. Besides, I have so much studying. I told you—the retreat—I'll see you the weekend after—for the dance."

Jesus, back on the August beach the absurd toy chaperone guaranteeing evasion, words pale as moonless, dismal starlight. Doubts crashed like angry surf across his nerves.

"Oh—sure—the weekend? You're all set?"

"Yes. I'm getting the three. The three o'clock train."

"The three. Okay. I'll meet you."

Squeezing his way through the outer rooms, packed now with political mourners, red beefy Irish faces, strange, suddenly more than strange, malevolent, laughing at little Dick Thornton who has come all the way from Hicksville. And what does he have to show for it? Humiliation. Rage pulsing in his chest, gnawing at his brain. Rage at the mere suspicion that he may have been lured down another more ingenious garden path.

On the shadowy sidewalk outside the funeral home, Faith and Larry seem extensions of his laceration. "I won't let you talk that way about him. Not any more," Faith cried, and ran sobbing past him into the night.

"Emotions," Larry says. "Sometimes I think emotions are the ultimate evil, Richard."

In a downtown bar, Jake O'Connor, slightly drunk, as usual. "Richard," he booms. "What brings a fine upstanding thirty-third-degree Mason to Immigrantsville?"

Larry: "He's looking for a job."

"What happened to Dwight Slocum? You mean all the sucking around you did with that shithead is wasted?"

Nod, shrug, what else?

Now you know what everyone else called it, Richard. Maybe it is about time you saw it the same way.

"Not that I ever blamed you. Somebody's got to wind up taking care of all that money."

"Yeah."

"So what are you going to do?"

"I'm looking around."

"You want some advice? I'd go right back to Paradise Beach and open a law office if I were you. Get into local politics and keep in touch with people like me and Larry up here. The guys running this town aren't going to last forever and when they go, we're going to change a few things in this state. The old idea of the city rolling up the killer vote can't last. People are moving out. We're going to need people like you all around the state–"

He was not really listening as Jake O'Connor went on to analyze with cool precision the way he saw the balance of political power shifting during the next ten years. It was amazing on several levels. For one thing it was clear that that laugh-it-up, drink-it-down Jake O'Connor was only a facade, that he, like everyone else, was shrewdly, carefully measuring his world for size. But Richard Thornton was not really listening after he heard the words Paradise Beach. They all saw him the same way and nothing he could do or say, tricks of the intellect, declarations of independence, could alter their image. Small-town. Don't call us, we'll call you. *Jesus, he would show them. He would show them how wrong they were.*

How? mocked a spectator voice.

"Believe it or not," Larry Donahue was saying, "I think O'Connor's making sense. You're a helluva bright guy, Richard, but if you don't make it at Stapleton Talbot, there's not much left for you in this town. Everywhere else a lawyer's got to have political weight, and let's face it, you don't have any."

"Well–I appreciate this tender loving care, fellows, but I've got to figure this out for myself."

"Sure, sure," Jake said. "Say listen, are you going to that Old Home dance?"

"Yes."

"I'm dragging Dolores Talbot. Why don't we sit together?"

"Sure. Thanks again for the advice."

"Forget it."

"I think I'll stay for a while," Larry said. "I haven't seen this clown in a couple of weeks."

A soft May breeze swirled around him as he walked to his car. Forget it. That is exactly what I plan to do, Jake. If I only could forget it. If I only could forget a lot of things. Jesus, what was happening? Everything was unravelling or unravelled.

Around and around the city, past the darkened houses, the groaning buses, through the business district where lights still burned in the tall buildings above the flashing theater marquees, he drove. Around and around and always there were more houses, more buildings, more cars and buses, more people striding purposefully along the darkened sidewalks. Around and around until the massive weight of the place seemed to loom above him like a great wave. You thought you could swim in this water, Richard. You fool, only those who are born here, who have inherited the skill to manipulate this mass, or the money to buy it, can possibly survive.

Suddenly he lost control. He pulled over, walked a few steps to a cigar store on the corner, past an old man behind the counter who looked more dead than Judge Kilpatrick, into the dark coffin of a phone booth.

"Dwight, this is Dick Thornton."

"Well, Richard, how the hell are you?"

"Fine. Dwight, I'd like to see you."

"Have you taken any boxing lessons lately?"

"No."

"And you're still chasing that reincarnation of the Virgin Mary?"

"Listen, Dwight—"

"Richard, you know you're really almost pitiful. I got a friend of yours here with me. She feels the same way."

"Hello, Richard," Vicky said, picking up an extension.

"Dwight, I'd like to see you—alone."

"For what, Richard? You want me to run you down to Stapleton Talbot and carry you upstairs in my pocket?"

"Well, I thought you might be able—"

"Oh, there's a lot of things I might be able to do, Richard. But you flunked out of the club, remember? After all those tests you helped me pass, you flunked the big one."

"Dwight, for God's sake."

"Get lost, will you, Richard? You interrupted Vicky and me in the middle of our favorite extra-curricular activity. But you wouldn't know about that any more, would you?"

Vicky began to laugh, shrill and savage. Dwight joined her, booming, explosive. "Richard," Vicky gasped, "be sure and give Margaret my very best."

He walked slowly back to his car. Across the street a pair of teenagers necked in a doorway. You have done it now, Richard. You have done the unthinkable and the taste of it is in your mouth and throat and belly. The taste of shit. You have eaten it and you will carry it in your blood and bones for the rest of your life. Jesus. And give your best to Margaret.

Yes, Margaret. Remember those several promises you have made to keep her separate, Richard. She is separate. And yet tonight she is anything but separate. She stands in the center of this ghastly vision of yourself surrounded by the city and its mocking, blank-eyed smiles. Faces as empty as these dark houses and as meaningless as those glaring street lights, as aimless as those buzzing cars and lumbering buses. You don't know where anything is going, Richard. You don't know where you are going. You don't even know where you are now.

There is a street sign, of course. You are on the corner of Garden Avenue and McDougal Street. But that tells you nothing. Everything tells you nothing. Somewhere on another street Margaret Connolly slept, beneath mother's ominously approving eye. And only a week ago she was in your arms on the beach. His hand touched the cold metal of his car. Coolness like that wind in the grass. Above, the sunlight warm on your face. You could have taken her then. Your hands were reaching for those sweet young breasts, your manhood was hard and long and hot in your pants. You could have taken her, murmuring love and it would have been right, it would have been in the name of love, which is what you felt then and what you do not feel now. And when Dwight asked you could have said, *Last week on the beach I scored like you've never scored. I play the game my own way, Dwight.*

You slob, you slob. Keep her separate. Make her the only thing you've salvaged from the wreckage. She is enough all by herself to let you graduate a winner.

But you have no power there either, Richard, you are up against the Catholic Church, as massive and as unknowable as the city. You are all alone, Richard, you and your straining mind against a system that has endured two thousand years. How many other lovers have those priests and nuns destroyed in the name of eternal happiness? You have heard of Héloïse and Abelard. But those other thousands, those legions of weeping eyes and drooping mouths, they have gone nameless into the dark.

He drove back to Larry's apartment and spent a night of semi-sleep on a lumpy mattress. In the morning when he awoke, there was only one word in his mind: Margaret. He had to know. He would call her now and demand the truth one way or the other. But with his hand on the phone, pride whispered no.

Yes, pride. On the beach, after the visit home, you had almost lost control of your pride, you had almost blurted the words of classic romance: *I love you, Meg. Tell me you love me too.* But pride had whispered no. Too much about the way she had acted, even then, had made you uneasy. No, if you crawl to her, you could crawl for the rest of your life. The words, when they came, should be a flowing, not even an exchange, but a communion—as simple as breath. They could never be a craven plea on the telephone. That was only asking for humiliation.

He turned his back on the telephone. But he could not turn his back on the angry suspicion whispering deep in his mind. It brooded there throughout the long, wearying funeral Mass for Judge Kilpatrick. The chanted Latin, the incense swirling above the crowd, the black-robed priests moving monotonously about the altar, the meaningless standing and kneeling and sitting, dripped on his brain like the famous Chinese torture. You are going to let your children grow up to believe in this, Richard? There was not a hint, a trace, an iota, of America in this religion. Its face was turned backward into that medieval world where death was the basic reality. America needs a God of light, of life, not death.

No sign of Margaret among the mourners. She must have gone back to school. But as the crowd streamed out of church and scattered toward their cars, a voice began calling his name. "Mr. Thornton. Mr. Thornton."

Mrs. Connolly bore down on him, wearing a silly plastic-looking hat from which a small black veil dangled. "Mr. Thornton," she said, "I was hoping I'd meet you. I wanted to ask you something rather important. This weekend Margaret's going to a week from Saturday, is it well chaperoned?"

"Definitely."

"Good." Mrs. Connolly gave him a small, faintly triumphant smile. "Margaret and I have had a long talk. She's agreed that after this date she'll stop seeing you. I want you to know there's nothing personal involved. You may even find it hard to understand. But for a Catholic it's—very simple. You see, Father Malone feels certain Margaret has a vocation to the religious life. Father Malone—remember you met him?—feels you and some other people have been distracting influences and that's why he asked me to put my foot down. So it's nothing personal, you understand? They're having a marvelous priest for their senior retreat and he's sure Margaret'll come to the right decision now. Not that we ever thought that there was anything really *serious* between you—"

He left her in mid-sentence and strode to his car.

It was absolutely logical and undoubtedly true. Margaret was incapable of telling a lie. She was also hopelessly sentimental. One more weekend together. *It will be so sad and noble. I may even let him kiss my sanctified lips again. And pray, of course, that my heroic sacrifice will turn him into a pillar of the one Holy Roman Catholic Church.* It was too ridiculous.

But you have not touched bottom yet, Richard. It could be much worse; the possibility that she had never even toyed with the thought of loving you, that she had been a puppet of that priest all along and had been experimenting with you to prove to herself the stupidity and vanity of the world she was giving up.

Stop. You have no proof. The rules of evidence. The reasonable man facing reality. Oh, yes, all the shibboleths, all men are created equal but some less equal than others, among them Richard Thornton. Who he? Oh, that clown from Hicksville. Just about everybody is defecating on him these days.

# Chapter Twenty-three

*How could he do it?*

The absurd, sickening question swelled inside Faith Kilpatrick's body for the thousandth time. There was no answer, of course. No one dies deliberately. It was ridiculous to accuse the Judge of deserting her at this excruciating moment of her life, of running away into eternity without even saying goodbye, leaving her to argue with a voiceless ghost. It just happened, Faith told herself again, also for the thousandth time.

But as she trudged from class to meaningless class at Mount St. Monica's, this answer only created another more enormous question. Why did it happen? Wasn't it God's way of telling you that the Judge was wrong, his whole way of life was wrong, and your way of life (if this suspended animation could be called life) was wrong and Larry Donahue with his vile denunciation of everything, the Judge included, was even more wrong? There had to be an answer to this pain that coursed through her mind and body day and night, and this was the only one that Faith could find. She detested it, every time she blundered up from sleep or a daydream to find it confronting her, like the raven in Poe's poem. It too was absurd, as silly as the fear that Poe, with his gift for third-rate melodrama, had tried to create. But the mind's analysis did not make the answer—or the fear go away. It just crouched there, croaking.

She had to talk to someone about it. Margaret was useless. In fact,

Margaret was suddenly meaningless. The symbolic game Faith had played with her became appallingly childish. Why had it taken death to make her see that the Judge had been the real symbol from the start? He was the one who had given her the strength to defy the idiocies of Mount St. Monica and the Catholic Church. Margaret receded to an almost indifferent figure on the horizon of other meanings, as Faith thrashed in her sudden, brutal vacuum of loss.

Inevitably, she was driven to Sister Agnes Marie. Had she (chilling thought) known it would happen? Was that the reason for her patient, apparently emotionless waiting? No, Faith, that is the highroad to lunacy. As usual, Sister Agnes declined to expose herself to the grandstand play. She simply listened to Faith's babble of guilt and grief and suggested that she see Father Nathaniel Lewis again.

That night, Larry called. He wanted to see her. "No," she said.

"Why?"

A voice within her whispered: *because I cannot expose my soul to you now without losing it.* But she said: "I have studying—exams."

"Listen. Get the hell out of that school. Now. Forget about graduation. You're in no shape to handle those people now."

"Maybe I need them now—more than ever."

"Don't be a damn fool. If you—"

She hung up. Twenty-four hours later she sat down in the study of the white clapboard house that was Father Nathaniel Lewis' rectory. Father Lewis' knowing eyes studied her tear-swollen face, and Faith realized with a sinking, dooming gush of pain that she knew precisely what was going to happen, and both wanted it to happen and dreaded it with all her soul.

Tall, white-haired Father Lewis was kindness, gentleness personified. He talked about her father in the most understanding terms. He even forgave his last decision, condemning that Negro boy to five years in prison. He assured Faith that God understood far more about the interior of a human soul than we imagined. He urged her to stop tormenting herself with images of the Judge writhing in hell for all eternity. "He is beyond our help, though not our prayers, Faith. It is the state of your spiritual health that troubles me now. At such times, it is an opportunity to make a genuine, profound reassessment of our values."

Precisely the opposite of Larry, who said it was the worst time. Did you expect anything different, Faith? Yet you are totally helpless before the soft serenity, the obvious intelligence of this tall, patient man. His white hair, his vivid, angular face somehow reminded you of the Judge, without his anger, his passionate egotism. You remember words from your earlier meetings. *Is a person ever justified in leaving the Catholic Church, Father? I left it myself for five years.* You respected this man. He had been chaplain at Mount St. Monica and resigned because Mother Catherine refused to go along with some of his ideas, such as unrestricted weekend permissions and the end of compulsory daily Mass.

Father Lewis sighed and ran his hand through his gray hair, rumpling it and giving himself a less organized, more uncertain appearance. He got up and poured two small glasses of sherry. "Was there ever a time when you got something out of Mass, Faith?"

That was easy to answer. "In the summer between high school and college. I was feeling very devout. I went to Mass almost every day at our parish church in Bay Head. There were never more than five or six people there. The church was quiet and full of—peace, I guess you'd call it. I felt so close to God. I remember—I even remember the words in the missal that used to mean so much to me. 'I will go unto the altar of God, unto God Who givest joy to my youth.' "

Faith suddenly found her throat was tight with emotion. "It's funny," she said, looking past Father Lewis at the books on the long desk. "I've never forgotten that summer. It was so different from every other Mass I ever went to. I was too young to think about what it meant then."

Father Lewis' voice was low, almost cautious: "Then you know what I mean about something real being there?"

"It was real that summer," Faith said.

"It is real now, Faith," Father Lewis said. "It will be real for the rest of your life if you can meet one of the greatest spiritual challenges."

"What?" Faith said uncertainly.

"Forgive your enemies, those who have trespassed against you."

"Forgive them? Who are they in the first place?"

"Everyone in the Church who has ever damaged your ability to believe in God's grace, who has failed to be perfect as Christ called him to be perfect, who has failed, most of all, to put love above all the laws. These people have wounded you, Faith. You're not the type who sees herself as wounded. You're too proud. But you are."

Faith shook her head. "I . . . never thought of it that way."

It was very still in the small study. The afternoon light was fading rapidly from the windows. Father Lewis got up and went over to a cupboard. "Would you like another glass of wine?" he said.

"Yes," Faith said. Her voice sounded small and distant to her. She felt strange. *Awed* was the only word that described it.

Father Lewis took a sip of his wine and cradled it in his hands. "Then there are a few truly evil people in the Church, people who have lost their capacity to love entirely. Their lives are usually dedicated to achieving something which is not evil in itself, of course, but they are prepared to sacrifice all the truly human values if these come between them and their desires. It is harder still to forgive them. But forgiveness, genuine forgiveness, is always worth the effort."

He leaned forward and the intensity crept back into his voice again. "If you can do it, Faith, then no one can ever interfere with your Mass, your communion with God, again."

Faith met his eyes and knew that he was speaking from experience. For a moment an enormous excitement raced through her. Then she cut it off. Better to wait and see how she felt when she was away from his spell. "I'll have to think about it, Father."

"Of course," he said, smiling.

"What about other people, people like my roommate? You see them ruining their lives because they're so absolutely obedient."

"I'm sure God loves your roommate for her obedience just as He loves you for your rebellious independence. He is watching over us all, you know."

"I think—that's the hardest thing of all to believe," Faith said.

"It is," Father Lewis said. "It is something we can never prove, not in our own lives or in the lives of others. Sometimes I think the Church puts too much emphasis, particularly in school, on merely believing in God's existence. It's not so hard to believe He exists, but to believe He watches over us and cares for us." He shook his head. "Everyone is shaken by doubts about that from time to time."

"But does that mean that we shouldn't live our own lives, that we shouldn't make our own choices? That's the most important thing of all to me. It's what people like my roommate seem to deny."

"Not everyone has the strength to make their choices with your ferocious independence. But eventually they do make them. Everyone has to say yes or no to life at least once."

"That's true," Faith said slowly. "Margaret does make choices . . . in her own way. Maybe that's the only way she can make them."

Father Lewis finished his wine and put it down on the desk. "Don't be afraid to be yourself, Faith," he said. "If we don't have the courage to be that we are nothing. But never run away from anything you find in life either. If you've found something solid and real in the Mass once, try to find it again. And remember this, too. You are young, and when you are young you are quick to say you want everything arranged in a certain way. You want things to be the way they ought to be, but you find out after a while there is a great deal that can't be changed by words, even by actions, not just in the Church, but in life itself."

"But that's giving up," Faith said.

"No, you don't give up wanting a change, working for it. But you don't give up in the other direction either, by quitting, as long as you feel there is something real there to make the fight worthwhile."

"Then you don't think I should leave the church?"

"Only you can answer that question, really. But since you ask my advice, I say no. Because that is where your challenge lies."

"My challenge. I like that word for some reason." Yet at the same time she hated it, dreaded it. She saw with bitter clarity that it was the perfect way to seize her combative soul in a new, more subtle vise. She saw, above all, Larry's contemptuous, denouncing face. But she was helpless to say or do anything about these thoughts. Fate had taken charge of her life. God had spoken in a voice too enormous to deny.

"Goodbye, Father. Thank you."

"Tomorrow is Saturday, Faith. Come to Mass tomorrow. Here."

"I will, Father."

The next morning was radiant with May sunshine. Why had she been hoping for rain, gloom, gale winds, Faith wondered as she trudged down the road to the village of Weston. She stared out at the plowed fields and tried not to think of the Judge lying beneath the soft silent earth in the archdiocesan cemetery, only a few miles away. When she came to the curve in the road, she stopped. There was the village and the church gleaming whitely through its grove of trees like a mute insistent question. Wouldn't it be better to turn back, forget the whole thing, take Larry's advice as a summons and run to him, to his sheltering arms and absolute voice?

Slowly, as if each stroke was an effort, the church bell began to toll. It had a dim, distant faery quality. But it was a voice, answering. You must go and face your challenge.

The small church was almost deserted; the dozen or so Mass-goers were scattered through the pews on either side of the center aisle. Father Lewis came out on the altar a moment after Faith sat down. She watched him prepare the missal, place the covered chalice in position. He seemed taller, heavier, than when she had seen him in his study. Perhaps it was the bulky green vestments.

She did not kneel as he began the prayers at the foot of the altar. She had come to watch, not worship. But she opened her missal in her lap and began reading in English the words which Father Lewis spoke in Latin. She wanted to face not only the ritual of offertory and consecration but also the words with which the priest, in the name of those present, supposedly communicated with God.

*I will go in unto the altar of God. Unto God, Who giveth joy to my youth.*

*Judge me, O God, and distinguish my cause against an ungodly nation: O deliver me from the unjust and deceitful man.*

*For Thou, O God, art my strength: why hast Thou cast me from Thee, and why go I sorrowful while the enemy afflicteth me?*

*O send out Thy light and Thy truth: they have led me and brought me unto Thy holy hill, even unto Thy tabernacles.*

*Then will I go unto the altar of God; unto God, who giveth joy to my youth.*

A twisting spear of emotion ran through her. It was unbelievable that these words, which she had read in sleepy boredom when she read them at all during the last three years, could say so much to her now. But it was a fact she could not deny. Again and again the words caught at her, sometimes because of the memory of their meaning, sometimes because they spoke with staggering directness to the person she had become.

*Why art thou cast down, O my soul? and why art thou disquiet within me?* And the next line: savage irony. *Hope thou in God, for yet will I praise Him, the health of my countenance, and my God.*

*Take away from us our iniquities, we beseech Thee, O Lord, that with pure minds we may worthily enter unto the holy of holies.*

Would her mind ever be pure again? Or would it always be buried beneath this jumble of guilt and bitterness?

*Kyrie eleison. Lord have mercy on us.* Father Lewis intoned the plea for mercy uttered by Christians in the catacombs, haunted by torture and death.

*Gloria in excelsis Deo.* Now he was praising God, recalling the promise of peace Jesus had brought to Bethlehem. *We glorify Thee. We give thanks to Thee for Thy great glory.*

Even the gospel's words were a thrust of anguish. *Truly truly I say to you that ye shall lament and weep but the world shall rejoice and ye shall be made sorrowful but your sorrow shall be turned into joy. A woman when she is in labor hath sorrow because her hour is come: but when she hath brought forth the child she remembereth no more the anguish for joy that a man is born into the world. So also ye now indeed have sorrow but I will see you again; and your heart shall rejoice, and your joy no man shall take from you.*

This was only pain, she thought, staring numbly up at the tall priest on the altar. But did pain mean belief was not over yet, it had not quite died yet inside her—or did it mean that it would never die? Was this blunted yearning, this sorrow, flowing from a part of herself that could not be destroyed without destroying herself?

*Accept O holy Father, almighty everlasting God, this stainless host, which I Thine unworthy servant offer unto Thee, my God, living and true . . .*

Father Lewis began the prayers of offertory. She was still a spectator but now the words crackled through her mind like gunfire.

*. . . Grant that by the mystery of this water and wine, we may be made partakers of His divinity who vouchsafed to become partaker of our humanity . . .*

*I have loved, O Lord, the beauty of Thy house, and the place where Thy glory dwelleth.*

*Holy Holy Holy, Lord God of Hosts.*

The Mass bells rang and the others knelt. She remained seated. She was a spectator, she told herself, an outsider revisiting a childhood place where she had once been happy. A moment later, so it seemed, Father Lewis, his body bowed like a symbol of sorrow, was murmuring the words of consecration.

*Who the day before He suffered took bread into His holy and venerable hands, and with His eyes lifted up to heaven, unto Thee, God, His Almighty Father, giving thanks to Thee, He blessed, broke and gave it to His disciples, saying: Take and eat ye all of this, for this is My Body.*

The bells rang and Faith watched the round white Host rise above the candle flames in Father Lewis' upraised hands. Suddenly, out of the pain and confusion and despair, words flowed up from her body, from her childhood, from the quiet church in Paradise: *My Lord and My God.*

Slowly Father Lewis lowered the Host and bowed his body above the chalice:

*In like manner, after He had supped, taking also this excellent chalice into His holy and venerable hands, and giving thanks to Thee, He blessed and gave to His disciples saying: Take and drink ye all of this, for this is the chalice of My blood of the new and eternal testament: the mystery of faith: which shall be shed for you and for many unto the remission of suns. As often as ye shall do these things, ye shall do them in remembrance of Me.*

The bells rang once more and now the golden chalice, wine, supposedly transformed to Christ's blood, gleamed in Father Lewis' hands. Again the words came, out of the depths beyond knowing, beyond understanding, a thrust of light in the darkness within her, a sharp silent cry in the still church: *My Lord and My God.*

Much later, alone in the empty church, Faith knelt, absorbed by a new bittersweet sorrow. Now you really know how deep it goes. This belief was not something that was going to end soon. With anguished, clutching prescience she saw her whole life revolving around that upraised Host and chalice. Years and years and years in which Faith would neither escape from the virus of doubt which her father and Larry Donahue had implanted in her soul, nor from the hoping, wishing, clutching spasm of belief those other words, those bells, drew from her. An enormous sadness engulfed her. Life—this one life she was living in this unique nation, this America of the twentieth century with its heritage of individual choice and freedom—had fatally divided her. She was drawn and quartered between past and future, between old and new. She could not really believe that this man, Jesus, who appeared on the hills of Galilee 1900 years ago, was truly God, and had founded a church which, with the arrogance of divinity, could regulate and rule her every thought and word and deed. The revulsion in her American soul at this idea was too intense. But there were still the words, the memory of the warmth and peace created by the idea of His transcendental love. She could not deny the reality of that memory, which flowered so easily into wish and trembled on the edge of belief, any more than she could deny the reality of her own yearning flesh.

Mournfully, Faith turned her back on the white altar and walked into the May sunshine, thinking: *How can I tell Larry?*

# Chapter Twenty-four

Weary. That was your state of mind, Margaret. Weary from sleep and no sleep, from stupid arguments and profound arguments and no arguments, from words and no words. Weary, walking in your black academic gown beside your friend Faith into the chapel on Monday morning. The first day of the last retreat. You should be very good at it by now, Margaret. You have been retreating for a long time. Look back down that empty highway stretching into the past. What were you running away from all this time, Margaret? Where are the pursuers? Vengeful cyclists in gleaming, beaded black jackets and visored caps low over hawk faces? No, empty. Running away from emptiness, Margaret, from nothing. That is the story of your silly little life.

And now? How wooden Faith looks. Her face might have been carved by a Bavarian toy maker, the sad little pug nose, the drooping child's mouth. She too is retreating. Her father's death has shattered her. How terrible it must be to love someone so desperately that his death is almost your death. How did those people find the power to drag others down with them into darkness and sorrow? Faith has had a long, long talk with Sister Agnes Marie. Marvelous mystical woman, Sister Agnes Marie. She has a supernatural effect on people. Sister Agnes Marie may be a saint. Faith said it, wonderingly, almost fearfully, when she came back to their room after their talk. You sat there calmly listening to one more proof, Margaret, as if you needed it, that the power of God was infinitely superior to the power of this world. Remember the arrogance with which Faith had strutted about the room, trumpeting her father's victory over Mother Mary Catherine. Yet you did not think these thoughts with the least trace of smug satisfaction. No, you recognized that you too were mysteriously involved in the Judge's collapse. As long as he reigned, rowdy and raucous in his irreligion, there was always a whisper of doubt in the back of your mind. Hardly strong enough, of course, to interfere with your ultimate decision, but now it too was gone. The highway stretched into the future, as empty as the one that ran out of the past.

Yes, empty. Face the truth, Margaret, there was none of the joy you dreamed would leap in your soul when you knelt in the chapel and offered your body, your mind, your heart to Christ. Father Malone had explained it, of course. You were making an extraordinary sacrifice. You were involved with Dick Thornton and you were surrendering him. There was bound to be a sense of loss. We are natural beings, Margaret. When we lose things, we feel them, just as our Lord felt the pain of the nails in his hands, the sorrows of Gethsemane.

Yet, in spite of those words, in spite of the vision of the polished empty highway, there was still this contrary dream, as persistent as it was impossible. A garden, miles from the highway. A garden shaded by tall trees with a lovely flowing fountain in the middle of it. A lush green-grass garden within sight of the sea. The wind soft in the trees and the muted crash of the waves beyond the dunes. A garden for walking with love. A garden where warm and cool air mingle on sweet flesh, touching hands, trembling lips. Why can't I rest in that garden, Lord? I am so weary.

In this garden there is a grave. The grave of a girl named Margaret. She is buried beneath years of Masses, prayers, communions, meditations, the commandments of God, the commandments of the Church, words like chastity, purity, slowly, inexorably, like lava rumbling from a volcano down a newsreel slope, a spiritual avalanche buried her. Yet when the lovers come to visit they pretend she is not buried, they act as if her saintly feet do not even touch the muddy earth. Oh, oh, oh, we do touch the earth. We dig our toes into the warm sand and feel the coolness underneath it. Warm and soft sand and wind in the coarse grass on the dunes above. The kiss. Coarse grass waving in your open eyes and the blueness of the sky absorbing every other color in the world. Even his hair, dark, colorless. Only blue infinite sky and sloshing over the muddy campus lawn to that small cottage in the twilight. Good and bad, Margaret. Upside down, downside around. Actors play multiple parts. Masks. Now you are able to see his anguish too.

Father: *I think you should know—I'm not trying to influence your decision in any way—but I think you should know. Dick has missed at Stapleton Talbot.*

Oh, my beloved, come to my garden and rest. You want things so terribly, heartbreaking boy's eyes conquering life when I don't care, I only want you alone with me in my garden. We can rest there and begin again together.

Another beginning. There strides the retreat master onto the altar. Father Matthew Reilly is his name, a big solid man with a shock of white hair and a face like an underdone side of roast beef. A small, pursed mouth that looks almost lost between the wide crimson cheeks. He kneels before the tabernacle for a moment's prayer. Watch him now as he walks slowly to the altar rail and stares intently at the senior class. Watch his expression slowly change from blankness to a mysterious disappointment and finally a solemn concern. Still he does not speak. He waits until the chapel is absolutely silent, until the last echo of murmuring and shifting has changed into expectant curiosity.

"I met a woman last night coming back here on the train from New York. It was a crowded train. I sat down next to her not by choice but necessity. It was the only seat left in the car.

"It didn't take me three minutes to see that she was drunk."

A small breath is drawn in the single creature which his audience has already become.

"Out of the corner of my eye I saw two sailors across the aisle passing a bottle back and forth and laughing between themselves. I heard one of them gurgle:

" 'Poor Betty. Her supply line's cut.'

"I made no attempt to talk to Betty. But I had a feeling, amounting to a certainty, that she would try to talk to me.

"I took out my breviary and started to read my office. Before I had gone a page, she said:

" 'I suppose you think I'm not much good.'

"I looked at her and shook my head.

" 'No,' I said, 'I don't. I don't think anything of the kind. But I do think you've been drinking too much.'

" 'I met them in the station,' she said, motioning to the sailors. 'I was just lonely, I guess.'

"In the next hour, she told me about herself. Her mother and father were divorced. She had gone to college for two years—one of those modern progressive schools—and dropped out. The only person she had in the world who cared anything about her was a married sister in Syracuse. She was coming back from a visit to her, now.

"Up until last month, she had been 'living' with someone in New York. A middle-aged man separated from his wife. But she had reached the point of no return with him and had fled one night, leaving behind all the jewelry and furs and dresses he had given her.

" 'And now where are you?' I said to her.

" 'Father,' she said. 'I don't know where I am. I'm just drifting from one day to the next, hoping and looking for something.'

"I asked her what that something was, and she said she honestly didn't know.

" 'Do you believe in God?' I asked her.

" 'No, of course not,' she said. 'I sort of did, when I first went to school, but they laughed at me, so . . .'

"I waited for her to say what I knew she was going to say.

" 'But I don't know why I feel so empty, so afraid, all the time. I want to be going somewhere and I want to have some place to go to. And oh, how I wish I had something to look back on. Something that would give me some idea of where I am. That would tell me where I'm going. Instead I have nothing. But it can't be just not believing in God.'

" 'Why not?' I said.

"She looked at me, startled.

" 'Maybe,' she said. 'Maybe . . . it is.'

"I was with that girl until the small hours of this morning. But what I want you to think about is not the possibility of her saving her soul. Much more important is her state of mind—*it can't be just not believing in God.*

"Here was a girl who like so many millions of others does not even think God is important. Think for a moment of the tremendous advantage *you* have over her, with your Catholic education. Yet again, this is not the whole meaning. In spite of the fact that you know God is important, you may someday find yourself feeling as empty and pointless as she. Because you, too, may have nothing to look back on, nothing by which to judge your progress, or lack of it.

"This is what you can find, what you can create, in this retreat. You can make this retreat your spiritual landmark, a supernatural oasis, that you can always come back to in memory and refresh and re-estimate your strength. Then you will never have to fear that terrible sense of emptiness, that premonition of abandonment, that intimation of . . . *hell.*"

Father Reilly stopped speaking. There was not a sound, not a movement in the chapel. He drew in a slow, careful breath.

"It's that important," he said.

"And because it's that important, talk as little as possible. Try to keep silence. It is the best way of making this retreat a record, a statement—for a lifetime. Meditate now, at the end of sixteen years of religious education, in the full flower of your idealism, on what you really want to be. How close to God you want to come. And you will, I promise you, someday come that close.

"It's that important."

Three quick strides and he was gone.

"Wasn't that wonderful?" Esther Sugrue said as they filed out into the bright May sunlight.

"Wonderful. Wonderful," other voices echoed around you. But you can only see the failure in Faith's eyes, Margaret, the shadow of terror on her once laughing face. No murmuring wonderful for Faith, or for Margaret. We are separate, separate from Father's magic words, for these sweet murmurers and their pale eyes and pale thoughts.

"I bet he does *Hamlet* before we're through. That will be the Wednesday matinee," Faith said.

Oh. Those words, the flicker of old impudence echo wildly down Margaret's long retreat. The garden stripped and bare by a furious wind and the waves thunderously mounting. Cold reaching fingers of water rush up the beach. Cold reaching fingers of fear. Oh. The intimation of hell, the intimation of loss. The four days were beginning, Margaret. How long can you hide behind your weariness?

They were eating lunch. Sister Mary Benedict stood at the far end of the dining hall and in a straining voice cried out: "There is a schedule of personal interviews with Father Reilly posted on the main bulletin board. Read it immediately and write down the time for your appointment. Do not be late for your appointment because it will only delay the girls behind you." Routine. Everyone had an interview with Father Reilly, ten minutes per girl. That is the way we save the souls, save the souls, save the souls, ten minutes per soul. Margaret, Margaret, you must go to bed early tonight.

The chapel again. The Stations of the Cross. Father Reilly's voice, loud but droning: "And when I see the wounds in Your dead body, oh my dear Saviour, and I realize they were inflicted by me, with an overwhelming heart I beg Your forgiveness and dedicate my gratitude to You forever, who could hope to repay You, no one, Lord, but I shall struggle in my small way to preserve and increase the graces You have won for us that I may someday join You in everlasting bliss. Amen."

Recitation: "I adore Thee, oh Christ, and I love Thee."

They answer: "Because by Thy holy cross Thou hast redeemed the world."

"Our Father—"

"Give us this day our daily bread—"

"Hail Mary, full of grace—"

"Holy Mary, Mother of God, pray for us sinners now—"

Kneeling, standing, kneeling. Up and down, up and down, fourteen times reciting the same prayers. No wonder your back aches and there is a shine of sweat on Faith's toy forehead. She is suffering. But you are not suffering, Margaret. Maybe that is why you will never be a saint. You have never suffered. Little twinges of humiliation and embarrassment, yes, but in love's furnace, that is where the suffering begins. Remember standing with your father watching him shovel coal into the fat furnace's small gaping mouth, the flames roaring inside. What would happen if you put your hand into that furnace, Margaret? Suffering.

"If we have said the Stations the way they should be said, my poor words are unnecessary," Father Reilly said. The majestic face with crinkly lines of care around the eyes. "The Stations sum up this retreat. They tell us all you need to know about the spiritual life. They tell us how you shall live if, as I pray, you make this retreat with an open heart. Why? Because they lead us to the model on which you can base your lives in complete confidence—

the figure who stands behind the suffering, who knows its meaning and endures Christ's anguish a million times more deeply than we—Mary, our Mother.

"I hope that we can all make this retreat with Mary. Let us take her hand and walk with her and talk with her and see the things she sees and love what she loves, above all, our purity and all the other things Christ teaches us. Let Mary be our philosophy of life for these four days and she will live in your hearts forever, your bodies will become her temples, your souls her chambers. Think of that, your soul her chamber!"

Silence in the church. Sister Agnes Marie plods up the center aisle. "Sister Librarian has made a special collection of books suitable for spiritual reading. They are on the reserved bookshelf but seniors will be permitted to take them out." Flat, matter-of-fact message from matter-of-fact Sister Agnes Marie. Take life calmly, Margaret. Drink the calm from this quiet woman as she vanishes down the aisle once more. Drink calm from her slow steps across the sun-drenched green lawn, calm from the budding trees in the spring woods, the soft winds of May, calm before those words that sow hysteria in your weariness, like the laboratory scientist who inserts his little sack of drugs beneath the rabbit's trembling skin. You could not look, Margaret, that visit to the drug company's research center during freshman science. Those poor quivering animals stretched out by the dozens, their bellies sliced open to the microscope, their hearts beating, beating, beating. Suffering. Maybe you are simply a coward, Margaret. You fear suffering and therefore you fear love. Very, very logical. And if love and sin are fatally intertwined, what of it? Suffering.

The library. *This Tremendous Lover.* That is about Jesus, a swinging title about Jesus. You love Jesus, you love Mary, you love your mother, you love your father, you love Dick. *Plunk.* That key is dead. We must get the piano tuner in. The key D is dead, or perhaps all the other keys are dead and this one rings out sharp and clear to wit, to woo a lovely note. He wants, oh, what does he want? His hand on your breast, Margaret. His hand against the blue sky of your body and you are offering it to him with terrified refusals on your lips. Suffering.

Back in the room. Faith lies on her bed. She stares at the blank ceiling with its plastered cracks and bumps. A blank map of nowhere. "He's getting to me," Faith said. "This afternoon, that sermon."

"Yes," Margaret said.

"When I was little I used to pray to the Blessed Virgin. All the time. He made me want to pray to her again."

"Yes," Margaret said.

But you did not feel any need to pray. You are saying yes because Faith needs a yes. To save her soul she needs a yes. Faith's soul, black with sin, yet Faith remains white, ghostly white, a clown face with the button nose and the staring eyes. White suffering. But Margaret needs nothing. She only wants them to let her alone, to stop dragging yes and no out of her when it is all perfectly simple in the garden by the sea.

Dreaming. A railroad train chugs endlessly down the highway. CHUG CHUG JUG JUG. Clanking restlessly into the past. The iron wheels mashing your weary footsteps. Alone in the last car in a bathing suit. Soot on your legs. Brush it off. It does no good, the soot rubs into your skin, ugly. Your clean white body is ugly, Margaret, black with the stain of sin and where is your ticket? Any moment the conductor is coming for your ticket and you do not have it. You threw it away on the wind, remember, that morning on the beach watching the ticket float idly out on the wind into the jaws of a thundering wave. Laughing, goodbye, ticket, goodbye. But you are not laughing now. Soot is on your hands, on your arms. Brush it away and it only blackens you a little more. Margaret, Margaret, any moment the conductor is coming. Clang goes the door. *All Abooard. Tickets for . . .* Dick smiles down at you, absurd in his brass-buttoned suit. *Tickets for Everywhere.* Weeping. I have no ticket.

Dreaming. The chapel in ruins, wrecked by some mysterious explosion. You crawl across overturned pews, loose bricks, great splintered beams, Esther Sugrue, Dolores Talbot, Rita Conboy, faces beneath the rubble. Weeping, you try to free them, tug massively at timbers. The altar is dark, the sanctuary lamp blown out. By flickering candlelight, the statue of the Virgin, hands outstretched, headless. All dead. All dead. All dead. Everyone is dead and you are alive, Margaret, and your fault. You stare in horror at the grimy seating chart still in your hand. You made them come. You marked them present and killed them all with your dynamite wish.

*Oh, I'm so sorry, I'm so sorry you are dead. I loved you all very much. . . .*

The fog creeps up across the long, low meadows and through the shrouded woods. They walk, ghostly creatures, to the phantom church. But it is real now, Margaret. No more dreaming. Father Reilly raises the round white Host, the gleaming golden chalice. *This is my body, this is my blood, My Lord and my God.* The long line of bowed heads at the altar rail, the Host, flat and dry on the morning tongue. God's body, grace. Then Father Reilly at the altar staring out at them once more, his words echoing above their heads in the brown rafters, telling them to find reality by seeing Christ with Mary's eyes.

Silence and shadow and tears on Faith's eyelashes, glistening tears. Suffering. You must flee again, Margaret, flee into the sweet-smelling spring woods and repeat over and over the careful words: *Everything he said is true. Everything he said is true.* Oh, true, true, the failure to see with Mary's eyes Christ, the heart of reality. His service, the invitation to the truest, purest vision, besmirched, warped; the heart twisted, shrunken and dry by Dick Thornton's smile, words, eyes.

"A penny for your thoughts, Margaret."

Sister Mary Benedict had come down the path behind her without a sound. They stood for a paralyzed moment face to face, her sharp eyes probing.

"Aren't you going to sell?" She smiled in her thin ironic way.

"What?"

"Your thoughts."

"Oh—I was just walking."

"What do you think of our retreat master?"

"Wonderful—just wonderful."

"He's a little too emotional for my taste, but I suppose it's needed."

"Yes."

"Father Malone tells me you're going to join this year."

"Yes, I—I—"

"It's just as well in my opinion. I stayed out for a year after graduation." Sister Mary Benedict gestured vaguely in the direction of the city. "I knew there was nothing there, but I thought it was a good idea to see it for yourself."

"Yes, I—"

"Once you get a good look at our stupid materialistic civilization with its idiotic advertising and radio and television and perverted sensate art—you're glad you have a vocation."

They were walking now out of the woods, onto the green lawn behind the chapel. The soft warm air was almost white with sunshine. Around them the trees whispered placidly, birds twittered. The chapel sat there looking old and tired, almost dozing in the silence.

"Peaceful, isn't it?" Sister Mary Benedict said.

"Yes."

"Do you date?"

"Well—yes."

"It's the best thing. If you go through the motions you find out the prevailing imbecility—"

*How stupid you are, Sister, sucking your dried up little lemon of a soul.* Margaret, Margaret, that is uncharitable, to say the least. Just because Dick Thornton is not an imbecile, that does not mean that Sister's judgment is not, on the whole, sound. Remember Dwight Slocum, remember Larry Donahue, remember—what? You have so little to remember, Margaret. Why bother making the effort?

"I—I think I'll make a visit."

Alone in the chapel's cool silence you walk slowly up the middle aisle to the altar rail. Suddenly it is all right. Staring at the red flicker of the sanctuary lamp, you are suddenly holding everything in your mind. Love for Christ and love for Dick. Somehow you would find the perfect words which would enable you to guarantee his happiness. He would understand with a purity, a totality, exactly why it was necessary for you to make this sacrifice. Because you are making it for him. That he might see the depth and magnificence and profundity of the Catholic faith. Yes, yes, yes, it is all right. It is all in your mind in perfect balance.

And then?

No, that would not happen. He would not thrust your words aside. He would not insist that love was possible, because he too had seen the futility and falseness of this world and was ready, even willing, to choose that garden by the sea. No, he would not say that, he would simply understand, and for the rest of his life the garden would be a shrine which he would visit, in memory of you.

Kneeling: *Thank you. Thank you. Thank you, dear Lord.*

That afternoon, after the Stations of the Cross, Father Reilly discussed the value and the power of sanctifying grace and counseled them at length on how to obtain and preserve it. He urged them to make a perfect confession and climax the retreat with a perfect communion so that they could go out into the world with all the perfection Christ willed in His words: "Be ye perfect as your Heavenly Father."

That night, suffering. Faith in the doorway of the room, her eyes glazed with pain, her little toy mouth moving, "I told him, Meg. I just told Larry I couldn't do it. I don't have the strength." She slumps in the lamplight and the titles of her books stare dumbly at her. *Beyond Good and Evil, The Golden Bough, The Future of an Illusion, Nausea.* "It isn't fair what he asked me to do, it isn't fair. I have to think—of my own soul. Why doesn't he think of it? Isn't that what love is supposed to mean?"

Say the automatic words, "Oh, Faith, it's for the best. If he really loved you—"

She shook her head. "No. You don't know how deep it goes for some people, the revulsion—"

Silence.

"To be free, Meg, to be free. To stand alone on the earth without God—"

"But He's there, Faith. Whatever happens to us, we can never stop believing that, can we?"

The voice thick with tears, the head bowed.

Suffering.

Oh, Margaret, Margaret, the taste of it is in your mouth, dry and salty. The harsh saline runs in your veins. But the pain does not exist for you. The twisted convulsed body on the cross, the sorrowing mother. *We adore Thee oh Christ and bless Thee.* Turn to the window and confront once more the face of the girl on the other side. What is she doing out there in the darkness? Only a ghost, a ghost who cannot suffer. But her sadness is inside you, Margaret, a vast dry windblown beach of sadness, cold in a winter wind while the sea recedes across the horizon. Who can rescue you from this emptiness, Margaret, but God?

"Oh, Faith, Faith, I wish I could help you, but we really can't help each other very much, can we?"

"Just knowing someone listens—someone cares. I think you're the only person who does now."

"Your father cared."

"He never showed it."

"Maybe he didn't know how."

"That's a sweet thought, a sweet, sweet thought. Thank you."

A wan smile on a toy face. Suffering.

The next morning Father Reilly discussed marriage and the family. He warned them about the dangers of mixed marriages and related a series of tragedies which seemed to follow almost inevitably from such unions. Then he talked glowingly of the joys of nuptial love, of the harmonious happiness which came from and through large Catholic families united by the liturgy and life of the Church.

Clearing his throat then and adding a postscript, as he called it. "If this were a high school retreat, I would give at least as much time to a talk on vocations, but you are four years older and far more capable of making such a decision without my help. But I would feel derelict if I did not at least mention the subject. I am sure that some of you are fortunate enough to have received Christ's blessed call to imitate Mary in the greatest, most perfect way, but others, after a year or so in the world, may suddenly find themselves hesitating about what to do with their lives. You should have at least the memory of these few thoughts.

"Because God is the whole of reality, nothing fills up a heart more than He does. To become a bride of Christ, then, is to lead a life of extraordinary fullness. Of magnificent plentitude. You share all the attributes of Christ, His peace, His charity, His kindness, His love. You come, in effect, as close as any human being in the world can come to taking Mary's place, to living with Christ as closely as Mary lived with Him.

"Think of the glory, the happiness of that privilege. And along with it there are the transcendent values of a life always rich in purpose, always full of opportunities to do good. There is the peace of poverty. No checkbooks to balance, no budgets to worry about, no anxieties about possessions and clothes and keeping up with the Joneses. There is the peace of chastity and obedience. There is the certainty of a glorious reward.

"So if you stop and wonder between now and graduation, for now is the time to do such a thing, recall these brief inadequate words. Perhaps they will guide you and help you to cooperate with that grace of God, that beckoning hand of Christ urging you: Come. Follow me."

Do you need more questions, more answers after those words, Margaret? Yet, the wish, if only the words somehow did more than swirl around you like hungry, skittering birds, if only they penetrated your flesh, like arrows. Remember the picture of St. Sebastian in the Italian church, with a hundred arrows in his writhing body? You would welcome even one. Without suffering, how can you truly know the reality of your sacrifice? How do you know this person named Margaret Connolly even exists? Wouldn't that be the ultimate joke? Margaret Connolly was not real, she never existed, she was only an idea invented first by her mother and father, then by Faith Kilpatrick and Dick Thornton and Larry Donahue, and finally by Father Malone. No, no, stop those thoughts, Margaret. There is too much terror in them. But terror is not suffering, at least not the kind of suffering you desire.

"When are you seeing him?" Faith asked.

"Seeing him?"

"For your interview."

"Oh, I never even found out the time."

There it was, her name on the long list: Margaret Connolly—4 P.M., Wednesday. Only two hours away. And what would they talk about? Would it be possible to tell him everything. Yes, why not? Then, miracle of miracles, Father Reilly frowns, his fingers drum upon his desk. "Miss Connolly, it is quite obvious to me you do not have a vocation." Imagine, carrying that message to Father Malone, Margaret Connolly on the high wire, balancing faith and revolt, yes and no, belief and doubt, cowardice and courage.

Suffering? Closer, closer draws the chaplain's cottage and Father Reilly sits behind the familiar desk, ample in his wisdom and grace. "Margaret Connolly," he says, glancing up from a list. "A good Irish name."

"Yes, Father."

"Are you getting anything out of the retreat, Margaret?"

"Oh, yes, Father, a great deal."

"Good. How has your spiritual life been up till now?"

"All right, Father, I guess."

"Do you go to communion often, Margaret?"

"Every day, Father."

"Well, I can see we don't have anything to worry about." He put a large check next to her name on his list. "Nothing very serious can happen to anyone who stays that close to the sacraments."

Leaning back in the swivel chair, Father Reilly gave a large sigh and patted his stomach contentedly. "Ah, it's really heartwarming to give a retreat in a school like this, Margaret. There are so many girls like you who live quiet, uncomplicated, Mary-like lives. It's such a contrast to the world outside."

"Yes, Father."

"All right, Margaret," Father Reilly said, "is there anything special you want to talk about?"

Oh, yes, Father, I have this vision of a garden, a dream of love by the sea, and I would like you to explain it to me, tell me why I feel this draining sense of loss when I have exchanged a world without grace for a God who is the fullness of grace. Will you kindly guarantee to me the unreality of this garden and the reality of my salvation and love's impossibility and the perfect understanding with which I must leave this love in order to achieve—salvation? Alas these are not questions you ask when other girls are waiting outside and the explanations are limited to five minutes, nor are they the sort of things a name on the list who is close to sacraments is expected to discuss, so you simply say, "No, Father, nothing special."

"All right, Margaret," Father Reilly said, "God bless you now and tell the next girl to come in."

You are back in the room and Faith Kilpatrick's suffering face reassures you, lifted up like a cry.

The next day Father Reilly talked about Hell, Purgatory and Heaven. He called them the three fundamental facts and he drew a number of useful lessons from them. Hell instructed us, he said, in the menace of evil. Purgatory in the goodness of suffering, and Heaven in the power of God's love. "These are the three realities which should overshadow every other reality in your life, my dear girls. If you shun evil and welcome suffering in the light of God's love, can there be any doubt that the end will be Heaven's eternal happiness?"

Over, over, over. The words of wisdom, the words of pain. It was a beautiful day. Sunlight glistened on the lawn, shimmered in the trees. "I went to confession this morning," Faith said beside her.

"That's good."

"I feel better about it, but not good."

"Oh, Faith, give it a chance. I know how you feel. It isn't easy to choose."

"You've made up your mind?"

Margaret nodded.

"I was afraid—but maybe it's for the best. I really don't know what I feel about it. What I feel about anything, now."

*No, no,* cried the distant voice inside Margaret's body. *You are supposed to denounce this choice, ridicule it, fling your very life in front of it as you once threatened to do, as it careens down the blank highway into the future. Faith, Faith, how can you fail me?*

"You're going to tell Dick this weekend?"

Nodding again, as casual, as calm as if you were discussing your next date.

"I wonder how he'll take it?"

"I'm sure he'll understand. He's known about it—I mean that I was thinking about it—for a long time. And we never made any—promises."

So calm, so sure, that voice in the soft spring air, and yet its very sound is a lie. Inside, Margaret is sure of nothing, believes in nothing but the wish to retreat, stumbling, crawling, weeping away from the highway in search of refuge, the garden, where love's blind, voiceless arms await you. *Abba Father, let this pass from me.*

"Larry was cold. Utterly cold. And brutal. He just told me to get out of the car and go back to my spiritual kindergarten. God, they don't know. They just don't know what it means to be a woman, to feel—"

"Yes," Margaret said. "Yes. I have to go now, the train leaves in an hour."

On the opposite side of the lawn, another voice. "Margaret?" Father Malone, black cassock shining in the sun, squinting at her. "How was the retreat, Margaret?"

"Wonderful, Father."

Automatic words. No feeling behind them. Just emptiness.

"I thought perhaps—your final decision—reserve a place at the novitiate." The wind, or was it the sunlight, kept tearing gaps in Father Malone's sentences. With stunning force, as if it were shouted by loudspeakers from the treetops, you realize you have not spoken the final irrevocable words to this man. You are free, Margaret, still free to hope, to pray, to dream about the impossible possibility of refuge.

"There's no doubt in my mind, Father, but I'd like—a few more days."

"I hate to press you, Margaret. But I've just received some rather dismaying news. I'm being transferred back to a parish in the city. I won't be in a position—to make arrangements—any longer." Suddenly, amazingly, Father Malone was almost weeping. "I can't understand what I've done wrong. It's punitive. The Archbishop knows I detest that sort of parish work." Struggling for control. "God is obviously testing me, Margaret. Give me your promise now. It will help me find—the spiritual strength to carry this cross."

Silence in the wind and sunlight. While the voice, even the echo of New Margaret dwindled at last into nothing, beneath this last lunge of the avalanche, the garden itself buried beneath tons of rocky, slimy debris.

Trapped now on the empty glistening highway, old Margaret sighed and said: "All right, Father. You have my promise. Now I have to go. The train—"

"Yes. Give my regards to Dick. Tell him if he'd like to talk to me —at any time."

That was so laughable it almost made Margaret weep. Then angry at herself: *If you truly believe, and you do, you do truly, utterly believe, love Christ Dick oh—*

She began to run. Rounding the curve in the path, she looked back. Father Malone still stood there, a lonely figure in black. Soon she would be another lonely figure in black. No, not lonely. A bride of Christ is never lonely. Christ is beside her. And the other Sisters. All sharing the same Christ. Seeing life through Mary's eyes. Yes, yes, yes.

If only you didn't look so lonely, Father.

# Chapter Twenty-five

Out on the brown greasy river a tug hooted derisively. From a nearby street a car horn sounded a plaintive reply. A bus motor groaned wearily. Radio jazz, so faint it might have been coming from a star, mingled with the chemicals on the desultory wind. Dick Thornton breathed the close, foul air. Night sounds of the sleepless city, and you are equally sleepless. Has God whom you so persistently deny . . . No, let us not become puerile, Richard. Let us simply face it, see it for what it is, failure. It is as simple and as dangerous as running a boat into Manasquerry Inlet in a northeastern storm. You hang out there, dancing on the swells like a toy balloon and pick your wave, not too big and not too small, gun your motor and go for the money. If your judgment is wrong, if you picked one too big, you can lose control and those glistening black rocks on either side of the river mouth bite through your hull like dinosaur's teeth. Too small, and there is a foaming monster right behind it, roaring over the deck, flooding your engine room. Dead in the water then, at the mercy of the next wave.

For a week you have plodded from law office to law office discussing your future with old men and young men, fat men and thin men, Catholics and Protestants, Jews and Italians. You even have an offer or two from law firms known only to the editor of the Yellow Pages. Dry-lipped invitations from men with faded ties and worn cuffs, men who could use a cut-rate patsy to do their brain work.

No, Richard, better to go home to Paradise and play the real estate game.

But first you have some unfinished, non-legal business. All week as you drifted listlessly from appointment to appointment (yes, you, the white-toothed charmer mumbling morosely, no wonder the interviewers looked bored) all week you have meditated on how to finish the business known as Margaret Connolly. Now you know, thanks once more to Lawrence Donahue. Two nights ago as you lay staring into the darkness something began happening at the other end of the apartment. Crash, clank, clunk. It sounded like an animal blundering around the living room, falling over chairs, bumping into walls. Then voices blaring: LOOK, BUDDY, IF YOU REACH FOR THAT GUN. An animal that could turn on television. Shoetree in hand, you had tiptoed cautiously down the long hall.

A man stood in the middle of the dark living room staring stupidly at the television set. The beaked nose, the bony profile, the domed forehead were Larry Donahue's, but there was no resemblance to Larry in the slumped shoulders, the drooping head, the swaying stance.

"Larry?"

"Hello, Richard. I wake you up? Listen, where the hell's the booze, I can't find a goddamn light switch—"

Flip on the light and see what strange catastrophe has overtaken your friend. Perhaps because his father was an alcoholic Larry seldom took a drink, but that night he had taken many. They stood there staring at each other in the harsh white light. Suddenly Larry began to laugh. It was not a pleasant laugh. It ripped and clawed at Dick's nerves like chalk skidding on a blackboard. Larry laughed and laughed until there was an edge of madness or, at least, hysteria in it.

"Oh, Richard, Richard," he finally gasped, "what jerks we mortals be. What jerks."

With no warning the bitter mirth fell off his face and his mouth drooped, his hand ran vaguely through his tangled hair. He weaved his way to the television set and smashed the off button with a wild swing. The set went dark and he bent over the big brown cabinet as if in pain.

"That little bitch. That no-good, stupid little bitch—"

"Larry, for God's sake—"

"Richard, it's funny." He spun around, wild mockery in control again. "Six or eight months ago I was lecturing you on how to rescue your beloved from the maw of Mother Church. Professor Donahue, the expert seducer of souls. And what happens? What happens?"

He barely made it to the fat easy chair. He threw his head back against the stuffed cushion and smiled up at Dick, who still stood in the middle of the room, the shoetree foolishly clutched in his hand. "What happens? *I* get seduced. Hooked. Oh, it was a beautiful performance all the way to bed and back, and tonight the big play, the tears, the repentance and 'Larry, come with me. Larry, Larry, I want to save your soul too—' "

The laughter again, the head rolling on the worn brown velvet. "And you know what happened, Richard? I almost went. I was falling in love with that rotten little bitch, all the time thinking I was one step ahead when she had two steps on me from the start."

"You mean Faith—?"

"I mean Faith. I had her, Richard. I had her. She was ready to come anywhere with me."

His hands clutched at the air in front of him, then fell into his lap. "Then her father—and this goddamn retreat. I told her not to go."

Now finally you are beginning to think, Richard. You are beginning to regain some semblance of self in this maelstrom. Your first thought, of course, is Margaret. No hope now, absolutely none. If they could do this to Faith, they are surely fitting Margaret for the nun's robes. But pride forbids you from mentioning Margaret to Larry. Besides you are genuinely disturbed by your old friend's hysteria.

"Larry, I always thought you took this religious stuff too goddamn seriously."

"I take it seriously because it is serious."

Larry's eyes glittered, the mouth became a cold line. "Let me tell you something, Richard. Something I've never told you before because I like you. Intellectually you're a lightweight. You think you can live your life with your eyes closed to the most important values in the human soul. You think you can be neutral about them. Well, you're wrong. That's what's wrong with all you thin-blooded ex-Protestants. You can't be neutral. Somewhere, sometime you've got to face up to what you believe, so why not now?"

What are you going to say? You are not neutral, you are not thin blooded, you have values? Another pious little speech from the ethical culture saint, Richard Thornton. "You sonofabitch, you don't think I've got religion in my guts, too? But I got rid of it. I started early and got rid of it."

The mocking laugh again. "You don't get rid of it with neutrality, Richard, that's your pale little Protestant heritage speaking. The agnostic, humble before the secrets of the universe. Shit. You get rid of it by making an absolute choice. Yes or no, and then living it. You don't chase Catholic virgins all over the state in your little car when you're rid of it. That's not getting rid of it, Richard. That's sneaking it in through the back door after you've made a big show of kicking it off the front porch."

Back to bed, to the city hooting and wailing and groaning in the chemical wind. I will not bother to defend my pale neutral thoughts to you, Lawrence. They may be bloodless, but at least they do not lead to the kind of humiliation you are enduring. And what would you say if I tried to convince you that I do have emotions? Why is it more admirable to curse and wail, rend garments, guzzle booze, shout, sneer, denounce, bemoan? No thanks. It would be easy to play that kind of scene with you and even with Margaret Connolly. But I have had enough humiliation for one week. I am going to play it Wasp, cool. There'll be no harsh words, never even a mention of the conversation with Mrs. Connolly after Judge Kilpatrick's funeral. Mother's move may not have been an accident, it may have been part of the master plan. By not mentioning it, you let Margaret worry about bringing up the bad news. She deserved to do a little worrying. As for Richard Thornton, he will be a model of debonair cheer. He will play her little game in reverse.

Now you have savored it for two days and it gets better and better. You have even dramatized a farewell scene, perhaps at dinner on Sunday. "Dick, I've got something to tell you," in her sweet, sympathy-winning way.

"Oh, yeah, your mother mentioned it to me. We won't be seeing each other any more. Well, we had some fun, didn't we?"

Careful, don't play it like an envious ingenue. It was just a new fact to absorb. No more important in the long view of your life than your year with Vicky Sand. Consider what you learned from this disaster. Vicky exposed your pretensions to sexual sophistication. Now you know you have the same weakness on the religious side. All right. Now that you know, you can begin doing something about it. Knowledge is power.

And suddenly the murky darkness is alive with sunshine. You are back on the beach, your hand moving toward her breasts, firm beneath the sweater. "Jesus!" The sound of his own voice steadied him. You are still alive. The world is still turning. She was coming. You had to face the weekend with her and stop acting like a seventeen-year-old. You are not going to let her make a fool of you in front of your whole fraternity. You are not going to let her hurt you any more, economically or emotionally.

The tugboat hooted again. He drifted into semi-sleep.

"Okay, law books," Jake O'Connor growled from the doorway. "I'm up on a two-count rap for grand L. They're going to cool me for twenty-five at least."

He threw a pillow at Jake. On your feet, Richard. You have completely forgotten that you are double-dating with this screwball. "Give me ten minutes, pal," he said, "and I'll draw up the brief of the century. But first I've got to shave."

"What goes with the minstrel boy?" Jake asked. "I saw him in a bar last night absolutely polluted."

"He and Faith have wrapped it up."

"Well, that's not exactly bad news," Jake said. "I wouldn't wish that little bitch on my worst enemy, much less my best friend."

"Still bringing Dolores?"

"According to the latest bulletin."

"Is it serious?"

He was in the bathroom now, lathering up. Jake was stretched out on the bed.

"Who knows, we're both a couple of frauds."

"You mean what's up front isn't real? Don't destroy my boyhood illusions."

"No, psychologically. All I've really got going for me is her mother. She hates the sight of me. That puts me right at the top of the list as far as Dolo's concerned."

"Another happy family circle."

"The world is full of them. Which reminds me, I hear you're going to start one of your own."

"With whom?"

"Your Virgin Queen—if that's still an accurate description."

"Goddamn."

Blood trickled slowly down his chin. It was the first time in years he had cut himself shaving. He rummaged in the medicine cabinet, found a styptic pencil and pressed it to the wound. The stinging burned into his jaw. It felt good, something else to fight besides the fantastic rage inside his body.

"You've been hearing the schoolgirl version, kid. As far as I'm concerned, it's just fun and games. And after this weekend—"

"How much fun?" Jake said.

"Enough."

"No kidding? You live and learn."

*After this weekend.* Yes, that could be the answer. Send her back to Mother and Father Malone minus that virginity they were so hell-bent on preserving unto death. That could be a very delightful, devastating answer.

He pressed the styptic pencil into his wound one more time and quickly finished shaving. He came out of the bathroom feeling almost calm. Swiftly he packed and dressed and in ten minutes he and Jake were on the road to the campus. They reminisced about prewar days at the shore all the way down and Dick found himself even calmer and more grimly determined at the end of the ride. It was good to recall years untouched by Margaret Connolly. Remember that for the weekend.

Dolores Talbot was waiting for them on the porch of the boardinghouse. She had driven over in her own car. "I was afraid you'd show up," she said to Jake.

"Your mother made me come," Jake said.

Dolores laughed. The sound went through Dick like a buzz saw. His eyes ricocheted from the soft white arm around the brown pole of the wooden porch, the sunlight on the golden hair, the bright, kissable mouth. It was impossible. He could not tolerate laughter, a woman's face. Only with an immense effort did he regain his grim, cold calm. He left Jake and Dolores on the porch and drove to the station. The train was late. He scuffed gloomily up and down the platform for a half hour, growing more and more depressed. Finally the big diesel engine came drumming around the last curve.

Confusion now. Waving, smiling girls in rose and violet and sky-blue suits and dresses, calling, offering their shining faces to kiss. Arms around waists, eyes meeting, laughter, laughter everywhere. And suddenly Margaret in the center of it, standing very still beside her bag, her eyes shy and vaguely frightened, an uncertain, slightly anxious expression on her face. It catapulted him back to that first day on the beach, and the rest of her completed his devastation. She was wearing a soft rose summer suit with a round white flowered hat that sat on the back of her head. Schoolgirl and woman. For a moment he was speechless.

"Hello," she said.

You know why there is shame and hesitation in her eyes, but ignore it, Richard, that is part of the game. "Hello," he said. "You're looking great."

"Thank you."

She took his arm as they started toward the gate to the inner station. "I had no idea this was such a big weekend."

"Big?"

"All those girls on the train. I thought it was just your fraternity."

"It's all the fraternities."

You were hoping for an *intime* little party, is that what's bothering you, Miss Connolly? An atmosphere with a little less oompah-pah, less carnival spirit? It would make it much easier to slip poor Dickieboy the news, at some unguarded, potentially tender moment. Well, watch out, because Dickieboy may slip you something before he's through with you.

In the car she spent most of her time looking out the window, as they wound through the downtown traffic. "I've never been to a university town before," she said. "I won't admit it to anyone but you."

"There's not much to see."

They said nothing for the next five minutes. He caught her looking at him in a more serious inquiring way. Finally she asked, "How are things on the job front?"

"Not encouraging."

"Oh."

It was almost too much. Not only was she prepared to save his soul, she was going to manage his career, too. What marvelous things supernatural wisdom did for the shy and simple-minded.

To his relief, Jake O'Connor and Dolores had vanished when they returned to the boardinghouse. He introduced Margaret to Mrs. Roundtree, the chubby, cheerful little landlady, and then he led his beloved up three flights of stairs to her room. "I figured we'd eat dinner alone," he said. "We'll be seeing enough of everybody in the next couple of days."

She smiled. "I'm not here to see everybody in the first place."

The total insincerity of that remark was almost too much. He almost cut her down on the spot. But play the game, Richard, don't show your ace card too soon. Wait for that moment when you can get more than a sweet little sermon. He took a deep breath and said he would wait for her downstairs on the porch.

Watching the sun vanish from the narrow little street of two-story houses, he realized it was going to be difficult to maintain the performance. Obviously she considered herself blameless. It was true that nothing specific had been promised. If the moment of confrontation came, she would undoubtedly play innocent and make this meaningless omission her whole defense. It fitted perfectly into their pattern. He tortured himself with the knowledge that he had allowed her to impose her pattern on their relationship—the indirection, the hesitation—it had all been her creation and now she was getting a superb dividend on it.

You are trapped, Richard, trapped by nonwords, unspoken promises, strangled adoration, voiceless love. Maybe it is really amusing. Maybe you should laugh. You had been more frank about your secret self with her than anyone else, and now it was ending in a weekend of double-talk.

Suddenly she was beside him on the porch, the same vaguely mocking smile on her face. "Here I am," she said, "getting hungrier by the minute."

He ignored that feeble pass at humor and led her to the car. Yet the mere fact that she had the gall to act lighthearted was enormously depressing. Supreme irony, Richard, she has found the happiness you had always wished for her in total surrender.

They ate in a small Italian restaurant in the north end of town. He was so tense, he found it almost impossible to talk to her. Margaret tried several topics: exams, the Communist takeover of China, earnest queries about his father's health. She finally relapsed into silence. He sat there sadistically thinking, *Let her squirm.* Gradually, he reached a kind of bitter equilibrium that made him feel almost buoyant. He began telling her in sardonic terms the story of his job search. Omitting the plea to Dwight Slocum, of course. Why not act perfectly natural? It was an experience, a unique experience. Why not get everything you can out of it: amusement, interest, disgust, and, for a climax, some nice horny pleasure?

It was not quite eight when they finished dinner and he suggested a stroll around the campus. The dance did not begin until nine-thirty. "Unless you need an hour and a half to get properly regal."

"You know I do that with no effort at all."

Once more he let her pale little pitch for humor expire in silence. She was reduced to asking polite questions about the various buildings and he gave her colorless, equally polite, answers. The twilight thickened and the buildings became indistinct blocks of darkness with occasional lighted windows from a night class or laboratory. His bitterness deepened with the darkness. Being here on the campus seemed to compound the irony. To meet the ultimate humiliation here, where you had spent those years of eager, confident dreaming. It was enough to make you wonder if some superhuman enemy was manipulating events specifically to torment you. Perhaps he was trying to get a message to you, Richard. *Face it, my child, you are a jerk, a small-town jerk.*

For a moment he teetered on the brink of total doubt, total terror, total humiliation. He stopped walking and a tremor passed through his body. *Beg her, beg her in the name of love.*

"Yes?" Margaret said softly. She stood only inches away, facing him. She seemed to be anticipating something. Jesus, was she that cold, that calculating?

"Nothing," he said, restored by new anger. "It's just getting late."

Jake O'Connor was already in the room, wearing his tux like he was born in it. Inevitably there was a drink in his hand. "Richard," he said, "where the hell did you go?"

"Oh, went to dinner, wandered around," he replied evasively. "I figured you wanted some time alone with the Golden Girl."

"Are you kidding? I need help with that girl. When I'm alone I can't keep my hands off her. You want a drink?"

"Definitely."

Jake pointed to the bottle on the mantel. Dick poured himself a double shot and raised his glass.

"A toast to the next man to die," Jake said. He squinted at him through the glass. "And I think it's going to be you, Richard."

"What the hell do you mean?"

"It's written all over your love-sick face. But rejoice, we've all got to go sometime and I think you're getting a good one."

"Thanks."

Dressing with Jake's cheerful gassing in the background. He was celebrating. He had decided to pass the bar exam honestly. "My old man wanted to put the fix in but I wouldn't buy it. Sometimes I think I've really got integrity."

"Where—what are you going to practice?"

"Criminal law, naturally, it goes with my background."

You are now downstairs with Mrs. Roundtree puffing around you, her eyes popping. "Oh, wait till you see her, Mr. Thornton, she'll just take your breath away." You smile and stare out the black window into the night until her step on the stairs. From the landing she meets your eyes with a radiant smile.

The dress is strapless, white lace at the bodice with a full rounded skirt of white silk faille banded with black chantilly lace. She carried a shawl of the same lace. The effect was regal. Her skin contrasted perfectly with the bands of chantilly, and her dark hair and eyes were a second perfect contrast with the faille. Her gloves were half length, accentuating the smooth rounded arms, symmetry of flesh rising to her strong lovely neck. In her hair she wore the single orchid he had sent her.

"Dolores said to go without them. They'll meet us."

Walking across the now totally dark campus, she was alive again for him. Scorn, bitterness, even hatred could not touch that moment of meeting on the stairs. You are conscious of her totally, every detail of that perfect body you have never possessed in that truly loving way you envisioned in your adolescent dreams. You are condemned to a vision born in madness, chaos, a desire that was mixed with disgust, yes, even with death.

Death. You are thinking death when you walk beside life, sex incarnate with your love. Why? She is marrying herself to death. You offered her life. Life rooted in freedom and love. She has chosen death, chosen to live out her life, day by withering day, in a pattern justified only by death. Again the stupidity of it convulsed him.

"Do you like the dress?" she was asking.

"I could only reply to that with understatements," Dick said. "That's why I said nothing."

"It's borrowed. It belongs to Helen Cudahy. I had to take it in—"

"It's a wonder you didn't have to remodel it."

They did not speak again until they reached the gym. The place was done in uninspired traditional style; streamers and crepe paper on the walls and girders, a mixture of school and rainbow colors. At the far end on an improvised stage, a band was playing a muted version of "Dancing in the Dark." The floor was not yet crowded.

Dick worked his way through the tables introducing her to several friends and noting with grim satisfaction how impressed they were. Get all the mileage out of her you can, Richard, while you can. What a repelling thought. He forced his way through one more introduction and hurried her to their table.

They sat down. He struggled for some completely innocuous topic, but it was like wrestling quicksand. A waiter rescued him temporarily. He ordered a double Scotch and soda.

"I'll have a Coke," Margaret said.

He led his little nun out on the dance floor. Give her a final whirl, Richard, before she gives up all these terrible vanities, like dance bands and Cokes.

"You are worried about the job problem, aren't you?" she said as the band swung into "Mamselle."

"I guarantee you I am not."

Concentrate on dancing. But the self-contempt he had felt in the room came raging through him again. He had never seen her dance so well. Their every motion was in perfect unison, as if they were one person drifting over the floor to the soft, sleepy music. She was weightless in his arms and yet he was acutely aware of her body. He held her a little farther away, deliberately choosing details, the thick soft quality of her hair, the perfect spacing of her eyes, the strong firm lines of her mouth, her breasts . . . They stood beside a window looking out on the sea. Passively, joyously, she let him undress her. He kissed her softly on the side of her throat as she slipped off each garment. Then she was naked and his arms reached for her, touched her, mouth half open, warm and sweet, in a long deep kiss.

No. Frantically he wrestled for control. It would never be that way. It would be brutal and snarling, a snide, sadistic gouging while she whimpered for mercy . . .

"Jake and Dolores are here," Margaret said.

"Oh, good."

Never did he think he would be so relieved to see Jake O'Connor's mocking smile. "Hello, Margaret," Jake said as they danced up to them. "You look good enough to make me swear off blondes forever."

"Don't bother," Dolores said, "blondes will soon be swearing off you."

Back at the table, the conversation rocketed around his ears like a train of roller coaster cars. Margaret showed she had profited from her tour of the party circuit, courtesy of Richard Thornton, by gamely joining the fun. It was, of course, also a way of avoiding the necessity of conversing with this tongue-tied sap, Richard Thornton. Maybe she is infinitely superior at a waiting game, Richard. After all, she has committed herself to a lifetime of it.

"In my opinion," Jake O'Connor was saying, "Miss Talbot is not a member of the ABA."

"What's that?" Margaret said.

"The Authentic Blondes Association."

"Oh no. I'm an authentic brunette. I know an authentic blonde when I see one."

"There are times when I suspect she's a member of another authentic association that begins with B."

"There are times when I know you are," Dolores said.

"The Authentically Beautiful Association?" Margaret said.

"That's right," Jake said. "How did you guess?"

"From the look on Dick's face, I think he's writing us all off as authentic bores," Dolores said.

Order another drink. Look interested and amused. You are having a wonderful time with these bright, merry, important people.

No use. It was not working. Nothing was working. He asked Dolores to dance. They talked about the wonderful spring weather. He watched Jake O'Connor dancing with Margaret. He kept whispering in her ear, making her laugh. She was having a ball.

"What a fantastic effect you've had on Margaret," Dolores was saying.

"What?"

"She was such a snail, always in a shell."

"Don't give me too much credit."

"Who else?"

Back at the table an old friend and amateur wit named Joe Cummings came along and began torturing Jake with visions of a stodgy married life. He was drunk and some joker had told him that his old buddy was engaged to Dolores. "She's a witch," Jake said earnestly. "You can't get engaged to a witch. Besides, her teeth are no good." He told Dolores to open her mouth and she obeyed. "Look at those incisors. This type of girl could cut your throat if you get too close to her."

"That will never be one of your worries," Dolores said.

"Besides, the condition of the bicuspids indicates she's really a hundred and twenty-two years old. I picked her up during the war. In this Tibetan valley . . ."

Have another Scotch and soda, Richard. Keep smiling. The waiter is slow, so excuse yourself and smile your way to the bar.

Two double Scotches later, dancing again. "Dolores and Jake are such fun, aren't they?" Margaret said.

"Yes."

"You don't sound very happy about it."

"I happen to think Jake O'Connor is an arrogant slob. Amusing maybe, but still a slob."

She looked confused. They danced for a long time in silence. "I wish Faith and Larry were here," she finally said.

"Why? They wouldn't be very good company."

"I'm assuming—things would be different."

"It's just as well. Watching those two in action makes me wonder if some people are born with a gift for making each other miserable."

"It's especially sad when both sides have the best of intentions," Margaret said.

A pregnant pause. He was supposed to come on now with the fateful question: *I hope that isn't going to happen to us.* Then would come the sad, dramatic tale of her supernatural decision.

Oh hell, oh hell, oh hell. Why was she so goddamn beautiful? Why was she acting this way? She had to be deliberately, consciously making a fool out of you, making you a fool not only in the eyes of Jake O'Connor, Dolores Talbot, all the others who would soon find out the last chapter of your little romance, but in your own eyes—the worst humiliation. Was she trying to be a living refutation of your arguments against her religion? It was possible possible possible. The whole thing was a fantastic, absurd maneuver to convert him. You had been out-thought by her, by the priest, every step of the way . . .

No. It is just sex that is bothering you—cold, meaty luscious sex. She has it and she knows it. Knowing it has nothing to do with her great supernatural decision. Sex was her natural weapon and she was using it with perfect confidence, without a trace of fear. And why not? Aren't you as good as gelded, Richard, thanks to the total surrender of your masculinity?

Across the dance floor through an accidental lane he caught a glimpse of Jake O'Connor and Dolores sitting at the table with five or six friends. The band leader announced the last dance. In five minutes they would be off to nightclubs, hotel parties, dancing till breakfast. It was impossible, you could not last. There was not an ounce of false merriment left in your body.

"Do you mind if we cut out and make it a short evening?" he said. "I don't feel very good."

"Of course," Margaret said.

He murmured a brief explanation in Jake's ear. Dolores smiled at Margaret. It was ghoulish. Everyone thought the lovebirds wanted to be alone.

The campus grass was wet and the night air cool. There was no moon and no stars. Margaret shivered and drew her shawl around her shoulders. They still gleamed whitely through the lace.

They walked in silence. Then Margaret said, "You are worried about the job, aren't you?"

"No."

"It will work out," Margaret said. "I'm sure of it. I'll say some prayers."

"I don't need any prayers."

She ignored the savagery in his voice. "I'll pray anyway," she said.

The boardinghouse was completely quiet. Everyone was making a night of it. The stairs were lit by single dim bulbs. He went down the hall with her to her room, not touching her. But he could not stop breathing her perfume in the close air. Margaret bent to find the keyhole, turned the lock and pushed open the door. The room was not entirely dark. From outside a streetlight filtered through the trees. He could see a fat dresser and a wide double bed.

She turned, solemn faced. Now was the inescapable moment of truth. With the perfect setting. The bed in the background, ironic commentary on her negation. They might even wind up sitting side by side, while she solemnly explained to him, good old castrated little Dick, about the power of God's grace.

Stop her, Richard, stop her. Only one way. Take her, as you dreamed of taking her that night at Slocum's party. Strip away dress, petticoat, brassiere until she stands before you naked and your hand goes out to seize one of those soft, coned breasts and the other plunges deep into the dark, hairy seat of love. Oh, the eyes will be closed, there will be tears on the terrified face, but that did not matter. Nothing mattered in a world presided over by a superhuman sadist. Larry is right, only an absolute No can survive this world, an absolute No to the Margaret Connollys and Father Malones.

"Dick. Do you remember that day on the beach?"

Was it her voice or someone from another world, whispering mockery? No, it was Margaret speaking across an immense gulf, a chasm of darkness, between them in the small still room. He heard his own voice echoing vaguely inside his body.

"How—could I forget it?"

"Why didn't you—say something?"

There was sorrow in her voice, sorrow and regret. And something else. A despairing, anguished honesty. Why, God why, was it despair that made honesty possible? Grimly, he spoke the truth.

"Because—because I was afraid."

"Afraid of what?"

*Of losing you?* No, that was the coward's romantic lie. "Afraid of admitting I loved you—because I didn't think you loved me."

There were tears on her face, in the lamplight. "Oh, Dick, Dick," she said. "Dick. And now I've promised."

"To go in the convent?"

"Yes. Who—told you?"

"Mother. To make sure I'd be a good boy."

"But the most terrible thing is happening, Dick. I can't stop loving you. I thought God—Jesus—would help me. But they haven't. And now the most terrible thing is happening. I keep thinking that you need me more than God. And I need you. More than God."

Words, words flowed from his lips. Where did they come from? Out of his whole life, his whole past, an answer to the choirboy years, Momma Glad and her Old Testament frown.

"I do need you, Meg. God—isn't telling you to give me up. God—Jesus—is there in history helping you to love me. Other people, Meg, other people have put orders on His lips. Orders against loving. Don't listen to them, Meg."

He drew her to him harshly, so harshly he could feel her breasts through the stiff dinner shirt. "I won't let you listen to them."

"But I promised. I promised Father Malone."

"The hell with Father Malone. The hell with those kind of promises. The old Margaret made those promises. The new Margaret promised me, that day on the beach. The Margaret I love promised me, first."

"But if I go back, it'll happen again, Dick. My Mother–Father Malone–will make me promise again."

"You're not going back. Jesus, Meg, when I think how close I came to losing you. You're not going back. We're going to get married. Now."

"Now?"

He drew her to him again, thinking once more how all his life was flowing into this moment, this freedom. "With this kiss, I thee wed."

Soft and warm and yielding, her mouth met his lips.

"We're going away. We both need to make a new beginning, Meg. We're going away to another state, in another part of the country. Not running away. Going away, together, Meg. Together."

"Yes. Oh yes, Dick. Yes."

He could have taken her, then, made her his triumphant defiant bride. But it was no longer necessary. It was almost necessary *not* to love her in that claustrophobic yet immensely victorious room. It was necessary to erase for all time the blunder he had come so close to committing, the loss he had almost inflicted on them, in that deadly room.

Swiftly they packed and drove to the beach. Margaret seemed to know, without even asking, where they were going. She felt the same need to return to where love had begun. As if they both wanted to be certain, one last time, that it was real.

Arms entwined, they watched the dark water hiss up the white sand. A half-moon glistened on the ocean's heaving eternal face. "Is the answer still yes?" he asked.

"Yes."

In minutes they were on the turnpike rolling west, the yellow lamps stretching ahead of them into the heart of America.

# Epilogue

I have, of course, corresponded at length with Margaret, Dick, Faith, and others to create this book. It seems simplest to quote from Margaret's letters to tell the rest of her story.

". . . We were married by a Justice of the Peace in Ohio, where we stopped while Dick negotiated a thousand dollar loan from his stepfather, a man named Stone. We honeymooned in motels between there and Denver. That's where we decided to live. Dick had an old Navy buddy in a law firm there, and he clerked for him, and I worked in a department store until he passed the state bar exam. I explained it all to my mother by mail. There was a lot of hysteria in the first few letters, but after a year or so, she calmed down, and even came out to visit. She died about five years ago, Daddy about five years before that.

"Dick and I both love Denver. It isn't perfect—what city is?—but it has that western sense of community that makes you proud to participate in charity drives and other kinds of civic causes. Dick dabbles in politics a little, state legislature stuff, but his law practice does not give him much time to concentrate on it.

"The Church? I just stopped going, when I married Dick. I knew he could not stomach it. I faced that, on the ride to the shore, that last night. I faced so many things that last night! But it was amazingly easy, once the facing began. It had all been *constructed,* so it seemed then, so that an absolute choice was the only way. So I chose.

"I haven't built Dick up into a god or anything like that, as a substitute. We've just lived a life together, a loving life. I still believe in a God that (I'm borrowing from Dick here) it is arrogance to define. Occasionally we go to the Unitarian church in our suburb. Our children (three girls and a boy) go to public schools. But I feel closer to God when we go skiing in the Rockies than I ever feel (or will feel, I guess) in church.

"Sometimes I look back on Old Margaret and wonder how I—or anyone else—ever stood that girl. Not that the new Margaret isn't creepy or morose at times. But for me marriage has been such a wonderful, continually *growing* experience—it has simply carried me through these occasional lapses. In the first years, when I had trouble sleeping after a party or when I was overtired, alarming thoughts would seep into my mind. Have I sinned? Will I be punished in some terrible unforeseen way? But I would just whisper: *Get lost, Old Margaret,* snuggle a little closer to Dick, and go back to sleep. I haven't had one of those episodes for years now. But perhaps the best answer to my stability—if I can dare to call it that—was the inner feeling I've never lost, that my prayers *were* answered. I honestly don't believe that the life I am living with Dick is in any way against the commandments or intentions of God. The absolute contrary, in fact, is what I feel, and hope I always will feel.

"In one of your last letters, you asked me if the new or post-Vatican II Catholic Church, with its emphasis on freedom and its tendency to abandon many of the traditional rigidities, has made it easier for me. I can see that you can't get that old adage, once a Catholic, always a Catholic, out of your head. It is obviously almost impossible to convince you that no matter what the Church did or said, or will do or will say in the future, it simply no longer matters to me. I've become something else—something better, I think: a free, adult American.

"I remember Faith, in one of her letters, lectured me intensively on that. She does not believe that Americanism can or should become a religion. But I don't worship America instead of God. I just mean that by choosing freedom, with Dick's help, I was able to escape that claustrophobic Catholic world that almost swallowed me. I say this as matter-of-factly as possible, without any bitterness, because by going away as we did, I was able to escape most of the personal recrimination and social ostracism that my apostasy—to use an old-fashioned word—would have brought me in the city of my birth.

"Dick just looked over my shoulder, and asked me to add a line for him. He said you should call the book *The Days of Our Adolescence.* I told him it was a good thing he had a law degree. As a novelist he would obviously starve to death."

Not all of us were able to escape the Church as easily as Margaret. Larry Donahue, applying his absolute nihilism to politics, descended from betrayal to murder to suicide. Jim Kilpatrick spent fifteen dwindling years with Esther before he faced spiritual bankruptcy. Then, leaving wife and children, he exposed himself to another kind of anguish. Faith, blundering into the blank openness of America with her burden of doubt and guilt, has veered close to tragedy more than once. But those are other books.

Looking back, I shed no tears for Margaret or Dick or Faith or Larry and the others. Perhaps because I am one of them, and tears would be that most repellent of all emotions, self-pity. But I also feel that tears would be a lie. Bad as it was, our youth does not deserve them. If I shed tears for anyone, it is for James Kilpatrick, Sr. Thanks to him, I know our time was better than his time. I know, too, it was he who helped to make it better by enduring the years of impossible but necessary compromise between old faith and new faith.

Oddly, in one of her letters, Margaret expressed a similar point of view. "The most important thing in your book is not my story (in my humble opinion)," she wrote. "At least to me. It was the chance to learn the whole truth about the Judge. It made me realize how little we really understand what is happening around us. I thought that the Judge's death almost trapped me, but now I begin to think that his death really freed us all. One thing I value from my Catholic past is the awareness of the mystery—and the value—almost always the hidden value—of suffering. Even this terrible war in Vietnam can be understood—perhaps only understood—in this way."

You, who are still time-bound, who refuse to forgive either the present or the past, may not agree. But I write with the confidence of a son who has regained his father, by patient historical effort. Only history can help us understand—and forgive—the struggles of earlier Americans to grasp our unique heritage—the possibility of freedom. Perhaps this history will help another generation understand our struggle—and forgive our failures. More and more, I see the story I have told as a paradigm of the American experience. All of us emerge in one way or another from the ghetto of our childhood, whether it be the narrow world of the small town or the smug one of the suburb, or the blindered world of a religion, an ethnic group, or a class. Even the Wasps, no longer a majority, must undergo the same, often anguished rite of passage.

It is time to stop. The sententious historian is endangering the novelist. I can almost hear Judge Kilpatrick saying: *Blow your nose, you weepy son of a bitch. Who the hell asked you to shed tears for us? We didn't ask for anybody's pity. We lived it high and wide and winging. Where the hell did you get the idea that we didn't enjoy our youth? We had a ball.*

Let's end it that way.